Tristan

Jesse Roman

cory roman natuik

officialjesseroman.com

First Edition February 2024

Published by Cory Roman Natuik

Paperback and ebook cover design by M O N O L I T H from 99designs.com

Hardcover design by ashous from 99designs.com

Interior layout created by Jesse Roman using Vellum

LGBTQ+ adult fiction / LGBTQ+ romance

ISBN 978-1-7381353-0-1 (hardcover) 978-1-7381353-1-8 (paperback) 978-1-7381353-2-5 (ebook)

For the LGBTQ+ community
and our allies all over the world.

1

Johnson had purchased a bag of popcorn from the Venus Valley Night Market last night. He brought it to work with him the following morning so it could be shared with his colleagues, all of whom helped manage one of America's most formidable supercenter chains: Brandon Save. The district and regional managers' offices were abuzz with the usual business jargon, keyboard clicking, voicemails and early morning store calls as they chowed down on Johnson's charitable gift of butter, salt and corn.

He dialed into the daily morning conference call and gave a pep talk to the opening managers of the stores in his district. He shared the weekend sales numbers, the stars, the losers, and asked each manager individually what their strategy was to help drive sales in their store today. He glanced around the office and resisted the urge to chuckle because that would only give away the secret he'd been guarding. Today, one of his colleagues would lose their job, perhaps even their career, and Johnson would undoubtedly replace the jerk, thus receiving a long overdue promotion. He could see his target now, sitting in his glass office, conceited and arrogant as he gossiped into his phone. There was a ridiculous overpriced globe on his desk that had been spun maybe once. *Cool, show me where Peru is, dumb fuck.*

Johnson was the workplace gay. But, there was *another* workplace gay. There were actually three (that were known), but only one of them would be the recipient of today's tragedy. The Other Gay was a problem. What everyone in the office didn't know was that the Other Gay liked to touch himself in his office, after hours, when his colleagues weren't around. To Johnson's wild surprise, the guy had an online cam account: *CorporateDaddyXL*. He stumbled upon it when searching for free porn on a site filled with ads and relentless viruses that would inevitably lead to the blue screen of death if you didn't have a proper virus blocker.

Johnson pulled out his phone and scrolled for the video he had saved to his camera roll. He could tell it was him just from the thumbnail alone. Someone out there had screen recorded a live video of the Other Gay, which they could only access with a paid subscription, and posted it to a free porn site. There he was, beating his meat in his office chair. It was the same chair that he was currently sitting in just across from Johnson, in his office, swiveling back and forth with that punchable grin on his face like he had just inserted a butt plug that fit oh so snugly. In the video, *CorporateDaddyXL* wore a black necktie with his shirt undone, wide open, and was naked from the waist down. He was twisting and turning the wheels of the office chair as he grinned sensually into the camera, taking tip and subscription money from his horny viewers. While performing his cock and ass tricks, he'd reach over to his left side and open one of the black filing cabinets where he kept dildos and Fleshjacks and small bottles of water-based lube. This was one of the company's regional managers; regional manager and regional daddy, all at the age of thirty. The ridiculous, inflated salary the company was throwing at him wasn't enough, apparently. This guy didn't deserve what he had. He was a joke, a sloth.

Johnson strolled over to the Other Gay's office and knocked on the door. The guy was busy speaking nonsense into his phone, still swiveling in his chair and grinning up at the ceiling. Johnson waited until he signaled for him to come in then stepped into the room. The Other Gay had brown hair: ordinary, plain. Not only was he the Other Gay, but he was the Basic Gay. He looked like one of those stock photos you find on the web when searching for *white office guy*. He was the type of guy you saw on Friday afternoons at your trendy downtown patio, wearing his Ray Bans and office suit, drinking from a tall beer glass, preferably craft, while talking business with colleagues. Johnson, on the other hand, had decided over a decade ago to shave his head. His strong rugged features were intimidating to most, and now, they went along with his shaven head and beard for maximum alpha dominance. His favorite pastime was going for morning jogs down his street and around the park on the weekends. He'd spend time at the local gym with the other gym rats, building his arms, chest and legs. He turned thirty-eight this year, and planned to live for a very long time.

The Other Gay hung up the phone as Johnson walked in. "Hey," he said. "How's it going?"

"Fantastic," Johnson replied, closing the door. His expression turned stoic as he looked the Other Gay up and down, as if expecting to find his pants down and a dildo sticking out of his ass. No doubt that's what would be happening later tonight, after everyone was gone and he came back in to use the office for after hours playtime. Johnson eyed the black filing cabinet behind the desk. It was, Johnson admitted, arousing to think about. Despite how much he detested the man, he still found him attractive, but also pompous and annoying and completely unlikable.

"I'm flying to Houston today. There's some drama going on in one of the stores," said the Other Gay, like it was a major inconvenience to him. "The new general manager and the assistant manager are fighting." He sighed loudly and opened a tab on his computer with a click of the mouse. "This new manager isn't working out. She seemed impressive during the interview, but you just don't know how they'll actually perform until a month in."

Johnson stared at him, no warmth behind his eyes, like an alligator watching a sloth on a comfy river bank. "Incompetent people are the worst," he agreed.

The Other Gay started rummaging around in his briefcase for probably a vibrator or ball gag. He was so fake. Fuck, Johnson couldn't stand him.

"Hey, before you fly out," said Johnson, casually opening up his phone, "could you explain this to me?"

"Yeah, what is it?" asked the Other Gay, flipping through sheets of positive STI results and bathhouse invites no doubt.

Johnson went around the desk and leaned down behind his shoulder. He swung his phone around and held the screen in front of the Other Gay's range of sight. Johnson kept his eyes on him, wanting to see his reaction and the moment he realizes that everything he had worked for, his career and professional reputation, was just destroyed. The Other Gay continued rummaging around in his briefcase as he looked at the screen, but gradually stopped. He squinted at the video then shoved the phone away. His face turned red, and panic set into the creases of his subtle forehead lines. You'd think the dumbass would get Botox with the amount of money he was making.

The Other Gay's mouth was open slightly, but then he quickly closed it. "What the fuck is this?"

Johnson could tell the Other Gay was trying to play it cool now, casual. "Let's talk," he said, straightening his posture. He looked through the glass walls of the office where their colleagues were busy with their morning work routine. They were making trips back and forth for more helpings of the popcorn that Johnson had put on some random table, like fruit flies to an open bottle of dark spiced rum.

"Why the hell are you showing me porn?" asked the Other Gay dramatically, his expression bewildered and annoyed.

Johnson opened the office door, and the murmuring from outside the walls spilled into the room. "I'd like to talk to you. Somewhere private."

"Close my door, please," said the Other Gay, forcefully.

Johnson didn't and wouldn't. He held his phone out into the office space where everyone was working, the blank screen facing them. "I'll just send your video to the corporate group chat then."

The Other Gay scoffed. "Why would you send porn to the group chat?"

Johnson raised an eyebrow at him as he resisted the urge to smile, his index finger tapping the top of his phone.

The Other Gay sat there, aghast, with his hands on his desk, his thumb rubbing against a red pen as he stared Johnson down, eye to eye. When a few seconds had passed, he hit his palms on the surface of the desk and stood up. "Fine," he said. Not wanting to draw attention to himself, he casually walked out of his office and made his way towards the door that led into one of the building's common hallways. He glanced behind him to see if Johnson was following, which he was, but when Johnson passed the table with the popcorn, he reached over and grabbed the bag before continuing on behind the fallen regional manager. They walked briskly down the hall, through a stairwell door and down a flight of stairs to a mid-level landing, stopping at a storage room door.

"Are we gonna blow each other in there?" asked Johnson, the smile finally spreading across his face as he locked eyes with the Other Gay. He tossed popcorn into his mouth as if a dramatic comedy was unfolding in front of him, his chewing echoing down the concrete stairwell.

"Why'd you show me that?" demanded the Other Gay. "Where did you even find it?"

"It's literally everywhere," said Johnson, stepping down onto the landing with him.

"Are there others?"

"Not that I'm aware of. Wait... There are more?!" Johnson pulled out his phone and juggled the bag of popcorn under his arm, laughing sadistically. "I'll look them up if you want. Should only take a minute."

The Other Gay slapped his hand against the phone, drawing Johnson's attention away from the screen. Johnson only grinned, looking at him for a moment with his dull grey eyes, then returned his attention back down to his phone, unbothered and giggling to himself. The Other Gay threw open the storage room door and ushered Johnson inside.

Johnson looked into the room, cringing. He shook his head and tossed more popcorn into his mouth. "I'm not going in there with you."

The Other Gay scratched his head. "So... Yeah, I've been camming. I'll delete it tomorrow. I'll delete it right now even."

Johnson looked up, deep in thought. "So, you're telling me, all those nights when you said you needed to stay behind at the office to finish up work, you were actually ejaculating all over our office spaces, sucking on dildos... Your naked ass on your chair in full corporate daddy uniform? Why pay for stage props when you can just use the real thing, right? Embarrassing. Just like your work ethic."

"Now it's about my work ethic," said the Other Gay, his face turning red again. "You're jealous that I'm better than you."

Johnson looked down and continued browsing through his phone.

"Tons of people are getting into stuff like this," continued the Other Gay. "This is the age we live in."

"Yeah," said Johnson in a nonchalant tone. "What *you* did was stupid, though. You whored out your job... Your career! Do that shit in private, man. Your office needs a black light inspection. It's like a jizz museum in there."

"Why are you even finding this so gross?" asked the Other Gay.

"Because it fucking is," said Johnson, dumbfounded.

"Right," said the Other Gay. "Because the thought of a guy masturbating in his office is such a turn off to you."

"So, now I'm locked into some sort of gay brotherhood bond of secrecy with you?" asked Johnson. "You've never attempted to have a real conversation with me in the four years that we've worked together."

The Other Gay stared at him. "I've talked to you, Johnson. Many times."

"Yeah, like, 'How's it going?' with zero interest behind it. That's not a conversation. That's what you say to a coworker when you're both walking past each other down the hall in opposite directions and don't want it to be fucking awkward."

"So, were you expecting us to hook up or something?" asked the Other Gay.

"That's really not the point here," said Johnson, his annoyance escalating. "You suck at your job, you suck at being gay, and now you're going to quit. Right now."

"What the fuck?" said the Other Gay, putting his hands to his head like he was speaking to a bald mental patient. "Suck at being gay?!"

Johnson threw the now empty bag of popcorn over the railing and walked right up to his face, sucking popcorn grease from the tips of his fingers. He held his phone up for the Other Gay, the video in clear sight.

"I'm not quitting my job," said the Other Gay. "Can't you just keep this a secret for me? I'll stop the account and won't do it ever again. I'll give you money."

"You don't deserve to be a regional manager," said Johnson, ignoring his offer. "I don't even know how you got it in the first place. Probably sucked Robbie's dick. He's always touching your fucking shoulder at conference meetings. You're his pet pervert."

"So, you're blackmailing me," said the Other Gay.

"You're going to go to Robbie's office right now, or Calvin's, and resign. You will say that the position has become too stressful and you can't handle the demands that the company is laying on you, let alone the demands that a future promotion would entail. It's too much work for you to handle. Unfortunately, you don't fit in with the culture of the corporate world and ultimately aren't a good fit."

The Other Gay pulled out his own phone and scrolled through it, his other hand running across his sweaty face as he started to laugh. "Is this actually happening? If you're taking me down, I'm taking you with me."

Johnson couldn't believe what he was hearing. "Excuse me? Who was the one recording porn in his office? You're expecting *me* to go down with you?! For what?!" He continued watching the Other Gay scroll through his own phone, thinking maybe he was recording him as they talked, but quickly realized that he wasn't. He wasn't smart enough to do something like that. The Other Gay bit his lip as he looked at his phone, tears welling up at the corners of his eyes as his situation escalated, the wheels turning behind his eyes.

"Looking for something to use against me?" asked Johnson.

"Trying to find my orgy fisting adventure video that doesn't exist? You'll find my online dating profiles, but that's it."

"Can't imagine anyone wanting to date a piece of shit like you."

Johnson's mouth twitched.

"I'll delete my account and all the videos and no one has to know," said the Other Gay. "I'll still pay you to not say anything. Please?"

"You can't just delete them," said Johnson. "You'll need some sort of income to roll in now that you're unemployed." His eyes lit up. "Was Robbie ever a guest in one of your videos? He always seemed like a creep." His eyes darted down to the Other Gay's phone, and he grabbed it out of his hand with one fast swipe. The Other Gay pushed him against the wall, pinning him against the concrete. Johnson put his finger to his lips, his eyes wide in fake terror, holding on to the Other Gay's phone for dear life.

"I'm *not* quitting my job," said the Other Gay. "I've worked hard to get here. Just like you."

Johnson flashed him a look of bitter resentment. "Worked hard... just like me? You don't have to *try*. You get everything handed to you."

"But you don't?"

"Unlike you, I've gotten ahead in life by being good at what I do. Not by being a flirt and kissing ass and swiveling in my chair all day long."

"And blackmailing others to get their position," said the Other Gay, his eyes like daggers glaring down at Johnson's face.

"I'm a vigilante," said Johnson in a helpless tone. "Hard-working people such as myself don't deserve measly crumbs while the sloths get served unearned rewards." He pried himself from the Other Gay. "It's game over, Jay."

2

Jay considered hurting him. He stared at Johnson for a few seconds longer then made his way up the flight of steps, slowly. When he reached the door, he paused. He balanced all the scenarios in his head. Could he possibly try to retaliate with blackmail of his own? What would stop Johnson from sending the video to everyone even after he quit?

Johnson looked up at him, stoic and lifeless. "Time's up," he said, lifting Jay's phone up. He had just shared the video to the company's group chat through Jay's own phone.

Humiliated, Jay stared at the phone in numb shock. He looked at Johnson, unable to move, hot blood rushing through his head, his hands clenched. Instead of going through the door, he descended back down the stairwell and took his place in front of Johnson. "Give me my phone," he demanded.

"Hurt me," said Johnson, gloating.

Jay grabbed his phone back and leaned into his face. "I'd throw you over this railing and watch you fucking die, you piece of shit."

Johnson licked his lips. "Want a blowjob to ease the tension?"

There was a ding from Jay's phone, the familiar notification when a manager messaged the group chat.

"Oh!" exclaimed Johnson, looking down with delight. "You have some new fans!"

Jay raised his hand and hit Johnson, hard, making him stumble back into the concrete wall. He stared at Johnson for a few seconds longer, ready to rip his face off, then escaped down the stairwell. He dug his hands into his pockets to check that he had his keys and wallet with him. They were all he needed, really.

When Jay reached the underground parking, he jumped into his car and drove away into the late Friday morning. His mind was a blur, rage pulsating in his veins, embarrassment emblazoned upon his face, and his destination hazy as his world was sent spiraling.

Jay couldn't concentrate on the road ahead of him. He had to stop.

He slowed the car down, parked on the side of the Goldenrod Boulevard in the heart of the downtown business district and got out, ignoring the persistent notification beeps he was receiving from his phone. He had no desire to mute them because that would run the risk of him glimpsing the notification screen in the process. Leaving his vehicle parked, he moved on foot and merged with the lunchtime pedestrian traffic. Moments later, a stone fountain caught his attention and he flung his phone into the shallow square basin without an ounce of hesitation.

Surrounded by dry terrain and canyons, mountains and endless highways, Venus Valley was famously known for its Valencia oranges. History revealed that the city was meant to be named Sunshine Valley, but it was deemed too "on the nose," so Venus Valley was chosen instead. It was an obvious nod to the planet, and most certainly inspired by the lustful Roman goddess of beauty, desire and sex. The city had its own gay village, and it was there that the name "Penis Valley" was coined, inspired by the God of Semen, naturally.

Jay was a thirty-year-old professional. Back at the office, all his colleagues were now in the loop as to what had just happened. He wouldn't just be known as Jay anymore: the five-foot-eleven, clean-shaven, brown-haired white guy. For all the Size Queens, he'd now be infamous for his dick size. *CorporateDaddyXL*. He was gross. He was a pervert... Just wait until they found the dildos, Fleshjacks and lube in the middle filing cabinet in his office.

As of today, he'd have a new reputation, and that concerned him a lot. He thought about his friends and family. Would they find out? Would news travel that far? Perhaps he was overreacting. His brain was a fried egg.

Jay was so lost in random thought that he stumbled over the leg of a blue aluminum chair that stuck out from a quaint bistro table in front of a tree. The tree partially blocked the side wall of an old three-story building that sat at the corner of two merging streets, one of which was the main downtown boulevard that Jay had parked on. The frontside interior on the main floor had been converted into a hummus bar called Lovely.

He slumped down into the chair, crossing his arms on the table and shoving his face between them. He ran his fingers along the aluminum floral pattern of the blue table. The butter smears left behind on his clothes from Johnson's greasy fingertips made him queasy. He couldn't bring himself to let out a deafening scream. His whole life had changed forever in an instant, just like that. Was he really that unsatisfied with his life that he resorted to exhibitionism for some sort of thrill? He had no real hobbies. He watched movies. He ordered dinner from food apps because he didn't like to cook. His last relationship was over two years ago and ended after only eight months, when his ex, Tyler, moved to Australia to work in his chosen field of marine biology. Jay had strong feelings for him at the time of their relationship, but he wasn't sure if the feeling was mutual, and he wasn't positive it could have been called true love. They both agreed that they wouldn't be able to sustain a long-distance relationship, so Jay let him go. When Tyler moved away, Jay started delving into the world of online porn. It was meant to fill the void of affection from a boyfriend. He wasn't doing it for the money. It was about feeling appreciated, wanted and noticed. The sadness he had felt when Tyler moved away was then compounded by the sadness piled on when both his parents died shortly after Tyler left. He wasn't ready to date again. He didn't want to go out. He, indeed, felt alone. His online audience was what kept him sane through all of this. Casual sex meant nothing to him. It often left him feeling empty. He desired passion, an exciting adventure that took him out of his humdrum life.

With his face resting comfortably in the crook of his arms, he stared down at his Calvin Klein loafers and the scuff marks along their tips. Johnson was a rotten man possessed of seething jealousy, disliking anyone more successful than he was at doing things he excelled at. Johnson hated those he perceived to be doing less, yet achieving more. But it was a distorted reality he invented for himself. Johnson despised seeing Jay smile, swiveling around in his office chair and being Mr. Chatty or Mr. Confident. He was most likely at this very moment pretending to be shocked and disturbed at what was happening in the corporate group chat. Truth be told, Jay never got along with him, simply because Johnson wasn't likeable. If it wasn't for his shit personality, cold vibe and creepiness, Jay would have been pals with him in a heartbeat.

It was nearing noon, and people were out and about grabbing a bite to eat at trendy eateries and food trucks or running last-minute errands. Jay reached for his phone, but remembered that he had thrown it into the fountain. Muscle memory. Phantom phone. His stomach rumbled when he smelled the spicy and savoury aromas from the food people carried in take-out bags in one hand, their phones in the other. He used to be like that. Now, he felt like a young adult or teenager again. Lost, confused and reckless. He needed a stiff drink. He needed to splurge. He needed sex. He needed to do something wild.

From his chair, he craned his neck to get a good look around him in search of any kind of food truck. He saw one that was conveniently parked several meters from where he was sitting. The truck was a cute purple, pink and blue color combo with glitter trim along the borders of the windows. Little Iris' Cupcakes. From the looks of the color palette, you'd think they were selling cotton candy unicorn farts in a jar. It was probably the gayest food truck he had ever seen. There was a middle-aged woman running the service window, her head moving back and forth as she tended to the customers, worked the register and shouted out orders to the preparation station. Taped next to the service window was a small promotional poster advertising their new unicorn cupcakes.

Jay grinned deliciously like some creepy fiend. Ah yes, it was all making sense now... a fucking unicorn cupcake. It was simply meant to be. He stood in line and waited for the few people in front to place their orders, loving the fact that he was going to have dessert for lunch. He folded his arms and glanced around casually, looking absolutely ridiculous in his work clothes that were so devoid of life that he felt like a black-and-white film grain against a children's fantasy spectacle of color and whimsy.

"Hello," said the woman enthusiastically, making eye contact with Jay when he was next to order. She was a bit overweight and wore purple glitter lipstick. Nestled on top of her pink wig was a neon blue ball cap that had a unicorn patch sewn onto it. It was all such an interesting mix, albeit a little ridiculous. She looked like a drunk unicorn ranch owner, appearing to be no older than fifty years old by Jay's reckoning. Everything about the truck and its owner possessed a fantastical arts and crafts aesthetic, and not quite a professional one. But he loved it.

"What can I get for you today?" she asked, her body in mid-turn as she waited for him to say his order.

"I'm curious about the unicorn cupcakes," said Jay, motioning towards the poster next to the sliding glass window.

"They're new," said the woman happily. "You'd be one of the first to try one. They're five dollars each, or two for nine."

Jay reached into his trouser pocket for his wallet. "I'll take just one for now. Do you take plastic?"

"Of course," she said, handing him a tapping device for credit card chips. "How's your day been?"

"Uhhh..." started Jay with a sappy smile. "It could be going a lot better."

"One Unicorn, Ben," said the woman over her shoulder.

Jay glanced into the truck past the woman and saw a boy working in the incredibly cramped quarters. His pace was quick and repetitive, knowing each station in front of him from memory. Jay stared at him, noticing his blond hair first. He was thin and looked quite boyish, probably seventeen or eighteen... and absolutely cute. Jay turned his attention away and continued minding his own business. Then, rather quickly, the boy placed the cupcake on the serving station and the woman retrieved it with a smile.

"Here you are," she said, handing Jay the cupcake.

Jay's eyes lit up. "Wow, I wasn't expecting it to be so big. Look at all that frosting!"

"That's what they all say," she chimed in, handing him a fork. "You may need this."

"Actually, I'll get two of these guys," said Jay, lifting the cupcake up.

"Most certainly. Another Unicorn, Ben," declared the woman.

Jay paid again and within seconds she handed him a second frosted confection.

He walked back to the bistro table and pulled the cupcake wrapping off one of the treats, placing the other in front of him. The fluffy cake portion was chocolate, with blue and purple frosting swirled on top, decorated with silver glitter and a piece of hardened sugar sticking out that was meant to look like a unicorn horn. It was incredibly pretty, like a periwinkle night sky. The frosting itself was several inches high. Jay bit into the cupcake and his eyes rolled back, the frosting smearing his upper and lower lips like a child. The horn slid down and knocked into his nose, leaving a spot of glitter on the tip. This was stage one of his post-walk of shame. The games were just getting started, and this cupcake was the starting line for the adventures that lay ahead of him. He demolished the first cupcake and gazed at the second, then reached forward and shoved it into his mouth as his body processed what was most likely sixty grams of sugar.

Realization struck at the exact moment of an intense sugar rush: he could just find another job. For the last half hour, all he'd thought about was the doom and gloom of almost certain unemployment. However, with his skills and tactical strategies of corporate chess, any company similar to the one he had just walked away from would be thrilled to bring him on board. He hoped. Better yet...

"I'll start my own business," he said to himself, swallowing down the last bit of frosting and cake. "Jay's Dildos and Lube."

"Where is that?"

Jay spun around, his eyes wide and his mouth splattered with unicorn glitter frosting. There was a guy standing next to where he was sitting, casting a shadow over him.

"You mentioned dildos and lube," the guy clarified.

Jay felt embarrassed. More so because the guy was cute. He

wiped his hands along his trousers, and cringed when he realized there was now blue frosting along the sides.

The guy's smile filled the awkward silence. "Hey, just kidding."

"I didn't get the joke," said Jay.

"No, I..." started the guy. "I was stepping out of Lovely when I saw you eating those cupcakes. You mentioned something about Jay's Dildos and Lube."

"Uh..." said Jay awkwardly. "Yeah."

The guy pursed his lips and looked down. "Hey, it's all good. Have a nice day."

Jay watched the guy turn and slowly walk away, like he was expecting Jay to call him back. "Do most guys call you back over?"

He turned around and flashed Jay a subtle smile. "Only the ones worth talking to."

Jay crumpled up the cupcake wrappers. "Sass," he said, returning the smile.

"Before class," finished the guy. He took the chair across from Jay at the bistro table. "Do you mind?"

Jay shook his head. Was this actually happening? Was he actually getting picked up outside a hummus bar next to a dessert truck selling unicorn cupcakes? His day had gone from being a tragic drama to a gay sitcom.

The Intruder was staring at him, wide-eyed, smooth. He was suave. That was easy to see. He was Latino and had glowing skin, like he'd just spent the morning at the spa. His black hair was curly and hung over his forehead, and he had a prominent jawline that could cut through butter. His facial scruff was perfectly groomed.

"What?" asked Jay, not knowing what to make of this. He had never had a guy come onto him this strong before.

"You seem kinda lonely," said the Intruder, cocking his head like a curious dog.

"I'm not," Jay protested, looking around out of awkwardness.

"People sit by themselves all the time. Look at that girl. She's clearly a loner."

The Intruder turned to look behind him at the stone steps of Lovely, where a small young woman wearing glasses sat on the bottom step, chowing down a hummus bowl with garlic pita bread. There were thick balustrades of carved stone slabs along the stairs that people often jumped up on to sit. She looked up from her food and waved at the Intruder, giving him a thumbs up.

"Oh, that's Kitty," said the Intruder, looking back at Jay. "She's my coworker, intern, whatever." That glint in his eyes. The swagger in his tone of voice was also playful, like a kitten playing with a ball of yarn. He wore a maroon bomber jacket that had some gold flower detailing and a black button-up shirt that was open so you could see some of his chest hair. Gold necklaces dangled down his chest, and he wore various tasteful bracelets and rings. The guy was fashionable, no doubt about that. He looked like a celebrity.

Jay looked him up and down. He was distracted by all the glitz and glamour and his overall aura.

The Intruder placed his hands on the table, his rings glinting sapphire and gold in the afternoon sun. "Kitty noticed you first. She thought you were cute and told me to go up and talk to you because she felt bad that such a cute boy was sitting alone eating all those cupcakes. As good as they taste, we were just concerned for you. She also said you looked sad and lost."

Jay licked his upper lip and laughed slightly, amused. "Well, thanks. But no, I'm fine." He scooped up the empty cupcake wrappers and scrunched them up in his hands.

The Intruder looked him up and down and drummed his fingers on the aluminum tabletop. "Well, I just wanted to fulfill her dare." He stood up and pushed his chair in. "Just remember though, you were the one shoving the gayest cupcakes ever into your mouth while muttering 'dildos and lube' to yourself. I've actually tasted dessert-flavoured lube before. Wouldn't recommend it."

Jay nodded. "Cool."

The Intruder looked at the ground. He stood across from Jay, his gaze coming back up and locking eyes with him. He turned his body midway to leave but stopped. "Would you mind giving me your name?"

Jay was always the first to break eye contact with a guy. Not this time. He rubbed his fingertips against the cupcake wrappers that were still in his fists.

The Intruder scratched the back of his neck. "I'm not usually this direct. You can just say no if you don't want to give it to me."

"No," said Jay immediately, "I'm going to say yes." He felt awkward, just as much as the Intruder probably did. He'd never dated a guy who wasn't white. In fact, Jay didn't have any guys in his friend circle who weren't white. He didn't know why. It never occurred to him until this very moment.

"My name is Jay," he said, smiling and reaching out his hand.

The guy smiled back. "Salvador," he replied.

Jay nodded his head. "Cool."

"I'm sorry my name isn't something like Chuck... or Nate... or Dan," said Salvador with another smirk, sexier than the last. He took the seat across from Jay again. "Mr. Blue Jay."

"Never in my life has anyone ever called me Blue Jay."

Salvador pointed to his own mouth. "It's because of the blue frosting on your lips. It's been there the entire time. I didn't want to say anything because it looks adorable."

Jay wiped the frosting off with the back of his hand, embarrassed... again. Salvador looked so put together, possessing an obvious edge. He had the most brilliant warm brown eyes, and was a couple inches shorter than him, which Jay liked. "I know the cologne you're wearing," he said. "Someone at my work wears the same one."

"I was at the store earlier and sprayed some," replied Salvador, smelling his own wrists, then extending one out to him. Jay smiled, hesitated for a moment, then leaned over and smelt his wrist. It was all so sensual. He felt euphoric. There was an aura and warmth that filled the space between the two of them.

"Are you on your lunch break?" asked Jay.

"Yes, actually," said Salvador. He snapped his wrist back from Jay and pulled his phone out. "I should've been back already." He spoke with a liquid sensuality and confidence, but seemed cavalier at the same time. "Oh well, they're not missing me," he said, waving his hand like it wasn't a problem, his rings clinking against the tabletop.

Jay laughed. Salvador was so mesmerizing. His mannerisms and personality... He was like a mystical pony.

"So, hey," said Salvador, tucking his phone away. "I'm sorry if I made you uncomfortable. I'm trying this new thing where I'm going up to guys instead of waiting for them to come up to me."

Jay leaned back in his chair. "It's working. I'm talking to you. Bless Kitty."

"She didn't think I'd do it," he said, turning to look at his intern on the steps, but she was gone. "And there she goes."

"Just like you pretty soon," said Jay, the disappointment ringing in his voice.

Salvador got up and placed his hands on the back of the blue bistro chair as he stood behind it.

Jay leaned forward and drummed his fingers on the table. "But we can talk later if you want... afterward. Whenever."

Salvador pulled out his phone and smiled. "What's your number, Blue Jay?" He typed away as Jay recited his number. "You want mine?"

"Um..." said Jay, briefly glancing at the fountain, which was only a few meters behind Salvador. "My phone is at work, actually."

"I'll call your phone so you have my number," he said.

"Oh, you can just text me," insisted Jay, getting up.

But Salvador had already hit the call button, and sure enough, Jay's ringtone gurgled out from beneath the couple feet of water behind Salvador.

Salvador craned his head around, threw his head back, then turned back to Jay with a raised eyebrow, dropping his hand to his side. "Nope. No way. I'm not leaving until you explain *that*."

3

Johnson flipped through his folder of various papers and notes for the weekly Friday meeting that was about to begin. His colleagues waited around the conference table, chatting about that morning's provocative turn of events. The door opened and Robbie stepped in briskly, taking his place at the head of the table. Robbie was one of the senior regional managers, and, of late, was given tasks that Calvin, the Regional Operations Vice President, would otherwise have done. Everyone accepted that he was Calvin's favorite for a long time now. In the last six months, everyone had noticed that Calvin had basically been training Robbie to take his place, much to the other regional managers' envy, especially Mary, who was a sharp no-bullshit-taker and undoubtedly the most qualified given her proven track record of success within the company. If Robbie died tomorrow, she would move up in rank to be Calvin's successor just mere seconds after the last breath left Robbie's lungs.

Robbie had turned fifty a few weeks ago, and there had been a big office party for him that was, from Johnson's perspective, overly cringe. Fake smiles and congratulations with copious amounts of food, alcohol and random expensive toys you give someone for these sorts of occasions, like a gold cocktail shaker. The man would soon be entering his twilight years, yet felt the desperate urge to cling to his youth by wearing skinny trousers that made his ass look as though it would burst out of the seams and a tight vest that most certainly suffocated him like a corset. He was tall, and looked younger than he was. He was also single, and held a stressful, highly demanding job. This was most likely the reason for the grey hairs that started to sprout a few years ago, so he had taken it upon himself to dye his voluptuous hair silver, saying he might as well embrace this new stage of life. They shared the same barber, Liam, and even though Johnson had been bald since his college years, he still had his beard professionally groomed. Johnson would be lying if he said he didn't find Robbie handsome. He liked assertive and aggressive men, and Robbie was both of those things. They hung out on occasion, but it was always strictly business-related, usually at restaurants with other managers, never one-on-one. There were times when Johnson thought about asking him out as friends, to go see a movie maybe, but the way Robbie gave him the cold shoulder during the work week made him shy away from doing so. Johnson had heard through the grapevine how in the '90s Robbie was a reckless slut who partied almost exclusively and did all sorts of drugs and worked menial jobs all through his twenties and thirties. As to how he got to where he was now, one had to wonder, and it didn't sit well with Johnson. Slowly, over time, he'd grown to dislike Robbie. It was hard for him because, in the beginning, he genuinely wanted to be friends with him.

"Alright," said Robbie, clapping his hands together and rolling up his sleeves as he laid his papers out like a storyboard. "Today we're going to run through next week's national promo and the new, self-checkout POS systems that a lot of stores will finally be receiving."

There was an awkward silence within the room; all you could hear was the shuffling of papers and scribblings of pens.

"Who wants to start?" asked Robbie, waiting for someone to speak up as he looked down at his collage of reports, highlighting random crap. "Beth, how about you? How's the new sales model for our underperforming stores, 219 and 274?"

This went on for fifty minutes. But the filthy pink elephant in the room was wafting through the air. When the end of the meeting rolled around, Robbie shuffled his papers together and sighed. There was obviously something else on his mind, other than the situation with Jay. He had been distracted not just during this meeting, but also for the last couple of weeks. Maybe it was turning fifty. Perhaps it was a midlife existential crisis.

"Now, as to what happened earlier today. Jay will no longer be with the company given his recent... extracurricular activities."

"Sorry, but what happened with Jay?" asked Wanda, another regional manager.

Johnson rolled his eyes and snorted quietly. Good, reliable, ignorant Wanda.

"He is no longer with the company," said Robbie directly. "His position will be filled within the coming weeks."

"Well, he was a joy to work with," declared Wanda with a smile. Her statement was met with a couple awkward coughs.

Johnson knew that Robbie didn't want to give further details on Jay's porn escapades because Robbie and Jay were buddies. He didn't want to publicly embarrass Jay any further than he already was. Favoritism. Nepotism. It was a deep and rotten sickness that ran rampant in the corporation. If Jay wasn't gay, Robbie wouldn't have given a shit.

"Are we looking externally or internally?" asked Johnson curiously. "For his replacement."

"Most likely internally."

Johnson grinned.

"But we're also looking externally," finished Robbie.

Johnson's eyes bugged out for a moment. He looked down and scribbled red circles on the corner of his papers like an annoyed high schooler.

"But we will keep you updated if any new developments arise," said Robbie. "Saying that, have a good weekend everyone."

Johnson gathered up his things and stood up with the rest. He knew it already. They would never give him what he deserved. Robbie needed someone who was strong, but also obedient and stupid for the role, not someone who would overshadow him like Mary. That's why Jay was selected to work here: to be Robbie's moronic puppy. He wasn't meant to last much longer, though. There was a tiredness about him that was showing through his overly moisturized face. Though everyone knew Robbie was being groomed for higher up, Johnson could tell that he wanted out from it all. Johnson, of course, would gladly help with the implosion of Robbie for mere shits and giggles. If he wasn't going to be awarded a shiny new position, neither would the Silver Fox.

4

Ben hurried down the stairs and into the kitchen as he hummed a song that was playing in his headphones. The clam chowder that was simmering on the stove had stirred his stomach and made it grumble, luring him down from his bedroom within seconds. His aunt's homemade soups were filling and delicious, creamy and flavourful, with a subtle kick of heat to them. He grabbed a ceramic bowl from the cupboard and served himself several servings of the good stuff with a side of garlic toast. He was ravenous when he ate, leaving hardly any leftovers.

His aunt Iris was counting cash at the kitchen table and examining the reports from today's cupcake sales on a spreadsheet in her notebook. Her house, overall, wasn't impressive. It was a modest 1970s design, and a house she had lived in for almost twenty years. Many of the appliances weren't of this century, along with the outdated furniture.

"We ran out of blue frosting today," said Ben casually as he grabbed himself a soda from the fridge. He awkwardly took a seat on the dining chair across from her, noticing the frustration on her face as her eyes scrolled the spreadsheet, the sales from her gourmet cupcakes plummeting further into improbability. She invested a large amount of her savings into the food truck, and the business did well, initially. During that first few months, she was the happiest Ben had seen her in a long time. She dressed up and would have fun with it, both of them optimistic that she'd be able to make some good profit. But eventually, sales tapered off and steady growth stalled. Iris would often argue with customers over the silliest things, and with any business, you're only as good as your online reviews and word of mouth. She strategized ways to get the flow back, but competition was intensifying by the year, and stress escalated. Her motivation took a steep decline. Ben couldn't be around her for long periods of time, for her negative energy drained him of any happiness he'd be feeling in any given moment. There was a distance between them, a coldness. He felt like a ghost in her house, even after all these years of living together. They'd go days without speaking to each other, even when they were both home.

Iris felt alien to Ben, and sometimes he even questioned if she truly cared about him. He had his father's blond hair and blue eyes, and his mother's smile. Nine years ago, Patricia and Russell were cleaning their restaurant, Divin' Seafood, when a driver, intoxicated from alcohol and heroin, crashed through the front window. Patricia was killed immediately. Russell had a fighting chance of surviving when he was transported to the nearest hospital, but succumbed to his injuries. Ben was only ten. Iris rarely spoke about his mom and dad, and he rarely asked her questions about them. When his parents died, he had no concept of inheritance. Then, when he turned eighteen last year, Iris sat him down and told him his inheritance was next to nothing. The restaurant Patricia and Russell owned had not been succeeding in the end, and they had to file for bankruptcy. Even Iris had chipped in with some of her savings when her sister, Patricia, had asked her for a loan. When Patricia and Russell died, their beautiful house was foreclosed. All their investments had gone into the business, so there was no money left.

"How was work this week?" asked Iris, taking a sip of her beer.

Ben turned down the volume of his headphones when he saw her mouth move. "What?"

"How was work?" she repeated.

"Insane," he said, breaking off a piece of garlic toast and dipping it into the clam chowder. "We were expecting a visit today from our district and regional manager, but it was canceled and now they're coming next week instead. Management was so pissy these last couple days trying to make sure everything was perfect for when they came. Then when the visit was canceled, it was like we could breathe again."

"Hopefully they recognize you," she said. "You've been there for almost a year. You'd think they'd give you a promotion to shift supervisor at least."

"I'm thinking about quitting Brandon Save," said Ben passively.

Iris looked at his bowl of soup disapprovingly like it had just called her a curse word. "But why?"

"Being a cashier sucks, and my supervisor sucks."

Iris shook her head in bewilderment. "Don't be ridiculous. You *need* a reliable source of income."

Ben spun the spoon around the rim of his bowl.

"You were planning that trip to New York. Are you still doing that? How will you pay for it?"

"I'm going later this year, hopefully. I'll need to save a bit more, though. New York is expensive."

"Then you'll need to keep the job."

"Brandon Save sucks," said Ben, becoming agitated. "My supervisor is an ass. No one there likes her except, like, one person. The company doesn't care about its employees. I'll just... find somewhere new that pays better."

Iris took a couple heavy sips of her beer just as Ben's phone began to vibrate from an incoming call. He glanced down at the screen to see who it was, then stood up and left the kitchen through the side door with his phone in hand. Seconds later, he heard a sharp shuffling of papers from behind him just as the door closed. He took a peek through the kitchen window and saw the reports scattered on the floor with the notebook lying open beside them. Iris was hunched over as she remained seated, holding her face in her hands.

Ben's body tensed up. He walked away from the window and down the gravel driveway as the sun started to set past the rooftops across the street. He accepted the incoming call. "Hey... So, eleven o'clock still works?"

"Yeah. Remember though, it must be discreet," said the voice on the other end.

5

There were dancing Blue Jays on his mind.

Once 4:30 finally came around, Salvador was more than ready to abandon Monroe Wealth Management and head home for the weekend. He was always working, regardless of what day of the week it was. Not only was he a wealth advisor, but he was also a wedding planner. Salvador often worked on his "days off" to satisfy all parties who needed his services from both jobs. Two birds, one stone. He enjoyed it. He liked staying busy. He dreamt of money.

"You think he'd actually call you?" asked Kitty, grabbing her jacket and purse from the filing cabinet she used as her own personal storage locker. Salvador's intern was short, just over five feet, and wore her black hair in a ponytail like a teenager. Her oversized black-framed glasses were probably from her teenage years as well. She wasn't a natural beauty, her face awkward and out of place, but her spirit was lively and pure at the age of twenty.

"I have no idea," said Salvador absent-mindedly as he closed down his laptop.

"What happened to that guy who you chatted up at the fragrance counter today? He was literally terrified of you."

"Kitty, all I said was I liked his sideburns."

"Is that why he never came back to the counter when he told you that he needed to check the stock room for the cologne you wanted?"

Salvador scratched his arm as though the bug of failed connections was biting at him again. "I'm awkward and I don't know how to flirt," he admitted. "Maybe he was straight."

"For a guy who looks as good as yourself, I'd think you'd be doing a better job at this," said Kitty matter-of-factly.

Salvador ran his tongue along his top lip. "You'd think," he mumbled.

"The Cupcake Boy wasn't straight," confirmed Kitty, smiling at him gleefully like a taunting child.

Salvador snapped his laptop closed. "Straight men don't usually smell other men's wrists."

"He's so cute," she said longingly, as though Jay had been in her nightly dreams for eons. "You *need* to call him."

"Why was his phone really in the fountain, though?" he asked as he clicked the charging cable into his laptop.

"Because it slipped out of his pocket when he was sitting on the ledge," she said. "That's what he told you."

"Oh please, he threw it in," said Salvador with a tender laugh. "The phone was sitting in the middle of the fountain like a rock."

"Why would he do that, though? Those phones aren't cheap. Maybe he's crazy rich and doesn't care." Kitty suddenly grabbed Salvador's arm in a way that made him jump in his chair. "You could be his wealth advisor!" she exclaimed, her eyes lighting up.

"Nah," said Salvador as he stood up, removing the grip of death from his arm.

"What if he's crazy?" she asked dramatically. "He seemed weird when he was just sitting there talking to himself. Also, did you see how he was eating those cupcakes? Imagine if that was your butt."

Salvador's mouth dropped open in amusement. "Sass, with zero class," he said, pointing his finger at her and making little circles in the air. "Most people come across as kind of weird when you first meet them because you don't know them."

"So... *call him*," said Kitty in desperation, her body all antsy like she needed to use the bathroom. She looked down at his phone on the desk, tempted. Salvador kept his eyes on her as he gathered his take-home bag of supplies that he would need for the weekend, monitoring his phone in case she decided to snatch it.

"You should be his sugar daddy," she suggested to him.

Salvador sighed loudly. Kitty was one of those girls who initially knew nothing about gay culture and was pure of mind until she met him. He feared his gay slang and sarcasm was having a bad influence on her. "People don't just throw their phones into fountains."

Kitty looked as though she wasn't paying attention to what he was saying anymore and instead made a sudden movement with her body, making Salvador jump again. She always did random, sporadic things. "Well, I'll be with my sister this weekend. We have our cousin's bridal shower to go to." She leaned over his desk to hug him goodbye. "Let me know on Monday what happened with Cute Cupcake Boy."

"I'm still disappointed that your cousin didn't choose me to be her wedding planner," he admitted.

"She couldn't afford you," said Kitty. "She also didn't want one. Wasn't in the budget." She gathered her things and made her way to the door, but then lingered in the doorway for one last word. "Just be careful," she said, "if you're going to meet him at his place."

Salvador scoffed, his mouth curling into a grin as he grabbed his bag and followed her out. "If I'm discovered chopped up into little meal prep containers inside his freezer, then please know that you were the voice of reason, and I was the idiot. That'll be my epitaph."

6

Ben didn't usually go out on Friday nights, but that was about to change. His aunt was usually out on weekends, so he'd have the house to himself. But he still didn't invite people over. He wasn't open about his sexuality yet, so having boys over was always risky, even when she wasn't home, since there was always the chance she could return unexpectedly. His short-term goal was to find his own place within the year so he could do whatever he wanted.

He left the house just before ten, taking an Uber to meet up with a guy he'd been talking to online. He had never actually met another gay guy in person, and the thing was, this guy had told him it needed to be discreet. He had sent Ben a picture of what he looked like, which was something Ben insisted on before meeting in person.

When Ben reached the address, he got out of the vehicle and walked the short driveway to a two-story house in one of the fancier neighbourhoods. He knocked on the ivory-colored door, nervous as hell. Just a few seconds later, there was shuffling from behind the door as it was unlocked. When it opened, Ben saw a man wearing light grey sweatpants and a solid white t-shirt. He was average build and around five foot eight, his beard scruffy and his black hair all a mess and slightly damp, like a dog after a bath. His eyes were big and cute, and overall, he looked like his picture. To Ben, he was essentially an Otter.

"Hey," said Otter Man, looking Ben up and down. Everything about him, from his mannerisms to how his voice sounded, appeared straight.

"Hi," Ben replied, waving to him as he walked into the foyer. He regretted the wave, feeling like an idiot already. The place had that "new house smell," and the aromatic essential oils were wafting through the air from a nearby diffuser. The lights were dimmed, creating an almost spa-like ambiance. Overall, the aesthetic was modern and tasteful, but boring. There was no real color to speak of in the home's entire palette, which was exclusively just ivories, creams and beiges with gold and silver accents. It was all staged in a way that made it look like a trendy furniture store. The white couch appeared expensive and looked as though no one had ever sat on it before. The minimal home décor was perfectly arranged, and there were silver picture frames up on the fireplace mantel with a white carpet laid out on the living room floor. The hardwood flooring of the hallway and foyer was slippery and smooth, like walking on butter.

"How was the ride?" asked Otter Man.

"Nice," said Ben, slipping off his sneakers. The guy's online profile said he was twenty-five, and he looked his age. Ben, on the other hand, was always mistaken for at least three years younger than he actually was.

Otter Man walked past him, a noticeable Old Spice deodorant scent lingering in the air. Ben could tell the guy got out of the shower just minutes before he arrived. When his back was turned,

Ben noticed the bottom curve of his white t-shirt and how it hung just above his butt. The swagger of his walk was... so sexy.

"Want anything to drink? Alcohol? Water?"

"Sure," said Ben. "I'll have whatever you're having." He followed him down the hall and into a kitchen that looked like no one had cooked in it before. The appliances were immaculate, and the table in the dining room might as well have been growing cobwebs.

"Your place is nice," said Ben, standing in the kitchen entryway. "Did you just move here?"

"Yeah, a few months ago," said the Otter, opening the massive fridge and taking out two cans of flavoured carbonated water. He cracked one open and took a few sips, then made his way back down the hallway, sweeping his hand along Ben's side. When he did that, Ben felt a jolt of warm arousal shoot through his body.

"Want to head upstairs?" he asked.

"Sure," said Ben, following him down the hall and up the carpeted steps to the second floor as the aroma from the essential oil diffuser filled the air. "Is that tea tree oil?"

The Otter turned his head and smirked. "Yeah. Good, ain't it?"

He led Ben down the second story hallway and into a spare bedroom at the far end that had a red suede armchair placed in the corner. It was hideous. The bed looked much older compared to everything else in the house, and the dresser across from the bed was something you'd get from a downtown thrift store, unloved and unwanted. It was the bedroom you put grandma in when she came to visit.

Ben sat on the edge of the bed as the Otter took his place next to him, placing the cans of carbonated water on the nightstand.

"It's Ben, right? Just wanted to make sure."

"Some people call me Benjamin."

"Benjamin is much nicer," said the Otter, smiling with dreams in his eyes as he held Ben's blue gaze.

"According to the girls from middle school, Benjamin wasn't a cute name. So, they would always shorten it to Ben, and it stuck."

"Either way, you're cute," said the Otter, shifting closer to him. "What could be cuter than you?"

Ben smiled, looking down the length of the Otter's body, his heart racing. It was the beard. Ben desperately wanted to kiss him. "What's your name?"

The Otter paused. "It's Martin." He surveyed Ben with his eyes, up and down, then scratched his head, his expression turning to awkwardness. "Hey, do you have I.D. on you? Just to be sure you're, what was it? Nineteen?"

"Uh, yeah..." said Ben, reaching for his wallet and handing him his high school student card. Martin's eyes widened as he looked at the laminated card. "Your high school card?"

"It says the year," said Ben quickly, pointing at it. "Bottom right. Grade twelve was last year."

"Where's your driver's license? Do you drive?"

"It's at home."

Martin handed the card back to him. He placed his hand on Ben's leg and slid it around his waist. Ben wished he had chosen something other than jeans to wear. They were too restricting, especially when he looked at Martin's looser sweatpants.

"You're so cute," said Martin quietly, looking at his lips.

"Thanks... So are you," said Ben, his heart racing even faster now. Martin leaned forward, took Ben's chin in his fingertips and placed his soft lips upon his, pushing his tongue delicately into his mouth. He put his hands on Ben's shoulders, gliding them down his back. Ben touched Martin's waist and slid his hand below his shirt, feeling his warm skin underneath.

Then, from downstairs, a phone started ringing. It stopped, but then it sounded for a second time.

Martin moaned at the shrill sound. "Hey..." he said, pulling away from the kiss. "I'll be right back." He left the room and Ben remained where he was, feeling like the ringtone had cut his horniness in half. Martin flicked on the light switch in a room just down the hall and closed the door halfway, taking the call from a computer. Ben could vaguely hear the conversation, but couldn't understand the actual words being exchanged, just the timbre of their voices through the wall. The other voice coming through the computer's speaker was clearly a female, her voice much louder than Martin's obscure mumbling.

Ben stood up, went down the hall and stood inside the doorway. On the left side of the room was a professional photography space complete with a white backdrop and a shiny white desk with multiple ring lights facing it from all angles. Martin was standing in front of a gaming station on the other side of the room. There were three flat monitors, expensive-looking keyboards, lights and routers. The setup also had a video camera that was secured to a swivel stand just above the monitors.

Martin glanced over his shoulder to see Ben and a look of panic appeared on his face like Ben was a random intruder. "Okay, I'll see you later. Bye."

The woman on the other end said her goodbyes and hung up. Martin sighed deeply and looked at Ben, an awkward smile spreading across his face.

"Are you a streamer?" asked Ben curiously.

Martin side-eyed his computers. "Yeah," he replied, swiftly exiting the room.

"You record other content too," said Ben, motioning towards the white desk in front of the backdrop.

Martin scratched his beard. "Yeah, mostly gaming." He started to close the door when Ben also noticed a bamboo tray on the floor next to the desk that was filled with all-natural air fresheners and essential oils.

"Do you do product reviews or something?"

"Sometimes," said Martin, closing the door completely.

Ben sensed a noticeable shift in the energy between them. When they got back to the spare room, it was too awkward. The mood was off.

Martin noticed the shift in Ben's eyes when they sat back down on the bed. "Sorry, that was my sister on the phone. She's been staying with me for the last few weeks." He smiled, returning his attention to the dream that was Ben's face. "Now, where were we, cutie?"

"Actually, I think I'm gonna go," said Ben, feeling like the moment had already come and gone.

Martin dropped his shoulders and arms. "Really?"

"Yeah."

Martin appeared both disappointed and annoyed. "Alright then..." He got up, a rush of cold air hitting Ben in the face.

Ben followed him down the stairs to the foyer, where he unlocked the door for him. Without another word, Martin turned around and made his way down the hallway towards the kitchen. When Ben opened the door to let himself out, Martin came back into the foyer. "By the way, this was pretty much a one-time thing."

Ben looked at him sheepishly. "Okay," he said, shutting the door behind him. As he pulled out his phone to order another Uber, he heard the door lock shut.

7

It felt strange to be stepping into his condo as an unemployed man. Jay was used to arriving home with work on his mind: what still had to be done that night, deadlines and meetings. This was the first time in his life where he'd wake up tomorrow, on a Saturday, and not have to think about work or school. He hadn't been without a job since he was sixteen when he first started as a sandwich artist in a grocery store. Even through four years of college, then as an intern, he worked as a waiter. Jay knew he was skilled at what he did for work currently. He had the résumé to prove it. He'd find other employment that was equally rewarding, or he might branch out and try something new and different. Maybe this was meant to happen. Breaking up with his boyfriend, then his parents dying, then turning thirty and now losing his job... Maybe it was time to start over.

Throwing his keys onto the countertop, Jay kicked off his loafers and slumped down onto his couch. He hugged a pillow in his arms and closed his eyes. The peace and quiet in his condo soothed him. The distant traffic down below lulled him into a sleep-like state of drifting imagination. His condo was located right in the hub of downtown Venus Valley, the popular entertainment and nightlife district. He could hear the chatty locals and tourists as music poured out from restaurants and into his condo through the open balcony door. To the eastern border, the sprawling forested and rocky hills of Larchdale Grove were the city's own private oasis of lush Arcadia amongst the dry terrain that surrounded the outskirts.

Jay got up, tossed back a shot of vodka to kick off the night, then stepped out onto the balcony to smell the aromas coming from nearby restaurants. There was fried calamari and perfectly seasoned steaks. Juicy ribs smothered in a rich sauce exploding with flavour. Fancy cocktails with aromatic botanicals and fresh fruit juices. Overhead, a plane flew past on its way to Venus Valley International Airport, and Jay's mind wandered to an adventure in a far-off land, some place different, some place exciting.

He reached into his pocket and pulled out his undamaged phone that he had managed to fish out from the fountain. He dialed Salvador's number, and he answered almost immediately. "Hey, you getting ready?" asked Jay, smiling into the speaker.

"I'm heading out soon," replied Salvador. "I'll be there in half an hour or so."

"Well, I was thinking," started Jay, "why not just come here instead of us going out? I have booze and food. We can sit out on my balcony. Or, if you want, we can still go out." There was a pause, and Jay heard a dog barking on Salvador's end.

"Yeah, for sure," said Salvador. "I'm down. What's your address again?"

"213 Evermore Street. It's a condo."

"I'm not driving home tonight if there's booze," said Salvador with a laugh. "I'm getting drunk, baby!"

"Are you now..." Jay teased.

"Sorry, did I come across as trashy?" asked Salvador. "I like to drink on weekends."

"Same," said Jay. "If you want, you can just–"

"I'll pack an overnight bag," butted in Salvador.

Jay pondered this. Though he barely knew the guy, the idea of hanging out with someone, as well as drinking and possibly hooking up with them, seemed like the perfect Friday night to him. There was no way he was ending the night sober and alone.

"Well, if you want, you can *probably* stay the night," said Jay, butterflies awaking in his stomach.

"*Probably*," said Salvador playfully.

"I mean..." said Jay, getting up and leaning over the railing. "It's up to you."

"As long as by the end of the night I'm not hacked to bits and put inside your freezer," said Salvador.

"What?" asked Jay.

"Okay, on my way. See you soon!"

Jay could hear Salvador's smirk on the other end as he hung up.

Jay didn't know what tonight would bring, but he was glad to have company over to help distract him from the chaos of his current situation. He put out a tasty display of various snacks and alcohol on the island countertop, then hurriedly went around and cleaned up some last-minute details before Salvador showed up. His condo was just a few years old, and it was his first real big purchase. His parents had even helped him move in. But a few months after settling in, his mom, Daisy, was diagnosed with cancer. Carey, his father, had already had health issues for several years, but was still managing to get by on routine doctor visits, prescriptions and lifestyle adjustments. When Daisy's health began to decline, Jay saw the devastation on his father's face almost every day. They'd all assumed he would be the first to go, not her. When she finally did pass away, his dad's will to live dropped tremendously. Some said it was the illness that finally took him, but Jay knew his dad had died of a broken heart. Jay's older brother, Bradley, was his biggest support during this time. Brad had been living in Portland and took time off work so he could come to Venus Valley for the funerals and to spend time with Jay. They hung out and made food and watched movies, brother to brother bonding, something they hadn't done in years. When Brad went back home, it took a year for Jay's isolation to creep up on him. The loneliness of no longer having his parents around during Christmas affected him. They weren't there for celebrations. He didn't get that phone call from his mom on his birthday anymore. He entered his thirties, and they weren't there to see it happen. He still had questions. An appliance would break in the kitchen and he couldn't call his dad to ask how to fix it. His mom wasn't there to offer him advice on any new obstacle that came into his life. They wouldn't be there to see him grow old.

His career kept him distracted during that time, which Jay was thankful for. He became a workaholic. He lost a few friends from not socializing and not maintaining a healthy balance between work and life. So, after all this time, he was excited that Salvador was coming over. He felt as though enough time had passed for him to be himself again. The last time Jay had a guy over at his place had been several months ago, when an eager bottom came waltzing into his condo. The guy surely looked like his pictures, but his overall demeanor was not what Jay ordered from the sleazy gay hookup app catalog. The spark didn't ignite, the chemistry was missing, but the blood was still rushing to his dick, and he needed to get off, so he might as well go ahead and fuck what was given to him. Once all was said and done, the guy just left, no chit-chat afterward.

Jay hoped this visit with Salvador would be different. There was a smile growing in him from deep down. He felt lightheaded. He put some music on his living room television, then poured himself a double rum and Coke, bopping his head to the dance track remix.

His phone vibrated on the marble countertop and he looked at the screen. Salvador texted that he had just arrived. After buzzing him in, Jay took a quick look at himself in the bathroom mirror. He jogged into the bedroom and sprayed himself with a new bottle of Azzaro The Most Wanted cologne, choosing to wear a casual plain t-shirt with slim-fit shorts and no socks. Grabbing his drink, he answered the knock at the front door. When it swung open, Salvador was standing there, smiling. Jay froze when he saw him. At twenty-eight, Salvador still possessed that youthful whimsy. His smile was perfection. His curly black hair was the second thing Jay noticed, and his face seemed to glow, his skin a gorgeous caramel. He had brown eyes, and there were some laugh lines and crow's feet on his face, which Jay found both masculine and sexy. It was a face filled with joy, and Salvador had the lines to prove it. He was some exotic bird to Jay, so different from the guys he had dated in the past. Who was this gorgeous thing standing in his doorway?

Jay stepped aside to let Salvador in.

"Look at you," exclaimed Salvador, looking him up and down, then briefly taking a look around his condo, the smile never leaving his face. He was dressed in a black button-down and tight black pants, the top buttons of his shirt undone, as they were when they first met, to reveal gold necklaces and his chest hair. "Now this is a first."

"For what?" asked Jay, making his way into the kitchen.

Salvador's hands glided towards the snack tray, the same rings he wore earlier that day dragging along the island's marble surface. "Food, drinks... and music! Most guys don't even offer me water." He leaned against the edge of the island. "Usually, it's straight to the bedroom."

Jay froze where he was. “Is this okay? Do you just...”

Salvador shook his head and quickly put his hand on Jay’s arm, laughing. “It’s all good. I’d like to do the same when guys come over to my place, but I don’t want to put in all that effort when they’re usually just there to... Anyway, whatever.” He sighed and placed his hands on the countertop. “This is nice, though. Thank you. None of that ‘blow and go’ happening here.” He grabbed a small handful of salted chips from the tray.

Jay smiled, really liking his personality. It was calm and flamboyant at the same time. “You want a drink?”

“Gin and tonic,” he said.

“Uh...” trailed Jay. “How do you make that? I’ve never had tonic water before.”

Salvador rolled his eyes playfully and hugged Jay’s torso before taking a seat on one of the stools at the island. “You can just give me orange juice with a straw.”

Jay gave him a sarcastic look. “Are you making fun of me?”

“You can spike it with something. I’m not picky.”

Jay grabbed a bottle of cheap tequila from the bar cart behind him. “Tequila?”

Salvador smiled. “Win.”

Jay took a highball glass from the cupboard and dumped in four ounces of tequila.

“Oh my... Tequila Blackout,” said Salvador, cringing at the glass comically.

“What?” asked Jay, pouring in the pulpy orange juice next.

Salvador smiled again and delicately placed his hand on top of Jay’s. “I mean, it looks good.”

“This bottle hasn’t been opened in forever.”

“Bad memories?” asked Salvador.

“It was the first liquor I ever bought,” said Jay, topping up his own drink. “I was nineteen, and my parents were out of town. I invited one of my close friends over and we drank shots of tequila all night."

"Did you puke?" asked Salvador curiously, sliding his stool closer like Jay was his grandfather telling a fascinating story.

"I remember waking up at 4 a.m. and my body lying on the threshold of the bathroom. My buddy had ordered two large pizzas with wings and was eating them by himself on the couch while watching reruns of *The Simpsons*, completely wasted and laughing his ass off."

"Was he gay?" asked Salvador. "Did he, like, put his dick through one of the slices and you sucked him off during this 4 a.m. drunken bro stupor?"

"Gross," said Jay, tossing back his drink. "We are not ordering pizza now."

Salvador shrugged his shoulders. "Hey, it's tequila. Expect the unexpected. Especially when you're..." he counted the shots Jay had put in his glass, "six shots in."

"Four," Jay reminded him, lost in Salvador's eyes. He couldn't look away. He knew what moments like this led to. When a subtle yet playful smirk popped up at the corner of Salvador's mouth, their eyes locked together. Jay wanted Salvador's tongue inside of his mouth with his warm lips pressed up against his. As if reading his mind, Salvador slid even closer to him with his drink in hand, their knees almost touching. He then turned his head and looked around Jay's condo, his eyes lingering on the door to the balcony. Jay poured himself another drink, then picked up the snack tray of marble cheese, salted crackers, bologna and salami and made his way to the open balcony door. "Want to sit outside?"

"Sure," said Salvador, following him. As he passed the television, he added swagger to his walk that was in time with the beat of the music. The sun had finally set, and twilight had spread across the sky. When Jay was going through his rough time during the last couple of years, he would often sit out on the balcony and live vicariously through the bar-goers down below. Almost every weekend, starting around eight, the noise lasted all through the night from restaurants and bars and people driving past or walking in groups along the streets. Girls wore their short sparkly dresses and stumbled around in their heels, slurring their words and laughing. The constant noise would have annoyed most people, but not Jay. It kept things electric, lively and not so lonely.

Salvador sat down on a plastic chair beside the patio door as Jay placed the snack tray on a glass table nearby.

"Nice setup you got," said Salvador. "Tourist central."

"You know it," said Jay.

"Seen any crazy shenanigans?"

"Not really," said Jay as he looked down at the restaurant and lounge that was directly across from his condo building. "Have you been to the Black Lagoon?"

"Several times," said Salvador, reaching for the snack tray and making himself a mini cracker, cheese and meat sandwich. "I've had meetings there with my clients."

"What do you do for work again?" asked Jay.

"I'm a wealth advisor for Monroe Wealth Management."

"I've heard of it before," said Jay.

Salvador raised his glass. "I'm also a freelance wedding planner."

Jay's eyes widened in surprise. "Really?" he rested his arms on the railing. "So, do you plan gay weddings?"

"More straight than gay," he confessed. "Why? Are you getting married, lover boy?"

Jay scoffed. "Not for a while. It must be fun, though."

"Getting married?" asked Salvador.

"Being a wedding planner," clarified Jay.

Salvador took several sips of his tequila and orange juice. "It can be. It's also stressful as hell sometimes. It's pretty cool, though."

"Isn't it a lot of work? Having two careers like that? You must never sleep."

Salvador shrugged his shoulders. "I'm in love with making money. I've been advising for almost two years now and I've been wedding planning for three. There's so much energy inside of me! I can't sit and do just one thing, you know? Otherwise, I'll get bored and... masturbate three times a day."

Jay tossed back more of his drink. "Totally understandable," he said.

"The salary from being a wealth advisor pays for necessary things like my monthly bills and food, condo expenses, savings and investments. The extra cash from wedding planning goes into my 'fun money jar' like vacations and clothes and meth."

Jay lowered his glass, his eyes widening.

"Kidding," said Salvador with a devilish smile. "I don't do drugs."

"Me neither," said Jay. "Sometimes an edible here and here. Fun money, though... That's cool." He knew the question that was coming next. The reason they were even here talking in the first place. The dreaded...

"So... What does Daddy Warbucks do for money?" asked Salvador with a curious smile.

Jay let out a sigh as he extended his arms out to stretch, trying to buy himself a few seconds. "Uh... Well, I actually quit my job today. Regional manager for Brandon Save."

Salvador nodded his head, and Jay could see the gears moving behind his eyes as he tried figuring out how to carefully ask his next question. "I'm getting the feeling that this might be a conversation better saved for another time," he said, gauging Jay's reaction. "Unless you want to talk about it. It's really none of my business or anything."

"Yeah..." said Jay. "Maybe another time."

"Great," he said, getting up and standing next to him at the railing. "I've quit jobs before."

"Not big ones like mine," said Jay.

"No," said Salvador, looking down at the people on the street. "Just small places like shoe stores. This was years ago during my assistant manager days. I remember this one boss, and she'd become the biggest bitch if you didn't know how to do everything she could do in the first few days of working there. She'd actually intimidate and threaten me–just pure negative energy. She didn't like me. Sometimes I'd walk into the stock room and she would be on her break, sitting at her desk and talking with one of the associates she did like. She'd be telling them how she always played the lottery, and hoped one day she would win so she could leave that store. For over twenty years she was a store manager for that company, and she hated it. So, I quit. After leaving, I told myself I'd never end up like her."

Jay's eyes wandered from staring down at the street to Salvador's face again. "Hey, can I call you Sal?"

"No, you can't," he said.

"Okay Sal," said Jay, jokingly.

"I mean it," said Salvador, his expression stoic, looking Jay dead in the eyes. "Don't call me that."

There was an awkward silence. Jay lifted his glass to take a sip and noticed it was empty, the half-melted ice clinking against the sides. He shook his glass at Salvador. "Gotta fill up. Want something different to drink?"

Salvador smiled. "Surprise me. Just no roofies, please."

Jay went back inside and worked his magic on Salvador's next drink, excited for him to try his concoction. Minutes later, he stepped back out with another rum and Coke in one hand and what appeared to be a frozen strawberry margarita in the other.

"Look at you, fancy guy," said Salvador, amazed at his host's unexpected skill.

"How's *that* for a frozen margarita?" asked Jay gleefully. "It's really not that complicated. Tequila, ice, strawberries, some other things and rim the glass."

"Rimming is good," said Salvador. "You always need to rim." He took a sip and cringed at what he tasted. "Wait, other things you say?"

"Strawberry jam to boost the strawberry flavour."

"Ohhh..." said Salvador, nodding his head with enthusiasm like a father would when receiving a hideous gift from his child. "It's very... disgusting."

Jay gave him a sassy look.

Salvador rolled his head and finished off his orange juice and tequila instead. "I'm firing you as tonight's bartender. See, you lost two jobs in one day." He bit his lip. "Too soon?"

Jay patted him on the back, laughing. "This next one won't disappoint you. I'll make a comeback!" He went back inside to grab the bottle of tequila, then ran back out, dumping several ounces of the gold liquid into Salvador's glass.

"Jesus..." said Salvador, laughing as tequila splashed everywhere. "God, this is going to be 'dick through a slice of pizza' territory soon."

"Do you want pizza?" asked Jay. "I'm sorry I'm not a proper bartender..." He slouched over the railing, looking down, his face somber.

Salvador slid his finger under Jay's chin to lift it up. "Don't hang your head down like that. You're too handsome to be hiding."

Jay smiled, but there was still uncertainty in his eyes. He lifted one of his hands and rubbed his eye with his fingertips as though he was trying to clear out a speck of dust.

"Are you okay?" asked Salvador, putting his arm around him.

Jay looked upward, into the blanket of twilight. He sighed.

"Not to sound nosy or anything," said Salvador, "but do you have money saved up?"

Jay nodded. "Yeah."

"Why don't you take some time off from work, then? You're a free man."

Jay looked at him. "I'm thirty. I can't just not have a job."

"Exactly! You're thirty. Take some time off."

"And do what?"

Salvador shrugged. "I still have no idea why you quit, but you've obviously been working a lot. You went to college?"

"Four years," said Jay. "I've never not had a job. I've always been so hyper-focused on school and careers that I've never had time for hobbies, really. My hobby is... watching movies."

Salvador rolled his eyes. "Everyone watches movies."

"Then I don't know what my hobbies are," said Jay. "I have no fucking idea... OH SHIT!"

"What?" asked Salvador, his eyes darting around frantically. He followed Jay's gaze over the railing, but Jay crouched down and pulled Salvador down with him.

"It's Robbie, my boss... Ex-boss."

Salvador's mouth fell open. "No..." He adjusted his sight through the gaps in the railing, trying to find him. Jay peeked through the railing as well, unable to miss that head of silver hair walking down the street with a few of his colleagues, including Johnson.

"Fuck," muttered Jay. Robbie knew Jay lived here, so Jay thought maybe Robbie would look up to see if he was out on his balcony.

Salvador peeked over the top of the railing. "Wow... He's a total Silver Fox. How old is he? I'd say around forty-five."

"He just turned fifty," said Jay.

"I'd blow him," said Salvador matter-of-factly. He then looked at Jay, smiling.

Jay met his glance. "I didn't suck him off if that's what you're alluding to."

"I didn't say anything," said Salvador, looking back down. "You said it, not me." He then glanced at Jay again out of the corner of his eye. "So, you did suck him off? Or..."

"You know, I still don't really know you," said Jay, squinting at him suspiciously. "Do you ever feel like you're being a little too intrusive with some of your questions?"

Salvador took a second to respond. "I guess," he said. "Why are we still crouching? He's gone."

"He went into the Black Lagoon," said Jay, standing up.

Salvador's eyes lit up. "I've seen him there before!"

"When?"

"Months ago. He was with some guy."

"What guy?"

"This really hot dude who looked South Asian... Pakistani or something. He had this muscular body, scruffy beard, buzzcut and wore sexy clothes."

"What was he wearing?"

"This fishnet shirt and tight jean shorts. You could actually see his entire chest through the fabric, even in the low lighting. He's one of those guys you don't forget seeing because of how sexy he is."

"Hm, doesn't ring a bell," said Jay. "Probably a rent boy." He snorted at the thought.

"The guy looked like he was in his thirties, though," said Salvador.

"So, a rent man," finished Jay.

Salvador took another deep sip from his glass, which at this point was just pure tequila. He looked at Jay, grabbing his arm. "Wanna dance?"

Jay puffed out his cheeks and exhaled a burst of air. "Sure. Where?"

"In there," said Salvador, pointing inside.

Jay looked over his shoulder as though he needed reminding of what was behind him. "My condo?"

"No, in Narnia," said Salvador, his voice drawling. "It'll be our little dance club."

Jay's drink splashed around in his glass as he stumbled towards the door, causing the glass to slip out of his hand and fall over the railing. "Shit..." he murmured, leaning over the railing to watch the glass tumble down nine floors and shatter when it hit the sidewalk. He took the tequila bottle and drank a shot from it, grimacing, and shook his head violently. "God. I'm nineteen again."

"Is this happening?" asked Salvador excitedly, taking the bottle back from him. "Is tequila the one that's gonna to do us in tonight? What's her name, anyway?" He looked at the label. "The cheapest bottom-shelf ho of them all."

Jay took the bottle and put it down on the table. He took Salvador's hands next and pulled him into the living room, where he took the remote and turned up the volume, changing the station to a dance club playlist. He threw the remote back onto the couch and pressed his body against Salvador, who gladly reciprocated the gesture and slowly grinded his pelvis against him.

"You're so handsome," whispered Salvador, pressing his forehead against his.

"You too," said Jay.

Salvador looked into Jay's eyes. "I don't normally do this when I first meet a guy. Like, become this way."

"Like what way?" asked Jay.

Salvador leaned in and kissed him on the lips, and Jay grabbed hold of the side of his face, tracing his hands down his back.

Jay started breathing on him, feeling Salvador's warm breath along his neck. "Your cologne is so sexy," he said, running his hand down the side of his face. "I'm so fucking happy right now."

Salvador smiled. "Me too." He let go of Jay and walked back out onto the balcony to grab the tequila. When he came back in, he took a sip and handed the bottle to him.

"Yeah, fuck glassware," said Jay, taking the bottle.

"Cheers," said Salvador.

Jay stopped the bottle halfway to his mouth, then raised it instead. "To being thirty." After taking a sip, he lowered the bottle and shook his head from the potent tequila taste.

"We're so dramatic," said Salvador, rubbing his hands along Jay's arms.

Jay placed his hands around Salvador and they started rubbing up on each other slowly as the throbbing dance track hit its chorus. Salvador smiled... His gorgeous smile. That was enough for Jay to lean in like it was the last time he would ever kiss a handsome man. Salvador stumbled back and dragged Jay towards him until they both fell onto the couch together. Jay struggled with putting the tequila down on the table, but managed to keep it upright as he fell against Salvador, kissing his neck up and down, rubbing his cheek along his face stubble.

Salvador reached for the zipper of his shorts, but Jay stopped him.

"There's more room on my bed," he said.

Salvador let go of Jay and lay beneath him, vulnerable as could be, and smiled. "You'll have to get me there somehow."

Jay grabbed hold of him and lifted him up into his arms. "You mean, like this?"

8

Robbie ordered another round of drinks for the table. His drink of choice was the Whiskey Sour, complete with egg white foam.

"Old Fashioned, please," said Johnson to the waitress.

Robbie rolled his eyes. He knew Johnson wasn't particularly fond of the Old Fashioned but reluctantly drank them to look suave and to impress others. His favorite cocktail was the Blue Lagoon, Robbie knew, having seen him order it multiple times before. Johnson came along to his first business dinner meeting years ago when he joined the team and most of the men had ordered an Old Fashioned or Negroni, and there he was, sitting with his Blue Lagoon, embarrassed. Never again.

The Black Lagoon, famous for its devilishly appealing cocktails and appetizers, was a popular restaurant and bar in the heart of downtown. Perfectly trendy with its dimmed lighting, black upholstered armchairs, tables of rustic wood and nautical décor mixed with pirate lore, it was a popular destination for business meetings. The weekends, however, were when the kids and tourists came out to play with their celebratory gatherings.

"At this point, why bother with an entrée when you're already two drinks in?" declared Mary, chuckling to herself as she dove into her Dark 'n Stormy. Mary was one of the senior regional managers, and although men often tried dominating her in business combat, she was indeed a complete savage cunt when it came to walking into one of her stores and making a manager burst into tears after a visit. Totally alpha and unapologetic. In the last year alone, she fired two store managers, two assistant managers and one district manager for their shit metrics and abysmal track record and, in her words, total lack of competence at what was expected of them. There were a couple times where even Robbie thought she would report him to *their* boss for his occasional blind eye. After all, we can't all be perfect at our jobs like Mary can. Since Robbie was next in line for Calvin's Regional Operations Vice President Position, Mary was bitter with the knowledge that she could do the job just as well, if not better than, Robbie. The only thing preventing her from getting that promotion was not having a dick.

Robbie held up the menu and scanned down the various categories. "I'm not particularly hungry," he said to the waitress as she held her electronic pad in hand, ready to take his order. "But I'll get the shrimp fritters."

"And for you?" asked the waitress, giving Johnson a friendly look.

Johnson put his drink down. "Thanks, I'm good."

"So..." started Robbie once the waitress walked away. This was it. The one word that made everyone at the table hush instantly and pay attention to him. Robbie had four sets of eyes on him, and the random clinking of a cocktail pick against the rim of a glass felt ominous. Mary sipped the last couple drops of her drink and crossed her legs, then folded her hands together and leaned back as if she was about to commence with an interview.

"What happened today was unfortunate. Let's not make it into some big ordeal. I'm sure most had a good time on their lunch breaks laughing about it."

"So gross," said Mary.

"People were sending me links to his profile," said Beth. She dropped her phone on the table as though it was suddenly unsanitary. "Like, stop please. I'm going to throw up. Literally, in our office? How did no one know?"

Mary shrugged her shoulders. "Maybe some knew but didn't say anything. It's easy for some people to turn a blind eye rather than to involve themselves in the situation."

Johnson drummed his fingers on the table and nodded his head. "You're so right, Mary."

Mary threw him a look.

"He may have to come back to grab some of his things," said Robbie.

"Um, no," said Beth. "We box up whatever there is and leave it outside."

"Good idea," said Mary. "The pervert can come and reclaim his bag of trash next to the... well... other trash." She shuddered and started fanning her face with her hands. "Whatever. This is making me angrier the longer we talk about it."

Robbie looked down at the table, twisting his mouth.

"He ruined his career," said Curtis, another district manager. "No one in the industry is ever going to want him." He scoffed. "What an idiot. You'd think he was only making a stock boy's wage working working here."

"I'm so embarrassed for him," said Beth, placing her hand to her chest.

"Yeah," said Robbie, his voice nonchalant. He downed the rest of his drink and got up. "Gotta use the bathroom."

He stepped away and, dragging his hand through his silver hair, sighed out loud; it felt like he could breathe again after suffocating for the last half hour. He didn't want to talk about Jay anymore. He knew about his personal struggles over the last couple of years. Just a few months ago, Jay confided in him about his mental state. Robbie was there for him when his parents died, and he tried supporting him in any way he could. He cared about Jay. Not in a romantic sense, but as a friend. So, when Robbie found out what Jay had been doing on company property, he felt betrayed. *Fucking stupid. Jay, you idiot.*

Robbie had found Jay's résumé online four years ago. Recognizing his talent, and finding him remarkably handsome, Robbie essentially gave Jay his career. He was supposed to be Robbie's prodigy, but he decided to piss it all away. Robbie would have given him a second chance. But this wasn't that world. He wasn't allowed to feel sympathy for Jay. He had to be a Mary, even though at times he would prefer not to be. For every talented person in their field, there were always others who could do the job better. Robbie knew there were smarter people who could do what he did better. But fuck them, and sorry, Jay, fuck you too.

Robbie slipped into the men's bathroom, went straight for the stall farthest from the door and locked himself inside. He knocked the toilet seat down to make himself a spot to sit for a moment.

Jay doing solo porn. The mere thought of Jay jacking off on camera for hundreds of horny dudes made him grin. He'd be lying if he said the mere idea of a man like Jay masturbating, legs spread, not just anywhere, but in his office, didn't cross his mind from time to time. Robbie needed to remain professional, even though the whole thing was comical in a way. Did Jay just not care? Did he want to get caught? All at the risk of losing not just his professional career but his reputation just for some extra cash.

Robbie felt an erection building in his trousers. He didn't cruise anymore, even though it was something he did a lot of in his thirties. Something happened when he turned thirty-two. He became a horndog, more so than in his twenties. His sex drive went from a solid eight out of ten to a twelve. Cruising bathroom stalls at malls, parks and libraries. Bathhouses. This was in Y2K, before social media and hook-up apps made it so easy. He was a reckless boy. The AIDS epidemic had ripped through the community in the '80s, and close to eighty percent of all the gay men he knew when he was a teenager had died. Then, as a twenty-something living in the '90s, he felt numb. He wanted to explore sex, so he became a young creature of the night, dipping into bars and going to underground parties and experimenting with every drug. He assumed he'd die, so he might as well live recklessly while he could since there wouldn't be a tomorrow.

In his later twenties, one of his hook-ups was looking for supervisors at a fashion department store. It paid more than where he was working as a supervisor in a pizza restaurant, making next to nothing, and going absolutely nowhere with his life. His dreams and aspirations for other careers from his youth had died long ago, so perhaps this was something that would set him in a new direction. So, he jumped at the offer. Robbie decided to follow the money. He was eventually promoted to assistant manager and later store manager. Once he realized he was capable of more than what he was doing, he enrolled in college and eventually got a degree in business and marketing. It wasn't something he ever saw himself doing when he was younger, but he was on to something now, and he went with it. From there, he job-hopped and climbed the ladder. When he grew tired of one company, he chased bigger corporations, higher salaries. Then one year, he was scooped up by none other than Mary herself, something she probably now regretted. He was hired as one of the district managers at Brandon Save and was soon promoted to regional manager, making more money than he ever had before. Having turned fifty this year, he found the world had become a much different place than it was back when he was a kid. The older he became, the more he felt like he was falling behind, out of the loop... irrelevant. He had recognized things were changing in his forties when younger guys would message him, calling him by the coveted *daddy* title. So, he kept up the persona, only because it garnered him the most attention. His hope was that eventually, someday, he'd find a guy who would only refer to him by his name. Luckily for him, it had happened. Robbie was waiting for his boyfriend's text telling him that his plane had landed, which would be any minute now.

Robbie's phone vibrated and he read the incoming text message.

> Hey babe!! Just landed. Gotta get to work. Staying at Larchdale tonight. See you tomorrow at the party. Can't wait!! :)

Robbie smiled and sent a reply, his heart doing somersaults in his chest. Before he finished typing, he heard someone enter the bathroom. The person walked towards the stall next to his, seemingly taking their time. They closed the stall door, then knocked down the toilet seat and sat down. Robbie glanced under the stall divider and saw a man's black loafers. The man was still at first, but then his left shoe tapped. Robbie put his phone away and stared down at the shoe long enough to realize that the man was tapping his shoe to the melody of the song that was currently playing from the bathroom speakers. Yet again, Robbie felt his dick growing excited, so he decided to quickly leave the stall. He went to one of the sinks to wash his hands, looking at himself in the mirror. The other stall opened just as Robbie turned off the water and out stepped Johnson, who walked over to the sink beside him and started to wash his hands.

"Couldn't go?" asked Robbie.

"Hm?" mumbled Johnson, looking at him in the mirror.

Robbie stared back at him. He had a gut feeling that Johnson wasn't nearly as embarrassed as he was in this awkward moment.

"Any word on a replacement for Jay?" asked Johnson.

"No," said Robbie right away, anticipating the question. He wiped his hands on a paper towel. "When there are updates, believe me, you will be the first to know."

"Am I at least being considered?" he asked, turning away from the mirror.

"Jesus, Johnson. You follow me into a bathroom to interrogate me?"

Johnson's face conveyed no emotion. Robbie honestly thought the guy was going to lunge at him at any moment.

"Listen, I'm sorry," said Johnson, sounding not sorry at all. "I just... really want this. I'm more than ready, and the money... Come on!"

"I hear what you're saying, Johnson" said Robbie in an honest voice. "But if you ask me again, you're really going to piss me off." He stepped forward and stood eye to eye with him. "Don't ever follow me into a fucking bathroom again."

Robbie tossed the crumpled paper towel into the garbage and walked out, letting the door swing shut behind him.

9

"Ugh!"

Carly threw her phone across the couch with a frustrated and dramatic flick of her wrist.

Martin looked down at where her phone had landed, then returned his attention back to his own. "What's wrong now?" he asked in a bored drawl, putting his feet up on the coffee table.

Carly snatched the phone back. "I lost eighty subscribers."

"Because of the ad placement?" asked Martin.

"I've been promoting the Super Banana Slicer during the first thirty seconds of all my videos. Don't they understand this is my job and there are companies out there who pay me to promote their products? It's a lifestyle channel, and this product was carefully selected by me. It's a cool thing!" She pulled out the ridiculous yellow contraption that cut a banana into perfect slices.

Martin stared at it. "Ever heard of a knife? If you're someone who would buy that, I'm judging you hardcore."

"It saves time!" countered Carly, opening and closing the hinge repeatedly. "It looks cute, it's in the shape of a banana, and it has a happy face on it! It just screams *use me*!"

"Great. People can store it next to their special apple slicer," said Martin. "Your viewers probably thought it was stupid." When he didn't get a reply from her, he pulled his eyes away from his phone and saw the annoyance on her face as she scrolled through her various social media apps. "Fuck them," he said, tapping her knee. "They weren't real fans of you to begin with."

"The Super Banana Slicer people paid me four grand," said Carly. "It's one of my highest sponsorships so far. I've been needing that Balenciaga bag for my trip to Miami next month–the new pink one that everyone is posting. Carrie already has one... and so does Sarah! Balenciaga has literally never released a bag in this exact shade of pink before."

"You don't need another bag," said Martin, slumping further down into the couch. "You have nine."

"Excuse me. You bought a pool table," she said matter-of-factly, her eyes widening. That seemingly ended the debate.

Last week, Martin did a stream for his twenty-fifth birthday where he got drunk with his viewers and the conversation turned to how he had never won a game of pool. So, right there on the spot, he pulled out his phone and ordered one live on stream. Martin used to be part of an immensely popular channel called *MarcVs-Martin* where he competed in daily video game challenges with his best friend, Marc, who had been his friend since elementary school. They had accumulated over three million subscribers over the span of six years and averaged hundreds of thousands of viewers each time they uploaded a video. However, over time, Marc became the favorite of the two. Two years ago, Marc decided to go solo, killing their channel and their twelve-year friendship. When Marc started his new solo channel, *Marc's Takes*, he became an even bigger star. He moved away from video games and jumped into commentary about any topic that was currently trending. He then started a podcast and was offered sponsorship deals left and right. Podcasts became Marc's new schtick. Within two years, he became a millionaire. Marc desperately wanted to keep expanding, so to increase viewership and notoriety, he started doing controversial shit. He got sued and people tried to cancel him, but he had already developed a cult following. Within months of *MarcVsMartin* ending, Martin's online presence dwindled to a couple thousand viewers a day on his own solo streaming channel, *OhHeyMartin*. It was a pun from the previous channel where viewers would enter a live chat of *MarcVsMartin* and greet Marc first, then afterward would drop a quick "hey" to Martin as though he was only an afterthought. Marc was the Freddie Mercury to his Queen.

Now, Martin played video games over and over again with interactive witty banter between him and his audience of loyal viewers. When Martin was no longer raking in the amount of money he used to, he still spent impulsively out of habit. Then came the interest and maxed-out credit limits that left him with fifteen thousand dollars in credit card debt. That was a tiny bit of information he was keeping from his new wife, Carly, whom he married six months ago, and who also happened to be an online personality. Her content was primarily beauty regimes, lifestyle advice and live streams. She was growing quite well for herself, much better than Martin's online presence. Two years ago, Martin had found her on a dating app and thought she was cute. Martin came from a large conservative family. He had two brothers, one younger and one older, and one younger sister. He was expected to go to college, establish a substantial career, pay his way, then marry a nice girl before he was twenty-seven. His parents were initially hesitant about his online presence with Marc when they were still in high school. When they started their channel, they were only seventeen. It was hard for his parents to understand that you could make money playing video games, thinking it was some sort of scam.

Then, once they saw just how much they were actually making through advertisements and sponsorships, they told him he still had to go to school. So, Martin went and got his marketing degree to get them off his back.

They assumed he was happy. He married Carly as a reflex, an expectation, especially after what had happened with Marc and the channel. She was also mixed race, her dad being white and her mother black. It was a surprise to his family. No one in his family had ever married someone who wasn't white. She was his beautiful royal duchess, a firecracker who possessed a feisty and commanding energy. Some would say she wore the pants in the relationship. He was a basement dweller who lived in his man cave and wore sweatpants and t-shirts with pop culture references on the front. He and Carly were able to relate to one another on a career level and each knew what it was like for the other to have a notable online presence.

Martin had known he liked boys since he was around twelve years old, but it was a feeling he had to repress right away. No one in his family was gay, as far as he knew. All straight. All white. All Christian. All conservative. The perfect recipe for no way out. His father actively hated anything he considered to be remotely abnormal. That rubbed off on Martin, and so he buried his feelings. He dated girls. He only masturbated to straight porn. He only dressed in masculine colors. When he was having sex with Carly on their wedding night, he felt emotionless. He felt like the women in porn who were completely submissive to the men, just wanting to get it over with. This was how it would be for the rest of his life. Sometimes he'd see a pink shirt in a store and have the urge to buy it. He wouldn't. He'd hear a catchy pop song from a female singer on the radio but would change the station rather than sit and enjoy it. He'd only groom himself in certain ways so others wouldn't think he was anything other than straight. He was always hyper-focused on what he should and shouldn't be doing at all times. It was all calculated. He was too self-conscious, not fluid or natural. He regretted marrying Carly the night he married her. The passion he faked was emotionally draining.

The other night he'd downloaded a gay dating app, and the adrenaline he felt was unlike anything he had experienced before. It was like he was eight again, doing something he wasn't supposed to. There was a blond guy that popped up on the grid, and Martin didn't message him at first because he looked younger than his listed age, which was nineteen. When a guy wanted to see a picture of him, he'd send one, but only hesitantly. He needed to be safe and discreet, not wanting to hook up with just anyone. He eventually messaged Ben anyway, assuming he just looked young for his age... and so damn cute. Martin sent him an obscure picture of himself in hopes he would at least be interested, and he was.

When Ben finally did come over the other night, Martin got butterflies in his chest from the anticipation of hooking up with a guy for the first time. It was a feeling he never felt when he was with a woman. Until meeting Ben, Martin had no idea what it was like to be drawn to someone sexually and emotionally at the same time. He hadn't even met an openly gay man before. So, when Ben decided to leave the other night after hearing him on the phone with Carly, it pissed him off. Her call arrived at the worst possible moment, and it scared Ben away. It was like she knew he was up to something. He deeply desired to sleep with a man and to feel his arms around him. He wanted to get down on his knees...

"There's a party tonight," said Carly as she bounced from side to side with excitement.

Martin dropped his phone and rolled over onto his side, looking at her. "You're going?"

"You're coming too," she said. "We have to go shopping!"

Martin grinned. He liked going out. He hadn't been to a party in months, so this was long overdue. "You have a ton of new stuff you haven't worn yet."

"Shopping for *you*," she clarified, flashing him a smile as her fingers typed away speedily without her even looking at the screen. "The invite says the dress code is glitz and glamour. You have nothing that fits that description, and no, you aren't wearing your suit from our wedding. Time to get out of your comfort zone!"

Martin ran his fingers along the tassels on one of the couch pillows.

"It's at Larchdale Castle too!" she yelled, her mouth dropping open like a reaction channel's thumbnail. "I've never been there before–I've only ever seen pictures. No way!"

Martin could see it on her face, that frantic high of ideas for new content for all her various social media channels blowing up inside her head. It was the same look she had when they booked their trip to Rome for their honeymoon.

"It looks like someone's renting the castle," she said. "Someone named Kim."

"So, you were personally invited?" he asked. "People who've rented that place before had parties, but they were always just private."

"The invitation just showed up in my DMs," she said, getting up from the couch and heading for the stairs with even more bounce in her walk. "Everyone is sharing and tagging the invite. It's spreading like wildfire!"

"So, anyone can just go there?" asked Martin. "Is that Kim chick even allowed to do this?"

Carly looked at him briefly, then scoffed like his opinion didn't matter in the slightest. "You should go to the mall right now and pick out an outfit to wear. Send me pics before you buy it, though."

She cackled excitedly as she ran up the stairs to get ready, her eyes glued to the screen of her phone.

"What kind of person throws a party at a castle?" asked Martin, clicking on the invitation he'd just received in his DMs. "Must be filthy rich."

10

Ben was thrilled that the day was finally over. He sealed up the last half dozen cupcakes that had yet to be frosted into plastic containers. It was five in the afternoon, which meant Little Iris' Cupcakes was officially closed for the day. During the week, Iris took her usual spot beside Lovely to take advantage of the foot traffic in the downtown business core along Goldenrod Boulevard. On the weekends, she parked at popular touristy locations like parks and busy entertainment hubs. Ben had been helping as much as he could now that he wasn't in school, as well as having to balance his other job, which he was still determined to leave so he could make more money elsewhere. Iris had told him that she would resume paying him once business picked up again, but he wasn't counting on it anymore. He decided to treat the food truck as a hobby or volunteer work, something that would look good on his résumé, which made him feel better knowing that he was at least getting something out of it. He thought if he invested more time into the truck, business would pick up again.

As much as he didn't want to see his aunt fail, he couldn't stand her business mindset. He'd never liked the design she chose for the truck. It looked tacky and garish and, quite frankly, embarrassing. Iris had let her two young nieces decorate the outside like it was a princess arts and crafts project. For years, friends and family raved about her delicious homemade cupcakes with their mountains of indulgent, colorful frosting and extravagant sugary toppings. She then decided to invest and turn her baking into a business on wheels, assuming the customers would come out in droves, which would've led to her gourmet cupcakes being the talk of the town. Venus Valley had countless food trucks all throughout the city, and selling cupcakes wasn't exclusive to just Little Iris' Cupcakes. Ben had counted two other cupcake trucks over the last year. They didn't necessarily taste or look better than what Iris sold. The owners were just savvier, had a more popular presence and were better equipped to do business than her. Just like Russell and Patricia's restaurant, though, the business just wasn't destined to succeed. Iris had grown increasingly frustrated, and she would often take her annoyance out on the customers and Ben, which added to the rapid decline in him wanting to be around her. He overheard her speaking on the phone one day about how his entire life had been a tragedy of bad luck so far, and he was messed up because of it. That comment really pissed him off.

Once the inside of the truck was cleaned, Ben sat down at one of the nearby picnic tables in the park to eat the pasta salad he had bought from Brandon Save. He put his phone down on the table and opened up a dating app he was actively using. Ben was still convinced that Martin had a girlfriend, or wife. It was obvious once he heard the woman's voice on the phone. He didn't want to leave Martin's place the way he did, but it all just seemed off to him. It was his first time going out to meet another gay guy and it turned out like crap. Maybe the guy wasn't even gay, but only curious. Maybe he was a serial killer.

Ben was scrolling through other conversations when he received a notification from one of his other social media apps. It was an invitation. Tempted, he clicked on it right away.

YOU'RE INVITED! YES, YOU!

COME JOIN US AT LARCHDALE CASTLE FOR A PARTY TONIGHT!

DRESS CODE: GLITZ AND GLAMOUR

TIME OF ARRIVAL: 10 P.M.

SEE YOU THERE! - KIM

"Ben!" his aunt shouted from inside the truck. "Could you help me with the window? It's stuck again!"

Ben wrapped his food up as he looked down at his phone, smiling and feeling giddy. He put his bag down on the steps of the truck and helped her pry the service window loose so it could close all the way.

"I've been telling you we need to get this truck fixed," said Ben, struggling with the stubborn window. The truck was previously owned, having once been used to sell gourmet fried pickles. Ben later found out from a customer that the owners had been arrested for dealing cocaine out of the truck and that's why his aunt got it for as cheap as she did. Ben was still finding hardened fried pickle grime in random crevices from time to time.

He could tell Iris was frustrated with the window from the way she impatiently shook it, her face turning red. She finally slammed her hand against it. "You deal with it."

Ben gave it another attempt, but couldn't get it to close.

"We can't afford to keep up with all these problems," said Iris as she threw all her might into it. She grabbed a nearby towel to help her grip the frame more firmly, her face red as a tomato.

Ben had learned not to say anything when she was angry like this. He would just drift off into his own world inside his head. He'd think about New York and the amazing experiences he'd have there for the first time. The city was known for its theatre, which enticed him. Ben was curious about acting, but had always doubted himself, especially when a lot of the kids in school were better than him. Most everyone from his graduating class last year had already finished their first year of college. He felt like he was falling behind, left alone, as they all grew up and became adults. The possibility of moving out of Venus Valley one day excited him. But knowing the repairs the truck needed, and how his aunt's business was suffering, he felt bad. He had to think about his life, though. The food truck was her dream, not his.

Aunt Iris had never married or had children. He heard rumours from his cousins that she was a lesbian, but as he got older, he learned that when Aunt Iris was twenty she was raped in her bedroom by a boyfriend that nobody knew about, not even her parents. She didn't say anything about the incident until years later. She was apparently raped again six months later in a park bathroom, and again, she didn't say anything until much later. Some within the family had said that these were made-up stories to hide the fact that she didn't like men, that her excuse for being single was because of the trauma she had endured from the men who had assaulted her. Iris had never liked Ben's father. Some in the family had said that it was Russell who started the rumour of her rape stories being fictional, and of her being a lesbian. This caused tension to spiral from within the family. It felt like an ugly smear on his dad's legacy, and Ben refused to believe such a blatant lie about him. There was no proof of it. Now, after nine years of living with Aunt Iris, it still didn't feel like home to him. The warm and tender love he felt from his mom and dad had died with them, and he hadn't felt it since. From anyone.

"All done?" asked Iris, exhausted, as she fiddled with the car key and slid it into the ignition. "There's a frozen pizza you can have for dinner tonight. I'll be back home early Sunday morning."

"Yeah..." said Ben, a smile spreading across his face as he looked down at his phone. "I'm heading to the mall." He walked breezily past the passenger door, shut it, then made his way down the gravel path towards one of the park's exits. Seconds later, he heard an aggressive jolt from behind him as Iris started up the engine and drove away, the wheels spinning furiously like someone's head was about to roll.

11

The tingling sensation of a tiny little bug crawling up his thigh made Jay bolt upright. He threw the bedsheet aside, expecting to see a black menace through the forest of hair on his leg. But instead, Salvador's hand rested gently beside him, drumming his fingers on his skin with a sly smile on his face. He was even sexier in the morning, naked.

"It usually works," said Salvador, placing his hand beneath his cheek like a cushion. His rings, which he still wore, glistened in the sunlight that seeped in through the bedroom curtains.

Jay rolled over to his side and placed kisses along Salvador's back. "What about kissing me awake? How about giving me a blowjob? That'll do the trick. No?"

"Do you think Prince Charming should have fingered Sleeping Beauty awake?" asked Salvador, pondering. "Equally romantic."

"Yeah, because you're a ho," said Jay, smiling and running his hands over his scruff.

Salvador placed his hand across Jay's chest, resting his chin on his shoulder. "You're really warm when you sleep."

"I'm a human furnace," said Jay. "There was... a lot of heat in this bed."

Salvador traced his hand down his chest and stomach. "You're the first white guy I've ever slept with."

Jay turned to him. "Really?"

Salvador nodded.

"Why did it take so long?"

Salvador shrugged.

Jay's eyes drifted to the side. "Wait..."

"No way," said Salvador, quickly catching on. "You aren't some sort of conquest."

Jay looked at him as though he needed further convincing.

"You're intimidating as fuck," said Salvador. "Really handsome, and just the vibe you give off. If it wasn't for Kitty, I'd have never approached you. Sober, anyway."

Jay nodded. "Okay," he said sincerely.

"What did you think of me yesterday?" asked Salvador.

"Really cute," replied Jay, running his hand through his curly hair. "Duh."

"*Duh*," repeated Salvador, rolling his eyes. "What else?"

"I thought you were just a little creepy. Intimidating, too. But those thoughts quickly went away."

Salvador looked as though he was going to protest what Jay had just said, but then stopped himself. "Yeah... That's totally understandable."

"Guys don't normally walk up to me on the street and start flirting," said Jay.

Salvador inched closer to Jay, their noses almost touching. "Tons of guys don't follow through with meeting up. There was once a guy who told me I'm too intrusive." He paused and gave way to a smirk. "I'm not a big texter. I'm a face to face kind of guy; that's how I like to get to know someone." Salvador sighed. "Do you ever feel lonely?"

Jay nodded subtly. "Sometimes... But I don't usually have time to think about being lonely because I'm always thinking about work or something else–like a hobby."

"What hobbies keep you busy?" asked Salvador. "Other than movies."

Jay paused. "I've been creating content."

"Like porn," joked Salvador.

"Yeah, porn."

Salvador scoffed and looked him up and down. "Yeah..."

"It's what cost me my job yesterday. One of my sociopathic coworkers found me out and threatened to expose me. Didn't matter, though. He still exposed me *and* everyone found out anyway."

"No shit," said Salvador in awe, sitting up. "No bullshitting me?"

Jay looked at him seriously. He was going to reach for his phone to actually show him proof, but he decided not to. Not just yet, anyway.

"What kind? Like hardcore?"

"No. It's just solo camming. If someone wanted me to do something, they'd tip me, and I'd usually do it depending on what it was. Well, you can imagine..."

"I really can," said Salvador, lying back down. He looked at Jay, lust in his eyes. "I'm horny now."

Jay rolled onto his back and put his hands under his head. "I'm really embarrassed, actually. In the beginning, I was only doing the videos here, in my condo. Then, one of my viewers tipped me a few hundred dollars to do a live show in my office at work. When I declined, he kept tipping me more and more."

"Holy shit," said Salvador.

"I finally caved. He also wanted proof that it was my office, too. So, I'd turn the camera so my viewers could briefly see the empty offices and cubicles through the glass walls. It was dark, though, so they couldn't see much. It was such a thrill, and it got me hooked. Then, the same guy tipped me to do it again, and so did others. Thousands of dollars, literally."

Salvador's mouth dropped. "I'm in the wrong profession."

Jay inhaled deeply, then puffed his cheeks out like a blowfish as he exhaled. "It's all... bizarre."

There was a brief moment of silence. The bedsheets crinkled together as Salvador stretched and readjusted himself, his pelvic region the only part of his body covered up. "You know what?" he said. "All those guys in your office, they probably jerk off every single day. Some of them, I bet you, jerk off on their break, in their office with the blinds closed or in the bathroom. The only difference is you got caught."

"Sure," said Jay.

Salvador leaned over and placed his head on Jay's shoulder. "You'll find another job."

"Making all that money was just so damn addicting," confessed Jay.

"Money *is* addicting," confirmed Salvador. "Are you going to stop camming?"

Jay shrugged. "I don't want to do anything right now. I need time to think and just... move on; readjust my life and all that shit."

"Tons of people do worse things behind the scenes at their jobs than what you did," said Salvador. "Some get caught, some get away with it. Why did you tell me, anyway?"

"Because you seem trustworthy," confessed Jay. "Maybe I'm *too* trusting."

Salvador rolled over onto his back. "Well, it's my turn then. Sal."

Jay looked at him. "You told me last night you don't like being called that."

"You actually remember that conversation?" asked Salvador, half shocked and half impressed.

"Only up to the part where we dropped down behind the railing," said Jay, laughing. "Everything else... no idea."

"You're lucky I didn't steal any of your stuff and run off," said Salvador, poking him. "You should be more careful when drinking with someone you don't know that well, and I'm not trying to sound like your mom or anything."

"No, you're right. I get it," said Jay. "You just got me at a weird time yesterday."

Salvador put his arm around him and stared up at the ceiling. "Salami."

Jay tilted his head, looking up at the ceiling with him. "Salami?"

"That's what kids in school called me. I was the only Latino boy in my class for a couple grades. But anyway, one kid decided to call me Sal. He would always follow it up with the word *salami* afterward. It soon caught on, and then the other kids were calling it out at me down the halls and on the playground."

Jay glanced at him. "Well, I promise you. *Salvador* forever."

"It doesn't usually bother me," he said. "For whatever reason, though, when you said it last night, it triggered me."

"I'm gonna throw out all the salami in the fridge right now," said Jay, getting up from the bed, completely naked.

Salvador smiled, then crawled over to the edge of the bed, just inches away from Jay's naked body.

"Don't even say it," said Jay, smiling down at him.

"Get rid of the salami if you want," said Salvador, looking up at him, "but I'm going to have a second helping of this all-American sausage."

12

The aftershave smelled of sandalwood and orange musk–typical masculine fare. Liam tapped his hands lightly along Johnson's freshly shaven head and lifted the barber chair into its upright position so Johnson could take a good look at himself.

"Smooth like butter," said Liam. "So, you never told me. Is this for a special date?"

Johnson scoffed at the comment, running his fingers through his trimmed beard and smiling at his rejuvenated appearance. "Not particularly," he replied.

"You look a whole five years younger," said Liam, looking at Johnson in the reflection of the mirror as he cleaned his blades. At the age of sixty-nine, Liam had finely combed salt and pepper hair that was styled to reflect a bygone era. He possessed one of those warm voices that you could listen to all day, like it was made for radio or broadcasting the news.

"All the gays will be crawling to me on hands and knees looking for the fountain of youth," said Johnson dramatically.

"What made you go the bald route?" asked Liam as he gently removed the warm towel from around Johnson's neck.

"It needed to be shaved off," replied Johnson, "before my hairline receded into oblivion. My beard will never go anywhere, though. If it did, I'd feel naked and just... ugly."

"It seems we have opposite problems, then," said Liam. "One of us grows his facial hair but doesn't want a full head of hair. The other..." he pointed to himself, "different story."

"You've never had a beard?" asked Johnson, surprised. "You're missing out."

"I didn't like looking older," confessed Liam. "I tried it once in my twenties, hated it, and never considered it again. Beards can do amazing things for a man's face, though. Like you, for example. But me? Nah."

Johnson appreciated the confidence boost from Liam. Since the '90s, Liam's Barber Shop had been a staple in the community for men's professional and stylish grooming. Built in the '60s, the interior retained its old-school aesthetic but had undergone modern improvements to the lighting, equipment and furniture to help keep the business hip, and also classic vintage. It was a time capsule of eras past: brick walls with warm overhead lighting, classic rock music coming from the retro wall speakers and a collage of picture frames hanging on the walls, displaying friends, customers and celebrities who had visited Liam over the past thirty years. You weren't just a customer, you were a friend.

"So," began Liam. "What's this event?"

"Some party," said Johnson as he scrolled through his phone. "My buddy, Tony, is being all dramatic about it. It's at a castle, big deal."

"Gotta look good to catch your Prince Charming then," said Liam, winking at him.

"Please. I'm not ten years old," replied Johnson, staring at himself in the mirror. "When it comes to the real world, there's no such thing–especially for gays."

"The castle you're speaking of must be Larchdale," said Liam. Just saying its name brought a smile to his face. "Oh..." He looked up, as though something had just crossed his mind. "Who is the host?"

Johnson checked his phone again. "Kim. That's all it says. She's renting the place. It must cost a bloody fortune to do that."

"Sounds intriguing," said Liam, marveled. "There used to be such big parties there. I'm glad to see the tradition carry on even after all these years. So many different kinds of people would show up, from all walks of life, wearing all sorts of wild and pretty outfits. There was always dancing, disco music, booze... Lots and lots of booze."

"Drugs," suggested Johnson. "Lots and lots of drugs. There's probably powder from the '70s still wedged between the couch cushions."

Liam shrugged. "Maybe. My purpose for going was to dance, have drinks and meet new people. It was always exciting to see who would show up, keeping an eye on the front doors to see which starlet or actor would walk through them."

"When was that?" asked Johnson.

Liam placed his hands on the edge of the countertop and thought for a moment. "The early '70s."

"Were you out?" asked Johnson.

"It was my early twenties... So, not just yet," said Liam. "There was one night at Larchdale that still stands out to me. It was a wedding reception for Mr. and Mrs. Kelly. When the dancing started, dozens of random people would show up and partake."

"So, you crashed a random wedding?" asked Johnson, laughing. "You weren't on the guest list?"

"It didn't matter," said Liam. "People showed up every weekend for a party, even if there was a wedding reception taking place. To get to the castle, you go down this long stretch of road through the hills... Some used to call it the Forever Road. You can feel your heart racing as you prepare yourself for the moment of revelation, when the trees finally part and the castle walls reveal themselves to you. Then it starts to sink in... You aren't in reality anymore. All your worries fall away, like a brisk waterfall. When you walk up the steps, the front doors are sixteen feet high and gorgeously detailed as though the engravings were paying tribute to a mystical story that no one's heard of before–a prelude to what's inside, the great surprise." Liam's eyes lit up, exciting memories thundering in his eyes. "Then the doors... They open up." He was standing in front of Johnson now, his hands spread open to emphasize his point. "When you walk in..." He paused for dramatic tension and looked down at Johnson as he did so, smirking, then continued with his cleaning, ending his story. "You'll like it there," he concluded.

Johnson was intrigued. "Well, this place has a lot to live up to. My expectations are high, Liam."

"It was such a long time ago. Just an old man's distant memory," recalled Liam, patting Johnson on the shoulder. "You should go out and meet someone."

Johnson's chin dropped. "My mom told me that the other day."

"How is Melinda, by the way?" asked Liam.

"She's well," replied Johnson. He turned in his chair and raised his eyebrows at Liam, causing the creases in his forehead to bunch up. "Why don't you come tonight? For old time's sake. I'm going with a couple friends."

"Oh, that's nice of you to offer," said Liam. "No thanks." He looked into the mirror and shook his head as though the mere suggestion was out of the question. "It's been almost fifty years. I'd like to remember those days as they were. Go make your own memories tonight, Johnson. They'll stay with you forever."

13

Carly gazed intensely at herself in the bathroom mirror as she put on the finishing touches of her makeup. She was sipping on a margarita–one of those canned premixed margarita beverages you find in the cooler section of your liquor store next to the seltzers. She set it down on the ledge of the bathtub without looking properly and it tumbled over the edge.

"Damn it," she said, craning her head down to see if there was any drink left to salvage from the can.

"Are you drunk?" asked Martin comically as he watched her from the doorway.

"I'm just distracted," she replied. "There's a million things running through my head about tonight." Carly returned her attention to her face, glancing at Martin in the reflection of the mirror as he stood in the doorway behind her. Her delayed reaction to what he was wearing finally caught up, and she spun around with her mouth open in shock, her reaction morphing into a smile of excitement. "Martin! Baby!"

Martin knew this would be the reaction he'd get from her, and he loved it. He was wearing black trousers and loafers as well as a shiny black shirt that was unbuttoned at the top and exposed some of his chest hair. The focal point of the outfit was a blue and purple iridescent suit blazer that was like liquid light under the bulbs of any room he walked into. Not only did his outfit delight Carly, but Martin's hair and beard were freshly cut and styled as well, giving her the ultimate lady boner. He was a superstar.

Carly started fake crying dramatically as she went up to hug him like a crippled old lady. "Where is my husband and what did you do with him?"

"So, is this a good reaction?" he asked, rubbing her back as she fake-sobbed onto his shoulder. "Hey now, you'll get your makeup all over the upholstery, babe."

"You look so good," she said happily, dragging her hand down his blazer. "It's like you're off to the discothèque." When she ran her fingertips down the iridescent fabric, it glowed like magic. She squealed. "You looked good at our wedding, but not *this* good. When did you buy this?"

"Like, last year," he said.

"How come I've never seen you in it?" she asked, slapping his arm.

He shrugged. "I thought it made me stand out too much. It was on clearance too, but no one else wanted it."

"Well, you do stand out because I can't stop looking at you!" She ran her fingers over the trimmed hair fades on the side of his head.

"I'm not a dog," he said, smirking.

Carly leaned in and kissed him on the lips passionately. He could tell she wanted to have sex now, but he was good at diverting when such emergencies arose.

"We have to leave soon," he said, between mouthfuls of tongue.

"My gorgeous handsome husband," she mused, "you'll have to be on my stream tonight."

"Sure," he said. "You'll need someone to help bring in as many views as possible."

Carly gave him a dumb look. "Mr. Cocky now. I'll repeat, where is my husband and what did you do with him?"

Martin leaned in towards her face dramatically. "He's gone," he whispered. In actuality, he hated being in her videos and streams even though her audience loved him. His role was to be the clueless, dumb husband. Every couple of months he agreed to participate in a video with her, producing such classics as *My Fiancé Makes Our Wedding Cake (EPIC FAIL!!!)* and *Pranking My Husband with a Quadruplet Pregnancy Reveal!!!*. The video *Sneaking Hot Sauce into My Husband's Body Wash (OMG!!! HE WAS MAD!!)* was peak troll era on her channel and had become her most viewed video to date with over fifty million clicks. The videos were all completely staged, of course. They even planned out scripts and what his reactions would be like before recording. On their wedding day, he couldn't even properly enjoy himself because he knew most of it would be recorded for hundreds of thousands of people to watch once the footage was edited together. He tried not to complain, though. She was the breadwinner between the two of them, so he had to play the game.

Carly turned back around and rummaged around the cosmetic wonderland that was spread out across the bathroom countertop. Martin rarely used their ensuite bathroom, knowing full well it was hers. The one in the hallway was his, but she still used it for more of her things. Instead of a standard frame, the mirror in *her* bathroom had an LED light around it, giving her continuous flawless glam for when she had to put on her face before recording or going out.

She pulled out a foldout director's canvas chair and placed it in front of the mirror, tapping the seat with her palm, indicating that she wanted him to sit down.

Martin pointed at himself. "Me?"

"Come. I'm gonna try something on you."

"That's your 'getting ready' chair," he reminded her, staring at it like he was unsure.

Carly tapped the seat again, smiling warmly at him.

Martin hesitated, then sighed and finally sat down.

"Don't worry. I won't make you look like a girl," she said. "Just wait and see." She took a black eyeliner pen and started outlining his eyes with it. Martin felt uncomfortable at first, wincing like he was a kid sitting in a dentist's chair. It wasn't until he saw the fruits of her quick work contrasted against the color of his green irises that he relaxed.

"You're making me into a badass," he said.

"Most of the biggest rock stars have worn makeup," she replied.

"But they were all confident and didn't give a shit."

"Maybe it's time you didn't give a shit about what others thought," suggested Carly. "You don't have to hide."

With those words, Martin's heart started racing.

"I'll sometimes see you gravitate towards things that I've never seen you interested in before," she continued. "Like this blazer you're wearing tonight. I knew you had it stashed away in the closet. But knowing you, I assumed you'd never wear it. Then I thought to myself, maybe you *would* wear it. Or maybe I just don't know my husband as well as I thought I did."

Martin didn't know how to respond. "I'm just... People are gonna look and judge me hardcore."

"Fuck them," she said, finishing his eyes with some black and plum purple eyeshadow. Then, she stood to the side so he could get a good look at himself completely. "I made it more masculine for you," she said, looking at her work in the mirror's reflection. "It goes well with your eye color and the palette of your outfit. What do you think of it?"

Martin leaned forward and moved his head from side to side, examining it.

Carly looked at her phone and suddenly panicked. She rushed into the bedroom. "Shit, I have to finish getting ready... You can wash it off if you want, babe! It was just a fun suggestion. I'm stressing over which shoes to wear! Like, do you think..."

Martin continued staring at his reflection, his face feeling warm and fluttery. He glanced down at the array of makeup before him and drifted his hand over the collection until his index finger bumped against a small container of eye glitter. He popped off the top and used the applicator to lightly spread some of it over his eyelids. The name of the color was *Midnight Dance.* When he finished, the LED light from the mirror caught the glitter and shine, twinkling like a mirror ball.

14

The night was restless with wicked anticipation. Jay and Salvador sat side by side in the backseat of a luxury rental car as their chauffeur drove them to Larchdale Castle. Jay had suggested they take an Uber, but Salvador wanted something fancier given that they were, well, going to a castle. Their chauffeur took the long and winding road that snaked uphill alongside the rocky forest along the eastern outskirts of Venus Valley called Larchdale Grove. The forest had completely darkened, the pine trees tall as their limbs reached to the blackened sky. Up ahead, shining above the treetops like a halo, was a distant white glow. It was the only beacon of light in the approaching dark as the trailing street lights guided ye weary travelers from near and far along the castle's Forever Road. Dozens of vehicles followed Jay and Salvador, and there were dozens more ahead, one after the next.

"That's it!" declared Salvador, looking up through his window at the white glow ahead.

Jay could feel his heart beating faster.

Salvador turned to look at him. "Look at how handsome you look."

Jay smiled and placed his hand on top of his. When he touched Salvador's skin, he felt a jolt go through his body that felt like a shot of ecstasy, right to the bloodstream. Earlier in the day, Salvador had taken him to his favorite men's designer store and dropped several thousand dollars on both of them. Jay had no intention of spending anywhere close to what Salvador had spent, but wanting to exemplify the dress code, Salvador had insisted they go all out, especially after the kind of day Jay had yesterday. Feeling inspired by Salvador, Jay decided to splurge on himself. He wanted to feel good, inside and out, and tonight to be special. Glitz and glamour meant opulence. It meant luxury. It meant showing who you really are to the world, without restriction. When Jay had finished deciding on what he was getting, Salvador went ahead and paid for Jay's items, with one added accessory: he insisted that Jay also get a royal blue bomber jacket with a red, orange and gold phoenix embroidered on the backside. Jay followed Salvador's instruction to not wear anything underneath the jacket, to leave it open with his torso exposed. Salvador also hung some of his own jewellery from his personal collection around Jay's neck to complete his look of transformation. He told Jay that he had planned weddings for millionaires in the past, and the newlyweds would receive many extravagant gifts from guests. As a tip for his services, those couples gifted him some of the things they didn't want. For tonight's affair, Salvador himself was dripping in gold jewellery and was wearing a sheer black top with gorgeous floral embroidery all along the front. His facial hair was perfectly trimmed, as always. He smelled of sensual toffee and amber cologne that made Jay want to rub his jaw along his neck and bite into him like a red velvet cake.

"You smell so good," said Jay, rubbing his nose along Salvador's neck.

Salvador kissed him. They grabbed each other and started to make out, both of them smiling between intervals. "One thing you should know about me is that I'm a total ho during the afterparty," said Salvador. "*Not* the preparty." He pulled away from Jay, teasing him, and leaving him with blue balls. He held Jay's gaze, his eyes dreamy as though Jay was putting him under hypnosis with his charm, stars dancing in his eyes. "Damn, you are so fine... and it's not the booze talking." He reached forward to their personal back-seat bar and took a sip of his gin and tonic. As he rubbed his other hand down Jay's bare chest, the rings on his fingers clinked against the gold necklaces dangling there. "You can keep those, by the way."

Jay's eyes widened, touching the chains around his neck. "No way," he said.

"They look better on you anyway," said Salvador, winking. He leaned back against the window, arm bent on the ledge and his cheek resting against his fist, staring at Jay in amused wonder.

Jay slid across the seat to be closer to Salvador, the sides of their bodies pressed up together. "Well, I guess I'll be picking up the bill for the next twenty times we go out."

"Nah," said Salvador, flashing him a confident smile.

"It's so much money, though," said Jay, reaching for his drink. "So... I'd like to ask you something that might seem a bit... tacky?"

"Am I rich?" asked Salvador automatically, grinning like a fox.

Jay cringed "Sorry... Are we close enough for me to ask you that?"

"I bought you a twenty-five-hundred-dollar jacket. By now, I should know what your high school locker combination was," said Salvador humorously. "Of course we're close enough. To answer your question, though... Yes, I'm comfortable financially. I'm not starving."

"I mean..." continued Jay, "wealth financial advisor... and you plan weddings for millionaires. You must have some insanely good connections."

"I've only planned two millionaire weddings," said Salvador. "If you give good service, people like to give you things in return." He placed a hand on his chest. "From my experience."

"You're good, though," said Jay. "I've never seen your work or anything, but just from your personality, I'm getting an idea of who you are. You're quick-witted. You're funny. You're cute..."

"Cute should have been the first on that list of flattery," said Salvador, smiling at him. "Thanks, though. Keep 'em coming."

Jay leaned in. "You're very cute... and a big slut in bed."

"Oh, don't worry, that was just a taste of what's to come later," said Salvador, leaning into him, his lustful voice intoxicating to Jay. "Are *you* rich?"

Jay paused and bit his lip, not knowing how to reply to that. "I..." he started. "Actually, can we discuss this later?"

Salvador nodded. "No pressure... Sorry."

"Don't be," said Jay. "Was I your first choice to bring with you tonight?"

Salvador looked offended, in a playfully dramatic sort of way. "What? I thought you were my boyfriend."

Jay's eyes widened as though he wasn't sure if Salvador was just being funny or serious. "Are we dating... officially?"

Salvador kissed him on the cheek. "How about tonight we party as friends. Then, we can see what happens from there."

Jay smiled as a warm energy overtook him. "Sounds good." He turned his attention back to the window, admiring the white aura above the treetops that grew brighter the closer they got to the castle. Salvador did the same.

After a few seconds, Jay turned to look at Salvador again, who was focused on what was outside his window. His eyes trailed down to Salvador's hand that was resting on the leather seat beside him. As much as Jay wanted to reach out and hold his hand, he instead turned back to his window and looked down at the city that sprawled out below like a sea of lights. Stars twinkled not just in the twilight above, but in Jay's eyes as well.

The air seemed unnaturally still as the vehicles weaved their way up the switchback road of the forested hills. Just as they rounded the final bend, the trees parted and the great walled French Renaissance structure of Larchdale Castle revealed itself in all its triumphant glory. Built upon forty-five acres of land, the 170,000-square-foot castle dated back to the late nineteenth century, 1895. It was reminiscent of a stately French countryside mansion, the facades made from green chlorite schist. Sculptural ornamentation decorated the architecture with various Gothic detailing, and plate and bar tracery stonework supported the glass in the countless windows. At each of the castle's four corners was a rounded French tower, with the top of each one ending in an imposing and pointed conical roof. The structure was four stories, housing over two hundred rooms, with the vast majority of its furnishings having come from overseas; tapestries, carpets and linens dating as far back as the sixteenth century. The long gravel driveway, the Forever Road, ran straight down the middle of the twenty-acre lawn. Exquisite shrubberies of all sizes surrounded the perimeter of the castle, and the rolling forested hills of Larchdale Grove continued into the distance.

Dozens of vehicles had been parked along the driveway as passengers converged on the steps of the wide stone terrace. The castle's front doors were sixteen feet tall and engraved with artistic vines and decorative patterns of a harmonious nature. Every window of the castle was lit from within, casting diffuse light down upon the guests below.

Just like the windows, Ben's blue eyes lit up as he looked out the car window. The driver was quick to find a spot to let him out at the front of the castle. Ben's head twisted left and right and all around him, marveling at the fantastical whimsy of the surrounding decadence. He merged with the forward momentum of people from all walks of life. Everyone had one thing in common: their fashion was particular to each individual, and no two people were dressed the same. There were the typical golds and silvers from the glamorous gowns that you would expect, and sparkling rhinestones on shoes that shone like chests of stars. There were new designer fashions of the most eccentric variety that were most certainly the height of the fashion world. Glittering makeup twinkled on lashes and radiant headpieces adorned perfect hairstyles that ranged from the simplest elegance to the most intricate arrangements. High fashion sophistication and indulgent costumes ranged from Cleopatra to Mark Antony, from gladiators to Bollywood masquerades and Renaissance kings and princesses, drag and disco queens. There was opulence all around, whether it be the black sheen of a man's tuxedo or the sultry beading of a woman's handbag that would make any formal red carpet blush a darker shade of crimson.

Before Ben had left the house, he downed a few shots of raspberry vodka that had been gifted to him from one of his coworkers on his birthday. He styled his blond hair with gel, shaved the sparse peach fuzz on his cheeks and put on black high tops that were purchased from a website that sold used luxury clothing at heavily discounted prices. The midsoles were in the shape of gold cobras, their heads meeting the top of the outsoles and their eyes embedded with fake red rhinestones. He wore a loose-fitting metallic gold top, a pair of black jeans that were torn at the knees and a silver bracelet that once belonged to his mom.

Ben waited around on the terrace with what seemed like hundreds of others, anticipating the opening of the front doors. The chatter was loud and intense mixed with screams of suspense and laughs of merriment. Then, the gossip was vanquished entirely when the front doors were pulled open to instantly transport the crowd to a world beyond Ben's own. He was pulled forward with the rest and was blinded by a blue and white light that flashed outward, gradually ceasing to reveal what was inside. Midnight blue swept forth and expanded into a cascade of silver and gold light that reached from wall to wall and ceiling to floor to form beautiful prisms that reflected off people's jewellery. If someone had been watching from above, they'd have been reminded of a river of sparkling diamonds as people flooded into the castle.

Ben entered a large rectangular ballroom where a titanic chandelier hung from an expansive frescoed ceiling. It lit up the entire room like its own personal sun, bathing everything in warm gold. The decorative gilded walls were extraordinary to him, and the flooring was polished parquet hardwood.

Like a moth to a flame, Ben's eyes trailed next to the grand staircase at the far end of the room. The railings were thick marble and had several pedestals decorated with gilded torchères that bloomed like radiant alien flowers at their bases. There was a landing several feet up the staircase that had diverging marbled stairs sprouting down from each side of it. From there, the staircase continued further up still, and separated once again at another landing into two sets of stairs that led into a mezzanine that ran around the entirety of the third floor. Extending out from the left and right sides of the mezzanine were six large balconies in total, three on each side, with pillared marble railings that overlooked the floor below like large theatre boxes. Each of the curtained balconies had its own theme: one was completely decorated in maroon and had an eagle-clawed bathtub filled to the brim with convincing rubies where a woman danced seductively, wearing nothing but long strands of jewellery that dripped down her body. There were couches, tables and a bar on each balcony that reflected the color and theme of each individual party. Down on the main floor, there was a cascading water fountain where entertainers dressed as mermaids and a merman cavorted, their green and purple tails splashing about. Constructed at the front of the first raised landing of the grand staircase was a small, oval-shaped makeshift stage. Curving out from the right side, a catwalk stretched towards a set of French double doors at the far corner of the ballroom, like a road, leading out into the backyard.

Ben couldn't stop smiling, for this continent of magical exuberance was seducing him. If the expression "died and gone to heaven" was to have ever been uttered from his lips, this would have been the moment. As his eyes trailed around the room, he locked onto a boy who met his gaze. The boy looked away after a few seconds, but the brief moment left Ben with a lingering, confident smile, and a hopeful outlook for the rest of the evening.

15

The loss of circulation in Martin's arm became more apparent the longer Carly clung to him for dear life, her eyes wider than the moon and sun, like they would pop out of their sockets.

"You look absolutely ridiculous," said Martin, his own face in awe as they walked through the front doors. He started pointing every which way like a kid in an amusement park, commenting on something that caught his eye here and there and everywhere.

Carly suddenly shrieked over the accumulation of voices and took a sharp turn left, pulling Martin along with her like a dog on a leash. Music was playing thunderously, echoing off the walls and floor; the party was officially and undeniably underway. There was something happening in every square inch of the ballroom. Scattered all over the main floor were bars that already had dozens of guests huddled around to be served the finest variety of cocktails, champagne and wines in glistening crystal glassware. There was a large dance floor next to the makeshift stage in front of the grand staircase, with a DJ recklessly spinning away.

"That!" demanded Carly, pointing her finger and running

towards an imitation regal throne that people were posing for pictures on. "Take a picture of me on this!" She handed her phone to him and opened the camera app, detailing exactly how to angle the camera lens when he took the shot. He couldn't keep proper focus, though, feeling like a kid in school whose attention kept drifting away from his humdrum teacher. All he heard were muffled voices as he sank deeper into a fantasy, sweat sliding through the hairs on his partially exposed chest. He was being seduced by the spirit of the castle. The energy was coursing through his throbbing veins.

Carly collapsed onto the throne, her baby blue puff gown billowing around her like a cotton candy cloud. She posed with her legs over the arm of the throne, her silver shoes dangling as she purred and giggled, flapping her hands widely. Martin saw a guy ogling Carly as she flapped away, so he handed him her phone. "She'll mention you in the photo description if you capture her at a good angle using this filter," he explained, patting him on the shoulder.

Martin trailed away and let himself be engulfed into the crowd. He looked up at the grand chandelier of centuries past, make-believing that it was some aristocratic spaceship that would shoot down its royal beam, suck him up, and turn him into a man of solid gold–an idol to be worshipped until the fall of the world. He wandered the ballroom as though in a fever dream. Faces made up in golds and hues of various blushes and shiny metallics winked past him in the constant sprawling lights. Tiaras and bejewelled bowties caught his straying eye... as well as all the beautiful men. His eyes knew what he helplessly desired.

He stood at one of the many bars, waiting to be served. The black marble bar top was lit with mini starlight glass holders.

"What would you like, man?"

Martin had caught the attention of one of the smiling young

bartenders, who was waiting for him to reply. "Uh, a beer? No, actually…" he said, leaning in a bit closer so the bartender could hear him through the blaring music and immense chatter around them. "Could you make me a fancy cocktail?"

The bartender smiled. "What kind of spirit do you want in it?"

"No, like, make me whatever you think I'll like," clarified Martin. "Surprise me!"

The bartender looked him up and down and nodded his head, accepting Martin's challenge. "I think I've got it." The man had the most vibrant smile Martin had ever seen from a guy, with a bottom lip that was so seductively plump. He rocked a goatee, and curly black hair fell to his jawline with twisted strands hanging down over his forehead. His black skin glistened beautifully in the aura of the lights around them, and Martin noticed a faint dusting of gold glitter along his bare arms, his biceps prominent and flexing. The man wore the biggest watch he had ever seen: the green, yellow and black dial was bigger than Big Ben himself.

Moments later, the bartender came back and slid Martin a chilled coupe glass filled with a pastel orange substance that foamed at the top and had a peach wedge secured on the rim next to a mint leaf.

"Excellent!" Martin exclaimed, his face excited like that of a child being given a milkshake. The smell alone was enough for him to identify what it was. "Peach Bellini!"

The bartender winked at him. He was most likely in his early twenties, and wore a sequined black tank top that glittered every time he moved his body. Martin dove into his peach Bellini, taking several long sips as the bartender took a drink request from another guest. Martin watched him move with a fluid precision that was second nature to him. When the bartender popped open a fresh bottle of champagne, he poured it into several glasses that were lined up on the bar top, one by one. Martin continued to stare at the man as he downed the rest of his peach Bellini.

"So... Never seen a black bartender before?" he asked Martin, cracking a smile. His voice was playful and upbeat, like he had never experienced a bad day in his life.

Martin's eyes widened in embarrassment. "Uh... It's cool watching bartenders do their thing, ya know? Like, when you shake the shaker thing, and all those hand movements and stuff." He cringed at what he just said, just wanting to walk away and shove his face into a pile of sand. Standing next to Martin was an older woman who was wearing a large rimmed peacock hat that kept getting in his way. She smelled like his mom's perfume: *White Diamonds* by Elizabeth Taylor.

The bartender flipped his cocktail shaker into the air and caught it behind his back. "That's all I've got right now. I'm still learning," he said. "Your makeup is cool... and that blazer you're rocking! You look like a disco man."

Martin felt his tension dissolve and smiled at him. He looked down at his empty glass and realized he had just downed the entire peach Bellini without paying attention.

"THE MIGHTY ZEUS!"

Martin craned his head around and saw a group of three guys walk up to the bar and high-five the bartender. They were young frat bros dressed as heroic gladiators, but without their helmets on. Their plastic swords bobbed around at their sides, awkwardly poking people in the waist with the tips and hilts.

"How's it going, guys?" asked Zeus. "Is this some Russell Crowe cosplay I'm seeing?"

"Shit, there's a fourth costume if you're down to try it on later," said one of the gladiators, Gladiator Bro One.

"I've always wanted to be a black Hercules," said Zeus, half sarcasm and half humor ringing in his voice.

"Can you make us some Black Thunders, then, mighty God of Thunder?" asked Gladiator Bro Three, handing him two twenties. "Make them doubles, too."

Zeus pulled out three high top glasses and two different spirits that were the base for the drinks he was about to prepare. Martin looked along the bar top and saw four other bartenders hard at work serving all the guests. Champagne seemed to be the most popular, followed by gin, gin and more gin. Moments later, Zeus passed the three drinks to the gladiators, leaving Martin impressed by the drink's presentation. There was a puff of smoke rising from each of the three identical concoctions, and the glass was filled to the brim with a black mixture. At the very bottom was a bright yellow substance. The entire drink looked like a lab experiment.

"Cheers," said Zeus with a smile.

Gladiator Bro One cheered. "Is this recipe on Tremble yet?"

"Not yet," replied Zeus. "I'm surprised you still use that app."

"Barely," said Gladiator Bro One. "The constant fucking ads make it unusable."

Suddenly, a girl wearing a sparkly bodycon dress pushed herself up against the edge of the bar top, her face astonished. "What was that drink?!" she asked desperately. "I'll get whatever drink you made them!"

"Yeah, I'll second that," said Martin, twirling the stem of his empty coupe glass. He felt a burp bubbling up, and he quickly put a fist to his mouth to help repress it.

"You're trouble tonight," said Zeus playfully, glancing over at Martin. "You're definitely getting a Black Thunder."

"It sounds like a superhero," said Martin.

Zeus finished constructing the cocktail, smoke and all, and slid it towards the girl. Martin would always get distracted for just long enough that he'd miss seeing how Zeus got the smoke to funnel out from the top like that, or what the bright yellow substance at the bottom of the glass was that was meant to resemble liquified lightning.

"CAN I GET YOUR ATTENTION PLEASE, LOVELIES!"

The lively music and chatter dissipated as a wondrous creature appeared on the makeshift stage in front of the grand staircase. Martin had personally never known a drag queen, having seen them only on television. Her personality was loud, exuberant and instantly contagious. Incredibly haute couture, she was dressed in a scarlet satin gown with a stream of roses and vines cascading down her side and front. Black satin gloves ran up her arms, and she wore fine jewellery that decorated as much of her body as possible. Her headpiece was shaped into a bouquet of roses, and her black hair was styled in perfected finger waves. To complete the look, she wore glamorous and sultry makeup.

"Welcome! *Bienvenido*!" she said in a lively Cuban accent. "Look at all you fine lovelies tonight!" She started fanning her face with her hands dramatically. "I'm already beginning to sweat, and it's not from all these damn lights. It's from all these damn fine boys around me! My name, in case you didn't already know, is Bailey Wondrous! I'll be one of your entertainers for the evening. Just a little about me first. Eight years ago, me and my family immigrated here from Cuba when I was fifteen. Thank God they chose Venus Valley, because in the last eight years this place has become one of the most popular gay cities in the country! Yes, you're welcome." There was a bombastic round of applause followed by cheers as she lifted her arms in the air and struck various poses. She pointed to the guests in the six balconies and waved to them. "I'm incredibly excited to be here with you all!" She started clapping along with everyone else, the collective sound like a thunderstorm. "Now to start the night off, we have a very special guest here for you all. She is a legend! She is an icon! We all know her, and love her to bits! Grab your drink, grab your boyfriend, your girlfriend, your lover or the nearest sexy motherfucker next to you and head into the backyard where you will see who I'm talking about! And no, it's not me. *That* will come later tonight! Stay tuned! *Los quiero a todos*!"

Several lights gathered into one single spotlight and lit up the French double doors at the far-right corner of the ballroom, leaving Martin to follow the sparkling lights to Oz.

Jay and Salvador walked among the other guests into the twenty acres of backyard bordered by sprawling forested hills of Larchdale Grove. There was a gravel trail around the castle's perimeter, and a small garden maze where within the center was a lush courtyard, bar and a disc jockey who greeted the guests who desired to revel in a more intimate affair. The backyard had a handsome conservatory, as well as Italian, rose and azalea gardens with lily-pad-filled pools nestled between various walkways meant for leisurely strolls. From inside the ballroom, the catwalk extended out through the French double doors and continued in a parallel trajectory to an impressive concert stage that was constructed at the very edge of the backyard–the pot of diamonds at the end of a rainbow. There was a delicate, sheer curtain that draped down from the corners of the stage and had embedded stones in the fabric meant to replicate hundreds of stars.

As people made their way across the lawn, the thunderous bass of the music intensified and the entire catwalk seemingly lit up of its own accord, as though it was fuelled by human energy. There were several elegant couches placed all over the lawn, along with other seating arrangements and bars meant for socializing. Random bits of décor were spaced around the grass alongside the seats as though they were part of some luxury yard sale or showroom.

"Bailey is awesome," said Salvador excitedly, taking Jay's arm and interlocking it with his.

Jay felt snug next to him, especially now that the cool breeze was sweeping past his open bomber jacket and grazing his exposed torso. "I've never heard of Bailey before," he said.

"You're not a real gay then," said Salvador humorously. "How do you not know who Bailey Wondrous is? She's one of the biggest drag queens in our city!"

"I've never been that involved in the gay scene until now," confessed Jay, which he didn't feel bad admitting. He grabbed hold of Salvador's hand, rubbing his fingertips along his rings. "Please, enlighten me."

"I'm pretty sure your head was shoved so far up corporate's ass for so long that you forgot what fun looks like," said Salvador, smiling at him. He rubbed his hand along Jay's arm as if to say he was only kidding. His spirit seemed so restless and alive, far removed from any sort of tired mediocrity. "Bailey Wondrous is only famous in Venus Valley. She hasn't really broken into the mainstream yet, but she will."

As they walked past one of the bars, Salvador paid for a couple drinks that one of the bartenders had just finished making and handed one to Jay.

"What is it?" asked Jay curiously, slopping some of the drink on himself as he took a sip. "Vodka cranberry," he confirmed.

"Show me drunk Jay again; that was entertaining!" said Salvador. He squeezed the lime wedge and dropped it into his drink.

Jay put his arm around Salvador's shoulders. "You do remember what happens when we turn into sloppy drunks?"

Salvador flashed him a gorgeous smile in response. It was just that simple. He was able to communicate anything he wanted to with just a single flash of his pearly whites. They copped a squat on a burgundy jacquard sofa next to an exotic potted plant that had leaves the size of baking pans. Behind them, there was a small platform where dancers in period clothing moved their curves to baroque music. The parade of fashion from all the guests was something that couldn't simply go by without discussion. Friends, lovers and acquaintances from young to old, gay and straight, walked in groups and pairs or solo. Men were openly kissing other men, while others were being thrust up into the air in celebration of their birthday. Jay looked up at the first and second story windows of the castle and saw people waving to those in the backyard as though they were setting sail on their maiden voyage, preparing to float away into the sky, above the clouds, and far far away. The front driveway was still swarming with activity as more guests showed up fashionably late in their exotic rides and vintage cars, engines revving up and headlights flashing about.

"I'm not on planet Earth anymore," said Jay, his head turning left and right, up and down. He looked at Salvador. "Who are you again?"

Salvador leaned in and placed his nose close up to his. "I kind of like you," he whispered. "I kind of like you *a lot*."

Jay's eyes trailed down his face, feeling like he was in grade school again, crushing hard for a classmate. "I'm feeling the same way, actually. I think you were meant to come into my life yesterday. Does that sound weird?"

Salvador shook his head. "No," he whispered again. "Blue Jay."

Jay put his drink down and leaned in to kiss him, placing his hands on the sides of his face. Salvador thrust Jay down onto the couch and rubbed his chest against his, which, expectedly, made passersby applaud and cat call.

"I forget how to behave when I'm around you," said Salvador lustfully. "Does that make you uncomfortable?"

Jay shook his head, gently biting on Salvador's earlobe. "No," he said.

There was a loud bass drop followed by an audible gasp from the audience as everyone turned their attention to the concert stage. It was awash in darkness as the lights dimmed, showcasing a tall set of stairs that gradually narrowed the higher they ascended. At the summit, there was a purple bench that a woman sat upon like it was her throne, her back facing the audience. She wore a white faux fur coat, her hair long, blonde and curled at the ends. She extended one glittering arm and turned her head so just the side of her face was revealed. An eruption of applause and screams poured from the audience as they rushed to gather around the catwalk, where they placed their drinks down like it was one long bar top. The glassware glowed as the catwalk lights lit their drinks from beneath, turning them into pools of neon, multi-colored liquid.

"No way!" exclaimed Salvador, his hand pressed on Jay's chest. He pulled Jay upright, desperately, and hugged him, his knees swinging every which way. Sabrina Elise, the United Kingdom's pop royalty of the last thirty years, had come to Venus Valley.

The instrumental began, and Sabrina started singing the opening notes to one of her most infectious uptempo anthems of all time, "Ask Me to Dance and I'll Dance with You." The song was expertly crafted to be a pop spectacle, its sole intention to persist as a timeless hit. As she sang the verse, Sabrina swung around on the bench to face the crowd, her face radiant, then stood up once the bridge of the song kicked into high gear. The coat fell away from her body to reveal a sexy gold catsuit. She descended down the steps that were lined with fit and shirtless male dancers who wore black pants and hints of makeup around their eyes, and the female dancers were some of the fittest women Jay had ever seen.

The chorus roared through the audience, who sang every lyric back to her in unison. Sabrina danced and pranced her way down the lit catwalk that extended from the main concert stage and towards the castle. She gestured to the audience all around, smiling behind her microphone headset and twirling around in her black heels. The dancers followed her pace for pace until the song hit the second chorus. She paused to do a quick dance number where the dancers circled around her and swung her up into the air. When she returned to the ground, they marched down the catwalk through the large French doors and into the ballroom, where they were greeted with uproarious applause. The song raged onward like a lit fuse to a stick of dynamite. People were jumping and throwing out their arms around the makeshift stage in front of the grand staircase as sparkling confetti rained down from the sky. In the balconies above, the most eccentric of people were dancing in full costume, watching over the railings as their diamonds twinkled far and wide. Sabrina left the catwalk and walked up the steps of the grand staircase until she reached the lower landing and positioned herself in the center, with the dancers lining the stairs around her. The final explosive chorus was met with exhilaration and immense heat as the lights were turned up to their maximum wattage. Bursts of sparks and smoke flew past as people's eyes reflected the iridescent lights in front of them and the confetti fluttered around like a blizzard. Two of the dancers lifted her up by her arms as the song wrapped up, a touchdown finale that was followed by continuous applause.

"Thank you!" she yelled, her mouth agape as she waved her arms in the air. "Enjoy the rest of your night!"

Salvador was apparently having dramatic heart palpitations as his body sank lower into the cushions of the couch.

"This is insane!" yelled Jay, feeling as though the air itself was giving him the biggest high of his entire life.

Salvador patted his knee. "You go find us another drink, and I'll go find our magical host who's been lurking around here somewhere. I've had a sneaking suspicion as to who Kim is."

"That will take forever!" shouted Jay through the electronic music. "Come on! Let's go do something!"

"Is that code for let's find an orgy?" asked Salvador.

"If that's where the night takes us, then that's where it takes us," said Jay, sass in his voice as he smiled.

"My God," said Salvador, terrified. "You're already turning into me." He smiled back at Jay, then got up, reaching out his hand to him. "Ask me to dance and I'll dance with you."

Jay smirked and took his hand, letting Salvador whisk him away to another adventure.

16

The Emerald Room was the name bestowed upon one of the ballroom's six balconies. Green velvet curtains with gold tiebacks and tassels had been hung over the archway, and green armchairs sat comfortably next to large areca palms. There were clear bowls filled with convincing emeralds on top of round side tables of green glass alongside the balcony's curved balustrade. The mini bar served green-hued drinks, in particular the Grasshopper, and martinis with not one, not two, but three garlic-stuffed olives. Snack trays and punch bowls of Watergate salad and sandwiches made with Havarti and Swiss cheese, sweet pickles, spicy mayo and black forest ham lay waiting for guests to devour.

Johnson was sitting on a chesterfield sofa wearing a midnight blue suit vest with a bejewelled bowtie and black button-up shirt underneath. Just moments before, someone had draped a green velvet cloak with white fur trim over his shoulders and placed a gold crown they had found in a nearby study on his head. He felt honoured, as well as ridiculous. He knew he could be pompous, but now this was just making it obvious. It was assumed that the rooms that had been left unlocked along the mezzanine on the third floor were open for anyone to enter and mingle within. Many of the other rooms and halls were completely off limits, with velvet ropes and security personnel preventing guests from wandering any further into the castle.

Johnson had arrived at the castle with two of his closest friends, whom he had known for over fifteen years. Back in school, the three of them were part of Nu Delta, also known as the Fisting House. It was a tragic nickname given to his fraternity when Johnson was found out to be gay, after some of his fraternity brothers found gay porn on his computer browser. Soon after, another student was outed, which led to extreme awkwardness from most of the straight men in the house.

Things escalated during the next couple of days at Nu Delta. One night, someone had poured beer onto his bed while he slept. That same night, he was pulled from his bed and forced to endure the most humiliating moment of his entire life: he was forced to get down on his knees and lick chocolate pudding off the bathroom wall that he, initially, was led to believe was something else. The following week, thinking the worst was over, Johnson went to bed only to be awakened when three of his fraternity brothers thrust him awake and shaved his entire head of hair off, as well as the hair on his legs and arms to the point where his skin had cuts from the dull blades they used. The other student in the house who was also outed, Glenn, was told that he'd have to have sex with a woman so that he could lose his virginity the right way, and refusal from him was not an option. The perpetrators who conducted the hazings threatened to blackmail anyone who ratted them out. Luckily for Johnson and Glenn, there were allies in the house who were disturbed by what was happening. One of these allies was a guy named Tony, who, at the time, was still in the closet. He was part of a group of students who went to the school's dean and reported what was happening at Nu Delta. The men involved in the hazing rituals were heavily disciplined, but not expelled. They still ended up graduating, and went on to live their lives and excel in their careers.

Johnson almost dropped out after what had happened to him, wanting to just give up his studies in business education. He developed a cocaine addiction that continued to this day, fifteen years later. No one but his closest friends knew. He assumed others suspected, but no one ever mentioned it to him in conversation. He had always been strong-minded, but what happened during those few weeks at college broke him, just as he had started to accept himself. During his first year, after the events that had happened to him, he came out to his parents. To this day, he still maintained an almost normal relationship with them, but he couldn't help but feel a sense of disappointment from them. He wasn't living the life that they probably envisioned for him when they watched him grow up. Perhaps they had accepted the reality of his life and learned to live with it, like how we accept the fact that everybody dies eventually.

Before he was outed at school, Johnson had just assumed he was the only one on campus who was gay until he learned about Glenn, then eventually Tony. They convinced him to stay in school and finish his education. They became his best friends. If it wasn't for them, he wouldn't be where he was now. They were with him tonight to revel in the evening's festivities and to perhaps let go of any lingering regrets over a more accepting life in college that could have been, all those years ago. Johnson went through something of a transformation after college, vowing to never let anyone take advantage of him again or take away his ability to succeed in life. He was going to run faster, even if it meant others had to crash so he could rise. He was going to excel and come out on top. Johnson had other goals when it came to his career, other motivations. He couldn't stand being just a district manager, even if it was for a prominent company that paid him well. There was more he needed to do with his talents, beyond what he was currently doing. It wasn't just about a promotion, or earning more, but proving to himself that, even if everything else in his life was out of his control, this was something he could steer on his own and get ahead at, regardless of the people he had to eliminate along the way.

"There are so many guys here I'd love to fuck," said Glenn, intoxication bubbling up as he started pointing every which way. "There's a hot one there... and there... there too. I'll just drop them all into my virtual shopping cart, please."

"You know, this balcony is going to get a reputation for being the place where all the slutty gays go," said Johnson.

Glenn got up from his seat and stumbled up to the balustrade. He raised his arms up into the air. "Hey, all you sexy boys! Come party with us!"

"Alright there, man," said Johnson, pulling him away from the railing. "You still have a job to get back to on Monday."

Tony was sitting still as a statue on one of the armchairs, wearing black sunglasses and looking like a gay assassin dressed all in Prada black. "Glenn, sit down next to me," he said, tapping the spot next to him.

Glenn tried reaching for Tony but missed his seat and fell to the floor instead, laughing hysterically with his glasses askew over his face.

The bartender looked at Glenn and shook his head, smirking to himself.

"You see that?" said Johnson, pointing with his thumb. "Even the bartender is ashamed of you."

"Nah..." said Glenn, looking up at him with a childlike grin. "He's seen worse shit."

"Martini, please," said Tony, speaking to the bartender. "Two olives only, and make it extra dirty for my dirty friend here."

"That's the name of my theme song tonight," said Glenn,

getting back up and balancing himself on the spot so he could get his grip. He straightened his glasses properly on his nose. "Alright... I'm good now."

"I'm tapped out of cash," said Tony, his voice disturbed as though he was embarrassed that he couldn't pay for the drink. "My cards are at home."

Johnson reached into his wallet and tossed a twenty across the bar top just as a group of four walked into the Emerald Room. Two of them were young women dressed as disco queens in mirror ball dresses, and the other two were cute boys that Johnson tried not to stare at. Given that he was in his late thirties, and he looked older than he actually was, he didn't want to come across as a creep. He always thought his ruggedness and fit body would suffice in attracting the right guys to him, and it often did. He wore shorts as often as possible so he could show off his muscular legs, which were the fruits of his labour. There was a cute blond boy who worked at one of the stores in his district, and Johnson liked to talk to and look at him when he visited the store.

Coincidentally, the boy was now standing across from him. He probably didn't even notice Johnson... or maybe he did, but was just being coy, playing the shifty eyes game. Johnson turned to his side so one of the areca palms covered most of his body as Glenn continued acting like a buffoon. Tony, being the silent snake charmer that he was, let Glenn continue with his antics for his own amusement.

Johnson finished his drink and stood up. "I'm stepping out for a moment."

"Yeah, exploring for dick," said Glenn, his voice slurring.

"Right..." said Johnson, humoring him. He swept past them and exited through the velvet green curtains.

Ben initially regretted not bringing someone along with him to be his party buddy. Following Sabrina's performance, he wandered the ballroom and noticed everyone was with someone, and there he was, the loner. That loneliness went away, though, because everyone seemed happy, whether they had come with friends or by themselves. He felt welcome, like this was where he belonged. When guys locked eyes with him, he knew he had a good chance of meeting someone new–he just had to come out of his shell. He decided that if there was someone he thought was his type, he'd smile and hopefully a spark would ignite between them. It was a good idea to have had those shots of raspberry vodka before leaving the house because he couldn't buy booze from any of the bartenders. When he gave it a try and was turned away without proof of his age, there was a boy next to him who looked to be the same age as him. They struck up a conversation about the party and ended up hanging out together. Shaun wore white pants and a tie-dye t-shirt underneath a lightweight leather jacket. There was gold glitter on his neck, and also in his dark brown hair. It was obvious he had just gotten a fresh haircut, and his face was completely smooth, just like Ben's. His skin was tanned, which made his white pants stand out even more. He was celebrating his twenty-first birthday with two female friends dressed as disco queens whom he had temporarily lost, but had since rejoined with. All of them, including Ben, were exploring the six balconies on the mezzanine floor and had made it to the Emerald Room, where they were now enjoying the sandwiches and snacks.

"You need a birthday crown," Ben suggested to Shaun as the two of them crammed themselves together on one of the armchairs. "That bald guy who just walked out of here was wearing one. He's my district manager at Brandon Save."

"Really?" asked Shaun. "He's hot. Do you like older guys?"

"Uh..." started Ben, "sometimes."

"Older guys are hot," confessed Shaun, tapping his foot to the beat of the song. "Forty is the cut-off though. Anything older, no thanks." He handed his drink to Ben. "Have the rest."

Ben took the glass and tossed back the remaining lemon-lime soda and vodka. It was exciting to hang out with Shaun. It was like they were already best friends after hanging out for just a short period of time.

"How many guys have you been with?" asked Shaun, putting his hand on Ben's knee.

"Just one," said Ben.

Shaun smiled and squished himself closer to Ben on the armchair. "Come over to my place later," he offered.

Ben could feel himself getting aroused at the offer, and also because their bodies were so close together. There was something incredibly brave and outgoing about Shaun, and Ben was drawn to him more and more.

Shaun leaned into his ear. "Have you ever tried acid?"

Ben paused, then shook his head. "No."

"Do you want to?"

"Uh, sure."

"Are you sure?"

Ben nodded and sat still, not really knowing what to say.

"Are you okay?" asked Shaun, looking into his eyes. "Are you nervous?"

Ben adjusted himself. "I'll be honest with you. I don't have very many gay friends. That's kinda why I'm here tonight."

Shaun grinned, his eyes lighting up. "Are you out?"

"Not really. You're, like, the first actual gay guy I've ever hung out with."

"You serious?" said Shaun. "Why are we just sitting here then? Let's go dance!"

"What about your friends?" asked Ben. He glanced at the two

disco queens, who were busy chatting with each other over a plate of celery and ranch dip.

"Pfft..." scoffed Shaun. "I'll see them later." He headed for the balcony's exit and pushed the green curtains aside, looking over his shoulder to make sure Ben was coming.

"By the way, I'm out," said Shaun as he walked alongside Ben through the mezzanine.

"Sweet," said Ben, smiling, as he rubbed shoulders with him.

"Hey, come here for a second," said Shaun, motioning Ben towards a nearby alcove. When they neared the opening, Shaun reached into his back pocket and pulled out two micro-sized squares of paper. He held them in his right palm as their chests pressed together. One of the treats had a heart, the other a happy face.

"Trick 'r treat," said Shaun quietly, his breath hot, as he leaned forward and kissed Ben aggressively on the lips. "Let's become fucked-up ghouls tonight."

Ben stared at the squares in Shaun's hand, his heart racing with the opportunity that was presenting itself to him. He reached out to take one, but Shaun stopped him. Instead, Shaun slipped the heart treat into his own mouth first, then held the smiley one close to Ben's tight, pink lips. "Open sesame," he requested deliciously.

Ben parted his lips and Shaun placed the square paper on his tongue. He let it dissolve away, and Shaun pressed his lips against his, shoving his tongue deep into the back of Ben's throat. He then took Ben's hand and led him to the top landing of the grand staircase, pulling his arm excitedly as they sped down the stairs. The pulsating beat from the DJ booth lit up the dance floor like fireworks as they joined in with the crowd of dancing stars.

17

It had been almost four months since he last laid eyes on him.

Robbie paced excitedly back and forth in front of an arched wooden door at the end of one of the first-floor hallways of Larchdale Castle. The area had been roped off, but Robbie was granted special permission to venture through via his special invitation. The hallway was truly aristocratic and held a prestige and elegance that was suitable for royal blood. The lower halves of the walls were carved walnut wainscoting and the rest done in the style of French Renaissance architecture, much like the rest of the castle. Moonlight glowed through the tall arched windows and spilled across the hallway and alcoves like you were standing in a ghostly underwater world, vacant of warmth but still rich with history. To the left of the wooden door was a landing of a wide spiral staircase to one of the corner towers of the castle. Robbie went and sat on the lowest step and fiddled with his phone, hearing the muffled thumping bass from the grounds outside and the ballroom.

From behind him, Robbie heard a subtle sweeping sound–like that of fabric dragging across the stone. He felt a chill go through him as a figure dressed in a seventeenth-century dress passed by him, having come down the tower stairs. Robbie briefly caught a glimpse of her snow white face and blood red lips. Her dress was similar to that of French royalty: lavender with silver detailing along the bodice and shoulders. She had heavily stylized brown hair with fine jewellery pinned to it, and curls ran down her pale, slender neck. Her arms were held daintily to each side, with her fingers outstretched and the sleeves of her dress stopping just below her elbows in large poofs of fabric. Robbie looked on in admiration, impressed with the care that some guests took in creating their costumes. He'd seen the belles of the ball and mid-century couture, modern-day disco kings and influencer princesses. The woman before him appeared lost and confused, though, like she didn't know where she was or where she was headed. She wandered down the hallway aimlessly, then disappeared into the darkness ahead.

There was a sharp creak from the door opening, and a bright, warm light escaped from within the room. Someone poked their head out and spotted Robbie. The man's expression transformed into joy when their eyes connected.

Robbie leaped up, entered the room, and took the man's arm like it was a life preserver. The man was still partially naked from having performed alongside Sabrina during her appearance earlier that night. Sarim was shirtless, wearing only black pants and leather straps around his shoulders. His body was built as though he had been designed in a gay man's laboratory: a hairy chest with strong pectorals, muscular arms, washboard abs, a buzzcut and a lush black beard. Sarim was thirty-nine, and of South Asian heritage.

"Look who we have here," said Sarim, taking Robbie into his arms and kissing him. Sarim's voice wasn't the most bombastic or vibrant, but it held a reserved yet smooth sensuality. His hands slid down Robbie's back and paused on the sides of his waist.

"It's been a wild four months without you here, honestly," said

Robbie. "You were fucking great earlier! The best dancer up there." His eyes trailed down his body. "You look great too, as always."

Sarim reached forward and adjusted Robbie's bowtie. "I've never seen you in a tuxedo before. It's really hot." He pressed his body up against Robbie, flashing his deep brown eyes and long lashes at him. Sarim had the cutest crow's feet at the corners of his eyes when he smiled. He nestled his face against Robbie's neck as though he was a vampire that was thirsting for his warm man blood.

Robbie ran his hands over Sarim's stiff shoulders and down his arms, feeling the veins along his forearms. "You'll have to put some clothes on soon, or mine are coming off."

Sarim grabbed hold of Robbie's crotch. "Come, I'll introduce you to the others. Maybe you'll see Sabrina walking around later."

Robbie smiled. It felt so good to be around him again. It made his heart flutter, and he felt warm all over. All he wanted now was to be alone with Sarim, to hold and be next to him.

The room was modeled after a knight's armoury and had three arches that led into a back chamber. Above the arches was a second-floor loft with a balustrade that no one was allowed to access. To make sure it stayed that way, a security guard kept watch.

Sarim took Robbie past the arches and into the unextraordinary chamber that was being used as the dancers' dressing room. There were dozens of suitcases scattered all over the floor and minimal furniture. Various food and drinks were laid as a buffet on a long table in the middle of the chamber. Pop music was playing from a stereo system, making it feel like this was their own private *end of the night* party.

"Damn, Sarim..." said one of the dancers as Sarim brought Robbie into their midst. "This is the Silver Fox?"

Robbie's eyes widened as he side-eyed Sarim, smirking. "So, that's my legacy. Do they even know my name?"

"It's Robbie," said one of the other dancers. She was holding a glass of wine as she swayed from side to side to the melody of the song.

Robbie pointed at her like a gameshow host would to a contestant who had buzzed in with the correct answer.

Sarim took him around like a prized pony he had just won at the local derby and got him to shake hands with everyone. Robbie noticed that some of the guys were checking him out, as he did in return, since it was hard not to. He was fit and devilishly handsome himself, but nowhere near the physical beauty that was Sarim and the other dancers.

"I'm the grandpa of the group," said Sarim with a sigh. "Everyone is under thirty–except Richard there. Anyway..." he slapped his flat stomach, "I'm excited to finally pig out. Want some cake?"

"Is that even a question?" asked Robbie. As they made their way towards the center table, he slapped Sarim's butt. "This is the only cake I'll ever want."

"It's begging for some creamy drizzle," said Sarim, turning around to smile at him. He abruptly stopped walking so Robbie would bump into him from behind, making his pelvis hit Sarim's backside.

Robbie slid his hands down Sarim's arms and kissed him on the neck, gently guiding him towards the table from behind. "So, you're sticking around in the city for a little bit?"

"Yeah," replied Sarim. "Sabrina wants to spend some time here with Owen. It'll be a nice break... until the shows in Europe continue."

"Owen is her boyfriend, I'm assuming?" guessed Robbie. "I'm not up to date on all the celebrity gossip."

Sarim nodded. "We met briefly. He's nice. Apparently, he's bisexual. Not like that matters, though."

Robbie scoffed. "Maybe he'll be interested in a threesome then."

"That won't be happening anytime soon," said Sarim defiantly. "Gaining personal time with him is like trying to reach a top tier boss in a video game." He grabbed a cheeseburger and consumed practically the entire thing in just a few bites. His eyes rolled back from the explosion of flavours that hit his brain, and he leaned over to rest his head on Robbie's chest. "I've really missed you," he said quietly. "I've been looking forward to sleeping in your bed again."

Robbie smiled. "It's been cold without you in it."

"I'm sure there have been other guys keeping it warm for me."

Robbie's mouth fell open.

"I'm joking," assured Sarim.

"Hey," said Robbie, looking at him seriously. "Don't even."

"I'm *joking*," reiterated Sarim. "Chill, baby."

Robbie scooped up a boneless chicken wing and dipped it into the spicy ranch dressing. "How about, as an appetizer, let's cruise down to the party downstairs."

Sarim licked his upper lip, his face beaming. He patted Robbie on the back then dragged his fingers down his blazer. "I'm going to finish up here and get ready. I'll meet you at the party in, like, thirty minutes?"

Robbie nodded. "Yes, sir."

Sarim casually looked down at the food table like he wanted Robbie to follow his gaze. When Robbie did, he saw a large strawberry cheesecake that had already been cut into. The message on it read: *Congrats Sarim! You get to finally fuck your boyfriend!*

"Yeah..." said Sarim, sighing to himself. "Everyone on tour had to put up with me complaining about *that*."

"I'd love to have seen the reaction of the baker who had to write that," said Robbie. "It's written in a fancy font too. That's fucking hilarious."

Sarim reached over and handed him a piece of cake on a plastic plate: the part that said *finally fuck*. He dragged his finger along the whipped cream frosting that decorated the sides of the cake and slid it delicately into Robbie's mouth. "You like that?" asked Sarim in a quiet voice, his finger sliding in and out of his mouth.

Robbie took hold of Sarim's hand and slowly pulled his finger out of his mouth as he maintained eye contact with him. "Why does it feel like we won't be going to bed until really late tonight?"

"You just turned fifty, not eighty," whispered Sarim. "Pretend you're twenty again."

"I'd rather not," said Robbie. He leaned in and kissed him. "See you soon."

"Meet me at the bottom of the staircase," said Sarim.

"Will do." Robbie gave Sarim one last look, then left the chamber. He exited the armoury with a smile on his face as he cut his fork through the *finally fuck* on his slice of cake.

18

Martin's wife was currently in her *influencer overdrive mode*, posting a picture every fifteen minutes to her social media stories so she could update her loyal minions and, more importantly, humble brag. It was impossible *not* to notice Carly at the party, for out of the hundreds in attendance, she wore the biggest and bluest of all the dresses. What pained Martin the most about her online persona was that the photos she posted rarely looked like the real her. They were so heavily filtered and edited that sometimes he believed he was married to a different woman entirely. He felt as though he couldn't breathe when he was around her sometimes. He knew how happy she was with him. But if only she knew how lonely he felt.

Martin stumbled into one of the six party balconies, its color scheme burnt orange with an African jungle theme. He leaned over the balustrade to catch a better glimpse of a bizarre outfit that had caught his wandering eye: a woman covered head to toe in zebra print, including a balaclava.

"Don't fall over," said a boisterous voice behind him.

Martin turned around and beheld a mythical creature. "Bailey

Wondrous!" he exclaimed, raising his arms like she was an angel that had fallen from the clouds.

"What gave it away, honey?" she said sarcastically, fanning her face with an African paper fan. She still wore her exquisite scarlet gown from earlier. It was blooming with roses and vines along the sides and up around her shoulders, ending with a full hat bouquet on top of her head. White pearls dangled from her ears, the same shade as her picture-perfect, infectious smile. "Wouldn't want you to lean too far over and take a tumble, Sugar Bear."

Martin placed one of his arms on the balustrade and raised his eyebrows at her. "That would never actually happen."

"Oh, this boy has some attitude," she said in her strong Cuban accent. "Sign me up!"

"Love the outfit, man," said a Korean man sitting next to Bailey. He looked to be in his thirties, and wore a sharp tuxedo. He was clean-shaven and had jet-black hair that was well-groomed and shined with pomade. There was a sense of authority about him, like that of a businessman who was just interrupted in the middle of a meeting.

Martin smiled shyly and downed the rest of his margarita. "You look nice and very good too, as well." He paused, then winced and sauntered away. His awkward response made him cringe and retreat towards the balcony's bar. "Give me one of those cool Black Thunder drinks," said Martin to the bartender. "With extra smoke and *pizzazz*!"

"Wrong guy," said the bartender. "The guy you're looking for is down there."

Martin looked over the railing and tried to spot Zeus, who should have been behind the bar closest to the castle entrance, but he wasn't there anymore. "Alright, give me something else."

The bartender pointed to another margarita that was already sitting on the bar top waiting for him. "Beat you to it," he said.

"Speaking of crazy, we just found my crazy husband!"

Martin felt someone grab his arm from behind. Carly jumped to his side with her phone right up in his face. She was live streaming on one of her social media accounts, and the comments were scrolling rapidly down the bottom half of the screen.

"This is Martin, the love of my life," said Carly in an airy voice. "Say hi, baby."

"Yo," said Martin with a limp wave. His eyes caught some of the scrolling comments, most of which showered him with affection and heart emojis.

"Are you live streaming right now, Lady Love?" asked Bailey Wondrous in a sweet voice as she stretched her arms out to Carly.

Carly skipped over and sat down next to Bailey, her puffy blue dress taking up most of the space on the couch.

The Korean man who was sitting next to Bailey stood up. "Enjoy the rest of the night, Bailey," he said. "I'll put a word in with Sabrina."

"Thanks so much, gorgeous!" said Bailey, flapping her gloved hand at him.

"Gorgeous, gorgeous, gorgeous. We're all gorgeous at Larchdale Castle!" exclaimed Carly as she continued to live stream. She lifted her arms into the air and cheered like she was at a sweet sixteen party, and Bailey started voguing with her hands and arms.

Martin rolled his eyes and slumped over the balustrade, looking down at the guests below. It was nearing midnight, and everything appeared to be blurring together for him. His eyes trailed from one place to the next, and all the women faded away, his eyes only fixated on the men, with their handsome faces and sculpted arms. Martin felt a new sensation in his chest, and at first, he thought it was the alcohol. There was a warmth spreading through him, and he gripped the marble balustrade hard as his eyes drifted towards the merman splashing around in the fountain, his bare chest exposed. Finally, it dawned on him. In all his twenty-five years, Martin had never confronted a feeling like this before. His whole life, he had been denying his sexual instincts. Seeing all these men now, he envisioned himself holding one of them. He wanted to wrap his arms around their waists and dance with them, to be with them. Martin turned and looked at Carly as she continued to engage with Bailey on her live stream. He felt a cold detachment that was distant and emotionless. She didn't feel like his companion. She felt like a good friend.

The men below flooded him with a warm sensation once again. He closed his eyes and thought of the man who had been sitting beside Bailey just moments before and how masculine and gorgeous his face was.

"Fuck..." he whispered, breathless. For the longest time, he'd avoided looking at men on the street. He never allowed himself to revel in the bliss of feeling any sort of romantic feelings towards them. In this moment, as sure as the sun is yellow, he himself was experiencing real, unhinged lust and romance.

"Why is your man not part of this stream, darling?"

Martin turned to look at Bailey, then Carly. When he met their glances, he looked as though he wanted to cry.

Carly's smile faded when she noticed he was visibly upset. She lowered her phone. "Baby, what's wrong?"

Martin leaned back against the balustrade and dropped his glass to the ground, rubbing his eyes with both hands as though a bee had just stung them. He felt ethereal, like he'd been suddenly dropped into a washing machine. His world was spinning, ringing all around him, and he was starting to perspire.

"Oh shit," said Carly. She got up and rushed over to him.

"Damn... boy, someone spiked your drink," said Bailey. She turned to the bartender and pointed. "I'm looking at... you!"

"Hey," said the bartender, raising his hands to his chest as though trying to prove that he was innocent.

Carly put her hands on the sides of her husband's wet face. "You're sweating like crazy."

Martin started laughing and put his arms around her. He began kicking his feet, legs in the air like they were in a production on Broadway. "I'm going to dance!" he blurted excitedly.

"Not now," she said, annoyed. She leaned into his ear. "Did you take something?"

"No, but I'm gonna give *you* something," he whispered back, thrusting his pelvis at her, still laughing.

Two boys walked in through the orange drapery covering the arch, and like most people would, the first thing they noticed was Carly's large blue dress.

"Twinks in, drag queen out," said Bailey comedically, lifting her scarlet gown as she stood up from the couch. "This bitch needs to perform soon." She turned to Martin and looked him up and down. "I'm sure you're in good hands."

"Let's sit down," said Carly, pulling him towards a bar stool.

"That's boring," said Martin, pushing the stool away. "Let's go jogging."

"Sure. You know what? Let's go jogging right off the balcony," said Carly sarcastically, her eyes betraying her annoyance.

Martin's eyes drifted to the two boys who had just walked in, one of whom he instantly recognized... It was the blond hair and blue eyes. Ben met Martin's eyes, his face stoic, then confused. There was a sense of questioning on Ben's face, like he was putting a puzzle together and realizing where he had seen Martin before. Then, Ben shifted his gaze to Carly.

Martin swallowed hard and turned away from him. "Oh shit," he said, turning to face the balustrade. He crawled up onto it.

Carly panicked, her hand reaching out to grab part of his blazer so she could pull him back down. "Martin, what the hell? Get down!"

Martin stood on the balustrade with his back slightly hunched, looking all around him, feeling nauseous. It all happened so quickly, and without any sort of rational thought. The people directly below the balcony pointed up, amused and concerned at the same time. It was so loud and chaotic in the ballroom that most everyone on the main floor was too busy in their own little world to notice what was unfolding above. Martin howled erratically and punched his fists into the air like he'd just scored a touchdown in the last five seconds of the game. He leaped off the railing and fell three stories, the swift, cool air rushing past him and against the sweat on his face. Just before Martin slammed into the ground, he was caught by several men. They all collapsed to the ground as more rushed to crowd around him to see that he was laughing hysterically like a lunatic. Martin jumped up to his feet right away. "Fuck yeah!"

Some cheered, some looked horrified and others just downright rolled their eyes. From out of the crowd, a member of security personnel came storming forward, grabbed hold of Martin, and dragged him towards the mermaid fountain, dumping him into the water. "Here, be a mermaid for the next thirty minutes," said the man as he placed a finger to the side of his headset and walked away.

The mermaids laughed as Martin attempted to stand up but then stumbled back down, the water soaking him up to his chest. One of the mermaids took his hand gingerly in hers and pulled him towards the edge of the fountain, where he kind of just floated and held onto the ledge.

"See, I knew you were trouble when you walked in."

Martin looked around, searching for the origin of the voice. "The water is speaking to me," he said desperately, his eyes wide as he turned to one of the mermaids. "It's the Water Goddess... isn't it?" He reached for the mermaid's tail and swatted at it like a kitten reaching for a fish toy.

Zeus tapped him on the shoulder and drew Martin's attention to him. Martin wiped water from his eyes so he could see better. "It's you," he said groggily.

"Maybe you should sober up a bit," suggested Zeus. "Especially after your flight of the phoenix act there."

"You should name a drink that," said Martin as he attempted to pull himself out with the help of Zeus.

"Hey!" yelled the security guard as he watched Martin like a hawk. "You ain't leaving until I say you can leave!"

One of the mermaids flapped her tail at Martin playfully, laughing with the other merfolk.

19

Jay watched the drunk man in the iridescent blazer jump from one of the balconies, and it was like a blip in time, nothing more. Everyone went on with what they were doing, with most oblivious to what had happened in the first place. He was initially concerned for the man when he hit the bottom, but the guy seemed to be doing okay, so Jay didn't linger on the thought. He'd been equally entertained by a guy dressed as Alexander the Great who was sitting on the imitation regal throne near the front entrance, his dusty blond hair wet like a mop. People were taking pictures with him like he was a movie star as girls poured red wine all over him.

Salvador was a great time to be around. They hung out and laughed, danced. Then Salvador, determined as ever, said he'd try to seek out the elusive Kim, a chore that Jay felt was a waste of time. As Jay waited around for him to return, he wandered through the crowd and took in the extravagance of the castle. He ran into a few people he knew, some of whom he had graduated from college with. There was just so much to see, excitement within every square inch of the ballroom. He had the attention span of a toddler, his eyes looking every which way. The floor was littered with confetti, glitter and balloons like it was New Year's Eve. Lights danced across the walls and floor, and Jay stared up at the frescoed ceilings, believing for a moment that he was in a European chapel.

He took a detour towards a long buffet table that was filled with fun finger foods like little cocktail sandwiches, ranch chicken wraps and fresh fruits, candies and chocolates. It was not overly fancy for a party where you would expect more complex offerings. There was also an array of cupcakes laid out before him. He selected a chocolate one with blue frosting and edible glitter sprinkled on top. Cupcakes. They'd follow him for the rest of his life. They'd be dancing in his dreams tonight, doing leg kicks like the Rockettes.

Jay took the dessert, wanting to hold on to it so he could give it to Salvador. He checked his phone to see if anyone had messaged him, and there was one message from a friend who asked what he was doing tonight and if he was at the party. He decided to open a dating app to see who was close by, and hundreds of profiles popped up on the grid. Jay was satisfied with the photo he used for his profile. It was a headless photo, with just his torso showing. He took the selfie two weeks ago when he was at the gym and feeling particularly good about himself. His profile caption was "let's grab some food." He had the urge to take a selfie of himself right now and use it as a new profile picture since he thought he looked pretty good.

He opened up the camera, about to take the selfie, then paused. Was it wrong to be on this app? Salvador said they would party just as friends tonight, but did he actually mean that? Jay hesitated. He didn't want to come across like he was bored with Salvador already. He wasn't, not even close. Maybe Salvador wouldn't come back, though, and that was that. Even if Salvador wasn't treating this like a date, Jay was, and he felt left behind. He knew they had a connection. There really wasn't a reason for him to believe that Salvador didn't want to hang out with him anymore, unless Salvador was a fantastic actor or just incredibly fake. Jay didn't get either of those vibes from him, so perhaps he was being paranoid. The guy bought him an insanely expensive jacket and gave him some of his own jewellery. You don't do that for someone you intend to blow off hours later. He liked Salvador, and Jay knew the feeling was mutual. He just wanted to be around him again, that was all. He missed him.

One of the waitresses walked past him holding a silver tray of Lemon Drop martinis, and Jay quickly grabbed one–his third one in an hour. It was essentially lemonade: delicious, potent and concocted with citron vodka and Cointreau. Jay got an alert from his phone that two guys had messaged him. He placed the drink and cupcake down on a cocktail table filled with empty glasses and looked at the first message. No profile picture, but Jay responded, humoring the guy.

Then right away, he received another message. The guy's picture was a headless shot of him in mid run wearing black athletic compression shorts and a tank top. His calves and thighs were huge. Jay replied.

The man immediately sent him a picture of his face, and Jay paused, his heart skipping a beat. It was Johnson. He had taken a selfie of himself at the party while wearing a crown and green velvet cloak.

Jay looked straight ahead, and, within seconds, saw Johnson standing next to the buffet at one of the cocktail tables with a few other people who may or may not have been with him. One of them was an elegant young woman dressed all in black as though she was attending a funeral for one of her dead supermodel friends.

It appeared that Johnson hadn't noticed Jay yet, his back turned towards him as he looked down at his phone, waiting for Jay's reply. Jay wasn't in denial. Johnson was handsome, with a rugged, bad boy aesthetic. However, Jay felt his adrenaline rise from anger. Friday morning's events flooded back to him, just when he'd been starting to move on and forget about them. Johnson was a complete and utter douchebag of the highest bro code. If he so much as approached him, Jay wouldn't stand for it. There was nothing Jay could do to change what had happened on Friday, so confronting Johnson was useless. He sent Johnson a response.

The woman's dress next to you matches your personality, you piece of shit.

Jay put his phone away, grabbed both the drink and cupcake and walked away, flustered. Odds were, Johnson would just smirk at the message while giving some asshole reply. In fact, Jay already felt his phone vibrating, and he knew it was Johnson. He chose not to look at it, anger rushing through him. He wanted to find Salvador instead so he could have a good time for the rest of the night and forget about everything else. Jay pulled out his phone and deleted the app, ignoring whatever retort Johnson had sent him.

It must have been his intoxication, because Jay stopped and turned around, having second thoughts about fleeing from Johnson and wanting instead to go up to him. He'd love to punch him the fuck out, but he convinced himself to just keep walking away. This wasn't the place for a confrontation like that.

Jay glanced up and saw someone else he could speak to instead.

Robbie finished the last of his *finally fuck* cake slice and licked the plastic fork clean of frosting. He left the plate on a nearby cocktail table and stood at the bottom of the grand staircase, waiting. He dragged the sole of one of his loafers along the step he was standing on, feeling like a kid at a high school party who stands by themselves like a dead houseplant while everyone walks past them. Given the countless pairs of shoes that must have gone up and down these stairs since the nineteenth century, they were in exceptional condition. The thick marble of the railings was identical to the marble along the balconies above. Pedestals loomed over the diverging flights of stairs at the top and bottom landings, where extravagant torchères glowed upon all who walked past. Robbie had been almost certain he'd look too proper in his tuxedo, having just pulled it out from the back of his closet. When he thought of *glitz* and *glamour*, this was the closest thing he owned that embodied such a theme. He felt pretty glamorous, anyway. Men and women looked him in the eyes, smiles creeping across their faces at such a fine thing. The only accessory he was missing was his boyfriend.

Robbie's brown eyes drifted to the party balconies above in search of some entertainment while he waited. He thought perhaps another drunk would take a dive off the balustrade again. There was so much to see every way you turned, of course, but there was one person in particular who caught his eye almost instantly. There was a blond boy standing at the balustrade of the nearest balcony, looking down, with another boy next to him. Their mouths were moving animatedly as they pointed down at things that caught their eye. Robbie's eyes glazed over, his mouth falling open a bit. He took a few strides backward up the steps so the balcony was at a better level with his sight, leaning forward, thinking his eyes were misleading him. As the blond boy scanned the party, he locked eyes with Robbie. Instead of looking away, the boy held his gaze, and Robbie wasn't able to look away. They were deadlocked. He felt his palms getting sweaty, his mind unable to think. There was nothing happening in his brain; it had shut off. He was confused. He lost his breath.

The boy was the first to break eye contact and went on scanning the crowd, leaving Robbie to look down, puzzled, mystified, and above all else, shaken. He looked back up at the balcony, but the boy was gone, as was his friend.

Robbie shook his head and wiped his left hand across his face, his eyes tearing up. He felt drunk, but without the alcohol in his system. If he didn't need a drink before, he certainly needed one now. Instead, he looked at the time on his phone. Only twelve minutes had passed since he left Sarim, so there were another eighteen to waste. The music played continuously, and the speakers blared into Robbie's ears. The dance floor was alive and spontaneous with people dancing like it was their last night on earth.

Taking one last look up at the balcony, he ran his hand through his hair and was about to leave the landing when Jay suddenly appeared in front of him. Now *for sure* he needed a drink.

"Hey," said Jay, intimidation noticeable in his expression.

Robbie gave him a stern look that suggested he wasn't in the mood to be talking to him at this moment. "Hi," he said.

"Did you see that guy jump?" asked Jay, looking over his shoulder as if expecting to see the same dude going for round two off the balustrade.

"Yeah," said Robbie. He couldn't help but glance directly at Jay's exposed torso between the open zipper of his bomber jacket–one of his nipples was partially visible.

Then came the expected awkward silence.

"So, why are you here?" asked Robbie, cutting to the chase. "Why are you here talking to me, specifically?"

Jay placed his left arm on the bannister. "Can we talk?"

"Really?" asked Robbie, annoyed, and knowing exactly what

Jay wanted to discuss. Tonight wasn't the night. "Here, Jay? Call me on Monday."

"I've been wanting to give you my side of the story," he persisted, "sooner rather than later."

"Oh God," said Robbie, in an even more annoyed tone than before. He pushed past him. "You're such a fucking idiot. You wasted a perfectly good career. Just... ejaculating all over company property."

Jay scoffed. "I wasn't ejaculating all over company property," he said aggressively. "I wasn't going around, room to room, jizzing all over the walls and Calvin's files. Looks like someone's been listening to Mary's exaggerations a little too much."

Robbie turned to face him, on the verge of laughing. "I can't believe we even have to have this conversation in the first place. Out of all the conversations I've ever had in my life, this one sits right at the top of being the most... just... weird, man!"

"I'm sorry," said Jay. "It must be traumatizing for you."

Robbie stepped towards him. "All your ex-coworkers are traumatized. Especially Beth. She's going around with fucking bleach and disinfecting everything you ever touched."

"She'll need more bottles then, 'cause my dick touched a lot of stuff," said Jay dramatically.

Robbie rubbed one of his eyes like the conversation was draining him emotionally. "Maybe you aren't as bright as I've been led to believe."

"You're a piece of shit," said Jay, pushing past him. Then he stopped and turned back around. "You want to talk about inappropriate workplace conduct? Remind me then, who made me suck his dick during my interview? Or did that just conveniently escape your mind? I'm sure your colleagues would love to hear that little tale."

Robbie glared at Jay, noticing the cupcake he was holding. He instinctively raised his hand and shoved it into the breast of Jay's jacket. "No one would believe you," he said in a frightening whisper. He stepped closer to him, the points of his loafers touching Jay's shoes. "If it wasn't for me, you'd be managing a chain of fucking hot dog stands. Show a little fucking respect." Noticing Jay's building anger at what he'd just done with the cupcake, Robbie added, "I'll make damn sure your reputation is slaughtered from here to high heaven to the point that you're blacklisted as far down as the fucking sandwich shops." He glanced down at Jay's torso, thinking Jay could possibly be recording their conversation, which hadn't crossed his mind until right this moment. Robbie pushed past him down the steps. "Come."

"Why?" asked Jay.

Robbie turned and stared at him.

"Why?" repeated Jay.

"Just come," said Robbie, rolling his eyes. "I've only got a few minutes to spare for this shit." He took the lead through the bustling dance floor and towards the open terrace that went around the perimeter of the ballroom, buried beneath the second floor. There were dozens of closed rooms along the terrace with security posted next to each one, monitoring the party and the rooms from the shadows and limiting the number of guests going in and out to three people.

Robbie opened one of the doors and held it open for Jay. The room was lit solely by a fire inside a large hearth on the east wall, its light flickering across the walls and leaving shadowed crevices and corners throughout the room. It was a study, the walls hidden behind shelves that held hundreds of books and small antiques. There was a seating area in front of the fireplace and a personal bar cart next to it. Heavy maroon curtains covered the high windows on the north wall ahead, shielding the room from the moonlight of the world outside. There were already three people in the room, sitting on a French mahogany sofa in front of the fire. They'd been talking amongst themselves until they were disturbed by the two strangers.

"Get the fuck out," demanded Robbie, standing next to the open door with his hand on the knob. The three got up as though he was the police doing a raid of the room. They exited, possibly thinking he was security, but also throwing him subtle dirty looks. Robbie swung the door shut behind them.

"I'd love to be able to command a room like that," said Jay, strolling around the room. "Thanks for ruining my jacket, by the way."

Robbie glanced at the blue frosting that was smeared along the breast of his jacket. "I'll buy you a new one."

"It was a limited edition," said Jay matter-of-factly. "Just a few grand, that's all."

"I didn't know our company was funding such an extravagant lifestyle."

"I guess it was a splurge from my porn money," said Jay bitterly.

Robbie sighed and sat down on the sofa, the heat from the fire ironically cooling his recent flare-up at Jay. There was an oil painting of two horses above the mantel, one grey and one brown, galloping free across a cobblestone bridge with a sunrise casting rays upon their backs.

"It was poorly handled," said Robbie finally. "What happened on Friday."

Jay rolled his head to the side. He walked over to the bar cart and poured himself a drink, looking around for soda mix. When he couldn't find any, he poured himself a shot of whiskey, his back still turned to Robbie. "Well, at the end of the day, there is no one to blame but myself."

"Were we not paying you enough?" asked Robbie curiously. "Did you really need extra cash that bad?"

Jay tossed back the shot, then licked the warm whiskey residue from his bottom lip. "It's whatever. Just forget it."

Robbie leaned forward on the sofa and put his hands together.

"I get it, though" continued Jay. "It was an idiotic thing to do." He looked at Robbie. "But fuck it. It just sucks that I'm being punished, and you aren't."

Robbie didn't look at him, not wanting to acknowledge what he was referring to. "I don't know what you're talking about, Jay."

Jay tilted his head, flabbergasted. "When my interview was done, you asked me if there was anything else you could help me with. Then you leaned back in your chair and spread your legs open."

"It was a long interview," said Robbie. "It was over two hours. Can't a man stretch afterward?"

"You tapped your fucking foot!" yelled Jay.

"I didn't make you do anything you didn't want to."

Jay put his hands on his hips. "So, when I casually moved myself closer to you and rubbed my knee against yours, it didn't occur to you that something was happening?"

"You forced yourself on me," said Robbie, finally looking up at him.

Jay stormed over and pushed his hands against Robbie, pinning him to the back of the sofa. "This is force," said Jay, his face inches from Robbie's.

"It was four years ago," said Robbie, letting Jay have his moment of hostility like a teenager going through a tantrum. "What happened... happened."

Jay paused. "Did you hire me because I was the right person for the position?"

"I always try to hire the best candidate," said Robbie. "Sometimes, my judgement isn't one hundred percent precise."

Jay looked as though his answer wasn't the one he wanted.

Robbie lightly sighed. "Most often, the best qualified aren't hired." He could feel Jay's grip on him loosening. "You're handsome," he continued. "At times during the interview, I'd be distracted and couldn't pay attention to what you were saying. Then I'd look down at my papers and try to zone back into the interview again. There were other candidates with more experience than you. More articulate and smarter–sorry. Better credentials." Robbie looked down. "But there was something in you that reminded me of myself. You had this willingness to learn, and your personality struck me."

Jay let go of Robbie and stood up, towering over him, his shadow casting itself over Robbie's body as the flames crackled and popped.

"I wanted to give you a chance," continued Robbie, "like how someone took a chance on me back in the day. You were someone who could be molded and made into something great. Then, in ten or fifteen years, you'd be unstoppable–my prodigy, perhaps. After leaving your interview, there was this guilt inside of me. It follows me to this day. It was wrong for me to throw those signs out to you, and I'm sorry if you felt like you were pressured or had to do it. But..." He shrugged his shoulders as his voice trailed off.

Jay slumped down next to him. "I don't know what I'm going to do for work." He looked at Robbie. "I didn't send that video to the group chat, even though it came from my phone."

"Of course you didn't," said Robbie.

"No one is going to want to hire me," confirmed Jay.

"You're good at what you do, Jay. You're headed on up."

Jay flashed him a small smile, his eyes trailing down to the carpet. There was a moment of silence between them as music from outside the room thumped against the walls.

"Well," said Robbie, "when you're ready to start making a regular salary again, shoot me a message whenever you want."

"Really?" asked Jay.

Robbie nodded. "I'll find you something that's just as good as what you had. Don't underestimate the gay network."

"The gay network?" asked Jay, smirking.

"You obviously have to be qualified for whichever position it is, though," said Robbie, "which you are. You'll also have my recommendation. Just promise me one thing: no more homemade porn in the office."

Jay smiled at him, feeling moved that Robbie was willing to do this for him.

Robbie returned the smile and patted him on the knee.

"Um," blurted Jay, looking down at his hand.

"Right..." said Robbie, taking his hand away. He instead placed it on his shoulder.

"That's not any better."

Robbie winced. "Sorry." They both stared at each other for a few seconds, then Jay slowly tapped his shoe a couple times on the carpet. Robbie felt a sudden rush spill through his body, but he quickly got up from the couch and walked towards the other end of the room. "I'm seeing someone," he said.

Jay looked surprised. "Who? You've never mentioned him."

"I've been dating him for a while now. We met a few months after... your interview." His eyes wandered around to all the relics and artefacts hiding on the shelves and displays within the shadows of the room. His attention came to rest on a decorative grand piano in front of the north window. It was completely gilded, with brass and gilt mounts. There were carved mythological characters among flowers, vines, scrolls and instruments along the piano's shell and lid. Robbie's hands wandered along the music rack, his fingers bumping against the artistry and detailing that looked and felt like gold treasure under his touch. In the middle of the fallboard,

TRISTAN was inscribed. The piano was a lovely old piece fit for a young prince.

"Can I meet him one day?" asked Jay. "Your boyfriend."

Robbie placed his index finger on one of the ivory keys and tapped it a few times, letting the rich tone fill the quiet room. He turned towards the window next to him, standing still as he slid his hands into his trouser pockets.

Jay got up and poured himself another shot of whiskey when Robbie didn't reply. "What a wild night."

20

The white glow from several solar-powered ground lights lit up the hedges of the backyard maze in the castle gardens. Simplistic in its construction, a small child could easily find their way into the heart of the maze, where, tonight, it had been transformed into a more secluded affair with its own bar and DJ for guests who desired something intimate. Couples and small groups danced merrily with cocktails in hand as they chatted with a friend or stranger while others sat at garden tables filled with dainty treats.

Owen walked the gravel paths of the maze leisurely with a Lemon Drop martini in hand, amusing himself by watching a girl live streaming his party. Free publicity at its finest. Nothing made him more pleased than seeing people enjoying themselves at one of his own events. It had turned out exactly as he had envisioned. People were now figuring out that it was indeed Owen whose name belonged to the mysterious "Kim" persona. He could just imagine the thousands of internet users searching his name online at this very moment, rediscovering who the man behind the sparkle was.

Owen returned to the heart of the maze and took a seat at the bar, ordering another drink from the bartender.

"Hey," said a reluctant voice behind him.

Owen put his phone down and turned his head, meeting the eyes of a young man who was smiling from ear to ear. "Hello," he replied, lifting his hand in acknowledgement.

The stylish man walked closer to the bar, his face glowing but also timid at the same time. It was like he was approaching an unpredictable animal, and caution had to be exercised. "Owen Kim?" he asked, his voice friendly and eager. He had beautiful curly black hair and was decked out in fine jewellery.

"Yes, that's me," responded Owen, reaching for his drink but not taking his eyes off the pretty Latino bloke.

"I've finally found you," said the man excitedly, his knees bending in awe. He extended his right hand, and a gold bracelet slid down his wrist. "I'm Salvador."

Owen was suave and untouchable in his dark suit, his black hair finely combed and shining in the surrounding ground lights. His eyes were confident and welcoming. Owen was Korean, but had a noticeable accent that sounded half British and half American, borderline Mid-Atlantic.

"Found me?" asked Owen.

"Yes. I've been looking for you."

Owen smirked. "Perhaps I should notify my security about you, then."

Salvador looked around, as if expecting to see them emerge from the shadows of the hedges. "I've been here the entire night and haven't really seen any security."

"They're here," he confirmed, reaching for his drink. "They're watching you right now. Wave to them."

Salvador subtly side-eyed his environment again.

"Don't look so nervous," said Owen with a laugh. "So, I'm

guessing you wanted to know who Kim is. Some have figured it out, but others don't seem to care."

"Whenever I'm invited to a party, I like to thank the host," remarked Salvador.

Owen toasted his drink to him then turned to the bartender. "Please, a drink for this determined man."

Salvador took the seat next to him, and the bartender served him a Paloma. "Tequila," he said with a smile, taking the drink. "Here we go again."

"Not my favourite spirit," replied Owen.

Salvador's lips wrapped around the salty rim as he took his first sip. "Did you want people to find you?"

"I'm offended more people didn't," he replied.

"You're famous, though. Don't people recognize you? You're dating Sabrina."

"I'm a bloke who made a popular bartending app," responded Owen. "I wouldn't expect many to recognize me. Maybe the techies. Also, bartenders. Maybe Sabrina's fans."

"I knew," said the bartender, her eyes lighting up, like she was expecting some sort of brownie point from him.

Owen smiled and placed his hand on top of hers. "Thank you."

"Tremble was pretty neat," said Salvador.

"Was?" replied Owen, glancing at him as he took a sip of his drink.

Salvador backtracked. "Well, it still is. It's installed on my phone, actually." He reached inside his pocket for his phone.

"You're right," said Owen. "*Was.*" He looked Salvador up and down. "You look familiar. Are you on television? You look like a designer from one of those home decorating shows."

Salvador hung his head and let out a subtle laugh. "I know who you're talking about. But no, that's not me."

"My mistake," said Owen.

Salvador spun his glass around on the bar top and took another sip. "Congratulations on making *Forbes 30 Under 30* a few years ago. I'd just like to say that you are an inspiration to me. You're someone I've admired for some time."

Owen tilted his head slightly. "Thank you. But, if you don't mind me asking, what makes me so inspirational?"

Salvador looked away. "It was your story. In the article, you said you came from humble beginnings and didn't come from wealth. You're self-made. That kind of gives hope to the rest of us."

The left corner of Owen's mouth curled up.

"When I read the invitation to your party," continued Salvador, "it didn't cross my mind that it could have been you. But once I stepped through those front doors, you popped into my head. There was a part of me that didn't want to believe it *was* you, though."

"Why?" asked Owen.

"It's like someone named Dalí inviting you to a party. You just don't think it could be Salvador Dalí because the odds of that are impossible."

"And Mr. Dalí has been dead for over thirty years," said Owen, raising an eyebrow. "So, yes, quite impossible."

Salvador looked down. "Bad example."

Owen gave him a warm smile. "Were you named after him?"

Salvador confirmed by nodding his head. "When I was a kid, my mom wanted me to be an artist. She hung a replica of his melting clocks in my room in hopes it would inspire me."

"And are you?" he asked. "An artist?"

"No," confessed Salvador. "Well, kind of."

Owen downed the rest of his drink and looked at his phone. "Your sense of style is quite artistic at least. Anyway... It was nice meeting you." He held out his hand to Salvador. "Duty calls. Enjoy the rest of your evening."

Salvador shook his hand and thanked him for the party. "It was really nice meeting you too, Owen."

Owen could see the disappointment on the man's face as he turned to leave, knowing the man wanted to spend more time with him, to be in his good graces.

Just another social climber.

The uptempo remix of Bailey Wondrous' original song "Dip Your Lollipop" filled the ballroom as she lip-synced on stage with her bedazzled microphone in hand.

Ben's forehead was glistening with sweat, his brain abuzz with the electricity that charged through his bloodstream. Shaun wrapped his left arm around Ben's lower back, and Ben reciprocated by placing his hands on Shaun's shoulders, feeling his soft leather jacket as they danced chest-to-chest and face-to-face to the pulsating beats. Neon blue lights shone through the crowd, and their shoes danced over glitter that had fallen from the ceiling. Ben rubbed his forehead against Shaun's while breathing on his lips, his own heart beating like a drum from feeling their hot skin touching. Then, when the final chorus reached its climax, Ben pushed his mouth forward and kissed Shaun, his hands sliding down his neck and shoulders. Ben felt his surroundings melt away. He wanted to be locked in this moment forever.

The song ended, and Bailey gleefully applauded the audience and DJ. The audience cheered in admiration, their enthusiasm and excitement contagious.

"Give it up for DJ SwitchBlade!" shouted Bailey. She waved up to the people in the balconies, who were showering her with love. "*Los quiero a todos*! Now, for my third and final song of the evening,

I'll be sharing one of my original songs with you called 'Nuestro Carnaval Es Pura Candela En La Pista De Baile!'"

The song's Latin pop instrumental began, then kicked into full swing when the chorus hit. The room was spinning like a hazy rainfall, and Ben started laughing for no apparent reason.

"You okay?" asked Shaun, laughing with him as his hands trailed down his back. "Are you having a good time?"

Ben nodded reassuringly. It was like they were both on the same wavelength, the sexual tension rising further and further the longer their bodies touched. What he really wanted right now was to have sex with Shaun, but at the same time, he was undeniably nervous. There was a tingling sensation that crawled up and down Ben's spine. The lines in the decorative parquet hardwood bent and twisted like ocean waves as he looked down at the battens beneath his dancing feet.

"I've been meaning to ask you again," said Shaun, "but do you want to come back to my place tonight?"

Ben didn't hesitate for a second. "Yeah."

Shaun smiled. "Are you a top or bottom?"

"Uh... Bottom," said Ben.

"Have you done it before?"

"Once," lied Ben. "It's still kind of new to me."

Shaun pushed his body up closer against him, his mouth right against his ear. "We'll go slow, though, right?"

Ben's heart started to race again, the raging erection in his pants feeling like it would burst through. His nervousness was entangled with raw sexuality. It was like a cocktail mixed with the highest proof alcohol and the sweetest of fruit juices sliding down his skin, down his throat and through his blood. He wanted it all, right now.

Shaun started laughing again. "How's the trip?"

"It's so weird..." said Ben. He tilted his head to the side as he became mesmerized by the specks of gold glitter in Shaun's hair–

they looked like hundreds of tiny light bulbs blinking at him as they caught the passing overhead lights.

"I'm gonna use the bathroom," said Shaun. He leaned in to kiss Ben again, then faded away into the crowd.

Ben kept on dancing. He spun his head around, and the colors around him mixed together like an oil painting that had been left out in the rain. The music became part of his breathing, his thinking and his doing. He moved and swayed along the floor, feeling stiff one moment, then like water the next. Fluid and elastic. Five minutes turned into fifteen, fifteen into a millennium. Shaun hadn't returned yet. Perhaps he had gotten lost, off on his own little adventure. Ben was excited at the prospect of actually going back to Shaun's place. He wanted to be with him, badly. He wanted to swallow every part of him, to taste him, and feel how good he was. It was more than that, though. He was also hoping to be friends with him. He looked down at his phone and realized he didn't have Shaun's number or socials. They were having such a good time that it hadn't even crossed his mind to ask for them.

Ben turned around and bumped into a bald, bearded man wearing a crown and green cloak. His face slithered as he danced, bugs crawling underneath his flesh, his dead, grey eyes focused on him. The crown was bouncing up and down on top of his head, in sync to the beat of the music, as though it was waiting for Ben to reach out and catch it before it hopped off into the lights. Ben's eyes trailed upward to the frescoed ceiling. Daytime clouds glided across the sky, revealing the heavens that opened up to him. Small cherubs swam along the many faces of the ordained, a scene displaying a peaceful world that made Ben feel envious of. Maybe that's where his mom and dad were.

The grand chandelier that hung over the entryway had grown and blossomed into a multi-tiered birthday cake of gold that was filled with hundreds of flaming lights. Ben thought about eating some cake to help him grow, just like Alice did, so he would be big enough to blow out the candles. Maybe he'd ask his dad for help, and his dad would lift him up and join him in blowing them out. Afterward, when Shaun came back, Ben would sing happy birthday to him, since it was his birthday, and then they'd go off to explore the castle together.

Shaun wasn't coming back, though. That made Ben sad. Ben wanted to go home. Not to his aunt's house. Home. He wanted to go home. He pushed his way through the endless stream of people, his mind reeling. He was swimming through the pulsations of the music, the sound waves liquifying all around him and waves of fabric from people's outfits blowing past as they walked by. Bodies crushed up against him, and a hand slipped up the back of his gold metallic shirt, fingernails dragging along his skin, deep voices whispering sweet nothings into his ear.

He walked through the open front doors and raced down the steps into the fresh evening air, where a train of vehicles lined the gravel driveway. Many of them were beginning to depart, carrying guests back home, while others were pulling in to drop off guests who had just arrived. Ben slapped his hands against the pockets of his jeans to make sure he still had his wallet, keys and phone with him. He breathed a sigh of relief when he felt them, then ordered an Uber from the app. There were several waiting in the driveway already, and within seconds, one of them pulled up in front of Ben. He jumped in before it had time to completely stop.

"Hey," said the driver, turning his head to look at him.

Ben looked up at the man, whose left arm was hanging out the window with a lit cigarette dangling from his fingers. Then, the cigarette started to move away from the man's fingers the longer Ben stared at it, like dozens of floating ants had grabbed hold of it and were now carrying it off into the night. Ben adjusted himself in the seat and watched orange specks of ash fall from the tip of the cigarette when the man tapped it. Then, when the man moved it, another cigarette appeared next to the first, vanishing within seconds.

The man stared at Ben through the rear-view mirror, blowing smoke out of the corner of his mouth. "Are we waiting for anyone else here?"

Ben turned to look out his window. He shook his head. "No."

21

It was just after two in the morning when Carly turned on the foyer light. The headlights of the departing Uber flashed across the floor as it backed out of the driveway. Martin trailed behind her, his eye makeup smudged and his hair a sweaty mess. He went directly to the living room couch and collapsed over the arm, falling face first into the cushion. Carly sighed and slipped the loafers off his feet as they dangled over the side like a dead giraffe.

"When did we get home?" he asked in a muffled voice.

"Just now," she said. "Please, get up. You'll ruin the upholstery."

Martin groaned, his face shoved into the cushion. He flipped over onto his side and wiped the spot on the cushion where his dirty face had been. "There was this bartender guy at the party, and he told me he used to watch *MarcVsMartin* all the time when he was in high school." Martin stared up at the ceiling, smiling, his eyes dreary and his speech slow and impaired. He turned to Carly. "*I'm* his nostalgia. He knew me!"

Carly opened her phone and smiled. "That's nice."

"His name is Zeus," continued Martin. "He makes this drink,

and it's like lightning in a bottle. There's this smoke that comes out of the top... and it was the most amazing thing I've ever seen."

"There's lots of people that know who you are," Carly informed him. "As of a few hours ago, you're now the *Jumping Disco Man*. You're trending worldwide–look."

Martin mumbled like he had no interest in looking, but she went ahead and shoved her phone into his face, showing him the fruits of his outrageous antics. His eyes were groggy, so all he managed to make out on her screen were brief clips of his infamous jump into destiny. His new moniker was being hashtagged endlessly down in the comments page. "I'm sorry if I embarrassed you," he said.

Carly slumped down beside him, her dress ruffling and crinkling as she did so. "It baffles my mind that you would do something like that. You literally could have died."

Martin sat up and flashed her sad puppy dog eyes. "I'm sorry. Someone put something in my drink. It was incredibly stupid. I'm surprised I've made it this far in life."

"You're going with that story, then?" she asked. "Someone drugged your drink?"

"I'm going with that story because that's what happened," he said as he took off his slightly damp iridescent blazer. "I don't want people to think I'm some attention-seeking idiot. Is that what your viewers are saying?" He carelessly waved his hand at her phone. "All those randos."

Carly browsed aimlessly on her phone, not responding.

"Well, that's probably what they're all thinking," confirmed Martin, throwing his blazer on the coffee table and accidentally knocking over a candle holder.

Carly put her phone down on the table and crawled on top of him, her body pressed down against his torso. "I'm just glad you're okay," she said in a sweet, comforting voice. "It was a good night, otherwise. Hopefully you learned your lesson." She tapped him on the tip of his nose. "Little puppet made of pine, you are now a real boy."

Martin felt like a dead fish underneath her. "I'll always let my conscience be my guide, going forward," he mused.

She straightened her back and unzipped her dress, letting it drop down to her waist. Her blue bra with lace trim was exposed to him, and her slim stomach was as flat as the glass top of the coffee table next to them. The rest of the dress slid off her body and she kicked it to the ground. Martin looked up at her, his hands on her thighs. It was at times like this that he had to find ways to give himself an erection, or else she'd notice. He felt ashamed for behaving this way, knowing how beautiful she was. Her femininity was meant to be caressed and admired and loved. Any straight man would already have his pants off, ready to indulge. He felt nothing, though, and he could feel his eyes getting emotional from coming to this realization.

Martin had been having sex with Carly every week (even multiple times a week) for the last couple years since they first met. It had been a gradual decline for him, though. In the beginning, he could get through it. For the longest time he had hoped it was just bisexual tendencies whenever he fantasized about men. Saying he was bisexual was a lot easier than saying he was gay. When he thought of the word *gay* in reference to himself, it sounded wrong. It didn't sit right with him. If he told people he was bisexual, maybe it would soften the impact and disappointment for others, more so than saying he was gay. He was initially going to tell Carly when they first dated, but he couldn't bring himself to say he was bisexual either. If he told her, he'd have to tell his family. In some ways, that was worse. Before admitting who he was to someone else, he had to first admit it to himself, and he couldn't. Then, it was too late to say anything–the point of no return. They got married. He chose to deny it. Homosexuality reared its bulbous head when he started watching gay porn out of curiosity, and he knew right away it was something he never should have started doing. Sometimes, when he was in bed late at night, he'd wrap his arms around the pillow thinking it was the body of a man. He felt happy when he did that, and it was something he couldn't stop doing now.

Carly undid her bra and let it fall down to his chest. She dragged her hands along the open part of his black shirt, unbuttoning it slowly, her eyes looking into his with immense desire. She leaned down and began kissing his neck, her lips trailing down his collarbone.

"This is really nice," he said. "I'm really tired, though."

"Alright," she whispered, followed by an intimate pause. "Martin... Can we have a baby soon? This year, maybe?"

He closed his eyes tightly. Then, he quickly opened them up again, knowing what he had just done instinctively was not the reaction he should have shown her. He smiled instead, backtracking. But any sense of romance had already fled. "If you're ready," he said, kissing her arm.

"Do you think we're ready?" she asked, placing her head on his chest.

Martin had to hold back the tears that were welling up in his eyes from the panic building inside him. "You deserve to be a mom," he said.

"You'll make a great dad," she told him.

"I'm just really tired right now. Is it alright if I sleep in the spare bedroom tonight? I'm a gross mess. I'm sure I'll be in bed all day tomorrow."

"Whatever you need to do to make yourself feel better," she replied vacantly.

When she didn't move her head off his chest, he awkwardly budged his body up so she'd get the hint that he was ready to go upstairs. Carly lifted herself off and wandered into the kitchen as Martin walked up the stairs to the bathroom to wash up for the night. Then, he stepped into the spare bedroom and closed the door. He undressed, crawled into bed, and wept.

22

Tonight, Owen had accomplished what he'd set out to do. The sheer splendor of the guests who had showed up to his party was proof of his continued success. They danced, they celebrated, they rejoiced. His second objective had been to light up social media with a chaotic firestorm that would be set off the moment people walked through the front doors. Never in his life had he hosted an event as gorgeous as this. This was validation. This was what he was good at.

The clock struck three in the morning. He climbed the grand staircase and stood at the top landing for a brief moment to watch the guests who still remained in the ballroom. Just a fraction of people remained, and there was enough food and drink to keep the booze flowing, the buffet filled and the entertainment rolling until the hours of first light. He walked along the various hallways and up stairwells to the fourth floor, admiring the fine architecture that surrounded him. He slipped off his blazer and hung it casually over his shoulder, thoughts running through his head. In particular, he went over events that had taken place over the last year.

Just over a year ago in London, he met a chef named Teddy.

When they had gotten to know each other on a more personal level, he asked Owen if he wanted to be his partner in launching a few state-of-the-art luxury nightclubs across Europe. Teddy, much like Owen, was an entrepreneur who had been immensely successful in the bar and restaurant industry. Teddy's vision was to branch out into larger endeavours that would require a great amount of ambition and a greater amount of cash flow. Owen had first gotten to know Teddy after selling his virtual bartending app, Tremble, which led to his reputation spreading roots within the industry. Owen was being invited to exclusive grand openings establishments all around the world, tasting cocktails from the best mixologists in the world. He never aspired to be part of the food and drink industry; it all kind of fell into his lap. He got the idea for Tremble while he was home for winter break from college, where he was studying engineering and technology. His cousin was hosting a holiday dinner and had been mixing cocktails in the kitchen with craft Korean equipment when one of them jokingly told him he should open his own bar. At twenty-two, Owen took that seed and started developing an app that simulated a world where any user could open a bar. You, as a bar hopper, could travel from location to location all across the globe, with your avatar, and check out virtual bars that people had designed and furnished. Upon entering a bar, you could chat with fellow patrons as avatars and watch live videos of talented and novice bartenders making drinks. Games were later added, as well as a Tremble reality show that grew into an obsession. During Owen's stint in college, he connected with people who were drawn to his vision, scooping up loans and investors along the way. Owen was surprised at how quickly it had come together. He didn't come from money, so he had to climb his way up a ladder that could have broken a peg at any moment during his ascent. Some thought the idea was stupid, and others didn't get it. But the rest, as they say, was history.

Three years ago, while visiting London for a couple months, Owen met Teddy at a restaurant called Wind & Rain, which Teddy had just opened. It was his second restaurant, having trained as a chef for seventeen years all over the United Kingdom and abroad since he was fifteen. It was here that Teddy and Owen began a friendship that evolved into something deeper. Owen grew to like him, and they ended up in an unofficial romance for just over a month, until he confessed to Teddy that he was already dating someone else–that someone was Sabrina Elise. As they'd been dating for three years, Sabrina knew about Owen's fluid sexuality. There was a mutual agreement between them that they wouldn't restrict their desires even though they were together. After agreeing to just remain friends, Teddy confided in Owen that he envisioned his nightclubs being among the best in the world. Owen liked what he heard, though the whole declaration of "the best in the world" was flippant. Still, given Teddy's success in his two high-profile restaurants, he knew the concept could be another success story for both of them. Owen also felt it could escalate his own brand after selling his app. Not only did he need to keep making more money, he wanted to invest in something that was truly special.

Unfortunately, within the first few weeks of planning, there was obvious tension with conflicting values and creativity between them. Some of Owen's closest advisors and friends told him it wasn't a promising endeavour. He was wasting his time and money. When he decided to exit the partnership, Teddy didn't take it well. He told Owen that he would regret it. Owen's rationale for the sudden change of heart was the lack of what Teddy had promised to him when he first signed on: intrigue. The whole concept wasn't special enough. Teddy eventually carried on with other partners, and went on to open his first nightclub in Liverpool.

Owen had thrown this party tonight to prove to himself that he'd made the right choice, and that he had the talent and potential to create something special, a worldwide event, in a place that was steeped in extraordinary captivation and history. If anything, this party had shown him the possibilities of what could be. When he sold Tremble for just over one hundred million dollars five years ago at the age of twenty-seven, it was a reality he couldn't believe. He had made it, but he still felt as though he had more to prove to the world, and to himself. He shouldn't want to sit back and retire, not now. He made *Forbes 30 Under 30*, and when the topic of his private life came up in a press release, people wanted to know who he was seeing. Owen preferred to keep his dating life private, but it was out in the open for all to read about when he started a relationship with Sabrina Elise.

Growing up, he had always known who she was, so it was a surreal moment when he was able to introduce himself at a celebrity afterparty they both attended. Rubbing shoulders with superstars. He was just some nobody from Middle America. The cards of life, however, had dealt him a different fate. He knew it wasn't just his money that attracted her to him, for Sabrina's own net worth was exceptionally high from being a pop star in Europe and around the world for the past two decades. Still, his sexuality was always being questioned by the media. Even though he'd been quite open about his orientation since his early twenties, there were those, the social media keyboard warriors, who believed that he wasn't actually bisexual. Sabrina was his beard. He was a closeted gay man, they said. No ands, ifs or buts. It was a stigma Owen had to live with. He knew he liked women. But he also liked men, perhaps just a bit more... Maybe a lot more. He had briefly dated men in the past, but Sabrina was the first woman he had gone out with since breaking up with his first girlfriend when he was in college. Whether he and Sabrina would eventually marry, he wasn't sure. She herself was divorced and had a fifteen-year-old son, which didn't bother him. Some of her fan base didn't like Owen. Some didn't like that he was

Korean. Some believed that he was just using her for her fame and to boost his own personal gain. It couldn't have been further from the truth. He liked the person she was behind closed doors, the real her, not the star that everyone saw her as on a day to day basis.

Owen opened a door to a state bedroom. It was dimly lit, an orange sunset glow seeping across the four corners of the room and fading into the shadows within the crevices that engulfed the room. The walls were lined with panels of beautifully detailed wallpaper of artistic twisting branches and swirling gold-leaf. The ornate gilded furnishings and hardwood were from the French Renaissance (as much of the castle's finery was), as well as the lush maroon textiles and linens. There was an oak four-poster canopy bed facing out from the west wall, with thick curtains tied at the corners with gold rope.

Sabrina sat at a large vanity that had carved scrollwork accents on the headboard–its bevelled mirror was fit for a noblewoman. She wore a blue silk robe that draped around her, with makeup and jars of skin care products strewn upon the vanity's surface. Next to the door was a small personal bar that Zeus was tending. When Owen accompanied Sabrina to Venus Valley as a sort of pitstop during her world tour, he had arranged to rent the entirety of Larchdale Castle so he could throw a party unlike any other. Naturally, he needed cool bartenders. They didn't necessarily have to be the best, just talented and charismatic. He hired a dozen after visiting multiple bars, lounges and restaurants around the city. If a bartender could make him whichever random drink he ordered, in a creative manner, they were a keeper. Zeus was interesting, as well as striking to look at. There was a calm confidence about him for such a young man, and he had a curious demeanor that made you ponder what he was thinking about. When Owen saw him mix his popular Black Thunder cocktail, Zeus became one of the bartenders who stood out to him. He appreciated his honesty when he told Owen that he never really used Tremble because it didn't interest him. To most people, as well as Owen, the app lost its appeal with the general public when it changed hands after he sold it. Tremble turned out to be a fleeting craze, a brief phenomenon, and Owen had been lucky to cash in when he did.

"Lemon Drop martini?" asked Zeus, already grabbing the citron vodka and pouring it into the gold shaker.

"Jesus..." remarked Owen, placing his hand on the bar top. "I've already drunk four tonight. Well, let's make it five."

"Another peach Bellini, Sabrina?" asked Zeus.

"No thanks, dear," she said, her eyes flashing to him briefly through the mirror as she applied night cream to her face. Her British accent remained strong as ever, having lived abroad in the United Kingdom for most of her life. "The Prosecco gives me a raging headache."

"You can go home after this one," said Owen to Zeus as he watched him shake and strain the drink into a Martini glass. "So, tell me. Have you ever made two grand for one night of work?"

"Never," Zeus admitted. "I've done a few private gigs, but nothing like this."

"There will be many more to come," said Owen, taking his glass and raising a toast. He reached into his trouser pocket and slid Zeus another one hundred dollars.

Zeus' eyes lit up. "Must be one damn good Lemon Drop," he said with a smile.

"They all were," replied Owen, turning to face Sabrina. "Things are winding down. The caretakers want the party finished by five, so I'll get Maxwell to start shutting things down at around four."

"What's with this *Jumping Disco Man*?" she asked as she combed her blonde locks. "Did you see that?"

Owen strode to an armchair by the window and took a seat. "I was holding my breath the entire time, hoping he wasn't dead. The whole party would have been disastrous, all because of one idiot."

Sabrina scoffed. "I've never had the urge to jump off a balcony."

"According to Maxwell, security only removed two people," said Owen.

"So, it was drugs," said Sabrina matter-of-factly. "The *Jumping Disco Man*."

Owen shrugged his shoulders.

"His name is Martin," said Zeus, chirping in with his smooth voice. "He's a popular content creator who played video games with his friend. He was a big deal when me and my friends were in high school."

"So, a has-been," said Owen, laughing.

"Don't laugh," said Sabrina. "That's what people said about me when my album bombed five years ago. People today do such insane things for fame." Her eyes widened in disbelief. "It *usually* seems to work."

"It's called their fifteen minutes, Sabrina," said Owen. "Then, poof. You'll never hear from them again."

Sabrina shrugged indifferently. "Whatever."

"What crazy stuff will you do then?" asked Owen. He bit his bottom lip and stopped talking when he realized he shouldn't have said what he did.

Sabrina threw him a dark look. "Well, that would suggest my career is falling off the radar and I'd need to resort to such embarrassing stunts for publicity."

"Which it isn't," he stated quickly.

Sabrina slammed her makeup down on the counter. "I had to fire Vic tonight."

Owen furrowed his brow. "Why?"

"He stole some of my rings," she said, her voice incredulous.

"One of them being the ring I bought with Mummy in Italy last year. That one was retrieved, thankfully."

"You caught him red-handed?" asked Owen.

"The cameras did. I noticed jewellery had gone missing from my change rooms, so hidden cameras were installed."

"Are you serious? He's been doing your makeup for five years."

"And it won't be six," she said sullenly, throwing her brush to the side. "First my dog gets hit by a car, then my song doesn't even chart... and now this."

Owen got up and stood behind her, rubbing a hand into her shoulder. "Sometimes, bad things come all at once," he said calmly. "Maybe now, going forward, a lot of good things will come all at once."

Sabrina looked at him like she didn't believe a word he had said.

"Dad used to tell me that," Owen said, shrugging. "Still does."

Zeus was packed up and ready to leave the room when he paused and turned around. "Hey, just throwing it out there. My sister does professional makeup. She's really good."

Sabrina eyes darted around as though she had forgotten that he was even there, then peered at him through the mirror. "That's lovely. Does she live here?"

"She lives in California."

Sabrina pushed a curly blonde strand of hair behind her left ear and smiled. "I've been there many times. Well, if she can make it down here by Monday, we can see if it's a match made in heaven."

Zeus grinned. "I'll for sure let her know. Oh, by the way, that was the very first song I ever heard from you when I was a kid. "'When Men Fall from Heaven.'"

Sabrina turned to face him. "*When men fall from heaven, and you don't know what to say...*"

"*You tumble down, you trip around, and they know just what you crave, oh no, oh no,*" finished Zeus, thrilled and looking like now he could fall over and die happy. "Oh God, my inner eight-year-old is screaming! Now *that* was the song that made me gay."

Sabrina flung her arms into the air, the sleeves of her robe sliding down. "Hallelujah!" she screamed. "It was great meeting you, Zeus."

"Oh... Totally. Same here, meeting you, um... I'll get my sister over here right away."

"I'll be waiting," said Sabrina. "Goodnight!"

Zeus left the room, closing the door behind him.

"He's nice," said Sabrina, "but don't you ever fucking do that again."

"What?" asked Owen.

"When you went downstairs just now. You left me alone with a complete stranger for twenty minutes. Not just a stranger, but an obvious fan."

Owen tossed back the rest of his drink, then placed the glass down on the vanity. "Concerned he would stab you with an ice pick and make off with your jewels like Vic did? You also have Maxwell's number. You could have messaged him at any time."

Sabrina shook her head, annoyed. "Owen, you can't forget how other people see me. That was the most intimate I've been with a fan in probably fifteen years. He was in the room with me, alone, for twenty minutes at three in the morning."

"And what happened in those twenty minutes?" asked Owen. "All my staff go through intensive background checks." He motioned towards the empty Bellini glass that was sitting next to her lotions and potions. "You even drank what he made for you."

Sabrina sighed loudly, her lips fluttering like a horse.

Owen smiled at her. "I'm sorry. It won't happen again."

Sabrina shook her head like the whole ordeal she had been chastising him for was irrelevant.

Owen leaned in and kissed her on the cheek, then went to the nearest window and parted the curtain, watching the vehicles in the driveway departing, one by one. He sat down on the stone window ledge. "I'm such a damn idiot..."

"You made the right choice," said Sabrina in a comforting voice. "Teddy's ideas were too typical. No one was impressed with his concepts. They looked good, but there was nothing meaningful or special about his clubs. The nightlife industry is deathly competitive, especially in Europe."

"I could have been such a great partner," said Owen in a bothered tone.

"He didn't want you for your ideas, Owen. He wanted you for your money and connections. There was so much weird tension between the two of you, anyway."

Owen looked at the floor, his hand running down the heavy curtain. "I just... can't be remembered as the bloke who made that one overrated bartending app that hardly anyone uses anymore. Something new needs to happen, and fast. When people first meet me, my net worth always precedes the introduction. It's also the first thing that pops up when someone searches my name online. What is Owen Kim's net worth?"

"What's the second thing that comes up?" asked Sabrina.

"You. We all know how much your fans *love* that."

"That doesn't matter to me," she said. "Don't read what they post. Most of them actually like you. It's just you choose to read the negative posts."

"It's hard not to," confessed Owen. "There's this page online where someone posts fake photoshopped images of male celebrities doing gay porn–*Thirsty4MaleCelebFakes* it's called."

Sabrina acted like this wasn't news to her. "You were posted on there," she concluded, holding back an incoming cackle.

"They put me in a threesome with Kurt Meyer and Richie Waters. I'm completely covered in photoshopped jizz."

Sabrina laughed. "Welcome to the dark side, baby," she said in a spooky voice.

"You seem awfully indifferent to this."

"I've seen it all," she said in a nonchalant tone. "I've heard it all. Another day, another drama."

"So, you just accept it?"

"You can threaten to have it shut down," said Sabrina. "But it's like a hydra. Three more will pop up in its place. All you can really do is ignore the unpleasant things. You'll need to invest in a pair of rose-colored glasses sooner rather than later."

Owen sighed, not wanting to just ignore it. He was bothered. "Your performance was great tonight," he said.

She smiled insincerely. "The song didn't chart, though."

Owen looked at her, tilting his head in confusion. "The one you did tonight? That's your biggest hit ever. It went number one all over the world."

"Not that one," she said. "'Betcha Gonna Miss Me.' The second single from the new album."

Owen sat down on the seat next to hers, his back facing the mirror. "You've been busy. It's your label who's dropping the ball."

Sabrina stared herself down in the mirror. "When the clock struck midnight on my fortieth birthday, everything stopped. It was almost instant, like the universe knew–the best-before date had finally come. I'm getting older, I'll accept that. What I can't accept is letting my talent suffer just because I'm not twenty anymore."

"Immortality doesn't age, dear," said Owen. "You are an icon."

"I've heard that so many times it's lost all meaning to me," she said. "Back in the day, everything I did would get noticed. It would be relevant. Now, I'm still doing the same amount of work, but sometimes there is nothing to show for it. It's like no one cares. Thank God for the fans who have been with me since the beginning. But even they can't stop the slow slide into irrelevance." She sighed, twisting the lids back on her jars.

Owen glanced into the glass of the vanity one last time, then stood, picking up the empty cocktail glasses by their rims. "Exciting things are always just around the corner," he said. "Trust me on that."

23

Sunlight was splashed across the floor when Ben's eyes opened. He'd never been this up close and personal with the kitchen tiles before. They were cracked, warped and smelled of lavender floor cleaner. He eased himself up onto his knees and looked at the time display on the stove. It was Sunday, just after nine in the morning, and he felt like shit. The afterparty for one had gone into full swing when he got home last night. He'd cranked the music up, pulled out the raspberry vodka from his bedroom closet and made himself two grilled cheese and bacon sandwiches. After all was said and done, he passed out on the kitchen floor. The freezer door was left wide open, and the frozen vegetables and meat were now thawed and soggy, the ice cubes having turned into little puddles. An open tub of cherry cheesecake ice cream lay forgotten on the kitchen table and had melted into a creamy soup with a spoon sunken into the bottom. The dryness in his mouth felt like a desert, so he poured himself a large glass of water and chugged it down in one go.

His aunt still wasn't home. If she was, he would have been woken up much earlier had she seen her nephew the way he was. He spotted his phone on the table, covered in melted ice cream. The battery was nearly dead, and there were a couple messages from his dating apps. There was also porn open on one of his internet tabs, which he quickly closed. Then, last night started to flood back to him–at least, the bits he could remember, like Shaun leaving the dance floor to use the bathroom. Dropping acid wasn't something Ben had expected to do, but he wanted to feel closer to Shaun. During their spontaneous adventures throughout the night, he'd forgotten to ask Shaun for his contact information. There was a part of him that thought Shaun had maybe intentionally ditched him, but Ben didn't want to believe it. Perhaps something else had happened that he wasn't quite remembering, like something he might have said or done that turned Shaun off from him. If he couldn't hang out with Shaun anymore, it would really suck.

Ben jumped onto his social media and was bombarded with posts from people who had been at the party, like his classmates from high school. The events at the castle were also making national and international news. Ben smiled as he browsed through the posts, reliving every moment. There were memes, gifs and stories about the *Jumping Disco Man*, a scruffy dude who wore a cool iridescent blazer and glitter eye makeup. Ben knew who he was. He was the guy he'd gone to see the other night. When he had returned home after that encounter, Ben felt bad, and had thought maybe he should have stuck around at Martin's place rather than leave the wait he had, uncomfortable. The woman on the phone could have just been a friend or family member. He was pretty sure she wasn't, though.

There was a sudden shuffling of feet entering the kitchen that made Ben look up from his phone. His aunt was standing in the entryway, looking dishevelled. The way she dragged herself towards the counter made it seem like she was heavily nauseous. She started preparing coffee as though he wasn't there, not even looking at him.

Ben's smile faded; he felt incredibly embarrassed for having thought he was the only one home. He quietly made for the stairs before any conversation could start.

"We need to talk," said Iris, her back to him as she continued spooning coffee into the machine.

Ben stopped where he was and looked at her. Iris turned and sat at the kitchen table, ignoring the melted ice cream in the center. It was almost like it took too much effort to care about such a small inconvenience. She placed a hand on the table. "I've been doing some thinking this last week, and I've decided that I'll be selling the house."

Ben was caught off guard. "Oh," was all he could say. In one way, he was thrilled that she didn't acknowledge the state of the kitchen, or him. He wasn't even sure that she was aware that he had been passed out on the floor just moments ago.

"We can't keep up with this food truck anymore. It's costing too much, and it's not worth the trouble. It's been very stressful for me." She looked blankly at the kitchen wall, like half of her wasn't really present.

Ben twisted his mouth. "Was it the rude customer we got the other day?" he asked. As badly as he felt, he really didn't care about the truck anymore–even he knew it was a lost cause.

"It was doing well in the beginning," she said, "but now there's competition all around us, and so many liars. Some of them are horrible thieves and just... not very good people. They've stolen some of my ideas, like those retro '50s cupcakes from a few months back. Then, there's the review bombing."

Ben licked his dry lips, real anxiety sinking in from the idea that she was going to sell the house. He'd been living rent-free with his aunt ever since he came to live with her nine years ago. It hadn't crossed his mind until now. He was just always taken care of.

"Where are you moving to?" he asked.

"An apartment," she said. "This business cost me a lot to keep it afloat, and with my surgeries... There isn't a whole lot in the bank." She paused. "You'll need to get your own place, so you should probably start looking soon."

Ben's eyes darted around as the words sank in.

"Your mom told me once that she and your father would have liked to put you through college. They opened a trust under your name that you've been able to access since you turned eighteen... My intention was to tell you about it when you finally decided to go back to school. There's just over nine thousand in there. It's yours now, so you can technically do whatever you want with it. The bank didn't get any of it."

Ben felt like the rug was being pulled out from under him. There was a life that existed prior to him waking up just a few moments ago, and another life that had just begun right this very moment. "I have no idea where I'll live," he said in a concerned voice.

"Maybe a cousin will let you stay with them," she suggested. "There's lots of roommates out there, too. Just think, though, your own place. You must know at least someone."

Of course, moving out was inevitable, and excited Ben, but he wasn't expecting to get the news today. He felt like a piece of trash that was being disposed of. He wasn't ready or prepared for a change like this.

Iris' eyes wandered around the kitchen, as though finally seeing the result of Ben's wild night. She got up and shut the freezer door angrily. "What on Earth were you doing?"

"I'll clean it up," he said, turning away and starting up the stairs. He felt his eyes beginning to well up as the aroma from Iris' freshly made coffee reached him. It reminded him of when he was a kid, being seven years old and waking up to the smell of coffee beans that his mom or dad had finished grinding. He'd sit in the kitchen and watch cartoons on the old portable television while eating cereal. Then, he'd walk to the school bus stop on a crisp fall morning, the smell of fresh dew still hanging in the air. His mom or dad would always pack his lunch bag for him. He could still remember what the bag smelled like, and the ice pack that kept his sandwich cool all day long. Sometimes, whenever he wanted a sandwich for lunch, his dad would jokingly tell him that he had better go to the backyard and get some sand from the sandbox so he could make one for him. There weren't a lot of memories he had of them. But the memories he did have were golden, almost fictional. How could something that happy be real?

When Ben got to his bedroom, he dropped onto the bed and stared up at the ceiling, unblinking. He pulled one of the pillows close to him, scrunched some of the pillowcase into his fist, then swung the pillow at the lamp on his nightstand. "Why did you have to fucking die?"

24

Jay took a seat at one of the French bistro tables on the sidewalk beside Lovely. It was only two days ago that he had been here, furious and disgraced. He felt so different now compared to then. When he and Salvador finally reunited at Larchdale Castle last night, they danced for a bit, revelled in the excitement, then went back to Jay's place. They were so drunk with alcohol and passion when they stumbled back to his condo that he barely even remembered the sex, having passed out soon afterward. He liked falling asleep and waking up next to someone. It was something he hadn't done since breaking up with Tyler.

This morning, Salvador had gone back to his place so he could check up on Peanut, his pet corgi, and to change out of his clothes from the night before. He suggested that they meet up for lunch at the spot where they first met. Truth be told, Jay was growing more attached to Salvador the longer they hung out, and he could tell the feeling was mutual. This little blue bistro table meant something special to them now. At least, it did to Jay.

Five minutes before noon, Salvador pulled up and parked along Goldenrod Boulevard. He got out and paid the parking meter. Jay noticed that whenever Salvador had to be somewhere at a specific time, he made sure to arrive several minutes early. He seemed like such a punctual and reliable guy, who drove a candy apple red Mercedes-Benz, naturally. Jay's car was a basic black Toyota that barely stood out anywhere he went. He admired how Salvador was always unabashedly himself. The man did what he did and was who he was. Today, he wore aviator sunglasses and a leather jacket with flashy studs and a red tank top underneath. There was a white bandana wrapped around his head with strands of curly hair falling down the front. He looked like a rock star. He looked expensive. In comparison, Jay wore a plain black tee with jeans and sneakers. The flashiest thing on his body was one of the gold bracelets that Salvador had gifted him the other night.

As Salvador waltzed up to him with a smile across his face, Jay felt happy. He got up from his chair and they embraced. Salvador was like a ray of sunshine, as cliché as that sounded. There was nothing cliché about falling in love, Jay found. He'd take it whenever he could, and however it was packaged.

Salvador leaned in and kissed Jay on the lips, his light facial hair rubbing against Jay's smooth cheek. "Long time no see," he said enthusiastically.

Jay saw his own reflection in the lenses of Salvador's sunglasses. He didn't like it when Salvador wore them–they took away from his pretty eyes. "How's Peanut?" he asked.

Salvador sat down on the other blue aluminum chair and placed his phone down. "One thing you have to know about me is that Peanut is my firstborn son."

"Totally understand," Jay wholeheartedly agreed. "When I was growing up, my parents had a cat named Tammy who they treated like the daughter they never had. She wasn't very interesting, but everyone loved her regardless."

"Unconditional love for the inferior pet," said Salvador matter-of-factly.

"Hey," said Jay sharply. "Cats are cool."

Salvador leaned forward. "When we were kids, my sister was scratched by a feral cat when we were playing in a random barn. The ugly thing almost scratched one of her eyes out. So, when we were growing up, we weren't allowed to have cats in the house or my sister would lock herself in her room and never come out."

"Yikes," said Jay, grimacing slightly.

Salvador shrugged. "Anyway, sorry for leaving so quickly this morning. Peanut didn't have a babysitter, and sometimes he likes to use my kitchen floor as his own personal bathroom if someone's not around to let him out. He's still being potty trained."

Jay couldn't help but smile at how tenderly Salvador spoke about his furry son. He liked listening to Salvador's voice. It was always so pleasant, like a warm, sugary dessert for his ears.

Salvador picked up his phone and showed Jay a snap of the fluffy corgi. "My brother and sister gave him to me as a birthday present last year."

"He kind of looks like you," said Jay with a smile.

"Shut up," said Salvador, laughing.

"He looks like you because you're both adorable," clarified Jay, "and you both have this dumb, happy look on your face; your tongue just hanging out."

Salvador kicked Jay's leg playfully under the table. "He is adorable, for sure." He put his phone down and reached over to stroke the side of Jay's face, but then stopped. "Is it okay when I'm doing things like this in public?"

Jay nodded. "It used to bother me, but it doesn't anymore." He could feel manic butterflies invading his chest. "Hey, you never told me, but did you find *her* last night?"

"I already told you what happened last night," said Salvador. "You just weren't paying attention."

"My drunk ass just wanted to dance, man," replied Jay.

"You're not mad at me for leaving you like that?"

Jay shook his head. "Nah… It's all good. You found her, though? This 'Kim' person?"

Salvador waved his finger at him. "She's a him. Owen Kim."

Jay looked puzzled and cocked his head to the side. "The name sounds vaguely familiar. Something about a cocktail app?"

"You're thinking of the Tremble app, which no one cares about anymore."

"I kinda recall some of my friends talking about it a couple years ago," said Jay, looking up at the tree's overhanging foliage.

"Apparently, he named it Tremble because of the cocktail shaker," stated Salvador. "When the shaker is filled with ice, and you start shaking it, the steel frosts over and your hands get really cold. When you shake it, your body trembles."

"Ah…" said Jay. "Creative. Imagine having that kind of money and just throwing a party like that."

"Well, he's dating Sabrina Elise," continued Salvador. "When combined, their net worth is around four hundred million."

"Shit," said Jay, his eyes widening. "Did you meet Sabrina?"

Salvador picked up a cork coaster from the table and started fanning his face with it. "She wasn't with him. But Owen… He's like the Korean James Bond."

"Shut up," said Jay as he reached for his phone to look up his picture online. "Like, he's handsome?"

"Yeah, but there was this mystery about him. You know how hot rich guys think they can do whatever they want? There was like this layer of invincibility about him. So calm and collected, like he was floating. He was nice, though."

"Hot rich guy," said Jay. "Kinda… like you?"

Salvador put the coaster down. "Depends on what you classify as rich."

Jay side-eyed Salvador's Mercedes-Benz that stuck out like a sore thumb on the side of the road.

Salvador turned to look at his car as well. "Alas, years later, I'm still not done paying her off. She was a splurge."

Jay wasn't comfortable with the direction the conversation was headed. He didn't like to probe into someone's finances when first getting to know them. "Sorry, it's none of my business."

"Hey, usually *it is* my business," said Salvador, smiling.

Jay suddenly remembered what Salvador had told him the other day about what he did for a living. "Right... Wealth advisor. Also, wedding planning."

Salvador leaned his head back in annoyance. "There's so much work waiting for me on Monday. Ugh..."

"Not me," said Jay, looking down.

Salvador leaned forward again and gently rubbed Jay's hand. "Did you see anyone interesting at the party that you know? How was Robbie?"

Jay sighed, the events of not only last night, but Friday as well, colliding inside his brain. "We talked briefly. It was pretty awkward. How did you know he was there? Did you see him too?"

"I didn't know he was there until you just told me," said Salvador, grinning mischievously.

Jay hung his head, his mouth breaking into a smile. "Nice trap."

"Do you like him?" asked Salvador.

"No," said Jay automatically, scoffing. "He's a friend. We just talked about what happened the other day at work."

Salvador nodded, his eyes still hidden behind his shades. "So, you two are good then? What about the other one... The bald guy. Was he there too?"

"Johnson? I saw him briefly, but didn't say anything to him. He's still trying to ride Robbie's dick to get promoted, no doubt."

"As goes the corporate world," said Salvador sweetly. "It's about dick riding and social climbing, a nasty game of snakes and ladders." He pointed to Lovely. "Do you want something to eat?"

"I'm not a fan of hummus," said Jay. "Actually, I'm visiting with my aunt today for dinner, so I'm saving my appetite."

"Do your parents live in the city?" asked Salvador.

Jay looked down and ran his tongue over his top lip. "They're actually dead."

Salvador slipped off his sunglasses, his brows furrowed in shock. "Oh no, Jay. I'm sorry."

Jay smiled at him like it was all okay. "They died two years ago."

Salvador reached over and put his hand on his arm. "Did you have a good relationship with them?"

"Yeah. We were close. What about your family?"

Salvador leaned back in his chair. "Well, both my parents are living in Arizona. My dad came here from Buenos Aires with his parents when he was three, and my mom was actually born here. Apparently, my mom wasn't interested in him at first but my dad was very persistent."

"Father like son," said Jay.

Salvador paused, then grinned at his remark.

"So, you have a good relationship with them?" asked Jay.

"I've been out to them since my fifteenth birthday. So, they've had thirteen years to mourn the loss of a straight son. Luckily my younger brother, Sebastian, was born two years later and he's pretty straight. There's also my younger sister, Maria, who is twenty-two... The one who almost got her eyes scratched out by the cat."

"I have an older brother named Bradley," said Jay. "He lives in Oregon."

"Cute," replied Salvador. "Jay is nice, though. Mr. Blue Jay." He craned his neck up and down so he could get a better look behind Jay. "The cupcake lady isn't here today."

"Maybe because it's Sunday," said Jay, turning his head to see for himself. When he turned his head back around, he caught Salvador checking him out.

Salvador blushed. "Well, can you really blame me? It might be stupid to say at this point, but the way you saw me dressed the other night at your place–you know, drunken tequila night–that's not my usual attire. I'm into wearing bold things, as I'm sure you noticed. I've found from personal experience that some guys get scared off by that, so I've learned to dress more conservative when meeting a guy for the first time."

Jay gave him a confused look, like the idea couldn't possibly have crossed his mind. "I'm lovin' fancy Salvador," he said, his eyes trailing down to Salvador's chest that was exposed just above his red tank top. Jay ran his sneaker along the side of Salvador's calf.

Salvador returned the gesture. "Not to sound like a slut or anything, but I'm thinking the hummus bar probably has a decent sized bathroom."

Jay swayed his body from side to side as though he was contemplating what Salvador had subtly suggested. "I've never done anything in a public bathroom before."

Salvador shrugged, as though he was leaving the decision up to him.

Jay reached forward, grabbed the top of his tank top and pulled him in for a kiss. He wasn't used to such displays of affection in a public place, but he couldn't help himself.

"You're a frisky boy," said Salvador, breathing on him.

"You're too good for a bathroom," said Jay. "We need something more comfortable."

"So you can toss me around," guessed Salvador quietly, his lips leaning back in.

"Fuck yeah..." whispered Jay. "This time, though, you're tossing me around like a fucking rag doll."

"Done," said Salvador, putting his sunglasses back on. He stood up and grabbed his phone. "I'm going to buy a bottle of water first because my throat is dry as hell. I'm still hungover, by the way."

"I'm literally not drinking again for a month," said Jay dramatically. He stood and followed Salvador, grabbing his butt from behind. As they walked past the tree, Jay's eyes caught sight of a name on the side of the building. TRISTAN had been painted in gold upon the wall.

"Tristan," Jay said distantly.

"What?" asked Salvador, turning around.

Jay pointed at the wall.

Salvador peered over his sunglasses. "Yeah, someone keeps repainting it when it fades."

"Is it, like, graffiti?" asked Jay curiously.

Salvador squinted at it for a moment longer, then slid his sunglasses back up. "Looks like it."

They walked up the stone steps at the front of the vintage three-story building. Half of the first floor was occupied by the actual hummus bar, and the rest was closed to the public.

Before opening the door, Salvador pushed Jay to the corner of the top landing where the stone balustrade met the wall and playfully dragged his lips down Jay's neck. Then, he reached over and opened the door for Jay. When Jay inside, Salvador kissed him on the back of his neck again. Jay was having so much fun with him that he didn't even notice the curious glances they were getting thanks to their brief public displays of affection. All of those concerns went away when he was with Salvador.

25

Sarim was unpacking his suitcase and laying out all his underwear like a gay color wheel on Robbie's bed. It was a collection of trunks, briefs, jockstraps, thongs and bikinis–each with its own story to tell. Like, this one was for when he danced on stage at a club in Montreal. That one was for when he ran errands. The other one was for... well, sex.

Robbie was lying on the bed wearing a white t-shirt and grey sweatpants, looking at the assortment of colors and logos stretched across the elastic bands. He picked up one of the jockstraps and spun it around his index finger. "This one is new."

"My ass hasn't even touched that one yet," said Sarim. "It's called the *Boyfriend Strap*. I've been saving it for you."

Robbie flung the jockstrap back at Sarim like a slingshot from his finger and it hit him in his hairy pecs. "We never fucked as hard as we did last night," he said, smiling.

Robbie and Sarim had been living together in Robbie's house for the last two years after two years of dating. When Sarim started talking about buying a small place for himself, Robbie took the plunge and asked him to move in. Sarim didn't have enough space in his apartment, and Robbie had too much space in his house, so it made sense to merge their separate worlds into one. Though he loved Sarim, Robbie was reluctant and nervous to introduce him to certain people in his family.

When he finally brought Sarim home to meet his mom, Judy, two years ago, it had been a big deal: she had been shocked and overjoyed. "It's about damn time" were her first words to Robbie after the announcement. The three of them sat down together and visited over a home-cooked dinner. Afterward, Judy told Robbie that she liked Sarim, but that she felt he was wrong for him, saying he was beneath Robbie career-wise. She didn't approve of Sarim's profession as a dancer, thinking that the two of them were trying to conceal from her that he was a stripper, or something else provocative. She thought Robbie dating Sarim would tarnish her son's reputation as a serious business professional, or that Sarim was just using him for his money and connections. Robbie knew his mother hadn't been expecting him to date a South Asian of Pakistani ancestry. Eventually, his mother's approval of Sarim came around once she got to know him better, which was a relief for Robbie. She appreciated Sarim's sensitive heart, and how well he was doing for himself when it came to his career. He even started teaching her choreography after a couple glasses of sangria. Given that his mom was in her seventies, her time on this planet was growing shorter. His dad, Oscar, died five years ago.

Even though Robbie knew his dad had loved him, there was always a certain awkwardness when the topic of his private life came up. Robbie had been out to them for half his life, but it still felt like he was trying to win their approval. His younger brother, George, was a dentist with his own practice. Miranda, his younger sister, became a politician in New York. George and Miranda liked Sarim, but he wasn't quite sure if they were just being flippant or actually genuine. His sister got married and had three kids; George followed suit. At least their parents finally got their grandchildren.

In his twenties, Robbie was unhinged, partying and working menial jobs while Miranda got her degrees, then married a well-off older man who worked for the federal government. George married a woman who gave him three girls. Robbie knew he lived in his brother and sister's shadows–they were the real success stories of their family. He had come a long way from where he once was, but to this day his lifestyle was still considered taboo for them all, and Sarim just added to that stigma. In his family, he was always the black sheep. It was something he had gotten used to.

"Did you enjoy the party last night?" asked Robbie, rolling over onto his side.

Sarim unloaded a pile of shirts from his suitcase. "It was great, but it didn't really interest me that much. I've been surrounded by music, dancing and entertainment constantly, day in and day out, for so many years now that it doesn't pull me in the way it used to. Maybe because it's part of my job now. Sometimes, I'll take the peace and quiet instead."

"It's too bad you have to leave again so soon," said Robbie, leaning back against the headboard and admiring him. "You just got here."

Sarim pulled out three pairs of jeans, his movements slow and somber. "To be honest, I'm not that excited for the next part of the tour. I don't like moving around from place to place all the time. Being homesick sucks." He closed his suitcase and jumped onto the king-sized bed with Robbie, happily closing his eyes and sinking into the comfort of the mattress and bedding. "When the tour stopped in Vienna, man, it was one of the most beautiful places I've ever been to. There was this restaurant called Steirereck that our whole group went to one night, and the food was..." he balled his hands into fists and opened them up dramatically next to the sides of his head like grenades, "mind-blowing. It was my first time eating caviar."

"I've been looking at all those pictures you sent me," said Robbie, snuggling up closer to him. "I'm so jealous."

"I'd like to go back there with you next year, or sometime soon," said Sarim.

Robbie rolled over completely onto his stomach and wrapped his arm around Sarim's chest. "Please. Any excuse to get me out of this city for a few weeks."

"Or forever," said Sarim quietly. He put his arm around Robbie, his beard rubbing up against his neck. Sarim's parents, Bilal and Aleena, emigrated from Pakistan to Chicago when he was still in his mother's womb. When he turned eighteen, his parents started pressuring him into finding a wife, saying his education was now top priority, and once he finished school he'd have to get married. They wanted him to come back to Pakistan with them one day, something he wasn't sure he ever wanted to do. Their plans for him led to the biggest upheaval of his entire life.

During a heated argument about his college enrollment and aspirations, he had blurted out to them that he thought he could quite possibly be gay. There wasn't a word in the dictionary to adequately describe his parents' reaction. They both assumed the Western society had influenced his immoral ways and were disgusted that he would entertain such a travesty. Furious, his father had flung him against the wall, thinking he was lying to them to get out of getting married. Sarim tried backtracking, claiming it was a joke, but the damage had already been done. Out of spite and anger, he told them he was indeed a homosexual, and would never marry. To make them even more furious, he said he'd never go to school. They didn't speak for weeks, and gradually they alienated him within their own home. Soon after, they announced they were moving back to Pakistan with his younger sister, Shaima, who, because of their parents' influence, also chose not to speak to him. Next came an ultimatum: he had to change who he was, and do what they asked of him, or they would never support him financially or acknowledge him ever again. They would tell family and friends that he went missing or drowned. Once again, out of spite, Sarim packed up what little he had and left home before they left him behind. No goodbyes. No good wishes. He would miss his sister the most.

At the age of nineteen, alone in Chicago with no family or friends, Sarim rejected his Muslim upbringing, his parents' cultural values, and everything they stood for. He hated his parents as much as they hated him. He lived on the streets and in the parks of the city for weeks. He needed money, and no one would hire him. Late one day in the park, a woman approached him and kindly asked him about his life, clearly noticing his dishevelled state. Emma was a social worker, and given how young he looked, she had assumed he was a runaway. After he told her his story, she managed to set him up at a homeless shelter and connected him with an employment office that would help him find work. He was almost in tears over this woman coming to his aid when he had no one. When he started submitting résumés in person, his limited experience was a challenge. One employer ripped his résumé to shreds in front of him and ordered him to get out. Sarim's only real talent was fixing bikes and doing minor repair work on cars, something he'd always done with his father when he was younger.

Thanks to the help of a worker at the employment office, Sarim got a position as a dishwasher at a South Asian restaurant. He was quickly promoted to server and was soon able to get out of the homeless shelter and move in with a group of five other Pakistani roommates. He was quiet and rather shy, so they never spoke to him. After a couple months working at the restaurant, he quit. The couple who owned the restaurant, though kind, reminded him too much of his parents, to the point where he couldn't bring himself to go to work and would instead stay in his flat, feeling down on himself. His parents didn't love him for who he was, and he knew his employers wouldn't either if they found out about him. He was lonely and even contemplated suicide, believing that if this was how the rest of his life was going to be, he didn't want to experience it any longer.

At twenty, he started prostituting. He knew full well it could end his life, and in some ways, he hoped it would. After just two weeks, he was held at knife-point and physically assaulted by a man. Sarim had to stumble his way to a nearby business so he could be taken to the hospital. He abandoned hooking after that. Someone was looking out for him, though, because he found work in a garage as a mechanic's apprentice. His name was Ralf, sixty-one years old and divorced, and he hadn't been able to hire anyone who would agree to his conditions until Sarim came along, willing to work for cheap. Ralf needed extra help, and Sarim needed money. Given that Sarim enjoyed fixing bikes and cars, it was a natural fit.

Sarim was still incredibly lonely, though. He convinced himself to try dating women, and even went on a few dates, but none of the girls stuck around long after he told them he lived with five other men in a small flat and worked as a mechanic's apprentice. He wore old, baggy clothes and his self-care was lacking in almost every way. He was scrawny and weak and got nervous talking on dates, having no confidence in himself. Sarim tried dating men again, but most wouldn't even give him a second glance. People harassed him on the streets, and would often push into traffic. When he was beaten up for the fourth time in less than two months, he avoided trying to meet people, thinking they were all the same.

During this period of depression, Ralf learned of the abuse Sarim had suffered and suggested that he start working out so he could build strength to defend himself. To this day, Sarim was thankful that Ralf had come into his life. Sarim was never treated as well and with such compassion by a white man as he was with Ralf. In the years he worked for him, Sarim began looking up to him as a father figure. Ralf told Sarim about his previous marriage, money, travels and cars. He educated Sarim on life. Sarim never spoke about his sexuality, having already learned his lesson the hardest way possible. Ralf was important to him, especially for survival, and he couldn't lose that. He decided to use the workout equipment that was gathering dust in Ralf's basement. It had belonged to his son who had died many years ago, by suicide. When Sarim learnt this, he told himself that he'd never take the road that Ralf's son did, and would fight through whichever hardship came his way.

Sarim started changing physically. He got himself a buzzcut and grew out his facial hair. The pounds of muscle he added to his body made him defined. The more he took care of himself, the more he noticed people wanting to talk to him in ways they never had before. People went so far as to start calling him handsome, and others would just stare at him. It wasn't a nervous or hateful stare, either, like the ones he was used to.

With this newfound confidence in himself, he had gone to a gay bar for the very first time and discovered a whole new world. It was the first time in his life where he didn't feel left out or looked down upon by judgemental eyes. After watching the go-go dancers and admiring their bodies and dancing, he asked the bar manager if they were hiring. The man seemed hesitant, but asked for his number and told him he would call if there were any spots available in the coming weeks for an audition. Sarim didn't think he'd hear back, but two weeks later the manager called, telling him that he had a practice gig for that coming Friday if he still wanted it. By then, Sarim had already found work in an underground nightclub called Boy Toys, where he was scooped up by the owners almost immediately when he applied. Men of his ethnicity were popular, and they wanted him as one of their Boy Toys. He was surprised at how much money he was making by not just stripping, but also renting himself out to men. Sarim quit his job at the garage and thanked Ralf for all he had done for him over the years. If it wasn't for Ralf, he wouldn't have made it out alive.

As expected, Sarim was popular at Boy Toys. The older, rich white men wanted to have sex with a young brown guy, and Sarim was their answer. He exercised and took care of himself as best he could, not just for his clients, but also for himself. As the years rolled by, things continued this way well into his late twenties. On one occasion, he had gone to see a concert with one of his clients who had bought tickets to attend the show together. The man treated Sarim as his unofficial boyfriend, showering extra cash on him every time they met. Sometimes, their outings were purely platonic. The dancers performing at the concert were what drew Sarim's attention the most. He loved their artistic agility, precision and how powerful they appeared. He noticed that one of them was South Asian, and in that moment, he knew he wanted to dance professionally, and not just at a nightclub. When he first started to dance, it was a way to express himself first and foremost, to show off his body, and to feel sexy. This was what he was meant to do with his life. He was about to turn thirty, and dancing was the change he'd been wanting. After doing a few more high-priced transactions with his wealthier clients and taking what he had saved up, he bowed out. He moved away from Chicago, finally leaving the place that made him into the man he was today. It was then and there that he made a promise to himself: he would never let anyone talk down to him about his ethnicity or sexuality ever again.

He moved to Venus Valley for its vibrant culture and beauty, loving everything the city had to offer. For the next few years he continued taking dance classes, did go-go dancing on the side, and became a personal trainer to pay for his life expenses. It was the perfect trifecta, and he was proud of how far he'd come. The only thing missing from his life now was someone to love. From time to time, he'd think about his family and sometimes their voices would burst through, bringing back unwanted memories. He tried his hand at dating women again, but he couldn't. He liked men.

One day, a tall, handsome brown-haired man walked into one of his exercise classes. Being thirty-five at the time, Sarim could tell the man was in his forties, having been with many older men before. His name was Robbie, and he was forty-six. They shared an obvious and immediate attraction, and Robbie was one of the reasons why he stopped working with male clients, because he'd always get aroused during training sessions. He'd get aroused by everything that had to do with Robbie, like his self-deprecation when he struggled with the routine or his butt when it arched into the air. Robbie's flirty smile arrested Sarim, and the way he talked... His aggressive demeanor... His hair. He wanted him to be gay, so bad. *Please, please, please be gay.* When these sexual urges became borderline unbearable, Sarim switched to training female clients exclusively. Then the women tried dating him, and he switched back to men, thinking if he was going to end up sleeping with one of his clients, it might as well be a man.

Robbie was someone he enjoyed spending time with, and they got along easily. Behind this intimidating man, there was a hidden sensitive side to Robbie that Sarim wasn't expecting to find. Sarim realized then that he had never actually dated someone for love–it was mostly just for money, or because he was feeling lonely and wanted to latch onto the first person who liked him. After a month of seeing Robbie at classes, Sarim decided to ask Robbie out. It was one of the most nerve-racking things he had ever done, and it took him days to work up the courage to do so. When he caught Robbie giving him flirty eyes, he knew a move had to be made. The gaydar was going wild. He was proud of himself when Robbie agreed to go out on a date, and also relieved. Even though Sarim had initiated the date, Robbie grabbed the reins and took him to an expensive seafood restaurant, where they chatted for over three hours until the restaurant closed. They just clicked. With Robbie, it was like several pieces of a jigsaw puzzle fitting together. Robbie made him smile. He made him forget about the bullshit in his life. He made him feel safe. He didn't even know what to call it at first, and didn't understand until weeks later that what he was experiencing was love. He hadn't expected to fall for Robbie as hard as he did, nor had he thought they would stay together for as long as they had.

Four years later, the passion was just as strong between them, but still, there was something distant about Robbie. Even after all this time, Sarim still wasn't able to tap into a particular piece of him. Their relationship was at ninety-five percent, but there was that missing five percent that Sarim couldn't place, an empty white canvas unknown to him. Robbie knew more than anyone about his troubled life, and Sarim came to learn about Robbie's own reckless period when he was young, but the finer details of Robbie's life were still vague in parts. Sarim accepted the fact that when Robbie was ready, he would share the missing piece with him. He just hoped that it wouldn't be something bad, something that would throw their entire relationship off the rails, which was one possible scenario. Sarim wanted to keep his rose-colored glasses on for as long as possible, until the day they would have to come off.

"Want to go to the bar tonight?" asked Sarim, as he ran his hand down Robbie's leg.

"I thought you were sick of doing that," said Robbie. "The nightlife scene."

"When I'm alone and you're not there, yes, but this is different. Let's go out and celebrate. Last night was too chaotic and I didn't really get a chance to enjoy it."

"I haven't been to a club since the last time you were here," said Robbie.

"Liar," said Sarim, teasing. "Just kidding."

"I'm serious," said Robbie, his voice going high for a second. "It's filled with all these young guys and I feel like..." He put his hands to his face. "I don't even want to say it."

"You feel like the daddy when you walk in," said Sarim, laughing, rubbing his shoulder to comfort him. "You are, though. It's hot, daddy."

"I don't even have a first name anymore at those places," said Robbie. "It's just daddy. Not, hey, what's your name? Just daddy. I've become a walking fetish. They're borderline aggressive, too. Even a bartender called me 'daddy as fuck' one time. At least you're still in your thirties."

"For less than a year," Sarim mourned, like it was the end of days. "My expiration date in dance has been long overdue, or so I've been told hundreds of times."

"You can obviously teach dance," suggested Robbie. "When the time finally comes."

"That's the plan," replied Sarim. "Or do daddy porn."

Robbie smirked. "I don't feel fifty," he said.

"You don't talk a lot about your twenties," said Sarim, guiding the conversation down a road he had tried dragging Robbie down many times before. "Your teen years too."

"It was the '80s... '90s," he said, looking down. "It was just... a weird time."

Sarim adjusted his body and cuddled closer into him. "I know it's something you avoid talking about, which is fine, whatever. But I've told you about my younger years. I'd like to know more about yours."

"So we can commiserate," said Robbie.

Sarim leaned over and kissed him on the forehead. "It doesn't have to be now. Whenever you're ready."

He saw Robbie's face turn glum and cold for a moment, so he slowly slipped off all his clothes to help cheer him up, his butt muscles clenched. Sarim crawled off the bed, went into the bathroom and turned on the shower, leaving the door open. Robbie turned his head to look into the bathroom, and the distant expression on his face gave way to a smile. Still fully dressed in his t-shirt and sweatpants, he stepped into the shower with Sarim. The hot water drenched Robbie's clothes and made his t-shirt cling to his chest as he pressed himself against Sarim's hard, naked muscles. Hot steam filled the bathroom, fogging up the mirror.

26

Marijuana smoke clouded the front of the television as Johnson poured himself another glass of vodka and lemon-lime soda. The thought of having to drag himself up into the kitchen just for ice was nonsensical, considering he had reached the point in the evening where it didn't matter if the drink was warm or cold, flat or carbonated. All he demanded of his drink now was for it to work its eighty-proof magic on his bloodstream. He was at Glenn's house with Tony, the three of them regrouping after last night. It was a familiar Sunday evening routine that involved pot, alcohol and a barrage of game show programming. They were currently watching *Wheel of Fortune*, a show that reminded Johnson of his grandmother.

Glenn stared at the puzzle on the television, taking a drag from his fat joint. He worked in IT, and he was hopelessly obsessed with computers, Reddit and cannabis. He rocked a man bun and almost always had something negative to say about the current government or world affairs. He liked to debate anyone he could if he detected blood in the water in the form of a viewpoint different from his own. "What the fuck is it?" he asked, squinting at the television through his glasses.

Tony looked up from his phone, also squinting, like he was taking a particularly strenuous eye exam. "Category is 'Before and After' ... Water under the Bridge to Terabithia," he said quickly.

"Shit," said Glenn. "That movie hit me hard."

Tony, the snake charmer, was an overall creepy guy. He was a professional photographer and video editor who traveled to other countries to take macabre photos of unsettling places. Last year, he'd been hired as the photographer for a vampire-themed wedding in Romania. Tony always sat straight like a ruler, his feet planted firmly together on the ground, and never slouched or relaxed his body. It was like he had a constant stick shoved up his ass, like a scarecrow. He wasn't known to wear any color other than black, and would wear a punishing number of layers even during the warmest months. His regular bedtime was five in the morning, for it was only during the early morning hours of darkness that he could be most creative, he'd say.

Johnson had been on his phone for the last hour browsing for a hookup, the nightly prowl for sex. It was only recently that he'd given up on finding a partner. As hard as he tried, finding a relationship was like navigating a maze of impossible complexity. He sometimes found it difficult to relate to other gay men, or perhaps he was just extremely picky about what he wanted in a boyfriend. He was often lonely and dreamt of the day he'd find his Prince Charming. This was something he learned to keep to himself, though, having been met with scoffs and laughter from people who mocked the airheaded whimsy of the fairytales he had grown up with and admired. Deep down, he was a hopeless romantic. He didn't want just anyone. He wanted *the one*. His biggest fear was that he'd go the rest of his life floating in the gay void of hookups and friends with benefits without ever finding a truly lasting relationship. Last month, he managed to find a couple of other guys to come over to Glenn's place, and the evening soon turned into group sex. It was great, of course, but it left him feeling empty as he drove back home.

Johnson had to be at work in a few hours, but he was a decent actor and had perfected the craft of appearing sober when needed. He stayed away from most drugs except cocaine, a habit he hadn't been able to kick since leaving college fifteen years ago. In the beginning, it was just once every couple of weeks to let loose, but now it had grown to twice a day, if not more, and the crack pipe was his new favorite toy. He trained himself not to do it at the office, not wanting his image to be tainted as that guy who did blow and crack in between bathroom breaks and conference meetings. Right before his eyes, he had become a walking stereotype. He had morphed into the gay guy he would often see in television dramas, the one who did copious amounts of drugs and engaged in constant random hookups and orgies at parties.

Johnson tossed his phone aside, the device hitting against the half empty vodka bottle.

"No one is interested tonight?" asked Glenn, looking at him.

Johnson tilted his head, annoyed. "Not really," he said.

"You're a good looking dude. You really shouldn't have this problem."

Johnson looked at Glenn as a desperate question came bubbling up and out of his mouth. "Do you think I'm *too* intimidating?"

Glenn blew smoke out of his mouth. "Like how?"

Johnson sighed. "I know I'm an asshole sometimes. Maybe I'm not likeable?"

An awkward silence ensued.

"Maybe just a little," said Tony.

"Yeah, well..." said Johnson, looking back at the television, "you're a freak, Tony. Does my personality suck?"

"Sometimes you are too straightforward and..." Tony trailed off.

"And what?" demanded Johnson.

"Maybe desperate is a better word," suggested Tony.

Glenn stepped in. "I've noticed during the last few months that you've been very on edge. You always seem so pent up, man, so maybe people are picking up on that energy."

Johnson leaned back on the couch and propped a foot up on the table. "Jay was at the party last night."

"You *need* to stop talking about him all the time," said Glenn, annoyed. "You embarrassed the fuck out of him and got him to quit."

Johnson scratched his arm, irritated. "Robbie was there too."

"They've fucked," said Tony matter-of-factly. "It's obvious."

Johnson scoffed. "They're probably fucking right now. Robbie knew exactly what Jay was up to the whole time. It's so fucking fake, everyone there. If someone makes your dick hard, they get a promotion. If they actually suck your dick, well, up and up they fucking go."

He leaned forward over the glass tabletop and did a white line, then grabbed his drink and downed the rest in several gulps. When he pulled the glass away from his lips, he noticed a streak of bright red liquid had drizzled down the inside like cherry syrup. There was a trickling sensation along his upper lip, like his nose was running. He touched one of his nostrils and looked at his fingertips to see warm blood smeared on the skin.

After staring at it for a few more seconds, Johnson looked at Glenn and Tony to see if they had noticed, and when he was sure they hadn't, he subtly wiped his fingertips along the sides of his shorts. He hunched over and furrowed his brow, staring at the floor, thinking. He then grabbed his hoodie from off the arm of the couch and headed for the front door.

"Where are you going?" asked Glenn, glancing at him quickly, then averting his attention back to the television.

"I'm heading out," he replied as he slipped on his runners and opened the front door to leave. Hearing the door open, Lil' Man, Glenn's kitten, came prancing out of the kitchen. Johnson bent down to pet him.

"It's the calm before the storm," said Glenn.

Johnson turned to Glenn as he continued stroking Lil' Man's back. "What?"

Glenn nodded to the television. "They're doing 'Popular Sayings' this round. Fuck, I'm good at this."

Johnson's gaze lingered on the television for a moment longer, then he looked back down at Lil' Man, who purred as he rubbed the back of his ear.

27

Several piles of photographs were laid out all over the kitchen table when Jay's aunt Louise added even more to the mix. The other day, she had told him she had something to show him, and that something was a box of family photographs from decades past. Some of the photos weren't new to him, but others were of moments he had never seen before. Louise was the wife of his mother's brother. She had also been close with Jay's mom, having known her since high school.

"This was at... my twenty-seventh birthday party," she said, handing him a photo as she sat down across from him.

Jay put his wine glass down and took the photo, smiling as he inspected it. There were aunts and uncles, but also older cousins who were still only babies and toddlers. He noticed his mom and dad were seated next to each other, with Bradley cradled in his mother's arms, still just a baby. She was so beautiful, and Jay could see so much of himself in his dad. Everyone was seated around a long picnic table in a backyard that had a swing set and sandbox in the background. Draped over the table was a plastic party tablecloth, with remains of a chocolate cake placed at the very end, already sliced up and served. Beer bottles, wine glasses, ashtrays and other dishes were scattered about. There were so many photos, just like this one, of various birthday parties, garage celebrations and backyard gatherings.

Jay put the picture down, feeling buzzed from the red wine. Louise poured more for the two of them, then picked up the empty dinner plates and cutlery and took them to the sink.

"Any idea what you'll do for work now?" she asked, turning on the tap and squeezing in bright yellow dish soap as the hot water ran. The artificial lemon scent hit Jay like a bright Sunday morning. Being that it *was* now Sunday night, the weekend was officially ending. It had been a fantastic distraction from what had happened at work on Friday. Monday was rearing its ugly head, though, and he'd have to face reality again. The magic of the last couple nights was turning to dust all around him, and he would finally have to come back down to Earth from his temporary kingdom on the moon.

"I'm still wondering why you quit," she said, probing him. "The last time we spoke at Easter you said you were on your way to promotions–even an executive role down the line."

Jay twisted his mouth, staring down into his wine glass. None of those workplace aspirations mattered to him anymore. They'd been carried off by the wind, and ceased to exist. "It was suffocating there," he said.

Louise looked at him. "Well, a job isn't a hobby. You can't just stop doing it because you don't like it anymore. Many of us have jobs we don't necessarily enjoy doing, but we do them because, well, we have to. The point is, you were doing so well and earning a great income. Maybe it wasn't your number one dream, but it's what you invested the most time in and knew how to do well."

Jay fidgeted in his chair. Truth be told, he *was* comfortable with what he had been doing for work. At his age, he was earning a real good salary and had surely been on his way to bigger career prospects. But things happen, and life has an interesting way of making you doubt and second guess things that you were otherwise satisfied with. His breaking up with Tyler was the first, then his parents dying, then what happened on Friday at work was the third. He was beginning to realize that life had other plans for him, and all of these unfortunate occurrences were life's way of trying to tell him something. Now that he wasn't working a steady job, new ideas were coming to light, ideas that he'd been putting off for years... The things he valued most.

"I've been working and going to school regularly since high school," he said. "I've never really had the time to take chances and do things that light a real fire inside of me: something passionate. I've been caged inside concrete walls for so many years now that it's pretty much all I know."

"It seems like a waste to just throw away all this experience that you gained through the years," she pointed out to him. "You have that wonderful business degree, and you still have all the skills and experiences from the other companies you worked for. Not to mention your school credentials and that great internship you got. It's only upward for you." She smiled at him, like everything would be okay again in a couple weeks once he regained his footing beyond this small twist in the road. The Earth would keep spinning, and he would continue to prosper. "You know, Sam is in marketing. You could connect with her sometime this week. You two are cousins, so you should be spending a bit more time together anyway."

"No," he said bluntly.

Louise's smile faded, her hands slowing as she gradually stopped washing the dishes. "You need to be smart about this. Do you really want to start from the bottom all over again? After everything you worked for? It just doesn't make sense to me."

"I'll take the next couple years off and figure it out," he replied.

"I'd expect a nineteen-year-old to say that, not someone at this stage in his life," she said. "Why can't you try something new while also working? At least then you'll be secure and won't have to worry about your expenses. Then once you get better at whatever it is you're wanting to do, you can take it more seriously. You can't just not work, Jay."

He looked at her. "Why not?"

She sighed, feeling like she was speaking to her own son. "It's the security. Your mom was a saleswoman and your dad worked at the ad agency for over thirty years. Imagine them being thirty and just stopping their careers to start something new. Not working for a couple years? How will that look on your résumé?"

"I've been saving money," said Jay. "I'll be okay. Also, the inheritance money." He didn't like bringing that up. The money he inherited was substantial enough, but he had yet to use it towards anything. It was mostly just sitting in his bank account and various investments, waiting.

"How many holidays with them did I miss because of work, or because I was busy with school... or because I just didn't care?"

"They knew how busy you were," said Louise sincerely. "They understood."

Jay balled his hands up on the table. "When Mom told me she was sick, I didn't take it seriously. I just thought she'd get through it, and life would move on. She told me she was doing fine, but she just didn't want me, Bradley and Dad to know how bad her cancer really was. Honestly, I don't think she wanted to know, either."

Jay looked down at the pictures, noticing one had been taken on his first day of grade one. "About a month before Mom died, she was in her bed, really sick, and I was reading *The Da Vinci Code* in the living room. She told me she had read it–twice. After a few chapters, I got up and went to tell her how much I'd love to go to Paris one day. I asked her if she had ever gone, and she said no, but would have liked to. Then, she closed her eyes and smiled. It was as though she was trying to picture herself there with me, or somewhere. Maybe we were all there, the entire family."

Jay turned his head and looked through the kitchen window, seeing his reflection staring back at him in the glass. "One of the last things she told me and Bradley was to live our lives. She never went to college. She never really traveled. There were so many things she was talented at, like baking and interior decorating. One thing I'll never forget is when she and Dad came to my college graduation. We were driving around the school grounds, and Dad was busy in his head trying to find somewhere to park. Mom was looking out the passenger window, staring up at the school. She said to herself, 'If I could do it all over again.' I knew she wished she had done more with her life–took more chances, I guess. Lived a life with passion. When Mom told me to live my life, it was like she was telling me to go out there, to see the world, and take as many chances as possible. Don't wait. Keep the fire burning." Jay turned his attention back to Louise. "I'm not returning to that concrete cage, Louise. That place doesn't matter to me like it did a couple years ago... or a week ago. It doesn't mean anything to me."

Louise stopped with the dishes and came over to sit next to him. She took his hand in hers. "That is *exactly* what she was telling you to do, Jay. So, go do it."

Jay packed the box of photos into his car, placing it on the passenger seat and wrapping the seat belt around it. Before driving off, he glanced over at a picture sitting at the top of the stacks, staring back at him. It was him, five years old, standing next to Bradley in front of their Christmas tree with their mom and dad. He remembered how Dad would take him and Bradley to the local ice rink to learn to skate because Bradley had grown interested in hockey after watching the Winter Olympics on TV one year. He recalled Mom asking him if he wanted homemade iced tea on any given day, and she'd make some for him, whether he was seven or twenty-seven.

He pulled out his wallet and unfolded the picture of his graduation ceremony from college that he kept inside. Bradley was standing next to him, smiling, with his arm wrapped around Jay's shoulders, as were Mom and Dad, the both of them beaming.

Jay started crying, his tears landing on the photo. He had to move the picture away from his face so his tears wouldn't stain the precious colors. When he came out to them in college, the love he felt from them, and the worry that was lifted from his shoulders when they hugged him, only confirmed to him that he no longer had to hide. They told him that they loved him, and that was all he needed to hear. He knew he wouldn't have grown into the person he was today if it wasn't for them, and he was proud of the man he had become. It was the greatest gift Mom and Dad could have ever given him.

28

Martin was going cross-eyed from continuously doom scrolling through post after post from hundreds of thousands of people tagging the *Jumping Disco Man*. Minute after minute, and hour after hour. He felt like he was stepping into a room filled with millions of people all looking at him, with speech bubbles popping up over their heads where he could read their opinions of him. He had become a meme, an idiot and a joke all at once. Carly took it a step further and asked him to record a video with her for her social media accounts, conclusively sealing his fate: *My Husband: The Jumping Disco Man*. In the thumbnail, they both wore their outfits from the party with a cropped snapshot from the infamous video of Martin jumping inserted between them. Their mouths were gaping open like blow-up dolls, and the color saturation was heightened to its maximum. She uploaded the video on Sunday night and it garnered five million views in just twenty-four hours.

His social media blew up, and people were following him in hoards, with some even recognizing him as one of the creators from *MarcVsMartin*. For every person that seemed to like him, there were three more waiting in the wings who hated him, calling him out in comments and private messages. He'd never been called so many horrible names in all his life. But, on the flip side, had never been complimented as much either. Countless news outlets from all over the world reached out to him asking for interviews and statements. He received emails from public relations and booking agents who wanted to represent him immediately. Every twenty minutes, Carly would scream out from somewhere in the house that there was another update in the *Jumping Disco Man* chronicles. He had no idea who came up with the moniker, but he hated it. The negative comments that called him a moron, bad influence, desperate fame seeker, drunk and drug addict made him angry. But the ones that put him most on edge were the ones suggesting he was a closeted gay man, and Carly was his beard. He was receiving messages left and right from gay guys–some of whom begged him to start his own gay porn channel. He tried to avoid those comments as much as possible and hoped Carly wouldn't give them much merit either.

"I'm scheduling your appointments," said Carly as she paced around the kitchen, typing away on her phone like she was trying to break the world record for fastest texter. "Starting tomorrow, you have nine interviews."

Martin's eyes bugged out of his head.

"I'm so fucking jealous of you," she said.

He dropped his phone into a cardboard box he called *the cellar*. Whenever social media became too much for him, he would drop the portable hate device into the box, place the lid over it, and leave it in there until he was ready to look at it again. "You're jealous that no one is calling you names every second of the day?"

"Hello! Your numbers are going up!" she blurted, in a tone that suggested that he should be feeling excited instead of downtrodden. "They can call me a moron, a bitch and a cringe slut all they want if those are the numbers they'll get me, honestly. Look–you gained twenty thousand followers in twelve hours!" She flashed his social media profile at him from her phone. That was the only good part of this circus, he felt. Though he felt nervous for how fast this was all happening, Martin was grateful that his follower and subscriber numbers were growing, and optimistic for all the money he could make.

"I'll want to be paid for all those interviews," he said, pointing at her as he went around the island to look over her shoulder at her phone.

"Do you have time for a quick phone interview right now?" she asked.

Martin scratched the side of his head. "I'm not ready... Tell them I'll do it, like, tomorrow."

"Be ready," she said, looking at him. "Twenty-four hours a day, seven days a week."

"You do realize that your poor husband was drugged," he reminded her. "Someone out there spiked his drink–probably a fucking bartender–and that's why he did what he did." It was half true, anyway. There'd been something snuck into his drink for sure, or maybe it was just the constant flow of alcohol to his system. Regardless, seeing Ben enter the balcony, of all people, had put him on extreme edge. Martin had thought Ben would say something incriminating about their meetup. Whether it was adrenaline, paranoia, stupidly, the drugs, the alcohol or everything slapped together, he had jumped. He just needed a quick getaway, from everything.

"Martin, you can't say that," she said, lowering her phone for the first time in hours. "You have to say that you were drunk and you didn't know what you were thinking. Don't mention drugs. You have to say you were an idiot, like it was a big mistake."

"It *was* a mistake," said Martin aggressively. "It could have ended really bad. You'd be planning my funeral right now, not all these interviews."

"That is terrible to even think about," she said in a sympathetic voice. "But people are going to ask why you did it. Do you regret it, do you think it was wrong... blah, blah, blah. Just tell them, and their audience, that it's wrong to act the way you did and to always drink responsibly." Her eyes lit up magically. "You could be a poster boy for bad choices!"

"What?" he asked, exhausted.

"You could be the spokesperson in those ads you see on TV for, like, drunk driving."

Martin just stared at her, completely incredulous. "There's an offer from a skydiving company who want me in their ad."

"You didn't tell me that!" she yelled, flinging herself at him. "That's great!"

"That's bad," said Martin, unwillingly enduring her embrace. "I don't want to turn something stupid like this into my public persona and be known as some idiot who jumped off a balcony at some rich dude's party. Also, I sure as hell don't want to be called the *Jumping Disco Man*, either."

Carly tried to relax him by rubbing her hands down his tense arms. "There are tons of people out there who are trying to make social media their career, and they're failing. They would kill to have what you're getting right now. They'd sell their soul. As we speak, people are making bank off you by putting out reaction videos and skits and writing articles and doing a multitude of other shit. People need to keep talking about you, or you'll just fizzle out. Gossip, mentioning your name... Those leads to popularity. That leads to money. Those equal fame."

"Infamy," corrected Martin in a soft voice. "I don't want this to damage my career."

"It will open doors for you," she said with a smile. Her brown eyes were lively and very convincing.

"As a stunt man," he mocked. "Who the hell is going to take me seriously now? Anyway, whatever. I'm heading out for a bit." He pulled his phone from out of *the cellar* and left the kitchen as Carly sat down and worked her social media magic for him.

"Be back here by dinner so we can go over your interviews!" she yelled back at him. "The first one is tomorrow at five in the morning! Also, we'll go out to dinner sometime this week to celebrate!"

"Sure..." mumbled Martin, sluggishly making his way up the stairs. He went into their shared office to grab his sunglasses and hoodie and pulled the hood over his head for comfort and protection. After glancing in a mirror, he went to the bathroom and grabbed his razor so he could get rid of the *Jumping Disco Idiot*.

"Don't shave off your beard!" yelled Carly from downstairs, hearing the buzzing and quickly running to the bottom landing of the stairs. "That's part of your identity now!"

"Fuck," he said, dropping the razor into the sink. Martin left the house, got into his car, and drove to a nearby public park. He parked in a secluded spot near some trees with long overhanging limbs that wasn't regularly frequented. He climbed into the backseat, pulled down his pants and settled himself in to watch non-stop porn.

29

"It's too pink."

There had been over twenty swatches laid out on the bride-to-be's lap, which she finally narrowed down to the ten she deemed to have potential for her wedding reception.

Salvador swivelled in his chair and leaned over the desk to look through the shades she painstakingly considered. "How about this one," he suggested. "This crêpe pink here."

Cher shook her head. "Too blah. That one's out."

"They're all too feminine," said her fiancé, his eyes drooping in boredom.

"Remember," said Salvador, "the curtains won't all be this one color. The pink will be an accent to the ivory. How about a blush pink for the blushing bride?"

Cher turned to her fiancé, seeking his acceptance. He just stared at the swatches, his face blank. "I don't want it to look like a baby shower," he complained.

She slapped her hands down on her knees like that was the last thing she needed to hear, causing the swatches to slide off her lap. "Josh, it won't look like a baby shower!" She picked the swatches up from the floor and showed Salvador which shade of pink she had chosen. "It doesn't matter what you think. It's my day! This is the color that me and Salvador want. If it was your way, everything would be blue, brown and seaweed green!"

Salvador's eyes darted between the two of them while he resisted the urge to cringe. He glanced at his watch. "Well, how about the two of you discuss this over the next few days, then on Friday we can touch base and delve into options for the dinner menu. Blush pink for the win, though!"

"It *will* be blush," said Cher defiantly. "Speaking of food... The cake. We'd like a fourth tier."

Josh sighed and looked up at the ceiling. "We agreed on three."

"The extra tier will almost double the price of the cake," said Salvador, scribbling down notes onto his pad. "Has the guest list increased?"

"We don't need a fourth tier," clarified Josh.

His fiancée was fuming. "It looks better with four."

"It doesn't matter!" he said, raising his voice. "People aren't going to eat all of it. It's a waste of money and our budget doesn't allow it!"

Cher placed a hand to her forehead like she was preparing to block an incoming headache from entering her brain. "It'll ruin the design if there's only three."

"What about a fake tier?" suggested Salvador. "No wasted cake, and the cost will be lower. You can also keep your original design."

"That would work," said Josh urgently.

"Don't use the word fake," she said, eyeing Salvador seriously. "Nothing fake–this isn't a fake wedding. That's not an option we're going to entertain."

Salvador's eyes widened. "Alright... Well, another option is the baker had said she can adjust the design to fit the three tiers. Given how many guests you have coming, the fourth would be a waste of money, like Josh said. You'll have a lot of cake left over. At that point in the evening, once dinner is served, you'll need to worry about having enough alcohol, not cake."

Cher stared at the floor as she appeared to weigh her options. She looked at Josh, as if expecting him to say something. "Fine," she concluded. "We'll meet on Friday to discuss the dinner menu."

They both stood up, took turns shaking Salvador's hand, then left his office. Salvador sighed, ripped off his bright blue bowtie and unbuttoned his paisley shirt so he could let the cool office air caress his skin. Working two careers was taxing on his social life, but he liked staying busy. Even on his days off from Monroe Wealth Management, he'd usually still be in the office tending to his wedding couples. He had built a portfolio of well-off clients, and given how charming they found him, clients would often thank him with gifts like jewellery, alcohol, gift cards and other random baubles to show their appreciation, on top of his fee. The women loved his personality and the husbands were exasperated by how he charmed their wives, sometimes even questioning whether he was a metrosexual straight man. Most other wedding planners in the city hated him and thought he was overrated and charged too much for his services, but Salvador prided himself on being proficient and successful at what he did. He built lasting relationships with his clients, and they appreciated his energetic demeanor and workhorse hustle. The other planners were boring, monotone plodders with elementary suggestions and "been there, done that" concepts. Salvador thought outside the box and liked to offer non-traditional solutions, and many clients were attracted to that.

There was a knock on his office door and Kitty poked her little head in, her glasses catching the glare from the sun. When she became Salvador's intern, she was instantly infatuated with him to the point where she fell in love in just a matter of weeks. She'd bring him homemade banana bread and would come into his office to chat with him all the time. In middle school, Salvador had experienced his fair share of girls who tried flirting with him, so he knew what Kitty was trying to do. When he broke the news to her that he was gay, she didn't talk to him for three weeks and wouldn't show up to work for several days in a row, almost getting terminated. When she finally recovered from the traumatic heartbreak, she accepted reality, thinking he would become her gay best friend instead but completely ignoring the fact that he was nine years older than she was. She became his matchmaker, bent on finding him a boyfriend after he told her that he was too busy with work to be dating. After some unfortunate attempts, she actually got it right with Blue Jay.

Salvador looked at his watch. It must have been almost lunch.

"Guess where little ol' me saw you on Saturday night?" she said in a teasing voice as she danced her way into one of the chairs in front of his desk.

"You were at the bathhouse on Saturday night too?" he asked.

She flashed him a horrified look. "Gross." She then gripped the edges of his desk like she was on a rollercoaster ride. "Let me tell you, that party will be the highlight of my entire life!"

"It was great," he agreed. "It was the best party I've ever been to, for sure. Who'd you go with?"

"Jill," she said. "My friend from high school." She paused, her beady eyes full of secrets. "I didn't say hi because you were with Cute Cupcake Boy."

"You could've said hi. Also, his name is Jay."

"Then I guess you're dating him now," she said as she fidgeted with her purse, clearly wanting him to get up already so they could gossip on their way to lunch instead of just sitting there.

He licked his upper lip and smiled. "It seems like it."

"Yay! He's really cute. Hopefully he's not crazy, though. That was my concern."

"He's just going through the ups and downs of life. Have you fallen victim to the *Jumping Disco Man* craze yet? It's sad that out of everything that happened that night, he became the top story."

"I'm following him!" exclaimed Kitty, like the words couldn't spill from her mouth fast enough. "So many people are following me now because of my video."

Salvador scrunched up his face and glanced at her phone. "What video?"

"The one of Martin jumping," she said. "I was going around, scanning the ballroom with my camera, taking videos and such, when it literally happened out of nowhere. There weren't many who managed to record it, at least, not from a good angle. Mine seems to have been the best one because it has three million shares and forty million views!"

Salvador dropped his pen. "Let me see it."

"You haven't seen it yet?" she asked, bewildered.

"I've seen it, but let me take a look at the original that you posted so you can show off all those crazy number counts to me."

When she showed him, his eyes widened. There were over fifty thousand comments. "So, you're the reason this thing blew up."

"I'm a pretty big deal now," she confirmed.

Salvador snorted.

"I need your advice," she said, her voice turning shy.

"For what?" he asked, re-watching the video on loop.

"People have been messaging me, asking to buy the original."

He looked at her. "For how much?"

"One person offered two thousand. That's a lot of money!"

Salvador leaned in closer, placing his elbows on the desk. "Did you monetize it yet?" he asked.

"Duh," she said, like he was her dumb dad. "As you know, I've been making 'people watching' videos, but no one clicks on them, so there hasn't been any money in that. Then all of a sudden, the revenue arrow spiked on my statistics page and my brain exploded into oblivion. The system must be overwhelmed or something because the revenue page is still blank and says there's a two-day delay. I don't know how much money I've made so far."

Salvador smiled at her. "Good," he said, satisfied with her answer. "I'm so proud of you! Keep me updated on that. I'd say you're in the tens of thousands of dollars by now. There's a wide range and tons of fluctuation when it comes to social media revenue like that."

"Are you serious?!" she blurted, her eyes bugging out of her glasses. Salvador knew the wheels were turning in her head as to how she was going to spend the money once it landed in her tiny hands. "Will I have to pay for your financial advice going forward?"

Salvador closed his notepad and grabbed his phone. "Think of it as a gift for finding a boyfriend for me," he offered. "Anyway, I'm starving. Let's head out. You're paying, money bags." His mind was spinning now, thinking of Saturday's party again thanks to Kitty and her eagerness to gossip about everything that had happened. His mind drifted to thoughts of Owen and their encounter at the party. He was kicking himself for not sharing with him what he did for a living, wishing he had made a stronger impression on Owen. If there was going to be another party at Larchdale, Salvador intended to keep his eyes and ears open for news of it. Having Owen as a possible business connection was a prospect that Salvador couldn't simply walk away from.

30

It was close to ten o'clock in the evening when Robbie knocked on the front door of the small single-story ranch house. The beige brick and white shutters were undeniably charming, originals from its 1950s construction, but the soil beds beneath the windows were sad patches of dirt, having long lost their greenery and flowers. As he waited at the door, he turned around and saw a stray black cat scurry across the road in his direction. It lingered on the sidewalk, its green eyes fixated on him like a patrol officer witnessing a potential burglary.

The door unlocked and was pulled open to reveal his barber, Liam, greeting Robbie with a wan smile. Liam had been Robbie's regular barber for the last several years, and they knew each other since the late '80s. He wore a grey cardigan and blue jeans with a baseball cap that bore the logo of his late father's favorite baseball team. This was Liam's family home, and it had belonged to his parents up until their passing ten years ago. He still maintained the place as best he could even though his older brothers had been wanting to sell it for years. Liam refused to comply with them, simply because there were too many memories attached to the place–almost seventy years' worth.

"Just finished supper," said Liam, greeting Robbie with a hug and a pat on the back. "You hungry? It's one of those frozen lasagnas from the store. They've been getting skimpy with the cheese lately, so they aren't as good as they used to be."

"I'm good. Just ate," replied Robbie. "Thank you, though."

"You're due for a cut," Liam observed, looking at Robbie's silver hair. "Letting it grow out now? Maybe one day I'll be able to convince you to go back to your beautiful brown hair."

As Robbie observed the state of Liam's living room and kitchen space, he felt his smile falter. The house smelt of pot and Hawaii Breeze air freshener, and the rooms were getting more cluttered with each of his visits. Robbie had been hesitant to come over recently given the house's fall into disarray, but also because of the noticeable shift in Liam's personality. The last time Robbie got his hair cut, Liam had almost clipped his ear, and on top of that, his professionalism wasn't on par with what Robbie was used to. Liam had said the marijuana was for his chronic back pain, and Robbie believed him, but the man seemed diminished. The passion was watered down, the twinkle had faded from his eyes, and his indifference to the world was growing.

Liam stepped into the poorly lit kitchen, where two of the three light bulbs in the ceiling fixture had burnt out. "Want something to drink? There's some beer or gin, that's about it. There's orange juice and soda if you fancy something non-alcoholic."

"Water will be fine," said Robbie. "I'm still recovering from the weekend."

"Ah..." said Liam as he bent down to open one of the lower cupboards. "You'll have to fill me in." When he stood back up, he held a bottle of gin in his hands. With a large cloth, he rubbed the dust from the glass. "This hasn't seen light for over ten years," he said, holding the bottle up so Robbie could see it. "What do you think? It hasn't been opened yet."

Robbie took a seat at the oval kitchen table. There was an antique lace cloth covering the table with a stack of newspapers piled on one of the chairs. "If you insist," he said, succumbing to Liam's hospitality. "Just a little bit."

Liam placed the bottle down on the table in front of Robbie. He didn't think much of it at first, but as the light caught the shimmer of the liquid within the glass, Robbie instantly recognized the label. It wasn't a bottle you could have bought at the liquor store. "You still have this... and unopened?" He ran his hand over the custom label that was scratched up and chipped at the corners. *Roger's 1920-1987.* Robbie smiled fondly like it was a beloved family heirloom.

"What happened to yours?" asked Liam curiously. "Drank it, most likely."

"It's long gone," confirmed Robbie, still staring at the label. There was something unsettling about Liam pulling out this particular bottle, at this particular time, given the reason for his visit in the first place.

All of a sudden, the television in the living room started blaring the local news, and Liam quickly picked up the remote to lower the volume. "They talked about the party the other night," he said, pointing to the screen. "You went, I'm hoping. Johnson did."

"For sure," confirmed Robbie, pulling out his phone. "Here's some pictures."

Liam looked over Robbie's shoulder as he scrolled through the photo album. There were snapshots of the performers with out-of-focus party guests lit up in their glamorous outfits in the background inside the ballroom.

"Mermaids," Liam said in a surprised voice, catching a glimpse of the fountain where the mermaids and merman were posing. "The place looks the same from back in the day."

"Were the parties like *this*?" asked Robbie, glancing up at him.

"No two parties were ever the same," Liam intoned, his eyes remaining fixed on the photos as they passed by, one by one, like a collage of whimsy and wonder.

Robbie smiled in unison with him. He let Liam take the phone and scroll through the images at his own pace. Halfway through, a selfie of Robbie and Sarim appeared. They were together on the dance floor, the sides of their foreheads pressed up against one another, with Sarim's arm wrapped around Robbie's shoulder. It was perfect, like a promotional photo for a nightclub.

Liam paused for a moment longer on this photo than he had for all the others. "How delightful it must be... to be with your boyfriend."

The joy in Robbie's heart was displaced by a sudden jolt as Liam swiped past the photo, onto the next one. His smile faded, and the photos seemed to have lost their magic all at once. "There's actually a more pressing reason for why I'm here to see you tonight."

Liam was only half-listening to him at this point, still scrolling through the photos. Robbie hoped he wouldn't scroll too far, or else he'd come across the risqué pictures he took with Sarim the other night. He monitored Liam's progress through his photo reel, and was ready to take the phone back before he reached the end.

"What's the special occasion, then?" asked Liam.

Robbie took the plunge. "Have you thought about Tristan at all lately?"

Liam quit scrolling and just stared at the picture he had stopped on, the hesitation in his breathing noticeable. Robbie knew he had caught him off guard. It got eerily quiet in the room, as if they had both stopped breathing altogether.

"Because it's all coming back to me," confessed Robbie. "You know how sometimes signs start popping up from out of the blue? For example, you might think about wanting to make applesauce. Then, a friend comes over and brings you fresh apples from their tree, but they didn't know you were planning to make applesauce."

Liam looked at him. "You've been wanting to make some applesauce?"

Robbie sighed and rolled his eyes, leaning his elbows against the table. "These signs, all around me–they're happening more and more. It's like I'm being pushed to remember." He picked up the gin bottle, the liquid inside hitting the sides of the glass. "What made you want to show me this tonight?"

Liam stared at the bottle as though he was about to speak to it, then turned away.

"I'm thinking of going back there," said Robbie.

Liam nodded his head, like he was expecting to hear that.

"I thought I'd never go back," continued Robbie. "I've always kept telling myself maybe one day. But now, I'm being pulled. Something is drawing me back there."

"No matter how much time passes, that pull will always be there," said Liam. "It's been over thirty years."

"I'd like you to come with me," said Robbie.

Liam shook his head and stood up, putting the phone down on the table. He went back to the kitchen counter and started fiddling with random objects that were out of place.

"It would really help me," pleaded Robbie.

"No," said Liam.

"I can't go there alone."

"Take someone else."

Robbie sighed deeply and looked away.

"I'm sixty-nine," said Liam. "I'd like to leave the past where it belongs."

"You don't even want to see it?" asked Robbie, curiosity rising in his voice.

"That's enough now," said Liam gravely, staring at him. "That's enough, Robbie."

"Maybe it's time to make peace with the past and finally move on from it. This will help."

"Have *you* made peace with the past?" asked Liam. "Have you moved on? Look me square in the eyes and tell me you have."

Robbie felt his eyes tearing up.

"I've moved on," said Liam distantly. He picked up the gin bottle and shoved it into Robbie's chest. "Officially, as of now. I've moved on. The best thing you can do for yourself is to go home and move forward with your life, not backward."

Again, Robbie felt his emotion building, but he remained strong and collected. "It's a sign," he said. "I feel it in my heart. It's something I've been *needing* to do."

Liam wandered further away from him into the dark living room. "You're on your own." He picked up a half-smoked joint and lit it, throwing the lighter across the table.

Robbie looked around Liam's living room again, noticing the disarray. "Do you need help around here?"

Liam took a few puffs of his joint, his knees rocking slowly back and forth as he sat on the edge of the couch. "Help would have been nice twenty years ago when change would have done something. It's too late now."

Robbie felt an immense wash of sadness, for everything.

"Sarim," said Liam.

Robbie furrowed his brow. "Yeah?" he asked.

Liam paused. "Don't let go of him."

Robbie's heart beat rapidly at the mention of Sarim.

"Does he love you?" asked Liam.

Robbie nodded gently. "He does."

"What about you?"

Robbie looked down and slid his foot along the tiled floor. "Whenever he's around me, it feels like home. Everyone else could turn their backs on me, forget about me, ignore me... But I'll always have that one person who looks at me like I'm more than enough. That's Sarim."

Liam stared at the living room wall, his vision unfocused, like he was looking through the wall itself. "Don't let that go, Robbie. Who knows when you'll find it again. You don't want to end up like me."

"You still have time," said Robbie.

Liam turned to look at him. "That boat has long sailed. The ones that got away... For some of us, love just doesn't work out. It doesn't reach us. I'm glad you were given a second chance at it."

Robbie drummed his fingers along the bottle of gin in his hand then stood up.

"Your pal, Johnson," said Liam.

Robbie turned around just as he reached the front door. "What about him? He's not really my pal."

Liam took another puff from his joint. "He doesn't have a lot of good things to say. It seems most of what he has to say is rooted in jealousy and bitterness more than anything. He feels invisible, you know. I'd like to see him be okay."

"Why wouldn't he be okay?" asked Robbie. "He seems pretty content with himself."

Liam shrugged. "I probably shouldn't be saying anything... He came here the other night, dishevelled and all out of place. There aren't many people that he feels like he can talk to. He's been really burying himself deep into the white stuff lately–now there's a pipe. Maybe you could try being there for him in case he needs you."

Robbie looked away, his hand firm on the door knob.

"You work together. I just wanted you to know in case he does something that seems erratic and not himself."

Robbie opened the front door. "Have a good rest of your night, Liam."

"Hey, good luck," said Liam with a small, sincere smile. "With the other thing you plan on doing. I'm sorry you have to do it on your own."

Robbie paused for a moment longer at the door. He tapped the bottle that fit snugly in the crook of his arm, and left.

31

Ben had assumed he'd be staying with his aunt for a little while longer. There was the planned trip to New York, his desire to go back to school and, on top of that, finding a job that would elevate his bank account and work experience. His brief outline for the next couple years had been neatly mapped out, but now it had to be shifted around due to the sudden revelation of him having to find his own place. When he sat alone in his room and contemplated his future, there was a sense of uncertainty of the changing times. It was the self-reliance that came with growing up, and confronting the fact that things never stay as they are forever. But soon, when he found his own place, he'd be able to do whatever he wanted and come and go as he pleased without the watchful eye of family following him. He also intended to use his trust money towards school, as his parents would have wanted. That brought him a sense of security, but everything else felt like a roll of the dice.

Right away, he started searching for potential places to live and job openings for supervisor roles. He felt qualified for a minor management role in a restaurant or retail store, given his experience in a food truck and the entrepreneurial mindset that came with it. After sending off a dozen résumés, he was browsing through one of the dating apps when he stumbled upon Shaun's profile. His main profile picture was a selfie of him in a bathroom mirror, wearing a black t-shirt and shorts, his expression sexy and stoic. Ben didn't think twice about messaging him. He did it right away, and within minutes got a reply back. He thought Shaun might not reply at all, so when he did, he was thrilled. When they got to talking about the party at Larchdale Castle, Shaun explained to him what had actually happened after leaving him to use the bathroom. Shaun had taken much longer than expected because he had gotten lost, and when he came back to the dance floor, Ben was gone. It was a relief to Ben that Shaun hadn't ghosted him. When he explained his side of the story (the parts he could remember), Shaun apologized to him and said he should have been there when Ben started tripping out, and admitted that he himself was tripping pretty hard. Ben liked Shaun; not only was he incredibly attracted to him, but he was fun. The prospect of fooling around with him made Ben eager and excited, and Shaun seemed to share the same mindset because he suggested they hang out soon.

On Monday, Ben was initially going to take an Uber to meet up with Shaun, but decided to take the bus instead because he wanted to save up more money, especially for a car. At eight o'clock, he got off the bus at a shopping strip where Shaun had said they should meet. There was a drugstore and liquor store as well as a coffee house, fishing supply store and a cheap pizza bistro. When the bus pulled away, he saw Shaun walking towards him down the sidewalk with a Keith Haring backpack slung over one shoulder. He was wearing jean shorts, a tank top and a backwards ball cap.

"Hi," said Shaun with a wave. He was the exact same height as Ben, and his skin perfectly tanned, just how Ben remembered it.

"Hey," replied Ben.

They both walked into the shopping strip parking lot. "Want to go to the liquor store first?" asked Shaun.

"Sure," said Ben. He wasn't expecting to drink today, but had no issues with it. Shaun picked out black spiced rum, which also happened to have one of the highest alcohol percentages. Ben offered to buy the soda mix from the drugstore nearby since he couldn't legally buy the alcohol. "I'll buy the snacks later," he said.

Shaun led them down the sidewalk to a nearby park. The early evening summer sun beat down as traffic rolled up and down the streets, and car horns echoed between the trees as birds rustled the leaves. When they found a spot next to a cluster of trees, Shaun pulled out a beach blanket and some plastic drink cups from out of his bag and poured them both a drink.

"Try to hide your cup," said Shaun, discreetly placing his drink beside his backpack. "I'm glad you messaged me the other day."

"There was a part of me that thought you wouldn't reply, actually," confessed Ben, spreading his legs out over the blanket. He glanced down at Shaun's toned knees and calves that were exposed just below the bottoms of his shorts as he sat cross-legged.

"Did you get home alright?" asked Shaun. "I might have invited you to come back to my place, but I can't remember."

"It's okay. I took an Uber home," said Ben.

"It was my first time taking acid," revealed Shaun. "My friends gave it to me. My roommate hates my friends, though, so they're never over."

"You live with a roommate?" asked Ben. "How's that been?"

"We live in this small rental house," he said. "It's kinda shitty. But it's just for now, so whatever. He used to be my boyfriend."

"Isn't it awkward being exes and still living together?"

Shaun shrugged. "Meh. We're good now. His name is Patrick. He goes to school, works full time and goes to the gym so he's practically never there. He'll usually come home at night to sleep and eat, then leave the next morning. Do you work or go to school? You said something about Brandon Save the other night, and a hot bald guy."

Ben noticed his drink was heavy on the alcohol and low on the soda mix. "Yeah. I'm a cashier there. How about you?"

"I'm majoring in psychology and working at the mall," said Shaun. "My parents wouldn't let me take time off after high school–they're paying for most of it."

"I'm going back to school soon," revealed Ben. "Probably next year."

"What will you take?"

"I'd like to take theatre or something creative."

"What do you want to do afterward? Become an actor?"

"Yeah. Or something else on the creative side."

Shaun looked down. "My parents wouldn't let me take any of those sorts of courses. I've been wanting to design music video sets or do graphic design... I'm still trying to convince them. I'm liking psychology, though."

"What else do you like to do other than work and school?" asked Ben.

"Jerk off," he said with a smile. "Play video games and watch movies. Go to clubs. You should come with me."

"That would be cool," said Ben, smiling, feeling happier with each passing moment.

"Have you been before? Wait, your dating profile says you're nineteen."

Ben looked down at his drink. "Maybe ask me out again in two years?"

Shaun smirked and took a swig from his cup. "We'll get you in... My friends know people at Fame. You should come with me on Saturday. I'm going with a couple people from work. One is a lesbian and the other is a straight girl, but they're fun. It's Men's Night."

"Isn't every night Men's Night?" asked Ben with a smile.

"Yeah. But it's more of a special event kinda night," explained Shaun. "There are extra go-go dancers, famous drag queen appearances, hourly drink specials and fun contests where you can win money. There's also Lesbian Night, which is whatever."

"I'm down," said Ben.

When they finished discussing general gossip and their favorite pop culture interests, the conversation seemed to fizzle out. Shaun reached forward and put his hand on Ben's leg. "Want to see my place?" he asked, downing the rest of his drink. "It's close."

"Sure," said Ben, finishing off his drink as well.

Shaun gathered everything up into his backpack, then walked alongside Ben down various sidewalks, side streets and parking lots. The sun's light gave off an early evening ambiance the hour before sunset, a sweeping aura that turned the world around them to gold.

"Do you drive?" asked Ben.

"I've been sharing a truck with my roommate," said Shaun as he casually rubbed his shoulder against Ben. "One week I'll use it, then the next he will. He still ends up using it more than me because he claims that he has to travel farther. Those days I'll just take the bus, which sucks."

As they walked down a back road behind a shopping strip, Shaun ran up a shipment ramp and slid down the railing, stumbling forward as he came off it. "What's the wildest, craziest thing you've ever done?"

Ben thought for a moment. "Honestly… I haven't really done anything wild or crazy."

"I went bungee jumping off a bridge," said Shaun as he started walking backwards. "I literally pissed my pants."

"That's insane," said Ben. "What made you want to do it?"

"Probably peer pressure. My cousins were making fun of me for being nervous. Heights are my biggest fear, so I'm happy I did it. I'll never do it again, though."

Ben's heart raced at the thought of what he was wanting to do for the last hour. So, he decided to go for it. He leaned into Shaun and kissed him on the cheek.

Shaun looked at him, smiled, and returned the kiss, taking Ben's hand comfortably into his. "You're adorable..." he said. "In, like, an innocent kinda way. We're gonna have a good time together."

They reached Shaun's small and modest rental home, which didn't offer much in the way of curb appeal. There was a chain-link fence with an overgrown front lawn and very little life to the sad, minuscule property.

"I swear to God it's not a crack house," said Shaun. "All of the houses down this street are mostly for students, so they look like shit. They're super cheap, though." He opened the front door and welcomed Ben into the living room, which was mostly bare except for some mismatched furniture and a long tank with some clown fish in it. The air was musty and the walls yellowed from decades of cigarette smoke.

"Patrick is obsessed with *Finding Nemo*," said Shaun, heading into the kitchen. "He's not home yet." After grabbing a bag of unopened dill pickle potato chips, he headed for the basement stairs. "Let's go down," he said. "It'll be awkward when he comes home and we're up here. He's weird."

Ben followed Shaun downstairs. The basement was one large rec room that probably hadn't been remodelled since the '70s, and still smelled like the '70s too. There was a short coffee table and a well-used vintage couch on the right side with an old television propped up on a dresser. The left side was used as a sort of storage space filled with boxes piled up high to the water-damaged ceiling.

There was also a pool table that had several more boxes stacked on top of it.

"How many parties do you think have happened down here?" asked Shaun, plopping his backpack down next to the coffee table and turning on the television. "The landlord said the pool table and dresser have been down here since the '70s. That's almost fifty years of pot and cigarette smoke and probably cum stains everywhere."

"Most from you," joked Ben.

"If we're talking about my bedroom upstairs, then yes," said Shaun, smirking at him. "Want to watch a movie?" He pulled out the rum and soda from his backpack and poured them another strong drink as he started searching for something to watch on the television. When they settled on an animated movie about a little alien rag doll, they both sat on the couch, side by side. Ben couldn't keep track of what was happening in the movie because all he could think about was being with Shaun. He hoped Shaun was thinking the same.

Ten minutes into the movie, Shaun turned to him. "Do you want to spoon?"

Ben had literally wanted to do that ever since the movie started. "Yeah," he said.

"Do you like being the little or big spoon?"

Ben smiled. "Little."

Shaun wedged himself between the back of the couch and Ben, wrapping his arms around him and pushing his pelvis up against Ben. There wasn't enough space on the couch for the two of them to lie down, which was a perfect excuse to be crushed up against one another. Shaun started to kiss Ben's neck, making Ben turn over onto his back to kiss him on the lips. After just a few moments, Shaun shifted onto his back and Ben got on top, their lips still locked together. Half of Shaun's body hung off the couch.

"Hold on a second," said Shaun, pushing himself up. He moved the coffee table further away, then threw down a couple square pillows and a vintage wool blanket. After spreading it out, he lay down. "Much better," he said, smiling up at him.

Ben lay down with him and they continued making out, his wandering hands gliding over Shaun's smooth arms, then down to his shorts, pulling them down to his ankles. Shaun's hands went up the back of Ben's shirt and slid it up over his head.

Then, footsteps from the main floor above shook the ceiling.

Shaun sighed annoyingly. "It's Patrick," he said, like it was the biggest inconvenience in the world. The light above the stairwell flicked on, and footsteps came creaking down the stairs, slowly. Patrick reached the bottom landing, the green light from the movie's color palette catching the glare of his glasses. The rest of him was just a dark outline standing still. There was an awkward pause as Shaun and Ben lay where they were.

"There's food if you want some," said Patrick, his voice low.

"Great," said Shaun. "I'll have some later."

Patrick lingered where he was for a moment longer, then went back up the stairs.

Shaun sighed again. "Let's go up to my room."

Pulling his shorts back up, Shaun took their drinks and led Ben back upstairs and into a small bedroom. Once inside, he shut the door and put the drinks down on the floor. He started playing some music from the laptop that was propped up on his bed, which was just a mattress on the floor with some basic sheets, pillows and a comforter. There were school books piled up in the corner, and some of his personal belongings were in random boxes.

Without even having to say anything, they both collapsed onto the bed and started making out once more, shorts and shirts flying off as their lips locked together. Shaun's kisses did laps over Ben's mouth as he grabbed his thighs. From the other room, Ben heard the shower turn on. Patrick sobbed like a disturbed ghost from inside the bathroom, his voice resonating through the walls.

"He's jealous," said Shaun, acknowledging the sound. "He still kinda loves me. It's annoying, actually."

Ben ignored the crying, albeit still feeling awkward about it. His lips went down Shaun's bare chest and he trailed his tongue along his smooth, tanned skin.

"Have you ever gotten a blowjob?" asked Shaun.

Ben ran his hand through Shaun's dark brown hair. "No."

Shaun immediately sank downward, making Ben's sensitive head explode within moments.

32

Jay had received a call from Robbie asking if they could meet to talk about something–a particular something that Jay knew referred to what happened at the office on Friday. This was it, the official be-all and end-all sit-down that he thought he'd be getting from Calvin, but seeing as Robbie had been stepping into doing some of Calvin's duties, it made sense. Let the gay handle the other gay. Robbie would discuss the incident formally with Jay over hummus and pita chips, then go over the terms of Jay's informal resignation. This was all just speculation, of course, but Jay felt this was the most logical reasoning for Robbie's invite.

Jay parked his car, then stood at the front steps of Lovely, leaning up against the balustrade. The stately, three-story building stood forty feet tall and was one of the oldest buildings still standing in Venus Valley, having most likely been built sometime during the 1800s. The exquisite architectural detailing was a love letter from a bygone era.

Robbie never showed up on time for anything. When he finally did arrive ten minutes past their scheduled meeting time, he parked his sleek Audi behind Jay's rather forgettable Toyota, then opened the back door and pulled out a cardboard box. Jay bit his upper lip when he saw it, knowing what it was filled with and hoping it was Robbie who had gone through his personal belongings at the office. The thought of someone like Beth finding the veiny dildos and lube in his filing cabinet next to his quarterly reports was horrific, but because it was Robbie carrying the box, he breathed a sigh of relief. If the toys had been left in the filing cabinet, well, the next occupant of his office would be in for a rather large surprise. Jay smiled at the thought, and that smile rubbed off on Robbie as he walked towards him with the box in hand, a grin spreading across his face. He handed the box to Jay like it was a special Christmas present just for him. "It really sucks to be doing this," he said.

Jay took the box and walked back to his car, placing it in the backseat. "As long as my laptop is in here, that's all that matters to me." He glanced into the box, but didn't see any silicone, butt plugs or lube bottles.

"Some things were thrown out," said Robbie, reading his mind.

"You should have donated one to Mary," suggested Jay. His face became red, and he paused, not wanting to turn around until his blush went away. He instead took a moment to himself and casually rummaged through the box. "You were the one who cleaned out my office, though, right?"

"Yeah, it was me," replied Robbie.

Jay finally shut the door and turned around. "Ready for some hummus?" he asked, nodding towards the building.

Robbie started walking towards Lovely alongside Jay.

"Does Calvin know everything?" asked Jay, realizing it was a stupid question considering everyone must have known by now. Like in any office, people loved to play tabloid and gossip from water cooler to cubicle any time the tiniest morsel of an embarrassing detail involving a fellow employee surfaced.

Robbie opened the front door for him. "It's all been taken care of. Calvin said it's unfortunate what happened given what an asset you were for the company. He wishes you well."

Jay felt embarrassed all over again. It was odd, though. It seemed that he and Robbie had already wrapped up the talk about his resignation. Jay had thought it was going to be a long, drawn-out thing, but the talk ended before they even entered the building.

The hummus bar was the size of a typical sub or burrito eatery. It looked exactly like you'd expect a hummus bar to look, from the wooden benches and stools to the array of plants and greenery along the walls and service counter. Fresh, dark panelling covered the walls, and the hipster lighting fixtures cast a warm glow. It was a hip and trendy place for its equally hip and trendy guests, which excluded both Jay and Robbie, but more so Jay. The aromas of garlic, chickpeas and spices wafted from behind the kitchen doors and straight into the customers' vegan-loving hearts. Jay had eaten here once before and didn't mind it, but he wouldn't exactly choose it for himself. He was more a greasy fast food kind of guy. Give him some takeout fish and chips or boxed macaroni and cheese, and you found the key to his stomach.

"Do you want anything?" asked Robbie as his eyes scrolled the menu options above the counter.

"What the hell is vegan knafeh?" asked Jay, his face disturbed.

"Knafeh is a Middle Eastern dessert," whispered Robbie.

Jay gave him the side eye. "You've had it?"

Robbie smiled. "Mhm."

There was an older gentleman with a black mustache behind the cash register, someone you wouldn't expect to work in such a youth-oriented restaurant such as this one. Jay would have expected to see some college girl with glasses and a ponytail who laughed at everything you said to her, not someone in their seventies.

Robbie bypassed the small lineup at the cash counter and made his way to the back of the restaurant instead. Jay thought perhaps he was going to use the bathroom, but when he stopped at the back wall with all the potted plants and random bowls of nuts, Robbie turned and subtly gestured for Jay to follow him.

Jay wasn't sure what was happening. He thought back to the other day when he was visiting with Salvador at the blue bistro table just outside and the topic of a bathroom hookup came up. This was the last thing he was expecting to happen, and he wasn't sure how to feel about it. When he started to follow him, Robbie took a sharp turn left through a white door.

Jay looked back to the front counter and caught the mustache man looking at him with his scary green eyes before returning his attention to the customer he was tending to. Jay was confused, but his gut was telling him to follow Robbie, because he trusted him. After a brief pause, Jay pushed open the white door to the left and emerged inside an area the size of a small kitchen. The walls were painted white, and garish lighting blazed down from above, making it feel like a dentist's office. There was a large white storage unit that took up most of the left wall, and it was filled with dozens of cubby holes where employees could place their shoes and bags. It reminded Jay of something you'd see at a bowling alley or a in children's classroom. There were a few uncomfortable plastic chairs up against the wall directly across from the cubby unit, and next to the chairs was another door that led somewhere else inside the building.

"Um, okay," said Jay, baffled. He then stopped where he was, his eyes widening as something suddenly dawned on him. "Did you find me a new job?"

"Isn't manager of a hummus bar below your pay grade?" asked Robbie casually as he turned to the cubbies along the wall and ran his hand along them.

From his left, Jay heard a key enter the lock of the door they had just come through, followed by an ominous *click*. His heart stopped as he stared at the door. When he jiggled the handle, it wouldn't open. He dashed to the other door next to the chairs, but that one was locked as well. Robbie was still at the cubbies, shoving aside random shoes and bags.

"Are you psychotic or something?!" asked Jay.

Robbie bent down and punched his fist through the cubby that was closest to the floor and second from the left, the cheap synthetic wood snapping. He reached into the hole, and seconds later, there was a subtle yet distinct *click*.

Jay raised an eyebrow as Robbie took hold of the side of the unit and delicately pulled it from the wall like he was opening a barn gate. Jay's mouth gaped. He was astonished, nervous and confused all at once. Robbie had opened up a gap between the unit and the wall, with just enough space for a body to squeeze past.

When Robbie stepped into the void, he looked back to see if Jay was following. "This looks weird, but trust me," he said.

"It's not like you've given me much of a choice," said Jay, stepping forward as curiosity got the best of him.

Robbie disappeared behind the unit and Jay cautiously tapped his foot behind it, feeling a stone floor. He pulled out his phone and turned on the flashlight as he slid himself to the other side, where he found a masonry brick stairwell and stone steps curving downward. It was crudely built, and certainly not constructed for lavish habitation. Robbie started down the steps, and Jay followed, making sure to watch every step he took.

"You're not going to tell me what this is?" asked Jay, his flashlight steady on the steps ahead of him.

"We're almost to the bottom," said Robbie.

True to his word, they reached a landing where they came to a wooden door. Robbie placed his hand on the wood and traced his fingers over the door knob and keyhole. He reached into the breast pocket of his jacket and pulled out a gold key that was dull and scratched up. He slipped it into the keyhole, turned the knob, and opened the door.

Instantly, a cold, musty draft washed over them as the door swung away. Jay aimed his phone's flashlight inside, breaking the spell of continuous shadow from within. The light caught something that sparkled just above, a cluster of crystals that revealed itself to be an impressive chandelier, emerging like a ghost ship from the depths of the sea. The crystals were knotted together in a beautiful artistic display, with a bronze frame and wooden light bulb holders around the circumference that resembled melted candles. Below the chandelier, Jay's light revealed a glint of gold. Railings curved along a short set of steps that led down to a lower tier that contained small round tables covered with white tablecloths and maroon leather chairs tucked beneath them. The room appeared to be a quaint, small theatre, and as Jay lifted his phone higher, he could see a modest stage at the far end of the room. There was a red velvet curtain drawn over it, identical to something you'd see in a typical theatre house, but on a much smaller scale. The carpeting was maroon, and in the middle of each table was a vintage glass lantern next to scattered ashtrays and glassware. The main level of the room where Robbie and Jay stood curved along the left to overlook the lower tier, with a gold railing around its perimeter. Set back from the railing was a long cherry wood bar lined with several gilded stools, and there were assorted cocktail shakers, bar spoons and strainers along the cocktail stations. Behind the bar was a beautifully carved wooden display with shelving for liquor bottles that went up to the decorative plaster ceiling. A large rectangular mirror formed the center of the display, reflecting the light from Jay's phone and making him appear like an apparition in the dusty glass.

Jay descended the short flight of steps down to the lower tier.

"This speakeasy was discovered in 1920," said Robbie, his eyes trailing around the room. "It's much older than that, though."

Jay walked between the various tables, running his hand over the maroon leather of the chairs and the fine art deco glassware. There were still cigarettes left in some of the trays with ash scattered around the sides. The beam from his flashlight would glide over a forgotten coin on the floor, or the occasional piece of glassware that still contained dried residue from a cocktail. He stopped and turned to face Robbie. "How do you know about this?"

Robbie's attention was elsewhere when Jay spoke to him. The light from Jay's phone caught the emotion in Robbie's eyes as they looked around, his memory off in a faraway place beyond Jay's limited understanding. Robbie walked towards the bar and took a seat on one of the stools, sweeping his hand along the counter, where a thick layer of dust had formed. There was an art deco drink coaster on the bar top that stubbornly remained where it was when Robbie tried to pick it up by its sides, having been stuck to the spilled alcohol and fruit juices that had long since dried underneath it. Jay returned to the main level and sat down next to Robbie, placing his phone down so its light shone upward, hitting the decorative white plaster ceiling.

"The last time I stepped foot in here was over thirty years ago," said Robbie, looking into the grimy mirror across from him.

"I've never heard of this place before," said Jay.

"It was a closely guarded secret amongst those who came here. The only way you knew about this place was if you were invited."

"Well, why bring me?" asked Jay, feeling honoured.

Robbie got up from the stool and walked behind the bar. "Support, mostly. Coming here alone would have been overwhelming for me. There were signs telling me to come back."

"Why not bring your boyfriend instead?" asked Jay.

Robbie closed his eyes and placed his hands on the bar top, his head bowing down.

Jay twisted his mouth at Robbie's reaction. "Did you... guys break up?"

"Maybe it was a bad idea to bring you here."

"It wasn't," said Jay quickly, getting up and coming around the bar. "I'm sorry. This is all just... very weird." He picked up his phone and shone the flashlight up along the back display to better inspect the shelving unit. Along the very top of the unit, just beneath the ceiling, was a collection of liquor bottles all in a row. They appeared to be full and unopened, with at least thirty bottles spanning the length of the entire unit. The ones closest to the left were the easiest to recognize, but the ones furthest away on the right side were more of a challenge. Jay walked the entire length, eyes and phone aimed upward. The bottle at the end was incredibly old and covered in a thick layer of dust and grime, its label so faded it was illegible.

"It's a wine bottle," said Robbie, standing next to him. "From the early to mid-1800s, approximately."

"You're kidding," said Jay. He looked at Robbie out of the corner of his eye.

Robbie glanced back at him. "No," he said. "You're not going to open it. It seems these bottles span the time period of this bar's existence. The two men who discovered this bar in 1920 concluded that it had been abandoned decades prior. They noticed a sort of pattern happening with the bottles. Each one was labeled with a year, and a new one got added every five to seven years like a tradition. At the time they found this place, the newest bottle up there was dated 1861, which meant this place was most likely abandoned around that time."

"1861," whispered Jay, the gears spinning in his head.

"Do you know your history?" Robbie asked with a smirk.

"1861. Well... That was an interesting time," said Jay, humoring him. It took him a few seconds, but it finally came to him. "The Civil War?"

"Crazy, right?" said Robbie. "This bar was just sitting here, forgotten and abandoned, for almost sixty years until 1920."

"Is there a record book or something?"

Robbie shrugged. "Maybe."

Jay shone his light around the room, into its corners and crevices. "Who else knows about this place?"

"Just the ones who used to come here," he said. "When this place closed for the last time in 1987, Christopher, the owner, wanted one person in possession of the key. It was bestowed upon me, and it was my responsibility to decide when the best time to come back was. During the first few years, people would reach out to me to ask about coming back. But that gradually stopped. They moved on with their lives... or died... or forgot. The last person to contact me did so well over ten years ago... Maybe I'm the only one left alive who still cares. City council doesn't know it's here. There's no record of it. You won't find it on any map or tourist pamphlet."

Jay raised an eyebrow. "How is that even possible?"

"Well, that's why it's a speakeasy," said Robbie.

"Yeah, but *someone* would have talked or said something. You're telling me that everyone who ever stepped foot in here, in, like, a hundred and fifty years, none of them had loose lips?"

Robbie simply smiled.

Jay couldn't help but feel honoured, like he was being initiated into a centuries-old brotherhood of secrecy. "It's a gay bar?" he asked.

Robbie nodded gently. "As to what it was back in the 1800s, some had said it was built specifically for gay men to meet in secret. The building above was a sort of cover-up. Perhaps it was someone's house originally."

"You haven't told me the name of this bar," said Jay.

"Because you didn't ask," replied Robbie, tapping the side of Jay's head with his finger. "It was called Roger's from the 1920s up until 1987." He picked up a martini glass and held the delicate stem between his fingers. "I'm still able to smell the vermouth and olives from the martinis," he recalled. "The smell is so nostalgic to me."

Jay directed his flashlight past the bar top and towards the wall next to it, where several photographs hung in gilded frames. They were organized in a grid of seven rows with ten to a row. The bottom row ended with only seven photographs. As his flashlight scanned them, Jay quickly recognized that they were all taken here in this bar, with each row representing a different decade. The black-and-white photograph at the top left was dated March 1920 on the bottom of the frame. Two smiling men stood behind the bar top in front of the mirror, with a portion of the photographer's reflection in the glass behind them. They wore black suit vests, and their ties were undone and their sleeves rolled up. One had a black mustache with a cigar in his mouth, the other was clean-shaven. They both had perfectly combed hair and held cocktails as though in celebratory toast. The photo next to it, dated June 1920, showed dozens of people gathered around the bar top during what looked like the middle of a celebration, all of them men. Some appeared to be women at first, but when Jay leaned into the photo, he came to see that a few of them were actually female impersonators complete with pearls and rouge. The years went on, picture to picture, down the rows with various depictions of joy and entertainment throughout the '20s but also the '30s,'40s,'50s,'60s,'70s and finally the '80s. Photos went from black and white to color, the guests becoming more diverse as the decades rolled on, and fashion and hairstyles changed with the times.

Jay shone his flashlight to the very bottom, the last photo hung, in August 1987. There was someone playing a grand piano on the speakeasy stage in front of a live audience. The photo had been taken from a distance, so you could only see the performer's silhouette as he sat and played. Groups of people were sitting around the tables and standing along the railings of the main level, looking out at the performer on stage.

Robbie's face dropped. "You know, when I was young," he said, "I didn't care much for the stories that people would share with me about this place. Over time, I'd just tune them out, but the odd exception caught my attention. There was a trashy club in Venus Valley that a lot of gays would frequent back in the early 1900s. It was called Majesty. The building is just a few blocks from here. It's completely different now, of course, and bears no resemblance to what it was a hundred years ago. It's some doctor's office now–something cold and dead, like walking into an empty freezer." Robbie's eyes searched all over the photos, like he was trying to watch dozens of different movies all at once but didn't know which one to focus on. "The club was known for having female impersonators who would put on shows not just for closeted gay men, but straight people as well. There were even back rooms where a man could go and succumb to his lust. It was where men could be with other men, but at a huge risk. One night, law enforcement raided the bar. Some of them were undercover. The entire club was trashed and shut down, with several men arrested for dressing as women, some for selling drugs and others for having sex in the back rooms. If you were a man, and were alone, or found with another man, you were arrested and needlessly beaten during the process. Majesty was shut down that night for 'illegal' and 'perverted' practices. The following day, there was a sign put up saying that homosexuals, or those suspected of homosexuality, weren't permitted to enter or they'd be arrested. So, it became a straight club for white people only."

Jay wasn't able to comprehend how something like that would

have felt. "I've watched documentaries about events similar to that," he said.

"Prohibition started in 1920," continued Robbie. "Most gay men couldn't express or show who they really were in almost any aspect of their lives, to the point where they entered into sham marriages with women, just so they could appear to be living normal lives. Because of Prohibition, the one thing that was helping them cope, alcohol, was also being taken away from them. There was nothing for closeted men to celebrate or be happy about because everything was against them."

"This speakeasy was used to combat all of that," said Jay.

"The building we're standing in was owned by a well-off married man named Dennis," said Robbie. "He had inherited it from his father, who founded a business that made work uniforms for other businesses across the country. Dennis was married, but was also in another relationship with a man named Roger. Dennis loved Roger so much that when he discovered this bar hiding underneath his building, he wanted to name it after the man he loved."

Jay placed his hand on the bar top. "What happened to them?"

"They lived their lives and died," said Robbie, leaning against the wall. "Back then, gay people had to be secretive. Whoever was invited here, they didn't have to be asked to keep it a secret because there was already an unspoken understanding and agreement between all of them that it *had* to remain a secret. This was their real home."

"Was there a code word?" asked Jay.

"Pink Flower," revealed Robbie. "From my understanding, Dennis and Roger discovered that Pink Flower was the original name of the club back in the 1800s, which meant it could have also been the code word people would have used to get in."

"So, a whole bunch of dudes just walked in and out of this building at night, and people on the street thought nothing of it?"

"Dennis continued to run his father's business after inheriting the building," said Robbie. "Everyone who was employed in this building to make the work uniforms were all men. Some worked during the day, some at night, and others came into the building pretending to be employees, but were actually using the club instead. There was also some sort of sex room set up on the second floor."

Jay was impressed. "It seems like a really thought-out system," he said.

"There was another door to get into the building," said Robbie.

"Where?" asked Jay, leaning forward. "This place has more secrets than a castle."

"It's covered up behind a wall now; that's why you didn't see it. Just outside, where you see TRISTAN painted on the side of the building. The original wall is underneath it, with the door. When the building was constructed, a side door was put in, which faced Goldenrod Boulevard. Some say this building was originally someone's house, and that side door led into a dining room or study, which is now the employee lounge that we just stood in earlier. It was a less devious way to enter the building than walking up the front steps and using the front door. You could just slide in and out at night, like a phantom. Most people assumed it was an employee entrance, and thought nothing of it. The door was still there until 1991, then Christopher decided to block it up because it was constantly being broken into by squatters trying to inhabit the upper floors."

Jay sighed and looked around the room. "It feels like a crypt..." he said, feeling the chilled silence within the darkness. "Why did it close?"

Robbie looked at Jay in a way that he found off-putting. "It wasn't a great time… near the end," he confessed. "When it closed in 1987, the name was changed."

"To what?"

Robbie was staring in Jay's direction, but he wasn't looking at him. He was instead looking through him, to a memory long ago. "Tristan," he said.

"Was Tristan an actual person?" asked Jay. "Like Roger?"

Robbie smiled faintly, his gaze sinking into the past. "He was… very special."

33

October 1919

Roger's fingers wrapped around the chilled tumbler that the bartender had slid to him across the bar top. The ice cubes were slowly diluting the drink, mixing with the delicate bitters and orange peel in the amber bourbon. He wore a tuxedo jacket, white shirt, vest and bow tie, and his brown hair was combed and styled with pomade underneath his black top hat.

He took a seat at one of the wooden tables in front of the small stage then pulled out his pack of Lucky Strike cigarettes, lighting one up and pulling the ashtray close to his elbow. Majesty was downtrodden, a dingy hole in the wall in downtown Venus Valley. The tables were sticky from the countless spilled drinks, and the floor planks were almost entirely faded from several decades' worth of drunken foot traffic. The drinks were cheap, and the entertainment and gorgeous boys made up for the otherwise unremarkable interior. The club's stage was smaller than it should have been, and shabby, having lost the luster from its glory years–tight quarters for a trombone, clarinet, banjo and piano where the band was crammed together. The musicians made do, though, and came together in unison to serenade the audience with youthful jazz and warm melodies that evoked lush daydreams and romance. The colored musicians were dressed in black suits and bowler hats, their attention locked into the expression of their talent as they performed for a crowd that was eager for a new decade to begin, and to bid farewell to the 1910s. Majesty was a club that attracted the curious. Girls of nineteen, all dolled up in their best finery, revelled in the male gaze and would float around and interact with the fairies of the bar–the men who liked to dress themselves to match the female form. It wasn't easy to differentiate the real girls from the boys in dresses and pearls, especially the young lads with their feminine features that took easily to their makeup and female mannerisms, easily confusing the soberest of men.

The handsome nineteen-year-old boys with their toned bodies were the main attractions that drove closeted male attendance at Majesty. If it wasn't the live music and drag comedy skits that drew guests in, it was for the beautiful boys after whom some men often queried. It took only brief eye contact between a boy and his potential client, or a solicitation such as the rubbing of a shoulder, for a transaction to kick into motion. For seven dollars, the handsome peddler boy would welcome a man into one of the back rooms and provide him with twenty minutes of pleasure. Sometimes, a man's only desire was to touch another male's body, to caress him, and nothing more. Starting at ten dollars, a wolf could take one of the boys home with him for the night, sometimes becoming the boy's ongoing daddy.

Roger's eyes wandered to a leather booth beside the entrance, where a black-haired man with a mustache was looking at him on and off, his mouth curling into a grin when their eyes locked. The smoke from his cigar would puff out of his mouth and create a perfect hazy halo around his head, evoking a type of handsome masculinity that Roger couldn't keep his eyes off, making him wild with lust. Roger grinned back at the man and blew a puff of smoke out, tapping the ash from his cigarette into the tray.

There was a whiff of sweet gourmand perfume behind Roger, signalling the arrival of a young dame who wore a headband and decorative feathers in her black hair. He'd been aware of her for the last few weeks only because she fancied him and wouldn't leave him alone–more so for his apparent wealth which he did not possess. The gold diggers were plentiful at Majesty.

"I've figured out why you don't look at me," she said when she sat next to him, her porcelain face flaunting a secret. She wore full-length white gloves and an elaborately draped and fanciful black silk gown that hugged her slim silhouette.

"We always seem to be here at the same exact time," said Roger, taking a good look at her. "It's either coincidence, or you're stalking me."

Vera's red baby doll lips pouted as though he had no right to speak to a fine treasure such as herself in such an ungentlemanly way. "Nancy says you're queer, and I'm starting to believe her," she said, placing her fingers on his left hand that was resting on the table. "She says you're a fairy-nice boy."

Roger turned his head towards the bar and saw one of the female impersonators, Nancy, looking back at him as she plucked one of the olives from her martini and put it between her red lips, her long eyelashes fluttering. Roger turned his attention back to Vera. "Is that what you accuse all men of if they don't take you out to dinner," he asked, gloating, "where you hope they marvel at your prettiness throughout the night?"

Vera intertwined the fingers of both her hands and placed them under her sharp chin, her elbows leaning on the table close to him. "Tell me again how pretty you find me," she said sweetly. "Take me to dinner this Friday, and the men at your office won't hear about you coming to this dirty little shack to throw money at the local boy whores."

"Ah... So that's your angle," he said with a smirk, pretending to sound surprised as he took another drag from his cigarette. He blew smoke in her immaculate face. "Entrapment. Blackmail. Don't you have anything better to do with your precious youth than incriminate men for enjoying a nice evening of good drink, swell jazz and comedy?"

"And a boy's lips wrapped around you," she added, her green eyes widening as a glint of madness sparked within.

"You can do what you like, miss. But I'll be sure to clarify to the men at my office that these accusations are from a dumb Dora who calls a man queer simply because he rejected her advances. She doesn't quite yet understand that the reason these men reject her is because, for being as young and beautiful as she is, she's looser than an old coin purse, and carries with her a stench that is beyond rancid. I'm not sure how that sort of gossip would fare for you, especially with all the eligible young men at my office. No man wants that sort of image in his head, especially in relation to a young beauty such as yourself. They'd be better off finding a whore, since she would most certainly be less trouble than what you would have to offer."

Beneath her makeup, Vera's face burned bright red as climatic frustration settled in. She pushed her chair back and fled the table, the smell of nervous perspiration trailing behind her. Roger downed the rest of his bourbon and glanced at the girl as she threw open the front door and left the club, her head held pompously like a tyrant queen.

"You've been making the babes cry since you were fourteen, I'd bet."

Roger put his empty glass down as Nancy sat down next to him, sitting herself on the very edge of the seat like she didn't intend to stay long. "Please forgive my rude accusations. Gossip travels fast when it comes to the handsome ones, unfortunately." She was using her falsetto quite distinctly, and her mannerisms were delicate and precise when it came to portraying a female presence. Nancy wore a small peacock headdress upon her brown wig and a white silk evening gown similar to what Vera had worn. Around her pale neck was a long pearl necklace that dangled down her chest, and her makeup was more dolled up than Vera's was, with the same red lipstick, white face powder and radiance of rouge. Under the dim lighting, Nancy would most certainly come across as all female.

"What made you think of me as queer?" Roger whispered. "Plenty of men come to see these shows."

"Plenty of *normal* men come to these shows with their wives," clarified Nancy. "They'd never be caught dead here by themselves. I've always been able to spot a man like you from a mile away." She leaned over, the smell of olive brine and gin still on her breath. "It's the way you pick up your drink, lovely."

Roger looked down and picked his glass up like he normally would–or so he thought.

Nancy shook her head and lowered his glass back down. "Not like that. You're being self-conscious now and aren't doing it normally." Nancy demonstrated for him with her own glass. "It's a sort of dainty gesture you do with your hand."

Roger wasn't liking this new observation of him, and it was plain on his face. "I'll continue to be self-conscious about that," he said, annoyed, "so adjustments can be made."

The immersive jazz instrumental from the band ended, and the instruments on the cramped stage were now being rearranged to open a space for the two female impersonators preparing to start their comedy routine. These skits were considered the highlights of the evening, and many people, straight and closeted, would come specifically to be entertained by the camp performances. The men in these shows had perfectly adopted the female bodily movements and feminine walks of their characters, often including lewd and hysterical comedy. Their falsetto voices and limp wrists poked fun at how straight people stereotyped their idea of what a homosexual was. The band often included their own bits of comedic timing with a blow of a horn at the right moment during a joke.

Roger's eyes turned again to the black-haired man with the cigar and mustache. He was still sitting at the booth, where a few more people had now joined him due to the club getting more crowded now that the show was starting.

Nancy looked at Roger, then followed his gaze towards the perfect man sitting like a statue in the booth. He wore a tuxedo and top hat, and his mustache added to his overall intrigue.

"Now *that's* a man," said Nancy, looking back at Roger out of the corner of her eye. Roger's expression started to droop the longer he stared at him, as though in a trance, both of them smiling subtly at one another. He was falling under this man's spell, and everything else around him faded away for just a few seconds.

"The rich men came out to play," whispered Nancy. "He's married."

"Most of them are," stated Roger.

"You're not," she said, glancing down at his left hand. "Forget about people finding out you're queer. At your age, if you're not already married and having babies, then it's as obvious as the rouge on my face."

"You don't need to be married to be in love," said Roger simply, his voice distant and undeniably happy.

Nancy noticed that the man would sometimes break eye

contact with Roger, but seconds later his stare would always return to him, his resistance failing each and every time. It was the same kind of longing that made the eyelids heavy, like seeing something so wonderful and beautiful that you succumb to its enchantment.

Nancy lifted her chin due to a sudden realization. “The real lovers,” she whispered, observing the two of them. She squinted across the room at the man’s hand that sat firmly on the table in front of him, a gold wedding band around his finger. “...and the sham,” she finished.

Roger leaned forward to light another cigarette. “Got any new boys?”

“You mean that fine specimen over there isn’t enough?” asked Nancy, flinging her body backwards against the chair like she couldn’t believe such a notion. “He’s the cat’s meow! How long have you known him?”

“Long enough,” replied Roger.

There was a roar of laughter from the audience, and Roger turned his attention to the comedy skit, seemingly having missed a comedic slap by only a few seconds. One of the impersonators was holding her cheek dramatically, gawking at the audience.

“We like to indulge in something new every little while, me and him,” said Roger. “As a sort of treat, if you must know.”

Nancy stood up and leaned over to Roger. “We have a new indulgence that started last week,” she whispered into his ear. “The cream inside will not disappoint.”

Roger was left alone once again, his eyes transfixed on the skit. He placed his hand on his upper thigh underneath the table and subtly ran his thumb over his trousers.

Minutes later, he heard the legs of the chair next to him scrape across the floor as someone joined him. Roger turned and saw the angelic face of a nineteen-year-old. He wore a black vest over a tieless white shirt with rolled-up sleeves, his muscles prominent, obvious and hard to look away from. His brown hair was tidy and his face clean-shaven, like Roger's, but much more youthful. The lines on his forehead hadn't come yet, and years of stress and vices hadn't yet taken away suppleness from his skin. The boy was clean and well looked after, not like some of the boys you'd find in the parks who were often desperate and didn't maintain their hygiene. The boy was watching the skit and laughed along with the rest of the audience, glancing over at Roger every few seconds. "You're a wolf, no doubt."

Roger's eyes darted back to the show, making sure their eye contact didn't last longer than it needed to. "Is that what Nancy is calling me now?"

The boy pushed his left loafer closer to Roger's foot. "It's what all the boys call the older men. You're very spiffy and handsome."

Roger adjusted his chair and casually turned his head to look at the boy, then to the man with the mustache and cigar sitting at the booth. The man smiled and gave Roger a small nod, as though he approved of the match, and returned his attention back to the show.

Roger glanced back at the boy, assessing him up and down. "Now," he demanded. The flames of lust burned in Roger's eyes. He couldn't help himself.

"Meet me at the back door in five minutes," said the boy, sliding a drink towards him. "I'm Timothy, by the way." He got up and drifted away.

The smoky haze in the club was becoming its most dense as the crowd lit up their cigarettes and revelled in the comedy before them. The first act had just ended, and the second was now beginning. It was finally Nancy's turn on stage, playing the role of Sir Harrigan's mistress, who was caught by Harrigan's wife in the act of fornication with her husband. The crowd laughed erratically, whether at the actual comedy itself or at the men in their dresses and makeup, like onlookers at a zoo watching monkeys. The straight men had come with their girlfriends and wives like this was all a freak show at the carnival–something absurd, abnormal and immoral that you pay to witness and get a good laugh out of. Hecklers would sometimes shout *fairy* and *pansy*, which the witty female impersonators would use to their advantage by incorporating improv jokes into their skits.

Roger took advantage of the loud engagement of the audience and slipped away from his table, heading to the back where the lavatories were. Sexual interactions were frowned upon inside the johns, as it took business away from the peddler boys, but promiscuity still happened almost nightly. Majesty had been around since 1899, having once been a gentlemen's club and brothel when it opened. Roger enjoyed the club in its current state, regardless of its reputation, since it was one of the few places where he could talk casually with other gay men, listen to some good jazz and have a decent drink. He looked forward to coming here every few weeks, but his reason for coming tonight was purely sex-related, and his object of desire was through the back door beside the bar.

When he knocked, the door opened and Timothy greeted him as promised. He led Roger down a hall that was covered in baroque wallpaper. The hardwood flooring was faded and unsightly, the floorboards creaking with each step they took. There were four doorways down each side of the hall, and one more at the very end. Timothy led Roger into the first room on the left and shut the door behind them. Roger took a seat on a wide cushioned bench against the wall that was fashioned with a headboard that had weaving around its edges. The headboard was divided evenly into three large squares where regal cushioning had been built in for extra comfort. The walls were painted a deep red, like Nancy's lipstick, with oil lamps flickering on Chinese lacquered tables in the corners, casting devilish, erotic shadows upon the walls.

Roger looked up at Timothy as he stood before him. Timothy straddled Roger's legs as he sat on the bench, his crotch rubbing up against his knees. Roger took out the money and held it out to Timothy, which he gently took and slid inside his trouser pocket.

"Do you have a squeeze, Mister?" asked Timothy, placing his arms around Roger's neck and settling himself down on Roger's lap, his legs wrapped around him like a tire swing.

"No..." Roger answered, looking into Timothy's chocolate-brown eyes. His eyelashes fluttered at him, and Roger felt a surge of heat. He touched Timothy's soft cheek and then slid his hand down his white shirt, where he started undoing the gold buttons, one by one, feeling the warmth of his skin through the fabric. Undoing the top button was like unleashing warmth from an oven that had been building up within, ready for something delicious to be slid deep inside of it.

"Sometimes, men just want to caress and hold me in their arms," said Timothy in a soft voice. "They're lonely. Sometimes they cry." He placed his lips on Roger's neck and started kissing his skin gently all around. "They just want to feel my body, nothing more than that."

"Do they kiss you?" asked Roger. "They have to kiss you. It's impossible not to."

Timothy undid the rest of his buttons and slid the shirt off, his pectorals quite defined for someone his age, his nipples hard to the touch. He leaned in, traced his nose over Roger's face and placed his lips near his, their warm breath mixing together. Roger took hold of Timothy and flipped him over onto the bench cushions so that they were lying side by side.

"You can do anything you want to me, Mister," said Timothy, his legs entwined with Roger's as he quickly undid his belt buckle. "Fuck me as hard as you want, or let me fuck you. I'll feel better than any woman."

Timothy already had Roger's pants down and was giving him head, his other hand climbing up Roger's chest and grabbing the lean muscle of one of his pectorals. Roger's eyes rolled back into his head as he thrust his pelvis into Timothy's mouth and grabbed his hair, his cock throbbing, warm pre-cum sliding down his head.

There was a sudden *thump* on the door as someone from inside the hall kicked and slammed themselves against it, making Timothy look up abruptly.

"Hey," said the demanding voice on the other side of the door. "Open up."

Timothy quickly pulled his shirt back on and did up Roger's pants in haste, all while signalling him to be quiet. Roger bolted up and off the bench, eyes focused on the door. "Don't say anything," mouthed Timothy as the impatient knocking persisted, the officer on the other side slamming their full weight at the door.

Roger's heart rate accelerated quicker and quicker, fear settling into his face. "Fuck," he said, panic in his voice, knowing what would happen once the bulls on the other side of that door got inside. It was his worst nightmare come to life.

Timothy crawled across the bench, hastily pried away one of the large cushioned squares of the headboard, and revealed a crude hole in the wall just big enough for someone to squeeze through. Roger didn't need to be told twice as he followed Timothy through the hole and into a tight crawlspace. Timothy grabbed the wicking of the piece he had removed and fit it perfectly back into place. Timothy led Roger a short distance to the end of the crawlspace, where he opened a makeshift sliding window. There was furious pounding from the room they had just left as the men, who had now forced their way into the room, banged at the walls and tossed furniture around. Timothy crawled out through the hole and out of the crawlspace, taking Roger's hand and pulling him out next. They were standing in a stale, dark pantry. Timothy pushed the door open and they stepped into Majesty's small kitchen that was all rusted and unusable, having sat idle for what seemed like many years. Roger quietly slid towards the kitchen entrance and peered through the small square window in the center of the door. There were policemen circling the club, kicking aside empty chairs and trashing the place, an act that appeared to bring them much joy from the sneers on their faces. Most of the crowd had left by now, but three of the female impersonators had been pinched, including Nancy, whose face was bloody from having suffered a broken nose. Roger's eyes shot to the booth where the man from earlier had been sitting, but it was empty.

Roger looked at Timothy. "Were there more boys in the other rooms?"

"There were three others," he replied nervously, heading for the back door at the other end of the kitchen. The sound of scurrying came from inside the crawlspace, and whoever was inside, they were nearing the pantry.

"Fucking degenerates," said one of the officers from inside the club, disgust in his voice after having explored the pleasure rooms. "There were some queers in the back, and in the johns," he said to the other bulls.

From out of the crawlspace, one other boy emerged with a man bringing up the rear. They made silent eye contact with Roger and Timothy as they passed and headed for the kitchen's side door that led into the alleyway. Timothy grabbed Roger's hand and followed the others out, poking his head into the alleyway first. Most of the action was occurring outside at the front of the club where police vehicles were lined up. Guests from the club were either walking home or getting into their vehicles, but the unlucky men who were deemed unlawful, whether because of female impersonation or lewd public homosexuality and perverted sexual activity, were pinched and thrown into police vehicles. Nancy had a smile on her face as she was tossed into one of the vehicles, as if to say that regardless of what was happening to her, she was still proud and held her dignity intact. The other boy who had come through the crawlspace ran down the alley and out of sight.

"It was nice meeting you," said Timothy, handing Roger back his money.

Roger pushed the money back to him. "Keep it," he said. "Your time was still worth more."

From inside the kitchen, a bull pushed the side door open and poked his head out, pointing his gloved hand at them. "Stay there!" he shouted urgently, reaching for his gun.

Timothy yanked the man forward and dragged him down the flight of steps. Being heavier than the scrawny officer, Timothy punched the officer to the ground, then planted his shoe into the man's face, blood splattering from his nose. Using his other foot, he slammed a swift kick into the officer's crotch. Timothy leaned into Roger quickly and planted a kiss on his cheek, then ran down the alleyway with the stamina of an athlete. Roger followed him.

Gunshots were fired in their direction, and by the time Roger made it to the end of the alleyway, Timothy had already vanished. Roger took his own route down the various side streets, walking as casually as possible. He stuck to the shadows that the buildings provided. It was a chilly October evening, and his jacket was still in his vehicle that was parked outside the club. He had no intention of going back to get it at this moment.

Twenty minutes later, he came to Venus Valley Uniforms right at the corner of Goldenrod Boulevard and Langley Street. It was a modest three-story office building that was once residential, but had since become a business space for the manufacture of work uniforms.

Roger paced back and forth, looking up at the windows, where he could see the occasional light aglow from within. As he took the first couple steps up towards the front door, he felt a hand touch his shoulder from behind. He spun around to grab the person who had laid their hand on him. The twinkling eyes Roger met were not those of an officer, as he had feared, but a familiar face, one that made him sigh in relief. The man with the black mustache that Roger was infatuated with at Majesty smiled at him, a warm comfort filling them both.

Dennis led Roger around to the side of the building and stood with him on the sidewalk next to the copper side door. Before anything else was said, and after looking nervously down both ways of the street, Dennis leaned in and pressed his lips onto Roger's mouth.

Roger placed his hands upon Dennis' arms, his heart beating wildly again, but this time for all the right reasons. "Of all nights, it had to be this one," he whispered.

Dennis pulled Roger towards the wall of the building, right next to the side door, so they were more concealed from the glow of the street lamps.

"That was some boy you went off with," he said, smiling at Roger, but with an obvious tinge of anxiety in his voice. "Please tell me the lad had you in his mouth at least, before the bulls arrived?"

Roger placed his hands on Dennis' shoulders and laughed softly. "If it wasn't for him, I'd most likely be in handcuffs with the lot of them."

"After you left your table," said Dennis, "a man came and sat next to me precisely five minutes later. He was too old to be one of the peddler boys, and wasn't charming in the least. It dawned on me right away that he was a bull, trying to entrap me. They aren't good at it in the slightest, and can't fake themselves into being attracted to a man. He wasn't queer, as hard as he tried to convince me otherwise. He looked at my ring and asked where my squeeze was. Then, almost on cue, having overheard the conversation, the dame seated next to me confirmed herself to be my wife. She pecked me on the lips, and that sent him off. Afterward, the girl didn't even acknowledge to me what she had done, but she most certainly was my saviour. It seemed to have angered the bull, though, because when he left my table, that's when the announcement was made that the club was being shut down. Many of the patrons were so horrified at the mere mention of queer fornication that they left without a fuss." He looked into Roger's eyes and stepped towards him. "I was most nervous for you. If I hadn't found you tonight, it would have been a sleepless night for me. The thought of you with blood on your face, in that cold prison, your hands in cuffs..."

"You could always play a better straight man than me," replied Roger, laughing. He leaned his shoulder against the wall and ran his hand down Dennis' side. They grabbed hold of each other, wanting to kiss passionately, but the occasional passing vehicle and glaring headlights prevented any such embrace.

"Ellie is expecting me soon," said Dennis. "I'm also expected to be incredibly drunk and quite merry. As I've told you before, she holds all the cards. If I don't play house with her, she has every intention of ruining me. My children will never speak to me, she said. Not to mention the shame and disgust that will follow me when people know the truth."

Roger looked into his eyes, heartbroken.

"It's a horrible life, I know," finished Dennis. "Whether I'm arrested or not, my life is a prison either way." He reached into his trouser pocket and handed Roger his car keys, fitting them snugly into his hand. "Take my vehicle to your place and wait there. Give me your keys, and I'll walk back to Majesty for your vehicle right now and we can swap them when I return to your place within the hour."

As he turned to walk away, Roger grabbed his arm and pulled

him back. "I'll get my vehicle tomorrow. You're not walking back there tonight. It's absurd."

Dennis smiled, pulling Roger towards his Chevrolet. Once they were inside, Dennis started the engine and pulled out onto the boulevard. Roger reached over and placed his hand on Dennis' knee as he drove.

34

January 1920

Dennis eagerly waited for ten o'clock to arrive. He shifted his paperwork around his desk, glancing up at the clock every few minutes. His office was small, cramped and provided little breathing room for tense moments such as these. Oftentimes, he'd have to step out into the reception area, or would leave the building through the side door in his office to take the air. The constant humming from the sewing machines and machinery in the other rooms was a welcome comfort, but being as late as it was, nearly all the staff had gone home. He was left with his own thoughts, the ticking on the clock the last frontier before complete maddening silence. Dennis arose from his desk chair and paced the tight quarters, the floorboards beneath the Afghan rug creaking under his loafers. He removed his tie and poured himself another glass of bourbon, having earned the right to be moderately drunk this Friday evening.

The door to the work room next to his office opened, and John, the last cloth butcher to leave, walked out wearing his winter coat.

"It feels like the coldest January we've had in twenty years," said John, walking past Dennis and towards the office exit. When he opened the door, he stood and looked back curiously at Dennis as cold air rushed into the office through the alcove. "Are you alright, Dennis? You appear worried. Would you like some company?"

Dennis reached for a new cigarette on his desk. "There's always something to worry about when you're the boss," he said, lighting up. "If there isn't, you don't have a business. Goodnight, John. I'll see you on Monday. Say hello to Katherine for me, will you?" He picked up the bottle of bourbon he had been pouring for himself and handed it to him. "It's better if you have it."

John took the bottle and slid it underneath his coat. "Have a good rest of your night," he said. When the door shut upon his exit, Dennis drummed his fingertips on the seams of his trousers, placing his cigarette on the edge of the ashtray. He stood in front of the large oak shelving unit next to the side entrance. Business strategies and fashion were the most common subjects found in the books on the shelves, in and around stacks of folders, empty tobacco tins and souvenirs that he had received from business associates, his wife and their two children, Lucy and Darla. The long middle shelf was reserved exclusively for bottles of bourbon and crystal glassware. He removed one of the unopened bottles and pulled the cork, refilling his glass halfway. This was the last of his own personal stock, and given the law that had passed last week prohibiting the sale of all alcohol, Dennis would have to start getting creative as to how to attain more of it. He refused to remain sober for the rest of his life. But his recent discovery earlier in the week, in this very room, had Dennis bouncing around with excitement. He couldn't wait to share the news with Roger.

Dennis positioned himself in front of the small square mirror hanging next to a cabinet and pulled a comb out from the top drawer. He dragged the teeth through his black hair, the pomade having not yet lost its lustrous shine.

The side door opened, and Roger came gliding in, his body shivering as he rubbed his hands together. The sudden jerk of the door opening made Dennis jump, but the mere sight of Roger cranked up his elation. He grabbed hold of his shoulders and kissed him, his mustache rubbing up against Roger's upper lip. Roger put his cold hands on Dennis' cheeks as he melted into his embrace.

"What happened to your leather gloves?" asked Dennis, feeling Roger's icy hands.

"My belief is that someone stole them from the office earlier today," said Roger in a sassy drawl. "If I hadn't been wearing my jacket all day, that too would have gone missing and you'd be left hugging a frozen ice cream man."

Dennis pushed his body closer into Roger. "Bourbon and a strong body provide the best warmth on a night like this," he said. He reached for another glass and poured Roger a drink. After retrieving the cigarette he had left cooling in the ashtray, he went to each of the three doors around the office and locked them. "There's something you need to see," he said, handing Roger his glass of bourbon.

Roger went and sat down at his desk.

"Don't sit down," said Dennis, moving frantically around the room. "You'll be going down soon."

Roger raised an eyebrow. He smirked and slid off the chair and onto his knees instead.

Dennis looked at him, tempted. "Tonight is for a different kind of going down... To start anyway." He rolled up his sleeves and crouched down at the left side of the oak shelving unit. Near the bottom was a square shelving space, and it was there that Dennis slid his hand inside. Roger watched closely, like he was waiting for a magician to pull a rabbit out of a hat. He soon realized that Dennis' arm had not stopped at the back wall but kept disappearing into the square, like it truly was a magic trick. Dennis' other hand was on his left knee with the cigarette between his fingers. His eyes snapped open at the sound of a subtle *click*.

Roger crouched down with him, trying to see what was going on. "You punched a hole through your furniture?"

"Kicked it in, actually," clarified Dennis, "pretending it was someone's face during a brief moment of hostility. Here, get onto my left side."

Roger did as he was told, and to his surprise, the entire oak shelving unit swung open effortlessly, making Dennis look as though he possessed the strength of Hercules. Everything on the shelves remained in place without any disruption except for a subtle vibration. He poked his head through to the other side and saw an old, stone staircase curving downward like a turret of a castle. Without a word exchanged, he took the cigarette from Dennis' fingers, inhaled a deep drag, then snuffed it out in the ashtray. He furrowed his brow. "Flashlight?"

Dennis got up, pulled two flashlights out of the desk drawer and handed one to him.

"Have you been down there yet?" asked Roger.

"Yes," he said, squeezing past Roger and taking the lead down the stone steps. He stopped and turned to face Roger. "There wasn't a question in my mind as to who I'd share this with."

Roger leaned forward and rubbed his arm. "Let's see it then."

When they reached the bottom landing, Roger placed his hand on the wooden door.

"It isn't locked," said Dennis. He twisted the knob gently and pushed the door open, their two flashlights aimed inward, straight into the depths of the solemn darkness. The cold draft was like a crypt, and the silence deafening. Roger was erratic in his flashlight maneuvers. He shone his beam up towards a crystal chandelier with a bronze frame and candle holders around its outer rim. Inside the holders, candles were melted down almost completely with solidified wax spilling over the sides.

"Have you tried turning on the electricity?" asked Roger, shining his flashlight every which way along the walls in hopes of finding light switches or a fuse box.

"Haven't looked that far yet," admitted Dennis, his attention monopolized by what he could see right in front of him instead. He walked down a short flight of steps, where small wooden tables and chairs were scattered unremarkably about a wide, open dance floor. In the middle of each table was a kerosene chamber lamp. To make do with what they had, Dennis pulled a matchbox from his pocket and lit the wicks of the lamps, one by one, lifting the chimney glass from each as he went along.

Roger's face was inscrutable as the lamplight filled the room with a lovely, haunting glow. From out of the shadows, a small stage appeared in front of them. The tattered maroon curtains had been left open, and sitting in the very center of the stage was a timeless treasure, a sparkle in the night. It was a gilded grand piano covered in layers of dust. But, if one was to shine a light directly on it, glints of gold would pop out from beneath the filth like the sun breaking out from the clouds after a long storm.

Roger joined Dennis on the lower level of the room and jumped up onto the stage. He ran his hand over the piano's elegant craftsmanship and its ivory keys, removing the dust in swipes with his palm. "It's gorgeous–a piece of heavenly art," he said, peering curiously at the mythological characters among flowers, vines, scrolls and instruments carved along the shell and lid. Prying his eyes away, he got down on the floor and slid underneath it.

"You're not repairing your vehicle, lovely," said Dennis as he pulled himself up onto the stage. "It's a theatre room... right underneath my building."

"Your father never told you about this room?" asked Roger as he slid out from beneath the piano and stood up, dirt covering his backside.

Dennis ran a finger over his mustache. "He mustn't have known about it."

Roger pointed his flashlight all over the room, up the walls and across the beautifully plastered ceiling. The light caught a glint from the gold railing that bordered the level just above them. "It's old..." he said. "When do you reckon the last people were down here?"

"Perhaps there's a record book that will tell us," said Dennis, jumping down from the stage. "We'll know more once we get more light in here."

Roger jumped down from the stage after Dennis and followed him up the steps to the main tier and towards the bar. The grimy rectangular mirror in the middle of the back shelving behind the bar caught the beams from their flashlights. Nothing sparkled on the rustic bar top; it was well worn from decades of use. The bar was exceptionally long, with many wooden stools tucked underneath. The shelves were mostly empty except for a few rows of glassware and random odds and ends. There was no alcohol to speak of, with the exception of the bottles sitting high up top, far out of reach without a ladder. Some rusted cocktail shakers, spoons and bowls were scattered around with little care, almost like everything had been dumped out and abandoned at the last minute. Dennis looked at Roger, a revelation coming to him.

Roger leaned over and grabbed Dennis' arm excitedly as though reading his mind. "This could be another Majesty, Dennis!"

Dennis was just about to reply when he noticed something folded at the far end of the bar top, his flashlight's beam on it like a spotlight. He went to pick it up, and when he did so, it unfurled down to his ankles as he held it up to his chest like a dress. It was a large flag with three bars across its length, the top and bottom bars red and the middle white. There was Bonnie Blue square in the upper left corner with thirteen white stars forming a perfect circle in its center.

Dennis looked at Roger, his reaction incredulous.

When Roger looked down the length of the flag, he noticed a yellowed piece of paper at Dennis' feet that must have fallen out when he unfurled the Stars and Bars flag. Dennis followed his gaze downward and saw the note at his feet. He picked it up. Careful not to rip the fragile paper, he unfolded it and started reading.

April 12, 1861

We leave the Pink Flower and head forth to war! Those who have shared their time in this bar have all agreed unanimously to enlist. Once this war has been won, our return will be triumphant and this letter will cease to exist. Should this letter remain, then misfortune has befallen me and my brethren. Death will have come for us at the hands of the Confederates! Let it be known that we died for a cause that was paramount to us. Please have many drinks in our honor! As you toast, the men who made this bar their personal sanctuary from the judgements of the world will be there with you in spirit. The notion that a pretty palace such as this should go uncelebrated and unfrequented is horrible indeed. My dear cousin Clarence, if it is indeed you who reads this letter, please tell no other persons about this place other than the men who exclusively enjoy the company of other men. This is a haven to us, and must continue to be honored as such. When the Union Army wins this war, please have it be known that all homosexual men, regardless of their color, will be welcome here. My hope is when you read this the war will have passed, and to that we say, drink, sing and love!

Lewis

Dennis looked over the letter again after he finished reading it out to Roger. After digesting the message, he handed it to Roger so he could look it over. "Clarence was my grandfather," he said, folding up the flag and placing it on the bar top. "This building has been handed down within my family. My father would regale me with stories about Clarence, who was once a boat captain who weathered treacherous storms, sought out hidden treasure and went on worldly adventures with his siblings. Such childish fantasies, of course. My father should have been a writer. This Lewis, though..."

Roger placed the letter on top of the flag as though it was a piece of delicate china. "Maybe Clarence was never made aware of this bar," he said.

"Then why did Lewis make it clear that my grandfather would have been the one to find his letter?" Dennis sat down on one of the stools, frustrated. "The most logical reasoning to me is that Lewis knew about Clarence's queerness, and confided in him about this bar." Dennis placed his hands on his knees, realization overtaking him. "My grandfather chose to deny himself, and married my grandmother instead. He never mentioned this place to anyone. Not to my dad… Not to anyone. My grandfather was gifted this building by his cousin Lewis, but Clarence chose to deny this bar, and himself. My grandfather was a homosexual, just like me."

Roger reached forward and put his hands on Dennis' shoulders. "You were meant to find this place, Dennis." Roger reached into his pocket and handed him a gold key. "This was underneath the piano. It's yours now."

"But I've done exactly what my grandfather did," said Dennis, feeling like he was about to choke as he looked down at his wedding band.

Roger shook his head at him. "Now it's up to you to do what he wouldn't," he said, placing his hand on the letter. "To do what Lewis and the others wanted."

Dennis took the key from Roger and rubbed his fingertips along it. "The bulls will never find this place. Majesty is over for us, so let's start something that is out of their reach." He picked up the letter and put it inside his pocket. "We'll continue what Lewis and the others started, before the war took them away."

"Maybe they didn't start it," said Roger. "Maybe they also were continuing it."

There was a sudden smash behind the bar top. One of the martini glasses had fallen from a shelf and shattered on the ground.

Dennis smiled. "They're here with us," he whispered, leaning into Roger. "I'll be right back." He left Roger at the bar and ran back up the stone steps to his office above. When he returned, he brought with him a bottle of bourbon. He went behind the bar, grabbed two glasses, and wiped the dust off before pouring them both a drink.

"But how do we keep it a secret?" asked Roger. "If we plan on letting others know, what will stop the entire city from finding this place eventually?"

Dennis handed him his drink. "Trust," he said simply. "It worked then, and it will again." He stepped out from behind the bar and walked over to the gold railing so he could look down at the lower level. "We will succeed Majesty and make this bar glorious. We will replace all the seating and décor. We'll replace the flooring with new soft carpeting and wood... Refurbish the bar, put in nice stools, new paint and wallpaper. This won't be a trash pit like Majesty. High class, better than world class. Queers only, of course. Degenerates only. Fairies only."

Roger went and stood beside Dennis. "The second floor can be used for special encounters," he said. "Strictly at night, though, and after business hours."

"Agreed," said Dennis without hesitation. "Nothing like that in here, though. This room will be for celebration, dance and music."

Roger nudged him with his arm, the glow from the lamps below dancing across their faces. "I'm very much happy right now," he said.

With his drink in hand, and overcome with joy, Dennis pushed Roger towards the bar top and pinned him against it. He put his drink down and started tearing off Roger's clothes, running his lips up and down his body. Dennis picked up his glass again and poured the bourbon down Roger's chest, making his smooth skin glisten as heat erupted around them. Dennis leaned down and ran his tongue over Roger's wet skin to lap up the liquid as it drizzled down onto Roger's pelvis, then undid his belt buckle and pulled his trousers down. After tasting him, he flipped Roger around and penetrated him, his face pressed into Roger's neck, his hand around his chin, and thrusting, hard. Two of his fingers went across Roger's mouth and inserted themselves between his lips, then he pulled Roger's head around so they could lock lips, their warm breath blowing into each other's mouths. Roger grasped the edge of the bar top with his sweaty hands so tightly that he could have ripped the bar from its foundation as his torso slammed into it from Dennis' passionate thrusts.

Minutes later, they both stumbled to the floor with their chests heaving. Dennis placed his head on Roger's shoulder as he recovered his breath. "I'd like to name this place after you," he said finally.

Roger traced his finger around the sides of Dennis' beautiful face. "Why?"

Dennis didn't attempt to hold back the emotion that overwhelmed him. "It's to make up for the one thing that I can't give to you," he said. "Every time we're away from one another, it leaves me angry. I've lost count of the number of times I've wrapped my arms around my pillow when I'm lying next to Ellie, wishing it was you. I'm sorry I can't give you the life that we both want for us. Maybe if we had lived fifty or a hundred years from now things would have been different. We don't live in that world, though. It's made up, a fantasy existence. If only we had lived during a time where I could have called you my husband."

Roger kissed Dennis. "I don't want us to ever stop, my love. It would break my heart if we did so. You might not be my husband by law, and no one will ever know about us, but you will forever be my one true love, Dennis."

"As you are mine," professed Dennis, kissing his hands. He pulled Roger up to his feet and poured them both another drink. They clinked their glasses together. "Here's to the '20s, the start to the best decade yet! May the booze be plentiful, the company fabulous, the music extraordinary and, of course, may there be beautiful men at every turn."

35

Ben looked around his room for another folded box, but realized he had just used the last one. Having to make do with what he had, he squeezed a pair of high tops into a box that was filled to the brim, crushing some of the clothes that were already piled up inside. As he folded up the top flaps and placed the box on the floor, there was a knock on his bedroom door.

"Are you busy?"

Ben paused. This was a first. Usually his aunt would knock, but then she'd just let herself in without waiting for permission.

"Come in," he said, skipping to the next song on his phone's playlist.

Iris walked in wearing a red bathrobe. She looked around the room, surprised. "You're packing up shop."

"I was going to tell you tomorrow... or whenever," he said, not making eye contact with her but instead browsing through his phone.

Iris strolled over to one of the boxes and lifted the top flaps to peek inside. Ben rolled his eyes, hating how she had a tendency to invade his privacy.

"I'm leaving behind everything that's on my desk," he said.

Iris went to the desk, where there was a tower of stacked CD cases. "You're not taking these?"

"I listen to music on my phone now," he said, pressing pause on the current song. "I haven't played a CD in, like, ten years."

She pulled out the second CD from the top. "I like this singer."

"You can have it then," he said.

Iris looked down at the blue ceramic garbage bin beside his desk and saw a birthday card sticking out from the top. She bent down and retrieved a pile of cards that he had thrown away. They were birthday cards he'd received from relatives as far back as his thirteenth birthday, including ones that Iris had given him.

"You're not throwing these out," she said bluntly, rescuing them all from the bin and bunching them together in her hands like a pack of playing cards.

"They just take up room," he said impatiently as he sat on the edge of his bed, still scrolling through his phone.

"Did you find a roommate then?" she asked. "Where's your new place?"

"I found a couple of roommates who live downtown," he told her. "It's close to the college."

The other day, Shaun had told Ben that he was going to ask him if he wanted to move in with him, but thought it wouldn't be a good idea because of Patrick. Instead, one of Shaun's friends was looking for an additional roommate. When Ben met Eddie, they connected, so Ben jumped at the chance, wanting to get out of his aunt's house as soon as possible. Eddie was twenty-two and studying business at Venus Valley College. He also worked at the same clothing store that Shaun did, both co-assistant managers. Eddie lived with his friend, who was also named Eddie, but went by Ed to avoid confusion. Ed was twenty-three and delivered food for a home delivery app called Let's Eat. Shaun, wunderkind that he was, set Ben up with an assistant manager position at a shoe store in the same mall where he worked. Shaun told him to lie on his résumé and to say he had one year of prior retail management experience when he supposedly lived in Toronto. During the interview, the manager, who was barely twenty-three, had seemed more interested in his "experiences" in Canada than his actual qualifications, and he was hired on the spot. She couldn't have cared less about the food truck, it seemed. Ben was surprised at how quickly everything was coming together for him within a matter of days.

"I'd like to talk to you about what happened the other day," said Iris. She took a seat on the desk chair.

Ben didn't want to have this talk. He could feel himself tensing up. "It doesn't matter," he said. "It sucks here."

"Excuse me?" she asked, her voice seemingly offended.

"I'm just a disposable piece of garbage," he said.

"Where did you come up with that?" she asked in a bewildered tone. "You know you need to start doing things on your own."

Ben sighed angrily.

"Why are you huffing like that?"

"It just feels like you don't actually care about me," he said.

"That's not true," she responded.

"Everything is changing so fast and I'm scrambling and..." He put his hands over his face as the stress accumulated in his voice and body.

"Where's the new job?" she asked.

"Some fucking shoe store in the mall," Ben said dismissively as he got up from the bed and gently kicked one of the boxes.

Iris paused. "Your mom and dad, I'm sure, would have been of better help to you."

Ben closed his eyes, wishing she hadn't said that. "You actually hated my dad. You still talk shit about him to family, and now everyone thinks he was a piece of shit when he wasn't."

Iris' mouth gaped.

"So, fuck off," he said, bending down to put his shoes on, deciding he'd rather leave the house than have this conversation.

Iris looked at him for a few seconds longer as he tied his shoes, then got up and turned to leave the room. She stopped. "You deserved a lot more than what life dealt you. I didn't set you up for the best success, and I'm sorry I couldn't support you the way that your mom and dad would have. It's been really hard for me, you know. My entire damn life has been hard." Iris' face was fraught with emotion. "But Ben..." She started crying, pointing at him. "Your dad said some really hurtful things to me. Don't you ever tell me to fuck off again!"

Ben stared back at her. "I'm sorry," he said quietly, looking away from her. "I just... wish they were still here."

Iris swept her fingertips underneath her bottom eyelids to rid herself of the tears. "You deserve to be happy, after everything that's happened," she said. "But the fact of the matter is... There are things about this family that you will never know, Benjamin."

Ben flashed his blue eyes at her, his jaw clenched.

"It might seem tough now," she said, "but you'll look back on all of this mess ten years from now and see that these were the years that helped shape you into the person you'll later become. Maybe, one day, you'll embody the shining example of what the childish, deplorable adults of this family should've aspired to be a long time ago."

Ben's mouth was glued shut, unable to form words, becoming mute. He just looked at her, the silence fuelling a dread that was building inside of him.

Iris turned and left the room, closing the door behind her.

36

When Zeus called his sister to inform her that Sabrina Elise was considering taking her on as her makeup artist, Lisa dropped everything and jumped on the earliest evening flight to Venus Valley. At first, Zeus almost didn't recognize her when she came through the revolving door of the airport. It was clear she had gotten a makeover worthy of any glam queen so she could make the best first impression possible on such a prominent potential client. Lisa was two years younger than Zeus, and ever since she moved to California, she had been trying to make it as a makeup guru. She wasn't struggling, she was growing, but it was a slow climb. She was a maestro at makeup; her eyes were sensual and smoky and her lips a deep merlot. She wore all black, down to her heels, and accessorized with jewellery and a punch of baby blue from the faux leather jacket that hugged her body tightly.

Zeus had been working as a flight attendant since he was nineteen. After being hired, the first place he had flown to outside of the United States was Brazil. It was there that he developed a passion for cocktails after visiting the bars and watching talented mixologists serve up exciting drinks to the locals and tourists. While bartending at a lounge in downtown Venus Valley one night, he was caught off guard when Owen Kim walked in, knowing who he was immediately. When Zeus made him his signature Black Thunder cocktail, Owen asked him to come bartend at Larchdale Castle for an event he was throwing. At first, Zeus thought it was a joke, or quite possibly one of the luckiest days of his life. Zeus had tried Tremble a few years back just to see what all the hype was about. It was cool, sure. He applied to be on the Tremble reality show, a competition for novice bartenders, but his application was rejected because he was under eighteen at the time. The app was immensely popular for a few years, until Owen sold it for a large payday. The new owners recklessly neutered its appeal and particular je ne sais quoi, and Tremble was officially no longer cool. Instead, it had become sterile and corporate and uncreative.

Upon her arrival in Venus Valley, Lisa immediately went to her job interview with Sabrina. Zeus knew what an opportunity like this would do to amplify her social media following and career. Lisa wasn't some pioneer in the makeup industry with an extensive portfolio, but she didn't need to be. Zeus told her that Sabrina was first and foremost looking for someone who was easy to talk to and whom she could be friends with. This wasn't fact, Zeus knew, but he wanted to ease his sister's nerves. When it was time to demonstrate her makeup capabilities on Sabrina's face, Lisa was unsatisfied with the final result and knew she could have done better. Later that day, she received a call from one of Sabrina's assistants telling her that, regrettably, she would not be moving forward. Lisa was so furious that she had no desire to stay any longer at Zeus' apartment. Rather, she wanted to fly back home that very same night. She had blown her big break. Doubt in her own skills started to rear its ugly head, and she no longer wanted to continue with makeup and no longer wanted to record videos for her channel. This had all been a waste of time. In her eyes, she wasn't talented enough or capable of keeping up with the demands of a job like this. The industry was too competitive.

As she was preparing to leave for the airport, Zeus had received a call from Owen asking to speak with Lisa. Owen told her he was sorry to hear she wasn't chosen, but there was someone else who was interested in her, as she had been recommended by Sabrina to them. Lisa saw this as a second chance, and refused to throw away her shot.

At noon, Zeus and Lisa arrived at Larchdale Castle. Zeus came along with Lisa as moral support. They were driven up the long gravel driveway of the Forever Road that cut through the middle of the expansive front lawn. The sun blazed down aggressively, casting heat upon the green chlorite schist facades as the castle's gardeners were hard at work, beautifying the castle grounds. Just as Zeus and Lisa started up the front steps, a tropical character came waltzing down a gravel path that snaked around the side to the backyard. Bailey Wondrous was dressed in a thin, transparent robe that was dyed blood orange. It was loose and flowed from his body like a blanket blowing in the breeze. His overall appearance made it seem like he had just returned from relaxing beside a resort pool, wearing black sunglasses and white flip flops, and holding a chilled glass of sangria. The only clothing he wore underneath the light fabric was a pair of white boxer briefs. Zeus was enthralled, having never seen Bailey out of drag before.

"Hello, Lady Love!" exclaimed Bailey, hugging Lisa excitedly. "Back for round two? This is my round two as well, wink wink." He took slow sips of his sangria and smacked his lips. "It's too bad this place doesn't have a pool, or I'd have invited you to a pool party in the backyard. Numerous shirtless men, all of whom are there to massage your toes and back. Delicious wishes! Let me be your tour guide to the tent, dear Lisa." He turned to Zeus. "Owen would like to see *you* inside. Giddy up, Black Thunder!"

Zeus saluted Lisa. "Good luck. You're gonna kill it." He spun around and made his way into the castle.

Bailey handed Lisa his drink and adjusted his shades. "Your brother is a cutie patootie. Anyway, walk with me!"

Lisa followed Bailey down the path and around the castle until they reached the backyard. "Wow..." she said, amazed, seeing the stage at the far end as well as the catwalk that extended out from it across the lawn.

"You missed an out of this world party last week," said Bailey, taking his sangria back from her. "There was fashion! There was drama! There was magic!" His voice was distinctly Cuban, Lisa noticed, and his mannerisms flamboyant and double extra. "In case you haven't realized yet, you're here today to do *my* glam."

Lisa smiled, finally realizing who her second chance client was. "That's great."

"Sabrina is practicing right now," he said, pointing towards the stage where she and her dancers were rehearsing expert choreography. "How has Los Angeles been this year? Is it just as hot and dry there as it is here right now?"

"Dry, like always," she confirmed. "It hasn't rained in forever it seems."

Just ahead, they approached what looked like a large fortune teller's tent in the same blood orange color as Bailey's robe; with gold moons, suns and stars printed all over its exterior. He lifted the flap and they stepped into a Cuban-inspired space filled with vibrant shades of orange, yellow, brown, turquoise and red. In the very center were large cushions laid out in a circle around a low table where bottles of water, a pitcher filled with sangria and various snacks had been set out. Lush rugs were spread out over the grass, and on the left side of the space was a vanity with an array of makeup and brushes scattered all over its surface. Mannequins wearing various colorful wigs of different lengths stood everywhere, and there were no fewer than four rolling racks that held some of the most extravagant clothing Lisa had ever seen.

Instantly, a white poodle that Lisa had mistaken for a fluffy white pillow jumped down from one of the cushions and ran towards her, its tongue flailing.

"That's Sugar Ray," said Bailey, scooping her up and placing her inside an open-top cage. "She's harmless, but fierce, and a little bit of a bitch–like me!" He put his sangria down on the center table and removed his sunglasses, plopping down on one of the cushions. "I'm ready for my glow up!" he declared. "I'm also kinda buzzed, so even if you think you didn't do as good a job as you should have, Yours Truly probably won't notice. There's some sangria over there on the table if you want any."

Lisa smiled and put her makeup bag down on the table to get set up.

"Have you ever done makeup on a boy before?" he asked.

Not wanting to appear as nervous as she was, she continued smiling. "No," she said. "You are the first. Honoured, really."

Bailey's skin was a dark brown with freckles sprinkled over his nose and cheeks. His lips were full and voluptuous, and his hair was a short jet black with streaks of blond.

"How old are you, if you don't mind me asking?"

"Guess," he said mischievously.

"Twenty," she replied, starting to apply moisturizer to his face.

"Damn it," he said, laughing. "People used to say eighteen. I'm actually twenty-three. So, I'm thirty in gay years."

"I'm twenty," said Lisa. "I don't know what that is in straight years."

"You're immortal-looking! Hello Naomi Campbell," he said, running his hand through her long black hair. "Oh sorry, is this creepy? I'm going to add your hair to my wig collection."

Lisa laughed as she reached for the primer. "Are your lips real?"

Bailey gagged. "These are my mom's lips. Zero injections and upkeep needed for these puppies." He reached over and flung her hair to the side with his hand. "Is this real?"

"Unfortunately, my hair isn't as blessed as your lips are in the family gene pool," she confessed. "I've always worn some sort of extensions." She was about to move on to the liquid foundation, but paused in midair. "I'm sorry, but I forgot to ask what you'd like done. Is it drag makeup?"

"No," he said. "My drag makeup is something I've perfected over the last eight years. I'd like you to give me something new and different for when I'm not performing! My fans want me to start posting pictures when I'm not in drag, and I've also been wanting someone to talk to when I'm getting ready..." He looked at her. "Do you still want to do this? You can leave if you want. It's totally fine. Run for the hills, honey! This bitch is a little crazy once you get to know her; I'm honestly demented."

Lisa shook her head and smiled. "You're being ridiculous now," she said, applying the rest of the foundation along his forehead. "We all need a little crazy in our lives... My hair is still intact and not sitting on one of your mannequins yet."

Bailey laughed. "Have you seen that horror movie? It's where this guy stalks the–"

"Nope!" cut in Lisa. "Nope, nope, nope. Horror movies are a big fat nope!" She steered the conversation in a different direction. "Is Bailey your real name?"

"Manuel is my birth name," he said. "At fifteen, I'd come up with all these different drag names for my alter ego. Then, Bailey Wondrous just popped into my head one night."

"You knew at that age that you wanted to do drag?" she asked.

"Oh, not right away. I knew I wanted to do something in the arts, but my parents couldn't afford to buy me art supplies. When we moved here from Cuba eight years ago, they didn't have a lot of money for those sorts of things that weren't seen as a necessity. I'd receive art supplies from friends and teachers on my birthday in December, but I'd always run out by the time April came along. So, to compensate, I would use my face as a canvas by using my mom's makeup when she wasn't home. I'd wear my sister's makeup too, but it was that cheap stuff for eight-year-olds that smells like fake strawberries."

Lisa finished with the foundation and moved on to the blush. "How did your parents find out about this?"

"When my mom discovered that most of her makeup was missing and started blaming my sister," he said, laughing. "I felt bad for my sister, so I told my mom that it was me. There was this awkward moment between the two of us, and I just blurted out... 'I'm gay!' My dad found out that night, so did my entire family. It was all they could talk about for days and days until it got boring and they moved on to something else like why my sister was getting so fat. When did you start doing makeup, Lady Love?"

"I've always liked makeup, and it became a hobby," said Lisa. "I started a makeup channel two years ago just for the fun of it, not really expecting much to happen. Then it just... took off! But then it kinda flatlined." She put the blush away and started with the highlighter and eyeshadow next.

"Are you passionate about it?" he asked, closing his eyes as she worked on his lids.

Lisa smiled. "There is nothing else that makes me as happy as makeup does."

"I watched some of your videos earlier today, and you have such great screen presence!" said Bailey. "You're not annoying or boring and you don't sound scripted."

"Aw, thanks," she said sincerely. "To be honest, my channel hasn't been growing as much as I had hoped it would. I always see how other creators do their videos and they all seem so on the pulse of everything. What I don't enjoy is the whole insincerity part: the flakiness and the lies."

"That's the thing about making content like yours," said Bailey. "You *need* to play the game. It's all about the algorithms and the clickbait and the pandering. If you miss any of those three ingredients, you're as good as extinct, honey. It's not easy being an honest bitch on the internet."

"I don't wanna sit in front of a camera all day and night in my apartment, applying makeup on myself and talking about products," she said. "I wanna travel to other cities and countries and do makeup for runway shows, magazines and celebrities... Not work in a mall boutique."

"If you could go anywhere right now, where would it be?" he asked.

"Paris," she said right away.

"Knew it," said Bailey. "Literally everyone says Paris. That, or like, Rome or something. The boys in France are cute."

"That too," she said, laughing. "I'll get myself a fine French man."

"And do the whole kissing portrait in front of the Eiffel Tower," teased Bailey. "Your brother is cute... Um, did I say that already? I'm sorry, it just has to be said!"

"Well, he's single," said Lisa, filling in the mascara on Bailey's eyelashes. "Unless he's still seeing that guy who lives down in Brazil, but I think he's more of a friend." She paused for a moment. "If you don't mind, I'd like your advice on something."

"Totally."

"How do you deal with online hate?"

"Not the question I was expecting," he said. "Um... It's kinda like a journey. Especially when you're first starting out and aren't used to people critiquing and saying things about you. It throws you off, especially when you think everyone will just like what you do. They'll start pointing things out about you that you didn't notice before, like some mannerism or how you talk. I'd get in these moments where I'd feel like shit about myself because of what they said. Then I'd talk back to them, because my ego and pride would get in the way. But eventually, you begin to learn that it doesn't matter how you defend yourself. They're still gonna think you're wrong, and they're right. So, you ignore them. The more they're mean to you, the more resilient you become and the more embarrassing they become. You get immune to their words because you've heard it all before, and it gets old."

"You need to find peace with who you are," said Lisa.

"You have to *own* who you are," added Bailey. "It took me years to figure that shit out! Your flaws, the way you talk... Everything! This is my personality, bitch! This is how I've chosen to do my drag! There's only so many times people can say the same shit things to you before you just start laughing at them rather than take them seriously. Especially when you see yourself getting better. That's the worst part for them. As you get better, the hate grows stronger. Then at that point, they just hate you because, well, you're you."

"It looks like I'll need to build a thicker skin," said Lisa.

"The only way to do that is to expose yourself more to the very thing that tears you down," said Bailey. "It's like a muscle. Every time someone says something that makes you feel like shit, you feel that instant pain and it tears you down. But if they keep doing it, and they do it long enough, you start to fight back. And when you fight back, they'll come harder for you, but by that point you've already won, baby! You get stronger, and they get weaker. Bitches want you to fail when they see you doing better than them. I've been dealing with jealous bitches for years. You can be the most talented person in the room, but there will always be people who will think you're horrible at what you do–untalented. It only takes those few people to say you aren't good enough for the doubt to start seeping in and making you second guess yourself. That's what they want, so don't give it to them!" Bailey fluttered his lashes, the final touches to his eyes complete. "I'm too busy to bother with those people, though. I'm booked, baby! I'm makin' money! I'm flying to places all over the country to do paid gigs because of *me*, *my* talent! Out of all the other queens in the city, Sabrina invited *me* to be here. I'm fucking fabulous! Let them seethe. Keep on hatin', baby! Keep givin' me that attention! I'm starved!"

"Are you where you want to be?" asked Lisa, applying a deep red to his lips. "In terms of your career?"

"Hell no," he scoffed. "I'm not at the level that I know I'll be at one day. People only really know me here and in Cuba. My main goal is to break out internationally. There's a lot more to show everyone, and a lot more to prove to myself. My ultimate dream is to be one of the greatest drag superstars in the world."

Lisa finished his lips and put the cap back on the lipstick. "Because you're absolutely amazing and wonderful," she said with a smile.

Bailey turned his face to the vanity mirror so he could see the tapestry that Lisa had created for him. "Because I'm a star."

37

Zeus entered one of the many castle's libraries to find Owen sitting in a blue and gold baroque armchair reading what appeared to be an old history book. He was wearing white trousers and a pink button-up shirt, undone at the top. No blazer, no tie and wearing white socks without loafers. The library must have had close to one thousand books on rows of shelves that snaked around the curved walls and up to a painted domed ceiling that depicted prancing deer in a summer forest. Sunshine poured in through the open windows, and with it came distant music from the stage outside where Sabrina was rehearsing.

Owen looked up from his book and smiled when Zeus walked in. "How's your day going, Zeus?"

"Not bad. Just a little sore," he replied, rubbing the left side of his neck.

"Did you strain it?" asked Owen.

Zeus shook his head like it was nothing. "What are you reading there?"

Owen flipped through the countless pages. "It's a history of bars," he said, "published in 1972."

"Getting any cool ideas?"

"I'm definitely inspired. I'll hand it over to you once I'm done skimming through it. There's a couple chapters on cocktails that might interest you." He placed the book down and got up to stretch his arms and back. "How's Lisa?"

Zeus sighed. "She at first didn't take the news well."

"Sabrina decided to hire someone who resides back home–a friend," revealed Owen. "It was nothing personal. Though Bailey did mention to me the other day that he was looking for someone to help with his various looks, so Sabrina suggested Lisa, and only Lisa."

"Her odds seem pretty good, then," said Zeus with a smile. "This would really mean a lot to her."

Owen returned the smile and walked towards a large, antique table in the center of the library. "You've lived here for how long?"

"For just a little bit," replied Zeus, rubbing his sweaty fingers along the sides of his green pants.

"So, you have a pretty good gauge for the nightlife scene around here," said Owen. "What's Venus Valley like compared to all the other cities you've visited?"

"It's decent," said Zeus. "When people come here from out of town, they sometimes tell me the city is like its own ecosystem... Its own little world. Lots of cool, trendy bars and clubs. The gay village is always fun." He walked to the center table and stood on the other side of it, directly across from Owen. "I've only ever gone to the gay bars, though. Sometimes I'll do shifts at a few lounges and the more upscale restaurants."

"Any of them stand out to you personally?" asked Owen.

Zeus noticed there was a large map of Venus Valley laid out on the table with books stacked at the corners so the map wouldn't curl inward. "There's the Silver Duck," he said. "It's very upscale and a great-looking bar. The gay bars are great too, but I wouldn't really call them standouts. They look and feel like so many bars you'd see in other states."

"The Silver Duck," said Owen. "Is it special?"

Zeus gave him an indifferent look. "It's beautiful, don't get me wrong, and it's money well spent when you go there, but it's kind of just... whatever."

"What... ever," said Owen, dragging out each syllable.

Zeus took advantage of this opportunity to conveniently bring something up to him. "Are you thinking of opening something up here? Like what you were going to do with that guy in Europe?"

Owen glanced down at the map to ponder his answer. "You know when something just feels right? You get that excitement in your soul. You feel happy, and there's that bounce in your step, like you're walking on clouds. It's similar to being in love. Except it's not a person you're falling for, it's an idea. That's what Venus Valley feels like to me right now. There was nothing special from that guy in Europe, Teddy. His ideas were like what you just said. Meh, not exciting." He focused on Zeus like a laser beam. "What... ever. Beautiful and seductive most certainly, and I'm sure they'll do fine for him, but they won't get top billing on a movie poster. There was passion, sure, but just... too on the nose. Not thought provoking. It's like being on a jungle safari and not a single person from your van gets eaten by a lion, or going for your daily jog in the park and not finding that secret tunnel that leads to a tropical oasis." He trailed his hand along the side of the table, his gold ring catching the distracting glare from the sunlight. "They're just nightclubs... Not destinations."

"Your party on Saturday was a destination," Zeus said admiringly, his eyes lighting up and giddiness coming through in his voice. "I'm not just saying that because it was your party, either. I'm still talking about it every single day to people. If you can somehow capture the magic of what it felt like to be there that night and turn it into some sort of nightclub downtown…" Zeus rubbed his hands together, the idea profoundly exciting.

"Stop," said Owen jokingly, "you're getting me hard just thinking about it."

Zeus pointed at him. "That's it, then! How many nightclubs out there get you hard from merely thinking about them?"

"Those are called gay clubs," replied Owen, but then he subtly bit his lip, returning his gaze to the map.

"It's going to be a gay bar?" asked Zeus excitedly. "Holy shit."

"No," said Owen.

Zeus' excitement faded.

"I mean, yes… and no," clarified Owen. "Given all the money and passion that will go into this vision, I'd want to maximize exposure and profit as much as possible. It'll be a must-see destination for everyone."

Zeus looked down, wanting to say something quickly before it got too awkward.

"What is it?" asked Owen, looking at him, noticeably sniffing out his dissatisfaction.

"It's just… Something special like this would have been great for the gay community, you know?"

"There's no doubt about that," Owen agreed. "You're so right, Zeus. But calling it a gay club will alienate a high percentage of people who otherwise would pay to be there. My party the other night wasn't a gay party. It wasn't a straight party. It was a party for everyone."

Zeus nodded, feeling like a stone was just dropped into his chest, squashing all the beautiful butterflies that he felt fluttering there moments before. He smiled at Owen. "It sounds great," he said.

Owen leaned over the table and intertwined his fingers. "When

Sabrina's social media promoter sent out the invitations, my intention was to see who would show up. The whole party was an experiment. When people eventually do come to my club, they will expect that same level of excellence. They won't just go there to drink and dance and socialize and be swept up in the fantasy. They will go there to be a part of something. When you leave my club, I'd want you to feel that you're taking a piece of history away with you, and you yourself become history just from being inside the place!" He looked at Zeus and smiled. "I'd like you to be my head bartender and mixologist."

Zeus' eyes widened. "Me?"

Owen turned his head and looked around the room. "Is there someone else here?"

Zeus' mouth was open in nervous surprise. "Sure, I'll do it... But why me?"

"You don't want to just say yes instead?" asked Owen. "What if I change my mind?"

"Yes," said Zeus quickly. "But I'm only twenty-two with not a whole lot of experience."

"And you're damn good for your age," said Owen. "You need to be more confident, man! I chose you because you're good as you are, right now. You're not the best, yet, but definitely skilled. You don't have an insufferable ego. You're not stuck in your ways. You're bright. You're fun to engage with, and you're mesmerizing to watch. You're professional. You're trustworthy and open-minded... Talented."

Zeus had never received so many compliments in a row like that in his entire life. He felt overwhelmed that someone would think of him that way, especially someone of Owen's stature. "The thing is," he said, "I like flying a lot. Being a flight attendant is great because of all the places I've been able to see."

"I'll bump up your salary," offered Owen.

Zeus smiled gratefully, but there was a lingering doubt on his face.

"I'll throw in a two-week all expenses paid vacation to anywhere in the world in the first year you work for me," countered Owen. "That's on top of your regular vacation time, plus the vacation time you would have received from working for the airline. That's... what? Five weeks of vacation? You'll be able to see the world, Zeus, the way it's meant to be seen: in style! Not wearing a stuffy uniform while on some overnight layover."

Zeus blinked quickly as emotion built up in his eyes. He placed his hands on his head, overwhelmed. "Is this even happening, man? Last week you just randomly walked into my work, and now here you are changing my life forever."

"It wasn't random," said Owen. "What will be, will be." He walked around the table and took a peek out of one of the open windows. "I'm having another party here on Saturday to kick off this new endeavour of mine. It'll just be acquaintances in attendance, nothing big. I'd like you to be there."

Zeus gathered his composure. "For sure. How many people?"

"Shouldn't be more than fifty. My dad is flying in as well."

"Oh," said Zeus. "That's exciting."

"Yes..." replied Owen as he stared out into the world. He turned to look at Zeus. "You mentioned that you know the disco jumping dude personally."

"Um," recalled Zeus. "Yeah. Why?"

"I'd like to speak with him. Given how many interviews he's doing with the media all over the world in regard to me and the party that so generously made him famous, he'd be well-placed to remind the people of who Owen Kim is."

"He also has a following," said Zeus, pulling out his phone. "It's growing a lot."

Owen smiled. "Fan-tastic. You know, my intention before going back to London was to only stay here for a couple weeks to relax while Sabrina did her rehearsals. But when I explored the venues of Venus Valley, I noticed something that was severely lacking. There is so much untapped potential in this pretty city. Such a gorgeous place like this, and there isn't a single defining nightlife landmark. You look at all the other major cities around the world, and they have at least one."

Zeus looked down at the map on the table, his eyes scanning the buildings and streets. "Do you have a name for your landmark yet?"

Owen slid his hands into his trouser pockets and gave way to a smile.

38

Martin downed the rest of his third drink of the evening, then shook the ice in the glass as though doing so would make more whiskey magically appear. Carly was an absolute vision in her red one-shoulder cocktail dress that had a large bow on the left shoulder. She opened her phone and took a look at herself in the camera. "People might be watching you," she said, glancing around the dining room. "Be very cautious of how you might come across to them."

"I'll bet you no one here knows who we are," said Martin, also eyeing the guests around the posh restaurant. Carly had suggested that they share a romantic Friday evening together at Set, a steakhouse and cocktail bar that was one of the most upscale restaurants in the city. She was nibbling away on her crab cake appetizer, and Martin his seared jumbo scallops as they waited for their entrées.

"I think it's about time for a story update!" cheered Carly. She slid her chair over next to his and held her phone up. Martin knew the routine. Any time they went out together, he was expected to be in a picture with her: smiling, elated. He had to exude the aura of a man having the time of his life... Happy and in love.

He smiled from ear to ear, exaggerating his enthusiasm to the extreme. The flash went off and he slumped back into his chair.

Carly sat tall in her seat, all gleeful and giddy. She picked up the cocktail menu and started browsing through it before slapping it down dramatically. "Martin, someone is coming." She said it with a mischievous smirk.

Martin frowned. "Uh... Who?" he asked, worried and annoyed at the same time. He rolled his eyes, assuming the worst. "Really? Like, an interviewer?"

"No way," she said. "It's your old buddy, Marc!"

Martin batted his eyes at her, registering this news. He didn't hate it, he just wished he'd had more time to prepare for this. "Uh, alright..."

"It'll be great!" she exclaimed with an optimistic smile. She looked down at her phone and feverishly tapped out a text, then craned her neck to the front entrance to see if their dinner guest had arrived yet. "He should be here any moment now. Surprise!" She glanced up to see his reaction. "You don't want him here?"

"No, it's fine," he said in a nonchalant voice. "Can't put the genie back in the bottle. It's just going to be awkward as hell."

One of the servers walked past their table, and Martin raised his hand to get her attention. "Hey, is it possible to get another drink? Just make it a whiskey on the rocks."

She gave him a flustered smile. "Your server will be right with you, sir."

"Do you not like what I'm doing?" asked Carly. "Are all these interviews too much? It's just, you need to strike when the iron is hot. If you want people to keep caring enough to want to talk about you, then you need to keep feeding the beast."

Martin scratched his forehead. "Well, you told me we were going out to dinner. That got me excited because it meant I could relax and not be stressed out for a couple hours."

"I thought this would be different because it's just Marc," she said simply. "He's not some random person. He's your buddy!"

Martin returned to his appetizer, burying his unhappiness under the scallops. As active as Carly was in being his unofficial manager, agent, cheerleader and wife, he hadn't told her about the message he had received from Zeus earlier that day. Zeus informed him that Owen wanted him to come to Larchdale Castle for a party on Saturday. He knew if he told Carly about the event, she would instruct him on what to say and how to act and what to do, even tagging along with him. He wanted to do this one on his own terms. "It would have been nice if you gave me more notice about him coming," he said. "We haven't spoken to each other in over three years."

"I'm sorry," she said, her voice sympathetic. "That was my mistake."

Their waiter, Devon, came back to their table. "How's everything here, guys?"

"Whiskey on the rocks," said Martin. "Make it a double. Gin and tonic for her, also."

"Can you put a sprig of rosemary in the glass?" asked Carly in her obnoxiously sweet voice that she used strategically with service people. Drive-throughs were the worst.

"Certainly," he said, his eyes switching back to Martin. "Hey... Aren't you that guy?"

"Which guy?" asked Martin, playing coy.

"*MarcVsMartin*!" exclaimed Devon with a smile, his eyes widening. "I always watched you guys in college while smoking a bowl. Now you're the *Jumping Disco Man*!"

Martin glanced at Carly skeptically. "Did you tell him to say that?"

Carly laughed, snorting as she did so. She looked at Devon. "My husband thinks you're acting."

"Dude, I'm not an actor," said Devon. "The commentary when you guys did those playthroughs was hilarious! If I had my phone on me right now, I'd show you that I'm still subscribed to your channel even though you guys haven't uploaded in years."

Martin was smitten, almost shy with pride. "Dude, thank you for being the highlight of my night."

Carly's expression dropped. She picked up her phone and started browsing through it with a dead expression, her vibe turning frigid.

"I'll be right back with your drinks, then," said Devon happily, walking away.

"Really, though," he said to Carly, "did you tell him to say that? We were just talking about Marc seconds ago."

"It's just a wild coincidence," she said, her voice dismissive as she carried on looking down at her phone. "People know who you are."

"Shit," he said, smiling.

Minutes later, Devon came back with Martin's drink and placed it in front of him. Disgusted, Martin pulled his face away from the stench of urine that came up from the glass. There was a grotesque piece of chewed gum on the rim, meant to imitate garnish.

"Enjoy, man," said Devon in a smug tone. "I'm glad there are pieces of shit like you getting famous."

Carly's mouth dropped open. Martin just looked up at the man, gobsmacked. It felt like he was just kicked in the stomach; he didn't even know how to react to something like this.

"You said you'd fuck an anorexic girl just to see if she'd snap in half," said Devon. "You're pretty gross, bro."

Martin's eyes narrowed, not comprehending what the hell was happening.

"How about this one," continued Devon. "You said you'd drive over a handicapped person because, I quote, 'What's the point of them?'"

"I never said any of those things," said Martin.

"Oh really? Because it's online." Devon pulled out his phone from his trouser pocket. "Everyone's been discovering the Jumping Disco Douche and what he's all about, so it's no surprise they're finding out about this kind of shit." He showed him a post from a social media page where someone had screen-recorded what Martin had said in one of his old videos with Marc from several years ago. The post had already been shared, liked and commented on thousands of times.

Martin looked incredulous. "That was eight years ago," he said. "I was, like, seventeen, and probably thought it was funny at the time." He looked up at Devon, who was staring back at him with a fun smirk on his face, like he was getting some real satisfaction out of this. "I'm sorry for saying those things," finished Martin.

"It really fucked me up," said Devon. "My sister was left paralyzed from the waist down when she was run over by a fucking drunk driver. When you said what you did, for humor, it left me feeling embarrassed for you. Then, what pissed me off even more was that a lot of your dumbass fans just laughed and didn't seem to care. They just continued eating out of your fucking asshole."

"So, you've never said something that you regret?" asked Martin, his heart racing with adrenaline. "That's not who I am, and it's not something I'd ever fucking think or say now."

"You graduated from being an asshole to being a complete moron who jumps off balconies at parties because you're so desperate for fame," said Devon, without a hint of hesitation in his voice. "You're so fucking gross. No one even watches your solo streams because they're embarrassing; half the time you're drunk in them."

Carly grabbed the arm of a passing server. "Get your manager, please."

"You know what, waiter Devon?" said Martin, looking him up and down. "I came here tonight to have dinner with my wife, and you just ruined it."

Devon scoffed. "It's disgusting that people like you become famous for being pieces of shit." He turned to Carly. "Please, don't have kids with him."

"Listen..." said Martin, taking the piss drink and throwing it at Devon with a quick flick of his wrist. The glass hit Devon squarely in the chest, and the urine splattered all over his face. Devon retaliated by kicking Martin's chair, knocking him abruptly to the floor, then briskly walked away.

Carly stood and looked over the table to see if Martin was okay, then sat back down and proceeded to stare into the void ahead of her. Martin got up, adjusted his clothes, and left the table. His heart was beating in overdrive, and his body perspiring heavily, as he slid between chairs and tables, heading for the lobby, feeling eyes following him like pestering mosquitos amongst the whispers and curious murmurings. When he made it to the front, Marc had just come through the front entrance.

"Fuck..." whispered Martin under his breath, walking past Marc and leaving the restaurant.

Marc paused, then followed Martin outside. "Hey, Martin!" he said excitedly.

Martin kept walking down the sidewalk, seemingly on his way to nowhere, deaf to all.

"Hey, what's happening?" asked Marc, his expression changing from excitement to confusion.

Martin turned around. "Why are you here?!"

Marc stopped where he was, his face turning serious when he registered Martin's wrath in his expression and his voice. "So, we're getting right to the point... I'm here because I've been wanting to talk to you. I've been in touch with Carly, knowing you wouldn't respond to any of my messages. This was the best way for us to meet, to kind of just spring it on you, or else you would have avoided me."

"You wanted to talk to me because I'm viral now?" assumed Martin. "The timing seems convenient. You didn't give a shit about me for the last three years. Now you do? You didn't even come to my wedding, man!"

"I'm sorry about that one," said Marc desperately. "The timing just wasn't good for me."

"You're such a shit liar," scoffed Martin.

Marc grabbed Martin's arm before he could turn away. "I'm sorry that I missed your wedding," he said sincerely. "It was a mistake not to go. I'm sick of it being awkward between us, and that's part of the reason I didn't go. Look at you, though!"

"Look at what?"

"I watched some of the interviews you've been doing and you don't seem okay, buddy. I've known you for years, and I can tell when you're faking it and putting on this mask. I'm not here to interview you or talk business with you or any of that shit. I'm here as a friend."

Martin sighed and looked down. He wanted to step in front of a passing car, just so he could end it. "I just had someone serve me a glass of piss," he said. "The dude used to watch our channel. He was willing to throw away his job just so he could get his fucking point across about something that doesn't even reflect who I am. I'm not that guy anymore!"

Marc placed his hand on Martin's shoulder, feeling the humid anger rising from his body. "There are people who want us to get back together. I've been getting so many requests from my podcast listeners. They've missed you. Let's sit down and talk about it, man to man."

Martin rubbed his eyes and dragged his hands over his face. "I can't do this," he said.

"Do what?"

"This fame shit! I'm just some loser to everyone. I really…" he looked Marc in the eyes, "I really hate my life right now."

Marc furrowed his brow. "Want to come over and talk about it? Kendra is home with the baby, but you can check out my new man cave in the basement."

"You have a kid…" said Martin. "Well, congrats man."

"She's six months," replied Marc, pushing up his glasses. "My offer is still on the table. Let's rip the Band-Aid off and say everything we need to."

Martin's phone buzzed with an incoming call from Carly. He ignored it and let it go to voicemail.

39

The brown-haired twunk felt every thrust that Johnson pounded inside of him. His calves were up on Johnson's broad shoulders, their eyes deadlocked on one another, the boy's head sliding up and down the pillow as he grabbed hold of Johnson's muscular chest. Johnson restrained the boy by grabbing hold of both his wrists and throwing them above his head, leaving Johnson in full control of him. The bottom he had invited over for a passionate fuck was his submissive slut, and the jock strap the boy wore gave Johnson easy access to his perfect, muscular ass.

"You like daddy fucking you like this?" whispered Johnson, sweat rolling down his body and drenching the bedsheets as he slid in and out of him, staring into his eyes.

"Yes, daddy," said the twunk, his voice desperate, yearning, his beautiful clean-shaven face giving Johnson the visual he needed to send himself over the edge into a bursting, gushing climax. "Fucking breed me, daddy," he pleaded, the bed frame rocking back and forth violently.

Johnson, needing to fuck as hard as possible, needing to see this boy submit and take every inch of him, reached forward and wrapped his hands around the boy's neck and started squeezing, rubbing his thumbs along his bulging Adam's apple. The boy gagged, tears welling up in his eyes from the pressure as he stared into Johnson's animalistic face. Johnson let go, just as his climax was fast approaching, but the boy forcefully pushed himself away and out from underneath Johnson. He threw himself off the king-size bed, distressed. Without even putting his clothes back on, the boy grabbed his belongings and bolted out of the bedroom, exiting through the front door of the house.

The electronic beats coming from the living room television echoed down the hall and through the open door of the bedroom. Johnson remained kneeling on his bed, his heart pounding, his dick raging hard. "Fuck," he said, using his forearm to wipe the sweat from his forehead. He threw himself onto his back to finish himself off. Within seconds, he climaxed all over his stomach and chest. He lay there in the dark, his chest heaving, his sheets drenched in a puddle of sweat. The boy had been turned off by him all of a sudden, even terrified. Johnson was as dominant as one could be in bed, and he loved seeing the expression on a guy's face when he had his hands around their neck. He couldn't control his actions in moments of lust. This was the first time anyone had reacted this way to him, actually leaving during sex. Men wanted to have sex with him, but they never stuck around afterward. Most of them just wanted to be dominated during a quick and intense session, and felt no romantic connection to him at all.

Johnson lay spread-eagle in his bed as emotion overcame the reality of what a sexual partner running out of his house meant. He had hoped to cuddle with him afterward, to fall asleep with his arms wrapped around him, but he'd ruined another moment of potential happiness. He didn't find anything meaningful at work anymore. His desire to move up the ladder of his career was diminishing with each day that passed. He was unmotivated to make more money if he couldn't share it with anyone. He didn't want this house if he couldn't live in it with someone.

It was like the universe didn't want him to be happy. Everyone around him seemed so fulfilled. They had lives. They went out on the weekends and did things. They had hobbies and purpose. Love. Johnson hadn't done anything remarkable with his life at all, really. He felt no real passion for things like others did. He didn't even have a loving pet to come home to, a furry friend to jump up onto his lap. He'd have conversations with colleagues and friends, and they always seemed to have such amazing stories to tell. His stories were blank pages. He was afraid that this was how it would be for the rest of his life–the blank pages of his journal colorless and wretched. He wanted to change the course of his life, he just didn't know how to.

Johnson turned on the lamp beside his bed. The crack pipe lay there on his nightstand, a cold hopelessness radiating from it. His hands were trembling as he dressed, and the high he'd been riding for the last little while would soon come crashing down. The reality of his loneliness was settling in, the reality of his existence. It was the grim realization that he wasn't good enough. For anyone.

It was the second time in a week that Johnson had come to see Liam. Before that, he'd usually drop by every few months. Being sixty-nine years old, Liam provided a different perspective to Johnson's life that most men his own age could not. He was an open ear for Johnson to spill out the contents of his mind to; like an unpaid therapist.

Liam's day-to-day routine had often consisted of doing the same exact things for the last decade. He went to work at his barber shop during the weekdays, then returned home. He'd prepare dinner, followed by relaxing on the couch and smoking a joint while indulging in a show or movie. He cherished the friendships he had formed with his clients at the barber shop, for having lived alone for most of his life, loneliness was an unwelcome friend that he dreaded coming home to each and every day. His barber shop was his little vacation getaway for eight hours a day, and his house the cemetery in which he wandered at night. It had become clear to him that the world of today wasn't built for someone his age. Everything was done online and through cell phones. It was all so advanced and quick that it was hard for him to keep up. When he went out on any given day, no one bothered to take a genuine interest in him except his clients at the barber shop and the girl at the grocery store who would ring him through every week. Little did she know she was one of the highlights of his week, just to see her smiling face and to hear her call him by his first name like a friend.

His biggest regret in life was never finding a soul with whom he could share his waning years. Any hope for that was long behind him now. He couldn't remember the last time a man, or anyone for that matter, had looked at him with desire. Everywhere he went, it seemed that people just passed him by, as if he was a ghost in the wind or a speed bump that slowed them down. Looking back, he could see all the opportunities he had taken for granted, laid out behind him like a time capsule. He had been reckless with his time, never imagining the day when he would be pushed aside for the young, modern and relevant. Life now felt stationary, flattened and meaningless. *He lived and died, but did not love*. That, he knew, would be his epitaph.

"You haven't said anything in five minutes," said Liam, turning to look at Johnson next to him on the couch as he watched the television. He could see that Johnson was staring aimlessly at the screen, having no idea what was happening because his mind was clearly racing with whatever distractions were keeping him from enjoying the show.

"Yeah," replied Johnson, the light from the television flashing across his face in the dark. "You're the only person I've been able to talk to on a more meaningful level. Yet for whatever reason, the words aren't coming out–even for you."

"What about your friends?" pondered Liam. "Those college buddies of yours. What's the name of the one who takes pictures of all those weird places?"

"Tony," said Johnson vacantly. "They don't understand. To them, I'm a guy who has a respectable job and a good body, who hooks up with hot dudes and owns a house and car. I'm their perfect life, a barbed wire fence disguised as a white picket fence."

"Maybe you don't want them to know what you're really feeling," offered Liam.

"They know," said Johnson. "They're too scared to bring it up." His eyes shifted down to the floor, where months-old newspapers were stacked beside the coffee table. "I've been trying to find someone to be with, but something always stops me from succeeding; like a curse was placed on me."

Liam pondered what Johnson had said. "You know, my life has been quite unremarkable. But your life doesn't have to be, and it shouldn't. You still have so much time left to meet someone."

"Stop it with the useless optimism," muttered Johnson. "I'd love to be the fun guy who smiles all the time and does stupid shit with his friends and finds joy in the smallest of things. I'd kill to have that life, but I'm always sabotaging it for myself. Going for daily runs was something that brought me some sort of joy, but I've come to realize that it's not working anymore." He reached down into the gym bag that he'd brought with him and casually pulled out a small sandwich bag full of crack. Next, a glass pipe that had burn marks around the bowl.

Liam watched Johnson and adjusted himself uncomfortably on the couch. He cleared his throat, uneasiness settling in. "You're not doing that in my house," he said bluntly. "I'm sorry, Johnson. I'd like to talk with you, but if that's what you came here to do, you can take it elsewhere."

Johnson looked at him, scrunching up his face like he'd just been insulted. "Really?" he said, feeling betrayed.

"It's hard to look at," said Liam, trying hard to avoid looking at what Johnson held in his hands.

"I've only been doing it sometimes," said Johnson, his annoyance escalating.

"The powder isn't just sometimes, though."

"Crack... Blow... It's the same fucking thing," said Johnson, raising his voice. "Plus, why are you judging me? Sometimes I'll smoke it, other times I'll snort it. Smoking it is a faster high." He looked around Liam's house and scoffed. "Clean up your fucking house. It's disgusting."

Liam got up and went into the kitchen. "I've seen enough of that crap in my life." Liam stared at Johnson from a distance, and Johnson returned the stare, dead eyes meeting dead eyes.

"You've done this shit before?" asked Johnson.

"No," said Liam. "But I've known people who've lost their lives to it. To disease, too. To hate. To self-loathing. You want to talk about being cursed? There's a constant black cloud that follows my life."

"Well, fuck," said Johnson, dumping the pipe and bag of crack back into his gym bag. He stood and headed for the front door, his face hostile as he looked back at Liam. "That's a real nice fucking image you painted in my head, Liam. If I ever want to feel like absolute shit again, I'll just come here."

Johnson pushed the front door open and slammed it shut behind him.

40

Fame nightclub was an anonymous sea of revelry and silhouettes as the steady, dark beats pulsated through every body and crevice. The humidity was a burning rush as people left drinks behind on tables for the lure of the dance floor. The mirror ball spun continuously and reflected the passing lights onto every man below, bodies undulating against one another as the mystery of darkness surrounded them, engulfed them, played with them.

Robbie watched from a stool beside the dance floor as Sarim seduced the crowd from his position on stage, his thighs rubbing up against a metallic pole, the metal hoops on his black chest harness glinting in the passing lights. He wore a ball cap that cast shadows upon his face, and his hairy, muscular chest flexed and stretched as he worked the stage around him for the creatures of the night. Robbie finished his drink and stared up at his man on stage, whose dancing lured in wandering eyes. The liquid movements of each limb in tune with the music was a gorgeous art form. Even though he couldn't see his face, Robbie knew Sarim was looking at him, and only him. Sarim thrust his pelvis down onto the floor, his plump ass gliding through the air as his shorts glistened.

Sarim slid off the stage and glided towards Robbie like a vapour, the passing lights distorting his approach within the shadows around them. He appeared in front of Robbie and pushed the stool next to him aside so he could stand between his legs. Sarim took Robbie's hand and brought him up onto his feet, then led him back towards the stage through the crowd of dance floor darlings. Sarim pulled Robbie up on stage with him, directing his body towards the pole with his hands. When Robbie's back was pushed up against the metal, Sarim leaned in, placing his hands on Robbie's chest and dragging his fingertips down his torso, letting them bump along his toned muscles. The heat from Robbie's skin collided with the fire from Sarim's exposed body, and their energies came together to form a heated mix of desire, masculinity and erotica. The entire room was hot and heavy, the walls melting from the stoked flames of desire. Robbie's eternally youthful spirit was busting through his veins. His tight black jeans and shirt were at the mercy of Sarim's advances as he slowly undid the buttons of his shirt. Sarim ran his fingertips along the pectorals of the man whom he'd helped define through countless workout sessions. Robbie's skin was both rough and soft, hairy and smooth. Sarim's facial hair made Robbie's body tingle as he stroked his lips down Robbie's chest and stomach, euphoric pings of orgasmic thrill shooting down every inch of him.

"You're mine," whispered Sarim. He pulled Robbie up close to him, away from the cold metal, and they started dancing, their bare chests pressed together, Sarim's thighs sliding up against Robbie's. The beat went on, ceaseless, drawing the moment out to infinity.

Robbie's face was up close to Sarim's, catching his eyes beneath the ball cap. Sarim's back was to the dance floor, but Robbie's eyes had wandered over his broad shoulders and into the audience. Some of the guys were focused on their dancing partners, while others were alone in complete oneness with the music as it seared itself into their flesh and blood: men with dark hair, pink hair, red and blue hair; light skin and dark skin; glitter and boy toys; tank tops and bare flesh. Robbie caught flashes of a young boy who danced along with another, his friend or his lover, or both. His blond hair was almost white underneath the passing lights. Robbie stared, squinted and watched. The boy made eye contact with him, his blue eyes prominent under each light that swept past his head. Robbie let go of Sarim with a jolt, his body flinching backwards.

Sarim grabbed hold of his shoulders. "Do you want to get down?!" he yelled over the music.

Robbie swallowed some nervous saliva that had accumulated in his mouth. "I'm gonna grab a drink!" He looked again over Sarim's shoulder again, making Sarim turn to see what Robbie had been distracted by.

"Did you see someone you know?!" asked Sarim.

Robbie regained his normal composure after having had the pleasurable moment with Sarim yanked away. "It's a fucking ghost," he said to himself, inaudible over the music.

Sarim continued dancing on the spot, then leaned in to kiss his cheek. "I'll be done soon!" he said into his ear. "Wait up, okay?!"

Robbie smiled briefly then jumped down off the stage and into the crowd. His body was swept along every which way, body to body, inside the endless maze.

It was 2:30 a.m. when Robbie and Sarim left. *Fame* didn't officially close until four, but many clubgoers were already leaving for after-parties or heading home for their own private soirees. Smokers stood along the street, chatting and laughing drunkenly as cars and buses drove past. Ubers waited along the curb as people rushed to be taken away into the night, while others headed down the street to catch a nearby bus.

"Were you fine with me bringing you up there?" asked Sarim.

Robbie smiled at him as they walked down the sidewalk, side by side, to Robbie's car. "It was great," he reassured him. "It made me feel young again."

"You weren't a stripper back then," said Sarim.

"No way," confirmed Robbie. "During my club hopping days, there were tons of guys who would get up on stage and start dancing during peak time. That's what it reminded me of."

Sarim slid his arm around Robbie's waist. "Did you see anyone you know tonight?"

"There were a few," said Robbie, looking straight ahead, his mind drifting.

Sarim sighed and put his head on his shoulder.

"What?" asked Robbie, knowing full well what his answer was going to be.

"We've talked about this so many times already," he said. "It's just... and you know what I'm going to say. There's a part of you I'm still missing–a stranger to me."

Robbie stayed silent, the city noises around them filling the void.

"Anyway, you know what I'm talking about," he finished.

This was the first time since dating Sarim that Robbie couldn't actually say anything in response. He was tongue-tied. The silence was uncomfortable.

"I'm in love with you," said Sarim, his voice quiet. "But I'm still waiting for the day when you feel like you can trust me enough to tell me more about everything... Your *whole* life."

Robbie looked at him, still unable to loosen his tongue.

Sarim stopped walking and stood where he was. "I've been hinting at it for the last couple years now, and you keep avoiding it."

Robbie kept walking ahead, leaving Sarim behind. Whether it was because he wasn't aware that Sarim had stopped and was no longer beside him, or that he had consciously chosen to leave him behind, he wasn't sure. He stopped and turned, waiting for Sarim to catch up. But Sarim wasn't moving; he just stood and looked at him as they remained feet apart from one another on the sidewalk.

"Would you trust me with your life?" asked Sarim.

Robbie stared into his brown eyes. The love he felt transmitting in the gap between them was like a rope pulled tight across a river. Robbie went back to Sarim and embraced him, kissing him on the cheek, wanting to feel his warmth.

Just down the sidewalk in the direction they had been heading, a bottle smashed on the ground several feet away, where two men stood. Both Robbie and Sarim looked in the direction that the sound came from.

The two strangers looked in their direction. "Get the fuck out of my country, faggot."

Sarim froze, the words hitting him hard. His body tensed up within seconds.

"Yeah, you," said one of the men, an aggressive sneer on his face. "Man, you're one ugly son of a bitch."

"I've lived here my entire life, actually," said Sarim loudly. He stared him down, unblinking, his heart beating out of his chest.

The man leaned forward, his face disturbed, like he couldn't believe Sarim was speaking to him. "What the fuck did you just say to me?"

Sarim's mouth was fastened shut, and his hands curled into fists. Robbie saw Sarim's body tensing up, his muscles clenched. The two men waited where they were, staring back at Sarim while they silently assessed each other, animal to animal.

The man turned to Robbie, then back to Sarim, his mouth

curling into a grin. "It was God's plan to wipe you all out–like the dinosaurs–for pumping another dude's ass full of AIDS."

"Fuck this," said Robbie, grabbing Sarim's arm and turning around.

Sarim turned slightly, but his feet were rooted to the spot, unable to move.

"You'd better fucking stop looking at me," said the man, his voice rising as he walked forward with a drunken swagger. "Get back on your little boat, and sail on home to your dirty fucking country."

Sarim turned around and pushed Robbie in front of him so they could start distancing themselves in the opposite direction. He stayed behind Robbie as he checked over his shoulder to see that the men had suddenly backed away, their guffaws echoing off the buildings and pavement.

"We could have fucking taken them," said Sarim. "We're bigger than them."

"No, they could've had a weapon," said Robbie. "It's a good thing you're not drunk." He reached behind him and touched Sarim's side. "Sometimes, you just need to walk away."

When they finally made it into Robbie's car, they locked the doors and sat in silence.

"It's things like that that just ruin my entire fucking week," said Sarim, sliding the key into the ignition. "I'm never going to forget those guys now. They're going to be imprinted in my mind for the rest of my life."

Sarim was staring angrily at the steering wheel when he turned to look at Robbie. He leaned in and kissed him, tracing his nose along his. "If this is so wrong, then how come it feels so right?"

Robbie felt tears welling up in his eyes as he returned his boyfriend's kiss. "Loving me was never wrong to begin with."

41

"Hey guys, how's it going? Thanks for all your support in keeping this thing alive. It's been a lot of fun getting to know all of you."

Jay looked away from the computer screen and over at Salvador, who was standing against the bedroom wall, off screen, in business attire. Jay smiled at him, then returned to the screen, the comments scrolling down continuously.

"Just wanted to let you all know that this will be my last session for a long time... Maybe forever." He paused. "So, let's make it a good one."

Jay rolled his home office chair back across the flooring and started unbuttoning his white shirt and removing his black tie as he remained seated. Salvador stepped away from the wall and entered the frame, standing beside Jay's chair with everything from his neck up concealed, keeping his identity anonymous to the audience.

"Hey, boss," said Jay, making eye contact with him, his chin raised.

"Everyone has gone home for the night," said Salvador, running his hand down Jay's leg. "You do know what you have to do now, right?"

"Of course, sir," said Jay, sliding off his chair and getting down on his knees so he could undo Salvador's trousers, feeling his erection through his pants.

"You gotta give me some of that overtime work," said Salvador, smiling down at him. "I'll spank you with my ruler!"

Jay looked up at him, wanting to laugh but trying his best to hide his smile. "You're not a teacher," he whispered.

"Oh..." said Salvador. "That's right... Your quarterly results were down. How are you going to make it up to me?"

Jay pulled down Salvador's pants, his boxer briefs following suit. "Slap me," he demanded.

Salvador reached down with his hand and struck him across the cheek.

"Ouch. No, with your dick," mumbled Jay. He shoved his face into Salvador's crotch, just in time to muffle his laugh.

"Shit, sorry," whispered Salvador, dipping back into character. He glanced at the screen when he heard a sudden *ding*. "What does that mean?"

Jay looked at the chat. "Someone tipped ten dollars to see you twist my nipples."

Salvador pondered the possibilities. "What does fifty dollars unlock?"

Two hours later, Jay shut off the computer, then slid down the side of his bed and sat on the floor, naked. He picked up his phone to browse his minimal notifications.

"It's hot in here," said Salvador as he strolled out from the hallway bathroom. He opened the window next to the computer, letting in a mild breeze. The chill swept over Jay's bare skin, evaporating the perspiration from his body. Salvador plopped down onto the bed and hung over the side on his stomach as Jay remained seated on the floor. Jay could feel Salvador's soft, curly hair caressing his neck when he rested his chin on his shoulder.

"So, how was it?" asked Salvador. "How do you feel?"

Jay let out a deep sigh. "What do you think?"

Salvador kissed his neck. "It's your decision. Is this really the end of *Corporate DaddyXL*? The end of an era."

"Do you think I'm, like, a slut for having done this?" asked Jay. "Honestly. Has your impression of me changed now that you've seen me do it?"

"No," said Salvador. "It's sex. Most guys jerk off, but you make it into a show so others can watch. We all gotta do the deed, one way or another. It's cool, actually."

"Cool?" asked Jay with a subtle smile.

"It's hot," reiterated Salvador, running his hand through Jay's hair. "You help people live out their fantasies. Do you feel ashamed about it?"

"I've felt ashamed for being gay for most of my life, said Jay. "So, this is just the extra layer to the ultimate shame cake."

Salvador lay quiet for a moment. "Do you still feel ashamed for being who you are?"

Jay turned to look at him. "Yes," he said. "That is, until we met the other day."

Salvador tilted his head.

"I've always been surrounded by straight people," said Jay. "As a kid, the word 'gay' sounded like a bad, dirty word. Dirtier than swear words. It was a word used as an insult. It was a joke. Abnormal. Being gay was worse than death it seemed. So, when my twenties came along, and I started dating guys for the first time, it felt unsanitary. The whole gay culture felt embarrassing to be a part of. I saw myself as normal, and them as the abnormal ones. I was so used to living in a plain world that once I stepped into one bursting with color, it felt scary. But over time, I realized there's nothing wrong with any of this. I don't have to bury myself into some deep dark hole to satisfy another person's expectations of me." Jay looked at Salvador, his warm brown eyes staring back at him. "It's because of you I no longer care what people think of me."

Salvador smiled, his face awash with joy. "Well, since we're being Honest Johns right now, do you want to hear a story?"

"Are we talking fiction here?" asked Jay.

Salvador slid down onto the floor next to him. He gazed at the blank computer screen ahead of him. "There were these two boys in high school, some odd years ago. They were two angry boys who liked to fuck shit up. All the other kids stayed away from them in fear that these boys might want to beat them up just for simply existing, or for getting in their way. Lots of the other kids in school had part-time jobs that they'd go to after class and on the weekends. Totally normal thing to do when you're a teenager. But these two boys didn't want to do that. They thought having a job was lame. They thought, hey, why not sell drugs instead? They got the idea to break into a pharmacy in town and steal a bunch of opiates, narcotics and other controlled drugs–literally thousands of pills. To do this, what they did was cut a hole in the drywall of the vacant office space next to the pharmacy to get past the cameras. When they were finished breaking into the pharmacy, they patched the wall up. They weren't caught. The boys were making thousands of dollars within days by driving out to other cities and towns to sell what they had stockpiled.

"Now, there was a third boy... We'll call him Sal. One day at school, Sal walked in on the two boys selling some of their stash to another student in the boys' bathroom. They thought Sal was looking to score, but Sal, on the spot, took the opportunity to ask if he could join in on what they were doing so he could make some money too. You see, Sal's parents would fight late into the night. It was mostly about money troubles, which led to threats of divorce. Wouldn't it be great if Sal could actually help alleviate his parents' money problems fast, before they could divorce? Next thing you know, Sal started hanging out with the two boys regularly. They threatened him, telling him if he ever snitched on them, they'd kill him. Sal gave them a spare key to his house as collateral, allowing them to come inside whenever they wanted, to do whatever they wanted, if he should ever betray them in any way. So, they took him on a run with them, and again, they pulled it off without issue. When it came to selling and negotiating with people, Sal was really good at it–something the other two boys had not expected, but which they used to their advantage.

"At some point, though, a rumour started going around school that Sal was a little queer. During gym class one day, he was caught looking at a boy when he was undressing in the change room. The two angry boys confronted Sal about this rumour, but Sal denied it. They weren't sure if they wanted him around them anymore, and they called him a dirty little fag boy, saying they'd shove a baseball bat up his ass if it was true. They had his house key still, so they'd taunt him with it, acting like they owned him, which they did. Before the night of the next pharmacy run, Sal secretly left a note for the pharmacist, telling him what was going to happen on the precise day and time. When the three of them got inside the pharmacy on the night of the break-in, the man was waiting for them. The two boys weren't expecting the man to be there, so they didn't have time to pull out their weapons. The man shot them both. Sal had already fled before the bullets started flying, having quietly walked away. The next day, Sal learned that one of the boys had died from gunshot wounds. The other was in the hospital, but later died from his injuries."

Salvador's eyes were focused on the blank computer monitor, a rerun of that night playing out on the screen in his mind. "Sal would wake up in the middle of the night with screams in his head because of the nightmares he now had to live with. The two boys would continue torturing him, turning his dreams into prisons, their cackling so wicked. They'd point a gun to his head and hold him hostage so they could claim their revenge each and every night, making sure Sal never forgot what he had done to them.

Salvador scrunched up his face, his eyes turning red from the tears that were building along his eyelids. "After they were both dead, Sal went and got the rest of the pills that were still stashed away in an unused bird feeder at one of the boy's grandparents' house. He sold everything that was left, then gave a good chunk of the money to his mom and dad, telling them he had won the money from a scratch card. Money was all Sal wanted from that day forward. Money was a thrill for him, and the power it provided was something he constantly desired. When he's not working, or when he has a day off, he thinks of it as a wasted opportunity to be making more money somehow." Salvador looked down at his right hand that was secure in Jay's palm. "The rest of the drug money went into a separate bank account, and Sal told himself that it was only to be used on people who make him happy." He looked into Jay's eyes. "People who bring joy into his life."

Jay rubbed his thumb along Salvador's hand. "The jacket you bought for me?"

"That was the last of it," he said.

Jay leaned over and kissed him on the cheek.

"Has your impression of me changed?" asked Salvador.

Jay's eyes trailed downward. "Yes," he said. "My respect for you has grown so much. I'm glad you made it out of that situation, and you're here talking to me. I'm glad you're safe now."

Salvador smiled at him.

Jay leaned his head back against the side of the bed and looked at him, placing his hand on Salvador's arm. "When you saw me that day, sitting by myself, with my entire world falling apart around me... What did you really see in me?" Jay felt his tears run down his cheeks and drip onto his chest. "Why do you want to be with me?"

Salvador looked Jay's face over, every fine line. "I saw a sad Blue Jay who needed a friend. Because of you, I'm finally free. My heart is beating wildly, and my dreams are now filled with the man sitting beside me. There are no more demons to haunt my dreams, because he chased them all away."

Jay smiled, falling deeper and deeper into a burning love that kept consuming him with each passing moment. "Can you keep a secret? I'd like to share something really special with you."

Salvador kissed him on the forehead. "Yes."

Jay looked him in the eyes. "Can you keep a secret?" he asked again, seriously.

Salvador met his gaze. "Yes, Blue Jay."

42

Martin walked into Marc's two-story house, disheveled and still fuming over what had happened at Set earlier in the evening. Marc's wife, Kendra, with Marc's collaboration, had gone for a nautical and rustic design aesthetic for their home that had warm tones, soft lighting and locally crafted wood furniture. She was in the kitchen doing dishes as May, their six-month-old daughter, was in her high chair with a puréed peas-and-carrots explosion all over her bib and face. Martin stared at the creature. Wide, mad eyes. Saliva dribbling from its slippery wet mouth. He knew, just from those first few seconds, that a baby wasn't something he truly wanted. Carly flashed into his mind, and the tragedy of his situation thickened. This was a life he had slowly built for himself, day by day.

"Hi, honey!" said Kendra when she saw her husband with Martin by his side. "You're back early. How was dinner?" She wiped her hands on a cloth and went over to hug them both. In her high chair, May began wailing the deafening shriek of a banshee from the black lagoon the moment her mom left the kitchen. Kendra was a good match for Marc, Martin realized. They were both average in appearance, so plain and unremarkable. Marc had worn contacts ever since he was a teenager, but it appeared he had now opted for regular use of his glasses. They were kind of adorable, like stuffed animals you wanted to squeeze.

"Dinner was cut short," said Marc. "Carly had a social media emergency to attend to, so we thought we'd come back here and I'd show Martin the basement."

"Wonderful," said Kendra, smiling as she headed back into the kitchen to attend to the drooling mess. "Nice to see you, Martin!"

Martin lifted his hand up as a sign of acknowledgement, then followed Marc down into the dark man cave. Marc flicked on the lights, and it was just how Martin expected it would be. Right smack in the middle was the pool table, racked up perfectly for a new game to be played. There was a nautical bar to the right, with pendant lights hanging over the bar top and swivel stools. The whole space had hardwood flooring except for the carpeted sitting area, where a big screen television was mounted on the wall in front of a leather sofa and two recliners. The walls were painted grey and had various memorabilia, framed movie and sports posters, Funko Pops and NECA action figures mixed in. Beside the stairs was a sign on the wall that listed the man cave rules, such as *My Cave My Rules* and *Hydrate with Beer*. Underneath was a turntable, floor speakers and a collection of vinyl records. Seemingly missing from the space was the obvious gaming and podcast equipment that Martin thought he'd see.

"Nice," he said, looking around. "Where are the games?"

"Like, video games?" asked Marc. "They're in storage. They haven't been a big part of my life lately."

"The podcast is more important anyway," said Martin as he took a seat on one of the bar stools.

Marc received a text message. "Kendra wants a picture with you," he said with a smile.

"I'm literally a meme," said Martin, his eyes rolling up to the ceiling.

"They're kind of funny," replied Marc. He walked around the bar and opened the mini fridge, grabbing a craft beer for Martin and pouring it into a tall beer glass. "So, any kids in your future?"

"Uh..." started Martin.

Marc looked at him, waiting for an actual response.

"It's been discussed," he finished.

"Do you want kids?" asked Marc. He paused after asking the question. "Sorry, that was rude of me to ask."

"Come on," said Martin, tilting his head at him. "I've listened to your podcast before. That's what you do, man. You always ask the probing questions."

"So, what's the answer, then?"

Martin took his beer from Marc. "Why did you treat me the way you did after we broke up?"

Marc fixed himself a beer as well. "That's something I've regretted. Looking back, my ego got the best of me. Don't get me wrong, my ego is still big. That's something I'll admit. But to be honest, Martin..." Marc sighed. "I used to think I was better than you."

Martin looked down, a part of him already knowing that. It just hurt to actually hear it from him. "You were," he agreed. "The viewers liked you more. You were more... You had that thing. You know what I'm talking about?"

"The *it* factor," said Marc.

"Yeah, that's the one. It wasn't until afterward when I started doing content on my own that I realized that I didn't have *it*. Most of my success had been thanks to you, and when you were no longer there, my luck dried up."

"You do have *it*, though," said Marc, leaning forward. "You've always had *it*. What you're missing is confidence. What's missing is you not being yourself; not being who you really are."

Martin looked down again and shifted in his seat. "It's like I'm up shit creek without a paddle… Unable to move or guide myself to shore." He started spinning his glass around on the bar top. "Be honest with me. Are you speaking to me right now because of the *Jumping Disco Man*?"

"I've been wanting to talk to you for a while now," said Marc. "This stupid moniker that was given to you, and seeing your mug everywhere online, it was like a constant reminder to me. All the signs pointed to this being the right time to reach out to you again." He took a seat next to Martin. "I'd like you to not only be a guest on my podcast, but if all goes well, I'd like you to be a regular. Perhaps, even, my partner again."

Martin scrunched up his face, surprised. "Why?" he asked.

"I'm tired of talking all the time," said Marc with a smirk. "For three hours straight, every weekday. Even with the guests, it's still a lot of me talking. Blah, blah, blah. It would be nice to have a second perspective. Someone to bounce off of and lighten the mood."

"It's not because I'm famous now?" he asked.

"No," said Marc. "I've been watching and hearing some of the interviews that you've been doing lately, and you seem like you have a lot to say. You're a funny guy. You seem like you'd be good at journalism, man."

"Please don't say I have a face for radio," said Martin, grinning, "or podcasting."

Marc chugged down a third of his beer. "I'm serious."

"I'm gay," blurted Martin.

Marc stopped in mid chug, the beer sitting in his throat for a moment. Martin was waiting for him to say something, his eyes shifting anxiously.

Marc swallowed and put his drink down. "Okay," was all he said, shrugging his shoulders.

"That's it?" asked Martin, looking him up and down. "Okay?"

He turned to his beer and chugged down the rest, wanting something heavier. "Did you know?"

Marc got up from his stool. "It's something I kind of assumed. I didn't think a whole lot about it, actually."

Martin watched him pour whiskey into a glass, like he had read his mind about wanting something stronger. "Is that assumption the reason why you distanced yourself from me?"

Marc dropped a couple ice cubes into the drink and handed it to him. He pushed his glasses back up when they slid down his nose. "We were friends for a long time. We grew up together, and because of that, we know a lot about one another. Even though you never came out to me back then, as a friend, it's just one of those things you pick up on over time."

"Answer my question," said Martin.

Marc scratched his neck as he looked down. "Back then, if you had decided to come out, I wouldn't have wanted people to think I was gay if they saw me hanging out with you." He dragged his eyes up to look at Martin. "I didn't want a gay friend."

Martin furrowed his brow, and his eyes drifted away as he fought back the sting of incoming tears.

"Listen, I don't give a shit about that anymore," said Marc desperately. "You are the only person on this planet who knows as much about me as I do. Even Kendra doesn't know everything that you know." He sat down next to Martin. "I've had gay people on my podcast, and the conversations we had led to some serious talks. We discussed things that really opened up my eyes. There was this one woman named Lindsay, who is transgender, and she talked about everything that she had gone through, as a man, and as a transgender woman. Then, when Mike Colvin came out on his stream last year, it got me thinking about how much I care about you. It wasn't right that I left you to die on that hill when our channel ended. It just took me a while to realize that."

Martin shook his head. "I regret getting married," he said. "Just over a month ago, a light bulb went off in my head. This is me, and there is no changing it."

"Are you going to tell Carly?" asked Marc.

Martin let out a sigh. "I can't do this for the next ten, twenty, thirty years. She wants to have a kid, and it scares me so fucking much that one day the kid is going to hate me for having lived a lie."

Marc put his hand on his shoulder. "I won't tell anyone," he said. "You have my word, okay? Even if you never say anything, and this is the last time you bring it up. It's your life, not mine."

Martin shoved his face into his palms and leaned forward in his stool.

"Do you feel better now that you've told someone?" asked Marc softly.

Martin nodded. "It feels good, man."

43

Shaun had offered Ben the truck that he and Patrick were sharing to help Ben move out of his aunt's place. Ben knew he wouldn't need anything bigger. He wasn't taking any of his bedroom furniture with him, just the possessions that were boxed up and ready to go. His television, which was secure in layers of bubble wrap, was the only thing he took that wouldn't fit inside a box. When everything was loaded onto the truck, there wasn't an inch of space left for anything more. Everything fit perfectly, like a jigsaw puzzle.

Shaun was sitting in the passenger seat with the door open and his feet dangling out as Iris came out of the house, hands on her hips and smiling.

"Look at that," she said, impressed. "You boys fit everything."

Ben looked at the truck, feeling a sense of pride wash over him. It was finally happening. He was leaving.

"Are you sure you got everything?" she asked, craning her head to get a better look in the bed of the truck. "You don't need any of the fold-out tables?"

"My roommates have everything already," said Ben.

"Well, if you change your mind, be sure to give me a call. Lots of the furniture will be donated once the house is sold." Iris glanced at the brown-haired boy waiting in the truck, browsing through his phone. "His name is Shaun, is it?"

"Yeah," said Ben, turning to look at him. At the mention of his name, Shaun glanced up from his phone and smiled, giving them a wave.

"What are the names of your roommates?" she asked Ben.

"Ed and Eddie" replied Ben, reaching into his front pocket and handing her a piece of paper. "This is the address. It's close to the college."

"Ed and Eddie..." repeated Iris, looking down at the paper. "Sounds like a comedy show."

"My work number is there too," said Ben, pointing at the number, "for whatever."

"Maybe I'll stop by your work and pick up some new fall shoes," she said, possibly joking, but Ben wasn't sure. "What's the name of the store?"

"City Shoes," he said.

"Well... That's very good," she said. "Being assistant manager of a store at nineteen is a great start. At your age, I worked in a bakery to help pay my way through culinary school and nursing school."

Ben looked at her, surprised. "You went to cooking school?"

"It didn't work out," she said regretfully.

Ben looked down, digging the tip of his shoe into the gravel. "Thank you," he said. "For everything you've done."

Iris smiled gently.

"You taught me a lot when we were doing the food truck," he told her.

Iris reached into her pocket and slid a folded piece of paper into his hand. "That was the plan," she said.

Ben opened up the paper and saw a check for ten thousand

dollars. His eyes widened in surprise as he stared at the dollar amount. "You sold the house?"

"Not yet," she said, "but soon. This is to help with the rent, food and school. Ultimately, though, you get to choose what to do with it. Take that trip to New York you've been talking so much about... Go see South Africa, maybe. There's also the trust money from your parents don't forget. Make sure to use it towards school, though, since that's what they would have wanted."

Ben looked at the check, completely blown away. It was the most money he had ever held in his hands.

"You were saying something about wanting to be in the arts," said Iris, "like acting. What about moving to Los Angeles?"

Ben looked at check for a moment longer, then tucked it away inside his wallet. "That's impossible," he said. "It's so expensive, and there's thousands of other kids like me trying to do the same thing. They're all more talented."

Iris shook her head at him. "If you're passionate about something, deeply, you don't think about who is better than you or say it's impossible. You just do it, get better, and believe that with time it will somehow work out like it was always meant to."

"What about your food truck?" he asked.

Iris shrugged. "Sometimes passion just isn't enough. That's the reality of it. The dream doesn't give up on you. You give up on the dream."

"So, I'll be a starving artist," said Ben, smiling and running his hand over his face at the mere thought.

"Whatever it is, at least you can say you tried." She rubbed his shoulder. "Your parents would have been proud of you. Finally, a young man."

Ben turned red. "I'm not a man yet," he said.

"Well, it'll be interesting to hear what the deciding factor was that made it so," said Iris. She reached behind her and picked up a sealed plastic container. When she handed it to him, Ben saw three cupcakes inside, each with a different colored frosting.

"Are you happy?" she asked.

Ben nodded, a hint of a smile revealing itself. "Yeah," he said.

Iris leaned in and hugged him one last time. "Well, go on!" she said cheerfully, flapping her hands at him. "I'm sure Shaun is bored to death."

Shaun looked up when he heard his name and smiled. Ben was halfway inside the truck when he jumped back out and jogged back to Iris. "Here's my house key."

Iris took the key from him and held it in her grasp tightly, the ridges of the metal digging into her hand. The engine started up as Ben jumped back into the passenger side, and Shaun put the truck into drive, leaving Iris in the front yard as they pulled away. When the truck reached the end of the street, it turned left and disappeared from view, the sound of the engine tapering off into the distance.

44

July 1987

It was close to midnight when Robert stopped on the sidewalk and scanned his surroundings. The tree obscured much of the building's left side at the corner of Goldenrod Boulevard and Langley Street. Cool Toppings Pizzeria was a popular favorite for teenagers looking for New York style pizza. Just one beautiful slice was a whole meal on its own. The smell of melted mozzarella and the satisfying crunch of their special buttered crust that burst with flavour brought foodies back time and time again. The building's weathered green copper side door was unremarkable. It was the door that Robert had been told to find by the mysterious drag queen at Rave last Saturday. Being only seventeen, he managed to get into the gay club with a fake I.D. that he got from a friend of a friend at school. It wasn't his preferred method of choice, but the urge to be around other gay boys was something he thought a lot about. He was your all-American teenager with dark brown hair and a fit body that suggested he was a jock. Basically, the type of boy a girl would bring home to Mom, who'd later remark to her daughter what a handsome young man he was. He wasn't out, at home or at school, mostly because of the gay cancer spreading across America for the past several years now. He didn't like to call the cancer by its name because it was uncomfortable to say, even in his head. It killed men who had sex with other men, and it terrified him.

Robert had a girlfriend named Meg. She was nice, but he felt bad for leading her on. His classmate Monica had been trying to match them up together ever since Meg confided in her that she liked Robert. Last month, Monica had told him to meet up with her and Meg outside her house. Meg stepped out of the house all dolled up, wearing a headband in her short brown hair and a pink jacket to go with her polka dot skirt: a pinup girl straight from the 1950s. He forced himself to be attracted to her, for he found himself being drawn to her personality, not her looks. They'd kiss, but it would always be a mercy kiss, to make her feel good and to keep things from becoming awkward between them. Then she'd get all giddy and smile, like he was the boy of her dreams. She'd call him every day at home, and if nothing else, her jokes were something that Robert looked forward to hearing. There was an offbeat and refreshing sense of humor to her that not many girls had. His mom would always ask him to invite her over for dinner, thinking this girl was quite possibly the one for him. He wanted to be her friend, not her boyfriend. But being with Meg was the only way to hide himself. He was concerned that if he did come out, he would forever be associated with the gay cancer, especially by his family.

When he went to Rave for the first time last weekend, it was exciting to see all the beautiful men. It was the embodiment of sex and lust and wanting something you couldn't normally have. He could feel that energy from them, especially when they rubbed their shoulders against him as they walked past. Robert was still a virgin, even with Meg.

His visit to Rave was a taste test for when he was finally ready to play around for real. Guys would hit on him, but still being in the closet, he simply didn't know how to react without looking awkward. It was a big enough risk even to be going there, but he hadn't seen any of his classmates or anyone he knew, so at least he didn't have to worry about his secret getting out at school. He felt like a bird locked inside its cage, watching all the other colorful birds flying freely around him in the club. It was sad to think that some of them were dying. He overheard one of them mentioning that two of his friends had died from the gay cancer just in the last couple of months, but it wouldn't stop him from being who he was.

When Robert paid for his rum and Coke, the bartender handed back his change with an extra ten-dollar bill. Robert flagged the man down and returned the bill, then took his drink. He was about to head for a free table when a drag queen standing next to the bar noticed the transaction between him and the bartender. She leaned down and whispered an address, a time and the random words *next Saturday*, *green door* and *pink flower* into his ear. *Don't tell anyone.* She then walked away into the shadows of the bar like a vapor.

Robert held on to this information for a few days, not quite knowing what to do with it. Several times after school he'd walk past Cool Toppings Pizzeria and see the green copper door on the side of the building facing Goldenrod Boulevard. He had no idea what it all meant. But tonight, he was finally going to find out as he stood before the door. Light traffic rolled down the boulevard as he reached for the door handle, and it opened without any resistance. He peered inside to find a narrow alcove that ended at a short ascending stairwell. Robert closed the door behind him and walked up the short flight of steps, where he came to another door at the top landing. Opening it, he entered a small room that looked like a manager's office. The walls were a hideous brown with water stains at the corners of the ceiling, and there was nothing remotely interesting about the wooden desk, metal chairs and office junk. Filing cabinets, folders and associated nonsense–it reminded Robert of his principal's office. There were two other doors, one across from the one he just came from and one to his right. Based on what he knew of the building layout, he figured that the door to his right led into the pizzeria, which was now closed for the night.

When he thought about turning around to leave, the door across from him opened and a man stepped into the room. Robert pegged him to be in his forties or fifties, someone who looked as though they had stepped out of an old movie that his grandma would have watched. His hair was jet black, and he had a mustache. Above all else, though, his green eyes were striking, almost scary. He stared at Robert as though he was an intruder coming to rob the place. "We're closed to the public."

Robert licked his upper lip nervously. "Someone at Rave gave me instructions to come here," he said.

The man stared at him like he was an idiot.

"Pink flower?" he offered instead.

The man stared at him a moment longer, then walked over to a wall comprised of several cubby holes next to the door that Robert had just come through. Most of the cubbies were filled with business documents and office supplies that were of no interest to most people. The man bent down to the bottom left cubby hole and reached inside. There was a subtle *click*, and he pulled the entire unit away from the wall as though it was connected to one large hinge. Robert saw a descending spiral stairway that was revealed to him, and tealights in glass covers on each of the stone steps.

Robert tentatively eased his way forward and looked down the ominous stairway, wondering if it led down into Dracula's crypt.

Before he could take his first step down, the man placed his hand on Robert's shoulder. "Do not tell anyone," he said gravely, his green eyes pinning him down. "This place doesn't exist. Understood?"

Robert nodded his head emphatically, feeling like this wasn't a man he should cross. "What's down there?" he asked.

The man gestured for him to go down to see for himself. Robert wasn't sure if he'd go at first, but the temptation was far too great. He walked down the steps at a steady pace until he reached a wooden door at the bottom landing. When he pushed the door open, the sound of a saxophone was the first thing to hit him, then chatter and laughter. There must have been thirty people in a room that was easily the same size as Rave. There was nothing modern about it. Vintage, classical and elegant, it was like something he would expect to see in an old movie. There were two levels divided by a gold railing: the main tier where he stood, and the lower tier where a short flight of steps led down to a dancing and seating area in front of a small stage that had its red velvet curtains parted. Much of the flooring was covered in red carpeting throughout, and the maroon leather chairs and rounded tables set in front of the stage were ideal for leisure and conversation while the music serenaded one's ears. The central dance floor was tiled parquet, polished to a shine. Hanging from the decorative white plaster of the ceiling was a dazzling gem of a chandelier.

Most everyone looked in his direction, curious: they were all men. Most of them appeared to be in their twenties and thirties. If it wasn't for their modern outfits, Robert would have thought he'd stepped through a time machine into the past. There was a saxophone player on the main stage, giving musical life to the space with a melody that lent the room a classy aura. Next to the man on stage was a gilded grand piano of radiant gold that was carved with fine artistry, and unlike anything Robert had seen before. It was a focal point of the room, as was the chandelier. As Robert looked around, his eyes were always drawn back to those two things. The piano was the most beautiful thing he had ever seen.

Not daring to go down to the lower level where most of the men congregated, he instead walked over to the bar on his left where he saw the drag queen from Rave schmoozing around. She wore all-blue sequins, including her hat, and a black wig cut in a bob. Her makeup was full glam with blue glitter sparkles. She was black, and looked to be in her late twenties, her loud voice full of sass, charm and mischief. When Robert sat down at the bar alone, and not knowing anyone at the party, the queen graced him with her presence, noticing his need for company.

"You made it!" she nearly shouted, bending down to hug him.

Robert had never spoken to a drag queen before. It was a bit shocking at first. "What is this place?" he asked.

"It's a bar," she said in a sarcastic tone. She backtracked when Robert responded with an expressionless, wondering face. It was like he had been hit with a taser and didn't know where he was or what he was looking at. "Sorry, I'm a smartass," she said. "Yes, it's a bar, but... It's a show! It's a special club."

Robert raised his eyebrows, his eyes checking out the surroundings, thinking there was something more to the place than what she was telling him.

She picked up on his concern immediately. "Don't worry. This isn't a drug ring or sex murder cult," she said, laughing. "You are safe here. It's a safe space to dance and laugh and talk with cute guys. Here, have a drink!"

Robert was thankful she cleared that up, and was beginning to feel the pressure leave him. He watched the bartender make the drink that the queen had ordered for him, and the man slid it towards him like the bar top was made of ice.

"You look like a boy who drinks these things," she said, looking into the red concoction of the Alabama Slammer.

"I've only ever had alcohol when it's mixed with soda," confessed Robert. "It's just to get drunk, anyway."

"You see, I was just like you," she said, pointing at him. "Vodka cranberry, orange juice and vodka. Don't get me started on tequila and grapefruit juice. I'm Eleanor, by the way."

"I'm Robert," he said, waving.

"If I had known you were still in high school, there is no way I would've hooked you up with this place," she said.

Robert scoffed and reached into his pocket. "I'm not in high school. Here's my I.D."

"Honey," she said, putting her hands together. "What year were you born?"

"1966. I'm 21."

Eleanor gave him a dubious look, then bowed down to him. "So let it be written, so let it be done. By the way, you can't tell anyone about this place."

"That's what the man with the mustache upstairs told me," he said. "What's this place called, if I'm allowed to know?"

"This is the one and only Roger's," she exclaimed, spreading her arms out.

"If I'm not allowed to tell anyone about it, why can you?"

"Well," she said, rolling her eyes, "technically you can. What we mean when we say that is you can only share your knowledge of this place with people who are like you and me. Like, gay people. They have to be trustworthy too, not just any cute guy you stumble across. When they come here for the first time, they get it. This place... It's a really special one. It's more than just a bar." She pointed to the nearby wall of framed photographs. "Take a look," she said, leaving him to continue being a social butterfly.

Robert turned and briefly checked out the framed photos

displayed in several rows on the wall. Losing interest immediately, he turned his attention back to the stage, where a boy sat at the gilded grand piano, about to play some music. The lights above the stage shone down on his blond hair. Robert could only see the side of his face from his vantage point. The gold railing along the edge of the main floor partially obstructed his view, but he could tell the boy at the piano was cute, and close to his age from the looks of it.

As the chatter around the bar carried on, the boy started playing, and the voices slowly died away as music filled the air. The ambiance of the room shifted, and Robert almost forgot about everyone else around him. Life sprang from the instrument like a songbird awakening in spring. The melody reminded Robert of a cozy winter evening in Moscow. It conjured an image of a blazing fireplace that illuminated a living room while snow drifted past the window and settled on the ledge outside. It was like someone had wrapped a warm blanket around him and rested their head upon his chest. Everything felt right in the world, like he was as safe as could be. The song was somehow cold and warm at the same time, sad and happy.

Robert sat on his bar stool, empty glass in hand, and listened to the full four minutes in wonder. The composition concluded to the sound of unanimous applause. Not a single person refrained from clapping their appreciation, including Robert. The pianist looked out over the audience with a subtle smile. Robert caught the boy's gaze when he turned his attention towards the bar, and Robert felt a spark go through his body when they met each other's eyes, brown eyes meeting blue eyes. Turning back to the piano, the boy began another song, this one more uptempo and wild, like something Elton John would play.

"Need a top-up there?"

Robert pulled his attention away from the boy and turned to the bartender. "Sure," he said, handing him his empty glass.

"How about something different this time?" he asked.

Robert looked down at his glass. "Sure."

The bartender started mixing him a drink. The man seemed kind, like one of those men who could have a conversation with anyone. His hair was light brown, and the subtle creases on his face and overall demeanor suggested he was in his thirties.

"What's your favorite drink?"

"Just whatever," said Robert. "Vodka cranberry, maybe."

The man slid Robert's drink across the bar top. "It's also known as Cape Cod. Squeeze a bit of lime juice in, some frozen cranberries, and you're on easy street."

Robert took the drink and tossed back a mouthful. "I'm not really into all those fancy cocktails and ingredients."

The man nodded. "Understandable. My name is Liam."

"I'm Robert." As he downed half his drink, he looked over at the stage again just as the pianist finished the second composition. For a second time, applause roared through the room, and Robert quickly put his drink down to join in. The boy surveyed the room once more, taking in the applause. He and Robert locked eyes again, and he could have sworn the boy's stare lingered a few seconds longer this time.

Liam leaned over the bar top. "You should go say hi to him. He only plays two songs, but he does come back every Saturday to play something new."

Robert swallowed the rest of his drink and rubbed his hands on his jeans, anxiety taking him over. "What's his name?"

"Hm... It's a mystery to me," said Liam, giving way to a smirk. "Why don't you go and ask him?"

Robert ran his tongue over his top lip, still tasting the cranberry and lime. He got up from the bar stool, but stayed rooted where he was as the saxophone player started up again. He saw the boy exit the stage behind the curtain. Robert looked down at the dance floor, where two men swayed from side to side, embracing one another. It was something Robert had never before seen in a public space other than Rave. He wondered if they had just met, or if they were lovers… He had never really spoken to anyone he already knew was gay. At least, he was assuming the pianist was gay, given where they were and how the boy made eye contact with him. Sometimes, when Robert was nervous to do something, he would count to five, then just do whatever it was he was contemplating. No hesitation.

He parted from the bar and made his way down to the lower level and zig-zagged his way through the dance floor of men, eyes following him. This was something he wanted to do. He wanted to be here. He went up the side steps of the stage and around the corner to the back. It was a narrow and cramped space. The floorboards were ancient and had probably never been redone from when they were first installed, which could have been a very long time ago. There were some random hooks and a few shelves on the wall where a cocktail glass was placed for easy access. He found the boy kneeling down next to a backpack and rummaging around inside, pulling out binders and paperwork and a couple of spare shirts. Eleanor was there, standing along the wall, flipping through a stage pamphlet and laughing at what she was reading. The second Robert entered, she looked up at him, but the boy took a few extra seconds to register his presence. When he finally did look up, his blue eyes were like bright summer ponds.

When neither said anything, Robert felt anxious again, but he knew he had to say something to break the silence. “Hi,” he said. “I just wanted to say how great you were just now.”

Eleanor put the pamphlet down and stepped away from the wall. “Going for a smoke.”

The boy smiled as Eleanor left through the side curtain, leaving the two of them alone. His button-down shirt was a light blue that matched his eyes.

"I don't think I've seen you here before," said the boy as he put his binders and clothes back into the backpack and zipped it up. "There's usually a couple new faces here from time to time."

"How long have you been coming here?" asked Robert.

The boy stood up. "Just a couple months."

"How did you find out about it?"

"This guy named Wayne heard me playing the piano in the park one day and told me about this place."

"How did he know you were gay, though?"

"Wayne?" asked the boy. "He kind of just... asked me."

"Just point blank?" asked Robert, surprised.

"Maybe he had a hunch."

"Guys usually lie when someone asks them."

"I'm out," said the boy. "I've been out since last year. Wayne loved my music and said he knew a place that was looking for a new musician–in particular, a pianist. It all seemed really weird, but since the place he told me to go to was at the pizzeria, it seemed okay. I'm glad I didn't chicken out."

The boy stared at Robert, and they endured another empty silence that spanned days and days it seemed.

Robert went for it and introduced himself. "I'm Robert," he said.

The boy lifted the strap of his backpack over his shoulder. "I'm Tristan."

Another silence.

Why me? thought Robert. Why was he always the one having to make the first move and fill the silence with talk? "Someone told me that those are original songs that you compose."

"Yeah," said Tristan, his smile so cute and handsome at the same time.

"You must love music, then," guessed Robert.

"Music is everything to me," replied Tristan. "My dream is to be a professional pianist and to play all over the world. I'd love to compose movie soundtracks one day."

"That's so cool," said Robert, his voice breaking for some embarrassing reason. "I've never seen you at my high school, though. Which one do you go to?"

Tristan sighed. "It's a private school," he said. "I don't like telling people that because they usually get the wrong impression of me."

"Oh," said Robert. He swallowed, looking down at the floor, trying to conjure up more talk. "Well, I like to sing."

Tristan smiled and leaned to the side with one hand on his backpack strap. "Like, in your spare time or at school?"

"Like, in the shower," confessed Robert.

"There's great acoustics in the shower," said Tristan. "I'll sometimes sing when I'm home alone."

"Maybe you can come hear me in the shower one day," said Robert, horrified at what he had just blurted out. He wanted to turn around and leave, which he started to do by slowly walking backwards, little by little. "Well, anyway… I won't keep you or anything."

"I'll be here again next Saturday," said Tristan, looking Robert up and down and walking towards him. "If they still want me."

"I'd want you," said Robert, feeling his face heat up like a stove.

Tristan stopped where he was. "Would you like to hang out before next weekend?"

Robert stopped walking backwards and nodded aggressively.

"Do you want my number?"

"Uh, sure," he said.

Tristan reached into his backpack and wrote down his home phone number on a piece of spare paper from his binder. He handed it to Robert.

"I'd give you mine too..." said Robert as he took the paper, "but..."

"It's okay," Tristan assured him. "If you like, we can meet somewhere... on Tuesday, maybe?" He took the paper back out of Robert's hand. "Can I use your back to write down my address?"

Robert turned around to let Tristan place the piece of paper on the top part of his back. He could feel the tips of Tristan's fingers pressed down against his shirt, just below the back of his neck, as he held the paper down in place to write. Robert turned back around and looked into his blue eyes, taking the paper from him again.

"I'll meet you outside my house," said Tristan. "Just wait by the sidewalk, and I'll look out my window to see if you're there. Whenever a boy comes over my parents get annoying, so we won't deal with that. We'll just go somewhere else."

"Okay," said Robert, feeling weightless. He didn't want to leave. He wanted to go with him right now, but couldn't bring himself to say it.

Tristan smiled. "I'd like to stay longer to hang out, but my mom and dad are expecting me home soon. I've already pissed them off by staying out really late last week... and the week before that."

"That's fine," said Robert reassuringly as he prepared to exit the back of the stage. "See you next week, Tristan."

45

Sarim's chest heaved at the end of the routine, having worked on the complex and demanding choreography for the last few hours. He thrived on the adrenaline. He savoured the sweat that poured off his body after a long session of high-energy dance. It lifted him to a cathartic state that he revelled in for hours on end.

Trish, the lead choreographer, urged everyone to take a ten-minute hydration break. Sabrina's Venus Valley concert night edged closer. When the concert downtown concluded, the tour would leave North America and return to Europe for its next leg. Sarim only had a few days left to spend with Robbie, and the fact that he'd be leaving again left him deeply saddened. That, plus the stress he felt within their relationship was doubling. With every day that passed, it was like he was being squeezed in a vice that was tightening around him, hurting him emotionally.

He picked up his phone, hoping to see a response from Robbie, but there was still no answer. Robbie was taking longer to reply to his messages, sometimes as long as a full day, which was never the case before. Robbie was always quick to respond to him.

"Hey, how's it going?"

Sarim looked up and saw Trish coming towards him, a wet towel around her neck and her face glistening under the lights. He shook his head, unable to form the words for how he was feeling. He placed his phone back down and dragged his hands over his face, trying to hide his growing panic while multiple scenarios ran through his head and twisted his nerves.

"What's going on?" asked Trish as she stretched her arms and hip to the side.

"It's..." started Sarim, his hand still covering one side of his face. He pulled his hand away and felt the sweat residue on his palm and fingers. "My mind is all over the place right now."

"I need you here, man," she said. "Like, mentally here. You have to shut everything else out and focus." Her face softened when she noticed Sarim's intensely worried expression. "Is it serious?"

Sarim nodded, his eyes tearing up. The more he thought about it, the more he felt himself breaking down.

"Sit down," said Trish as she motioned towards a chair. She put her hands on his shoulders as he sat, his tears merging with the sweat on his skin like one big oily mess. She knelt down in front of him, looking into his face. "Would you like to tell me?"

"I think he might be cheating," said Sarim right away, wanting to finally say it out loud to someone, anyone. "That, or he wants to break up. I've been getting these signs that just randomly started popping up... Something isn't right."

"You don't know that for sure," said Trish. "Just take a deep breath. Relax."

Sarim looked down at his hands as he rubbed them along his knees. "He's been gone from his house more than usual this week. We don't really talk about it, but when he does come home, he feels so distant when we're lying together." Sarim was trying his hardest not to sob in front of the other dancers, but he felt his control slipping. "There's been something on his mind for a while now... I really love him, Trish. I don't know what I did wrong."

Trish kept rubbing his shoulders. "Take an extra five minutes," she said. "We'll get through this, okay?"

Sarim nodded and wiped his hands on his clothes. "I know," he said. "Let's do this. I'll be fine."

Trish gave him a comforting smile, something he was glad for in that moment. "Let's talk about it after," she said, getting up.

When she walked away, Sarim reread the last message he had sent Robbie nine hours ago.

I'm at practice. Want to grab dinner after? :)

Just looking at it made his eyes tear up again. Instead, he aggressively forced the tears away by throwing his phone down and getting up to stretch like it was the last time he would ever dance again. He was now mentally preparing for what he expected to come in the following days. Before leaving Venus Valley, he'd make up his mind as to whether he'd continue living here. Sarim couldn't live in a city where he thought he had found true love, then had it crushed and ripped away from him.

46

Martin had been watching porn on his office computer for the last two hours. The white wine he'd found in the fridge helped escalate his desire for constant sexual satisfaction. Over the past week, he'd been watching his social media numbers continue to climb, as expected. They were over triple what they were just a week ago, and the larger audience took him back to his days of creating content with Marc. He wanted to interact with his fans, but his engagement with social media was non-existent because of the sheer anxiety he felt. He should have been taking advantage of this moment, milking it for all it was worth, and growing his ridiculous brand even further. Carly was sending him emails from businesses wanting to work with him, but he ignored most of them, and he knew it was pissing her off. Even the clothing brand that made the iridescent blazer he had worn wanted to collaborate with him, which, admittedly, he knew was pretty big.

For now, though, his attention was on the copious amounts of porn on his browser, distracting him from what was happening around him, which was becoming increasingly more unbearable as the days progressed.

His phone started to vibrate next to him and he looked down to see Zeus' number. The guy had messaged him a few days ago asking him to come down to an event that Owen was throwing at Larchdale Castle for some of his friends and business acquaintances. If Martin stood to gain from this transaction with Owen, he was all for it, albeit apprehensive at the same time. The moderate fame that came with being a successful video game content creator, and even as a low-key streamer, was something Martin adored because it was recognition for something that brought him happiness. In that spotlight, he wasn't considered a fool or attention seeker. He was a cool content creator, a guy you could see yourself hanging out with. Now, he was a dancing monkey for people to get clicks for their blogs and videos, to make money off his momentary lapse in judgement. How could he possibly be taken seriously now?

Carly would have suggested that he go to Owen's social orgy so he could use it to his advantage. But Martin wanted to speak with Owen as Martin the content creator, the online personality, the streamer. The cool guy. Not the *Jumping Disco Idiot*. His recent moniker was associated with an ideal that was frat house, moronic, fame-seeking debauchery. Martin was certain that a lot of the people who were now following him were only doing so because they wanted to see if he'd perform another viral stunt for them, not for his real content. Zeus had been a real fan of his for several years and knew him as what Martin wished to be portrayed as, before the *Jumping Disco Man*. Looking back, Martin knew he hadn't been perfect in some of the things he had said and done in his early content days, and the waiter who served him a piss cocktail the other night was proof of that. Even now he was still a work in progress.

"Hey," Martin drawled when he answered Zeus' call and muted the porn. "How's it been?"

"Great, man!" said Zeus, his voice full of life. "So, not to hound you or anything, but did you get my message from the other day?"

"Yeah," he said. "Sorry, I've been busy, as you can imagine. Forgot to reply."

"That's completely fair," said Zeus. "So, what do you think? Ready to come back to where it all began?"

Martin paused, suddenly turned off by what Zeus had just said. "Is that the tagline for the sequel?" he asked.

"It's just to talk," said Zeus in a reassuring tone. "You don't even have to stay long if you don't want to. Just come have a drink, a chat, and revel in the luxury of the castle."

Whether it was the alcohol or Zeus' charm, or both, it sounded like a tempting idea to Martin. No real pressure. "Definitely," he said. "When is it again?"

"Tonight," said Zeus. "At eight o'clock. It'll be a good time, dude!"

"For suuure," said Martin, dragging out the last syllable. Then, his phone suddenly beeped, indicating another call was coming through to him. "Zeus, sorry. I'm getting another call. I'll see you tonight." He disconnected from Zeus and let the incoming one come through. "Hi."

"Hi," said Carly, sounding rushed like she always did. "Where are you?"

"At home," said Martin, staring at the porn that was still on mute. It was POV porn, one of his favorite categories. The camera was focused on the guy's face as he looked up at you (presumably the aggressive top) the entire time, the hungry bottom's face enjoying every inch.

"Can you come down to the mall for a quick meet and greet?" she asked. "We can do some photo ops and do a video. People want to see you! It'll be great!"

Martin cringed. He was sure they weren't waiting with bated

breath. Within the last week, he'd been in two of her videos, five of her photo postings and seven of her live streams. She even used a smoothing filter on his skin and increased the size of their eyes and lips on both their faces for the photos, which made him look like a sadistic Ken doll. Several months ago, she posted a staged photo of them where they were posing and locking arms with each other on the couch. However, the photo she posted wasn't the original version. In the edited one, his biceps were enlarged. When he saw it for the first time, he didn't say anything, but it bothered him because she did it without telling him. He had never been bothered by how he looked, even in the *MarcVsMartin* videos from back in the day. But when Carly altered his images, he began thinking that perhaps he simply wasn't good enough, physically. Did he need to start working out more?

"I'm going to shave my face," he said, amused, wanting to hear her reaction.

"Don't you dare," she said dramatically. "People won't recognize you. You'll need to keep the beard indefinitely."

"What's indefinitely?"

"For the rest of your life," she said. "It's your money maker."

"Carly, people won't care if my face is smooth. It'll grow back."

"You'll look too babyish," she said.

Martin's face dropped. He ran his hand over his facial hair, letting the bristles echo into the speaker of the phone. "Have you always thought that?"

"I've always preferred guys with facial hair," she exclaimed. "So do all your fans! They're absolute hounds for it."

"Was this some study you conducted?" he asked in an overtly bored drawl.

"Why are you being so difficult?" she asked. "This is so big for you! You are literally throwing away what everyone our age wants. This is a lightning in a bottle moment! You blew off the last few interviews. The sponsorship with the Spaghetti Barn was a great one and now it's crickets from them. All you had to do was endorse their new cheesy garlic bread. Now that's easy money!"

"No one wants to eat spaghetti from a place that uses the word barn in its name," Martin explained. He brought his mouth right up to the speaker of his phone. "*Mooooooooo.*"

"That's not the point!" she finally yelled. "JUST DO IT! Actually, you know what you do? Reach into your wallet, pull out all your cash, and flush it down the toilet! Get the point?"

"*Mooooooooo.*"

"Martin! Are you drunk?"

"Maybe I'll do just that," he said, getting up from his office chair and taking his glass of wine with him. "In fact, I'll do it right now."

Carly scoffed as Martin strolled into the bedroom, grabbed his wallet from his nightstand and withdrew a couple hundred dollars. He flipped his phone to a video chat so they could now see each other's faces and went into the bathroom.

"Martin, you're–"

He dropped the cash into the toilet and flushed it, zooming in on it as it swirled around and around and out of sight.

"I've tried my very hardest to help you with this," she said. "Why aren't you taking any of this seriously?"

"Because this isn't me!" he shouted into the speaker. "I'm a joke!"

"It's fame and money!" she retorted. "How many people would kill for a chance like this?! I'd be so much further along if all of this had happened to me."

Martin slammed the toilet seat down, making it crack. "During all this time, did you ever consider asking how all of this made me feel?"

"Okay, how does it make you feel, then?" she asked. "Sad and mortified that millions of people know who you are? There are businesses eager to offer you tons of money to do easy, dumb shit. What happened at dinner the other night was an isolated incident, if that's your concern. No one gives a shit about the comments you made when you were seventeen except for, like, a handful of people. If it becomes a problem down the line, you'll apologize like a good little boy. You need to build a thicker skin and not let every random hater get to you!"

"Easier said than done," said Martin.

There was a pause on Carly's end. "Baby, this could help our lives so much. You're fucking it up for us!"

"It's already fucked up," he said quietly. "We're fucked up."

Martin promptly disconnected from the call, lifted up the toilet lid and dropped the phone into the bowl. Then, having second thoughts, he fished it out and started slamming it against the bathroom counter instead. When it wasn't breaking to his satisfaction, he removed the case, then continued bashing it again and again until bits of glass and debris flew every which way. Screaming, he gathered up all the pieces, dumped them into the toilet bowl and knocked the seat back down.

He took his wine glass, wandered into the bedroom closet and started sifting through his clothes. When he found what he was looking for, he took the iridescent purple blazer off its hanger and laid it out on the bed.

"Fuck you," he said to it. He downed the rest of his drink and started getting ready for the night ahead.

47

Robbie disconnected from the weekly conference call; one full hour of showmanship on his part, since Calvin had once again passed the reins on to him so he could lead the team in the executive's stead. However, Robbie's attention kept drifting back to the speakeasy, and then a terrible, aching feeling would wash over him. He'd think about Sarim, and his sadness would escalate to the point where he couldn't concentrate on his work at all. He'd gone back to the speakeasy by himself after Jay tagged along with him the first time. It was crushing to see such an important place fall to ruin, lying in its own waste, unloved and cast in a blanket of shadow below the earth. It was like finding a toy from your youth that you hadn't seen or touched in decades. Upon first glance, the nostalgia hits you hard. You might smile at the memories that cling to it like a fingerprint, but it doesn't evoke the same joy as it once did. So, you either lock the toy up again for several more years, or hold on to it and revel in the bygone life that you will never experience again. Or, you throw it away.

There had been a notable absence from today's conference call. It was never acceptable to miss one unless you were mutilated, dying or dead, according to Calvin. Robbie looked at his phone and the message from Calvin that simply said *ask him why*.

Robbie looked through the glass wall of his office and sighed as he remained seated at his desk. He wanted to get this over with, so he got up and left his sanctuary of glass for the buzzing beehive of colleagues. Mixed reactions from his coworkers followed him as he passed offices and cubicles. Some smiled, some greeted him; others were stoic, pissed off or uncertain as to how to be around him, given his obvious promotion looming ever closer.

Mary swooped in like an unwelcome hemorrhoid and started walking alongside him, shoulder to shoulder, matching every step he took. "How are you?" she asked.

He side-eyed her. "Fine," he said. "Once again, Mary, good job with your region. Record performances across the board time and time again. Brilliant."

"Flippant, are we?" she queried.

Robbie stopped walking. "What do you think of Johnson?"

"Nothing really," she said, her eyes widening. "He's always just there, in the background. His stores are never the lowest or the highest in performance metrics. I've rarely heard praise for him from Calvin or anyone because he's always so average. He wasn't on the call today, either. Is he dying or something?" She turned and saw Johnson typing away on his computer, his face pale and vacant. "That's all he ever does," she said in a disturbed voice. She lifted her hands to chest level and mime-typed in the air with a goofy look on her face. "Sometimes he doesn't even blink when he's at it, and it's fucking creepy. So far, you've been the only non-creepy gay guy working here out of you, him and..." she shivered dramatically and hunched her shoulders, "*CorporateDaddyXL*." She gagged and stuck her tongue out like a thirsty camel. "Anyway, I'll leave you to it."

When she walked away, Robbie stood where he was a moment longer, then went and knocked on Johnson's door.

"Hi," said Johnson from inside. He stopped typing and looked up from his screen when Robbie came in.

"How was your weekend?" asked Robbie casually, closing the door behind him.

"Why are you invading my space?" countered Johnson.

Robbie scrunched up his face. "Yeah, we work together."

"You have never asked me how my weekend was in all the years we've worked together," replied Johnson in a sluggish, monotone voice. "Get out."

Robbie stepped forward and stood in front of the desk, his eyes trailing around the shelves on the walls and the top of his desk. People usually kept things in their offices that reflected their tastes and personal lives in some way. Johnson had nothing.

"Why weren't you on today's call?"

"Do you enjoy being his dog?" asked Johnson, emotionless. "Licking his ass."

"Uh, it's training," stated Robbie. "We all know what's coming. Your performance these last couple of quarters has been waning."

Johnson waited, knowing there was something else Robbie wanted to say to him.

"I've had my own concern for you too," finished Robbie.

Johnson stared at him, then looked blankly back at his screen, not responding.

Robbie stood up tall and folded his arms. "Johnson, it's getting fucking obvious now."

Johnson's muscles started to tense up, and he clenched his jaw. "Well, say it then."

Robbie rubbed his nose.

Johnson sneered. "Well, you got me... But you're guilty too.

Calvin as well. You've both probably done lines off each other's dicks."

Robbie ignored the desperate jab. "I'm not talking about once in a while for social use," he said. "I'm not talking about going to a party one weekend and loosening up. I'm talking about excessive and obsessive use. You're high right now."

Johnson shook his head in disappointment. "Thanks, Liam."

Robbie raised his eyebrows. "No one told me," he said. "It's just obvious. It's affecting your performance."

"But Liam told you," demanded Johnson. "You guys talk! He told you!"

"Stop yelling," said Robbie. "He's really concerned for you. You can't blame him for that... and I'm concerned for you too."

"You are the fakest dick-riding piece of shit," blurted Johnson. "Since when did you ever give two fucks about me, Robbie? This is the first time you've ever come to see me in my office. This is the longest you've spent talking to me."

"That doesn't mean I've never cared about you, Johnson," said Robbie sympathetically. "I'm really sorry we never talk. I'm really sorry we never had lunch together or hung out."

"Just say it," said Johnson solemnly. "You don't like me. Which is okay, it's fine. No one likes me. But please, don't lie to me when you say you're concerned about me. If I decided to quit or was fired or dropped dead tomorrow it wouldn't affect your life in any way."

Robbie leaned forward and placed his hands on the edge of Johnson's desk. "That's not true," he said. "Stop putting words in my mouth."

"I have to because you won't say them yourself," said Johnson, his eyes welling up.

"Is it *just* coke?" asked Robbie.

Johnson glanced up at the ceiling. "It's the crack pipe too. What will it be next? I don't really know."

"Are you sleeping and eating okay?"

"No," he confessed.

Robbie stared at him. "Are you happy?"

Johnson turned and met his gaze. "No." He reached down to grab his work bag and shut down his computer. "I, uh... made Jay quit."

"I'm aware," said Robbie.

Johnson stopped what he was doing and sat still in his chair. "It felt good at first," he admitted. "But the satisfaction didn't last very long. Then you begin to think to yourself, was it even worth doing in the first place?" He stood up and pushed his chair in. "I'm the destroyer of–my own included. Everything that comes near me turns to shit. It's actually a good thing you never spoke to me."

Robbie was still looking down as Johnson headed for the door with his work bag slung over his shoulder. Before he left, Robbie grabbed his arm. "You're better than that," he said.

Johnson looked down at Robbie's hand. "It would have been nice to know this side of Robbie before today." He yanked himself away from him and exited the office.

Not one person looked up or glanced his way.

48

When Shaun had introduced Ben to Ed and Eddie a few days ago, Ben thought they were easygoing, talkative, and of course, pleasing to look at. They seemed like average guys who went to college, had jobs, smoked pot and liked to party. The rental house they shared was a small one-story with a basement similar to the one Shaun stayed in. College parties were frequent in the area, which made the move even more enticing to Ben. Ed and Eddie smoked pot everywhere inside the house, so it wasn't unusual to see a surplus of air fresheners lying around that supposedly emanated the fresh scents of Hawaii and apple tree groves. The furniture was bare bones and used strictly for functionality, not style. There was a vintage chest that served as the living room coffee table and was often riddled with empty dishes and bits of weed. They kept all their empty beer cans and liquor bottles in the corner of the kitchen beside the pantry and would dump them into the trash outside at the end of every month. Ed would often boast about getting hooked up with pot and other drugs from the people he delivered food to. Given what had happened to Ben when he took acid at Owen's party, he was hesitant to try it again, but wouldn't say no to another hit if it was offered.

The night Ben moved in, Shaun went back to his own place so Ben could get better acquainted with Ed and Eddie. From Ben's observations, Ed was the more dominant one of the two roommates. He didn't have a filter and would say whatever was on his mind. Even so, Ben felt a stronger attraction to Eddie. Ben found Eddie's personality hard to resist, but he still fancied Shaun more.

They ordered a bucket of chicken, opened a bottle of vodka, mixed it with orange soda, and watched random music videos that were synced from Eddie's phone to the television. Ben didn't want to come across as someone who had never smoked pot before, because he had tried it when he was in high school. Ed offered him his bong, and when Ben inhaled, he took in too much smoke and started hacking continually for several minutes. His face and eyes turned beet-red, making both Ed and Eddie laugh. Ben stepped outside for fresh air to help clear his throat.

"When was the last time you smoked?" asked Eddie from the living room.

"Like, a couple years ago," replied Ben, going back inside and instantly recognizing the song that was playing from the music video. It was Sabrina Elise's new video for her latest single, "Betcha Gonna Miss Me."

"Yeah, next time don't inhale so much," said Eddie. "We'll teach you."

Ed skipped to the next music video in the queue. "That song sucks," he said. "It's so mid."

"Meh," said Eddie, resting his joint on a green ceramic ashtray that had been molded to look like a marijuana leaf and said *GET HIGH* in squiggly typeface. "There are some good songs on the album, but she keeps releasing the wrong ones as singles. Her not putting out 'Icy Rain' as the second single is such a miss: the beat and hook slap so much harder than 'Betcha Gonna Flop Me.'"

"Are either of you going to her concert?" asked Ben.

"I'm going," said Eddie. "With Shaun."

"Would you fuck Owen?" asked Ed.

"Maybe," replied Eddie as he rested his legs on the arm of his chair. "I'm not really into Asians. Especially gay ones claiming to be bisexual. He's cute, though. Super fucking rich, too. I'd let him be my sugar daddy. Pay my way through school, dad."

Ed turned to Ben and smirked. "Eddie is a racist, by the way. If you're not white, or don't look white, he won't reply to you, regardless of how hot you are."

"Um, that's not true," said Eddie, looking mortified at what Ed had just said. "I've had lunch with a hot black guy from my class. And no, not just for the BBC."

"You still wouldn't fuck him," said Ed matter-of-factly. "That's the point I'm making."

"Hell, I'd ride that black monster cock," replied Eddie eagerly. "Rearrange my guts, please."

Ben's eyes widened. He then laughed, more so because he didn't know how else to react. "What ethnicity are you?" he asked.

"I'm half Russian and Armenian," replied Eddie, tilting his head back over the arm of the couch to look at Ben, making the veins in his forehead bulge out as the blood rushed to his head.

"I'm Turkish and Greek," said Ed. There was something about Ed that Ben found off-putting, like the way he would just stare at him. Sometimes, Ben would catch him doing it from out of the corner of his eye. It was as though Ed was digging inside Ben's brain with just his eyes, like an owl honing in on a mouse that was scurrying across the dirt. "You don't need to say what you are," he said to Ben. "Just fucking cute... Such a cute lil' ass you have."

Eddie smiled and got on his phone. Ben felt his own phone

vibrate and saw that Eddie had just sent him a message: a gay porn GIF. Ben looked at Eddie, who was watching him, his eyes smiling. He felt the impending arousal in his shorts, and the energy in the room suddenly changed dramatically.

"Idea time," said Eddie, cutting the silence. He got up and grabbed the vodka bottle. "Spin the bottle. We usually play this at parties, and this kind of is one, so it works."

Ed took a place with him on the hardwood floor, with Ben following suit. They sat in a triangle with the vodka bottle on its side in the middle, ready for its inaugural spin.

"So, rules," said Eddie. "Whomever the spin lands on, they have to do whatever sexy thing the spinner commands. For example, if it lands on you, let's make out." Eddie spun the bottle and they all watched until it landed on Ed. Without hesitation, Ed and Eddie leaned into each other and locked lips, their tongues sliding in and out of each other's mouths, lips gliding along lips. Ben stared at them, watching the intense moment unfolding. There was nothing hotter than watching two guys passionately make out with each other.

Ed grasped the bottle and swung it around again, and it landed on Ben rather quickly, as if the bottle had been drawn to him like a pendulum of lust and desire.

"Excellent choice," he said with a seductive smile, leaning into Ben and locking lips with him, tongue against tongue, intertwined. Still kissing him, Ben took the neck of the bottle in his grasp and spun it.

"Take off your shorts, sexy," said Ben.

"Hot," agreed Eddie.

Ed slipped off his shorts, as did Eddie when it landed on him next, then Ben when it landed on him after that.

"Whomever this lands on must remove their underwear," declared Ed. "Or in Eddie's case, a thong, probably." When it eventually pointed to himself, Ed stripped off his own boxer briefs and took a shot of vodka from the bottle, his lips wrapping around the opening, his Adam's apple bobbing up and down as the liquor slid down his throat. "By the way, if it lands on yourself, you also have to do a shot." He stripped off his t-shirt and sat naked now. He got onto his knees and motioned for Ben and Eddie to come closer. When they did, he started making out with the both of them together, exchanging one for the other between mouthfuls. Ben could feel Ed's throbbing erection rubbing up against his knee, so he reached down and took it in his hands as Ed reached around and grabbed hold of Ben's ass, working his fingers underneath his boxer briefs. "You should let me fuck that cute lil' ass," said Ed through mouthfuls of kissing, his voice deeper than usual now, the facial hair rubbing against Ben's smooth cheeks. "Yeah?"

Ben felt Ed's strong hand on him, the want overpowering him, fingers digging into his flesh. Half his mind was focused on the intimacy of the moment, and the other half on whether he wanted to have anal sex.

Ed slapped Ben's ass and started sliding his underwear off, dragging him closer into his embrace. "Yeah?" he repeated.

"Not right now," said Ben, feeling Ed's powerful lips against his. "Just oral."

Ed slapped his ass harder. "What if I don't want to do oral?" he asked. He pulled away from Ben and looked in his eyes, his body becoming motionless. "We could hold you down right now and fuck you, and you couldn't do anything about it." His arms were now wrapped tighter around Ben, and he was locked in, unable to move.

The room around Ben darkened, shadows eclipsing the walls, the vodka bottle on the floor like a wicked talisman as a surge of dread filled him. He didn't want to look scared. He wanted to appear calm. He forced himself to want it.

"Have you been fucked before?" asked Ed, rubbing his hands along Ben's back, thrusting his pelvis slowly against him.

"Once," lied Ben. "Like, last year."

"Too long," said Ed, his inhalations heightening, warm breath splashing across Ben's face. "Your ass is so tight. You like it raw?"

The longer Ed talked, the more Ben just wanted the moment to end. "Next time," he said. "I'm not ready right now."

Ben assumed Ed wouldn't listen to him, and that he'd just do it. In the seconds that followed, Ben prepared himself for the moment when it would happen–for the pain he'd probably feel. It was something he'd been wanting to happen for a while, having actual sex, so maybe he should just let it happen now. Maybe it'd be okay.

But when Ed let go of him, Ben was surprised, and he abruptly stood up. "I'll be right back. Gotta use the bathroom," he said.

Ed slapped Ben's ass one last time and let him leave the circle to use the bathroom. Ben didn't need to use the bathroom, but instead stood inside for a minute or so to make it seem like he was doing something. When he stepped back out, he went and stood at the threshold of the living room and saw Ed and Eddie making out on the floor, their naked bodies pressed up against each other. "Hey, that bong kinda fucked me up. I think I'll head to bed now."

"That sucks," said Eddie, looking at him over Ed's shoulder. Ed didn't even bother looking at Ben, for he already had his prized flesh underneath him. Ben turned and went down the hallway to his bedroom. He closed the door then sat on the edge of the bed. He could hear the escalation of their sex in the living room, until the air went quiet. There was no music, either. The house was still. Then, the floorboards in the hallway started to creak from the pressure of feet upon them, the sound drawing closer to his bedroom. Ben got up and locked the door.

"Hey," said Eddie from behind the door as he jiggled the door knob. "Are you alright?"

Ben's pulse raced as he glanced around the room. His eyes fell on the lamp sitting on the night stand. He reached over, unplugged it from the wall outlet and held it in his perspiring hands as he returned to a seated position on the edge of the bed.

The door knob jiggled some more. "Can you let me in?"

Ben was mute, frozen. He put the lamp down on the bed and unlocked the door. When the door opened, Eddie was standing in the hallway in just his underwear.

"Sorry if that was all too much," said Eddie. "It went from point A to point B pretty fast."

Ben's eyes drifted down the hallway when he heard music starting up again on the television. He rubbed his nose and looked down when he felt his eyes begin to well up. "Yeah, it was weird," he said quietly.

"Lots of people don't like Ed because he's kinda scary," said Eddie. "He's a little fucked up... It won't happen again, though."

"Yeah..."

Eddie placed his hand on the side of the door frame. "If you'd like, I can sleep with you tonight if that will make you feel better. Just cuddling, nothing else."

Ben looked Eddie in his eyes. "No thanks." He swung the door closed, locked it, then put his back against the wall, hitting the side of his fist against it.

49

July 1987

Tristan was endlessly interesting. Part of it had to do with how open he was about himself. He was only seventeen, and yet so sure of where his future was headed. He had everything planned out, ironclad. He told Robert about his intention to attend the Curtis Institute of Music in Philadelphia next fall and that he'd be submitting his application by the end of the year. He was worried about the low acceptance rate, but wouldn't let it discourage him given how much he believed in his natural gift for music. He was already planning for his audition at Curtis, having composed several different pieces, most of which he'd already played at the speakeasy and at the concert hall downtown during student nights. These were his test audiences, and he'd tweak the compositions at the end of each night if he felt they weren't quite right. He told Robert that he never felt shame about his sexuality, which was something Robert himself had struggled with. Robert was so used to being around the same kinds of kids at school that Tristan was like some sort of mythical entity–a fairy prince or brave knight. His blond hair was his crown, and his blue eyes dared you to sink deep into their depths. Tristan possessed an artist's soft temperament and an outgoing curiosity, which were both balanced with a sense of confidence in knowing who he was and where he planned to go in life. He wasn't willing to be humble or coy about what he wanted or what he was capable of achieving.

Robert had only known straight people his whole life. He'd see the boys and girls at school get together and flirt and date while he looked on from afar, watching the boys walking down the halls or sitting in front of him in class. He knew he was invisible to them, just a guy in their class. He had both male and female friends, but found it difficult to be around them half the time because of his secret. But now, in this moment with Tristan, he was beginning to feel what all the boys at school must have felt when they spoke to girls they liked. It was the same feeling he got when he looked at Tristan and when he spoke with Tristan and, best of all, imagined kissing Tristan. Here he was, the cutest and most interesting boy Robert had ever seen or spoken to, sitting next to him on the park swings at dusk on summer vacation. Robert felt like he was normal for once. When it came to Tristan, there was nothing to figure out. He wasn't hiding. He was out. He was happy.

Robert held on to the metal links of the swing as he swayed forward and back, with his feet grazing the gravel beneath his shoes. It was another warm summer night with just enough breeze to help cool down after the long stretch of heat from the day. They'd been hanging out for the last four hours, talking about everything from school to hobbies to life. The conversation flowed naturally, hitting on any topic they could think of. He was just as interested in Tristan as Tristan was in him. They ate at McDonald's, then walked the side streets towards the park. Strolling through the pathways and gardens, they ended up at the play structure just as families were heading home, leaving them alone to themselves. That was when Robert realized he wasn't just hanging out with him as a friend. This was a date.

"So, my parents are going away for a couple days to visit family outside the city," said Tristan. "If you like, you can come over when they're gone."

Robert smiled, not having to think about the answer. "That would be cool," he said.

"You can even spend the night," suggested Tristan as he swayed from side to side. The black plastic seat of his swing hit Robert's and their knees touched. "You can hear more of the songs I've been working on."

"Will you play them at the bar on Saturday?" asked Robert.

"Yeah. It doesn't do anything for me to perform them at home with no one around to hear. They're meant to be heard by people. Playing them for an audience really helps me improve on them."

"What about your mom and dad hearing them?"

Tristan rolled his eyes and smiled gently. "They've liked everything that they've ever heard me play. They're just happy to hear my music, and don't care about the critiquing part at all. Whenever they throw a dinner party, they always get me to play something so they can show me off to their friends, like I'm a new car."

"Do you have to dress up?" asked Robert, smirking. "Like, in a tuxedo?"

"Yeah," Tristan admitted. "It's not bad, though."

Robert wasn't sure if he was being sarcastic or not. "Really?"

"If you look through our family photos, you'll see that in all the pictures where I'm in front of a piano, I'm wearing a tux."

"When did you first start liking music?" asked Robert.

Tristan looked up, as though recollecting the precise moment it happened. "The musical score is what grabs my attention the most in every movie I've ever seen... That's probably where it started."

"Do you remember the first one you ever saw?" asked Robert.

"*Sleeping Beauty*. Tchaikovsky. I've been watching that movie, like, once a year ever since. It's also my favorite Disney movie. That and *Mary Poppins*."

Robert didn't even have to think about his. "Mine's *Pinocchio*."

"Another great score," said Tristan. It felt as though the longer they talked, the closer their swings became, their knees constantly bumping into each other.

"You can critique my singing, then," said Robert. "I'll sing, and you can play the piano. I'm definitely not as good at singing as you are on the piano, though."

"We'll be like Simon and Garfunkel," said Tristan. His voice echoed through the peaceful twilight and made the breeze happy as it played with his gold hair. "I'll compose, and you can sing."

"You could teach me to play the piano," suggested Robert.

"Have you played an instrument before?"

"Never. It's kind of intimidating."

Tristan looked down at the gravel. "So... I've been wanting to ask you something. But I'm afraid you'll get offended."

Robert cocked his head, feeling nervous all of a sudden. "What is it?"

"Your name kind of reminds me of a fifty-year-old man," confessed Tristan, half smiling.

Robert laughed; he'd expected to hear something worse. "My dad named me after his dad."

"You're little Robert Junior!" exclaimed Tristan, his face ridiculously excited. "That's really cute."

"You can call me Rob," offered Robert. "That's what most people usually call me."

Tristan pushed his shoes into the gravel and started swinging. "How about Robbie?"

"I've never been called that."

"What do you think of it?"

"It sounds pretty good," he said. "That'll be my stage name."

"Just Robbie?" asked Tristan. "Like... Madonna? I've been listening to her new CD *True Blue* and there's this fun song called 'Jimmy Jimmy.' I'm going to think of your new name now whenever it comes on."

Robbie blushed and scratched his arm. "My mom listens to that CD literally every day when she does the Jane Fonda workout video. Also, when she's cleaning the house... and when she's driving."

"My mom listens to Reba," said Tristan. "She has some good songs. 'What Am I Gonna Do About You' is nice." He jumped off his swing and landed a few feet away. "Do you want to walk again?"

"Sure," said Robbie. They left the playground and walked down the path that would take them out of the park. "Have you seen the abandoned stage? It's just further back."

"Yeah. It's sad, actually," said Tristan. "They need to repaint it or something."

The pathway lights turned on as the sun continued to sink further. Tristan suddenly stopped beneath one of the lamp post beams. "Hey... Would you mind it if we kissed?"

Robbie paused and looked around him in the fading dusk. There was no one around, just the crickets and distant cars beyond the trees. He wanted to ask Tristan if they could do it somewhere else, not out in the open.

"I've never kissed a guy outside before," said Tristan. "I've only ever kissed one other guy while in his car."

Robbie still felt nervous about the idea. He looked at Tristan, standing there in front of him. He didn't want to suggest that they go somewhere more secluded, private, even though he wanted to, feeling as though it might ruin the moment if he did. He was putting his trust in Tristan instead. He was putting his trust in him that everything would be okay.

"Okay," said Robbie. Instead of waiting for Tristan to make the next move, Robbie stepped forward and gently kissed his lips. He was not expecting to feel this way. Having kissed girls before, he thought it would be just another kiss, but he was finally realizing what it felt like to kiss someone he was deeply attracted to. He didn't care anymore if anyone saw them, because he could no longer think about that. The only thing he felt in that moment was how for the first time in his life, he knew what it was like to fall in love with someone.

Tristan pulled back and smiled at him, their noses just barely apart. He gently pushed Robbie backwards towards the base of the lamp post beside the path and started kissing him again. Robbie put his hands on Tristan's face, gently moving his fingertips down to the sides of his neck and along his shoulders.

"Are you nervous?" asked Robbie.

"No," whispered Tristan.

Robbie smiled. "You make me feel safe."

Tristan kissed him on the cheek. "If anyone has a problem with us, we'll kick their ass." He wrapped his fingers around Robbie's left hand as the budding white stars in the night sky bloomed and bloomed.

50

Lisa's fingernails were drumming along the balustrade of one of the balconies as she looked down at the guests entering the ballroom. They all wore posh, sophisticated tuxedos and dresses, their eyes surveying the architecture around them in awe, like it was the Sistine Chapel itself, the lights blazing gold around them. The extravagant chandelier that hung from the high frescoed ceiling, and the entirety of the ballroom itself, was so timeless and decadent that one felt like they had to be wearing gloves before touching anything. There was a gilded grand piano sitting upon the stage in front of the grand staircase, bathed in the light of the torchères. Just like every piece of furniture and architectural design in the castle, the marble grand staircase was its own piece of historical art, and would continue to linger in the minds of guests long after they had departed.

Lisa's slim plum-colored dress hugged her body, and her black hair fell to her waist, with her bangs casting a shadow over her smoky eyelids like a sultry femme fatale on a moonless night. "This is the closest I've ever been to feeling like a queen," she said.

Bailey was standing beside her in full drag, decked out in gold and silver. Her hat was a complex avant-garde statement piece, so unique that it could have had its own display in the MET. "Two queens–one good, and the other evil," she declared. "You're the good one."

"You're not evil," Lisa remarked. "Maybe a bit devilish."

"The villains always resonated with me more," said Bailey. Her Cuban voice was lush yet commanding, like an actress from the golden age of Hollywood. She twirled and arched her back over the balustrade, throwing her head back and touching her forehead, palm facing the ceiling. "Drama, darling."

Lisa spotted Sabrina as she stood with Owen at the front entrance, greeting everyone. Jack and Jackie. Beauty and the Handsome Beast. Sabrina in a strapless hot-pink dress, blonde hair curled, and flawless makeup done by her new makeup artist, Vanessa. Lisa still felt a sting of disappointment, having come so close to securing a once-in-a-lifetime job opportunity. On the flipside, she was glad to have gotten to know Bailey over the last several days. Bailey had opened her eyes to the realization that you can't succeed in everything, and when you don't, it's not because you aren't good enough. Not everyone will understand or like what you do, and that's okay. Bailey taught her that everyone is talented at something, but it's how you put yourself into your work that will get you not just seen, but noticed. Lisa was always copying what her peers did, by the numbers, thinking it was what would bring her the notoriety and success she desired. It wasn't until talking with Bailey and watching how individual and confident she was that Lisa began to understand the thing that ultimately made herself just another face in a crowd of good makeup artists. Bailey lived her life, passion and work to the beat of her own drum. The ones who stood out the most, the ones who were truly unafraid, were the ones who shined the brightest.

Lisa looked at her brother as he bartended down below. He

epitomized the essence of what she desired from life. She'd never realized it until now.

"Sabrina thinks Owen is going to propose to her tonight," said Bailey.

Lisa brought her attention back to Owen and Sabrina. "But will he?" she asked, taking the cocktail pick out of her Manhattan and sliding the Luxardo cherry between her lips. "Do you honestly think she wants to marry him?"

"Do you honestly think he wants to marry her?" countered Bailey. "They seem out of place and awkward together, even now. Look at them. They're too different from each other, except for the money part."

"Tell me, honestly," said Lisa, "do you think he's bisexual?"

Bailey flapped her hand in the air. "Honey, I'm over that kind of gossip. Someone's sexuality is their own business."

Lisa looked at Zeus again as he prepared drinks for the guests, excited chatter echoing all around them. He had such a radiant smile. You could prop him up in place of one of the torchères on the staircase and he'd light up just the same. "You said that your parents never cared that you were gay."

Bailey reached for her champagne glass and took a sip. "They never cared, mostly because they have two other sons, so thoughts of the family line dying out didn't keep them up at night. But yes, they were very accepting from the beginning. It's just how my family is. We're all kind of different and do our own thing. When did Zeus come out to you?"

Lisa looked up at the glittering chandelier. "He didn't," she said regretfully. "He was outed to our family... by me."

Bailey sucked in her lips. "Oh..."

Lisa caught the subtle reaction out of the corner of her eye. "My perception of him changed when it happened," she said. "He didn't feel like my brother anymore, but this stranger. Like everything I'd known about him prior was a lie. There was this panic inside of me when I found out about him–a rush to tell our mom and dad, and even our minister. I'd visit the church to talk to the minister and ask him what was wrong with me. Why was I feeling such ugly disdain towards my brother? He told me that my brother is still the same brother. His heart is the same. His spirit is the same. He is still there, unaltered, and just as loving." Lisa gazed ahead at the balcony across from her. "I later asked Zeus if he could find it in himself to forgive me for what I did to him... and he did. But still, I find I'm unable to forgive myself. Not just for outing him, but for thinking my feelings for someone I loved could change over something that was out of their control."

Lisa's gaze trailed downward and fell upon Zeus. She could see how happy he was, and it made her smile. "I wouldn't be who I am today if it wasn't for him. He showed me that the ones he cares for will always have a place at his side, regardless of their mistakes. Now, the ones I care for will always have a place at my side, regardless of who they choose to love." She looked at Bailey. "I have a fierce older brother, and his name is Zeus."

Bailey ran her finger underneath one of her wet eyes, her glitter and makeup getting smudged in the process. She reached over to give Lisa a big hug. "The three of us should start our own party service called The Three Queens! *Las Tres Reinas*! Singing and comedy, professional glam makeup and delightful cocktails! We'll also kidnap Sabrina's dancers and turn them into strippers. Owen can be the sugar daddy we'll rent out, too!"

Lisa smiled and finished her Manhattan. "That sounds absolutely glorious. I'm ready for some of that bubbly now!"

Jay was in a clearer state of mind this time around when he arrived at Larchdale Castle. He knew he'd enjoy himself tonight, instead of the anxious uncertainty that preoccupied his thoughts previously.

Salvador had managed to schmooze his way into tonight's event, naturally. Jay's arm was wrapped around Salvador's the way a child would grasp onto their mom or dad on the way to the ice cream parlour, excited and giddy for the treats ahead. When it came to dressing up for tonight's event, Jay was on it. In fact, he found himself dressing up a lot lately, a helpless victim to Salvador's wardrobe. For tonight, Salvador wore a navy blazer with an exotic print button-up shirt and his trademark gold jewellery. Jay had never cared for clothing labels, but Salvador opened his eyes to how a fitted wardrobe can do wonders for someone's confidence. The other day, Jay had gone out to buy a tuxedo by himself, and when he surprised Salvador with it, his response was one of intense sexual foreplay. Before last week, Jay would second guess a piece of clothing he wore if it made him stand out too much. The judgements from other people would often cross his mind. Did he look too gay? Would people think he was a materialistic snob who spent too much money? All those worries had gone away. Jay wanted to show off his boyfriend to everyone because he cared about Salvador, and couldn't care less what anyone thought about what he did in private or how he spent his money or who he dated. Salvador was changing his life.

Jay and Salvador had stepped into bursts of galactic lights, glitter and glamour the last time they entered the ballroom. This time, the theatrics were gone. Owen and Sabrina greeted each guest as they arrived, their faces joyful and welcoming for each and every person who had come.

"Nice to see you, Salvador," said Owen with a strong and commanding handshake. "Hey, do you mind being called Sal?"

Jay's eyes widened. He looked at Salvador to see his reaction.

Salvador smiled awkwardly at Owen, then quickly followed it up with a laugh. "I've never been a fan of it, actually."

Sabrina reached out to shake Jay's hand, her green eyes so striking that they almost seemed supernatural, staring into the very depths of his soul. He was starstruck, having to take a moment to register that he was in the presence of a singer that he had grown up listening to.

"Jay," he said, introducing himself. "I'm Salvador's frie..." he looked at Salvador, "boyfriend."

Salvador made a clicking sound with his tongue and pointed at him. "He finally got it."

"How nice," she said, smiling at them both. "Love the tux... and your shirt! So far, the best dressed guys of the night."

Salvador curtsied.

Owen stretched his arm out to the side, gesturing for them to make their way inside. "Have a good time, guys."

Jay knew that this would be a different experience than Owen's last event. Most of the people in attendance were friends of Owen, which meant they were incredibly well off. Within his own circle of friends, Jay did well for himself and was proud of what he had done for work and the income it had provided him. But within this circle, he was the peasant stealing fruit from street vendors. He felt as though he didn't belong, looking around at the top one percent who were milling about. They turned their heads at him and Salvador, wondering who the strangers in their exclusive circle were.

"Your hand is sweaty," said Salvador, loosening his grip. "You're nervous."

"Aren't you?" he asked.

"Just be confident. Pretend your family is really rich. Fake it, baby!"

"What if they ask me what I do?"

"You tell them you make your millions by beating your meat," said Salvador. "That'll get a reaction. I'm serious, too."

Jay pulled at Salvador's arm and groaned into his ear. "That's hot."

Salvador subtly dragged his hand down Jay's body. He pointed to the buffet. "I'll be devouring those mini sandwiches later." Unexpectedly, Kitty was at the buffet table, filling a glass plate with said sandwiches already. She wore a little black cocktail dress with an iridescent ribbon wrapped around her waist.

Jay pressed his cheek against Salvador's face and squinted out in the direction that he was looking in. "That's your intern, isn't it? The one who told you to talk to me?"

As if hearing Jay, Kitty looked up and waved to them with a smile. She put her plate down and took out her phone.

Salvador felt his phone vibrate and pulled it out to see that she had sent him a smiley face emoji.

"How did she get an invite?" asked Jay. "Maybe she's someone's plus one?"

"Some uber-rich silver fox magnate who looks like Robbie," joked Salvador. "She weaseled her way in because she thinks she's famous now, and flaunts that *Jumping Disco Man* video around like it's her golden ticket into every major event in the city. I'm surprised it's working out so well for her, to be honest."

"Want to go say hi to her?"

"Later," said Salvador, putting his phone away and steering Jay towards the bar. "How about a Tom Collins?"

"What's that?"

"You'll like it," he said, sliding his hand down Jay's backside. "You look so good in your tuxedo," he whispered. "Look at all these hoes eyeing you down."

Jay smirked and bumped his side into him. "Maybe they're

looking at you. Hey, if you could name a cocktail after me, what would it be?"

"Jay's Tropical Love Juice."

Jay snorted. "What the hell would be in *that*?"

Salvador looked him up and down. "Pineapple juice and something extra special." He wiggled his fingers at him. "Kind of like a Piña Colada."

When they were next to be served, Zeus glided over and placed his hands on the bar top, his smile contagious. "What would you guys like?"

"My Tropical Love Juice," declared Jay.

Salvador, in horror, blew his cheeks out like a blowfish. "Gross. Who is this guy? Sorry, I don't know her. Goodbye..." He pushed Jay away playfully, then put his hands together on the marble bar top. "I'd like a Tom Collins, double, and a Cosmo. Could you also add a bit of simple syrup to the Cosmo?"

"For sure," said Zeus. "We only serve doubles here, by the way. What's a single?"

"My thoughts exactly!" exclaimed Salvador. Once Zeus finished making their drinks with a showman's flair, Salvador took them both and handed Jay his Tom Collins. "We'll be back."

"What are your names?" asked Zeus.

"I'm Salvador."

Jay yanked the straw from his mouth to speak. "Jay," he said.

"See you soon," said Zeus, smiling at them both.

Salvador led Jay to an empty cocktail table and sat down. DJ SwitchBlade was positioned beside the grand staircase once again and filled the ballroom with his pulsating beats. Jay's eyes wandered around the room, noticing just how stripped it was of Owen's pageantry trimmings and the wild exuberance of the previous party. There were no gimmicks. No mermaids, or flashy costumes. Now, the ballroom revealed its true identity as a relic that was built as a nod to the French Renaissance and a gilded time capsule of the old world.

Jay looked down at his drink. "So, can you tell me again what the point of this party is?"

"Owen is pursuing the nightlife scene," said Salvador, his eyes shifting away for a second. "It's just a big, hyped-up announcement that he could have done via email blast but instead decided to throw a party for his friends."

"Why were you invited?" asked Jay. "You're not his friend. You guys met at his other party, but still."

Salvador just stared at him, sipping on his drink.

"You guys just met the other night. So, you're friends now? That's a pretty big deal. Did he reach out to you?"

Salvador remained silent.

Jay took a sip of his Tom Collins, his eyes glued on Salvador as he drank. "What kind of nightclub does he want to open?"

"Like... Maybe a gay club or something," he said in a nonchalant tone.

Jay downed the rest of his drink, then slammed it down. "Are you fucking kidding me?"

Salvador sighed and placed his hands on the table, about to speak, but Jay cut him off.

"What happened to *always* being able to keep a secret?"

"Will you let me explain?" asked Salvador.

"You know, a part of me didn't want to tell you about the speakeasy," said Jay, his face scrunching up in disgust. "But when we had that talk the other night, where you told me about your high school experience, it made me trust you. *A lot*."

Salvador's eyes looked suddenly distraught at seeing Jay angry. "My intentions were in a good place, Blue Jay."

"Don't call me Blue Jay."

"Why are we leaving something so beautiful down there like a rusty crypt when it can be opened and shown to the world?" asked Salvador. "Bring back the lights and breathe life into it again!"

"You haven't even seen the place!" exclaimed Jay. "You have no idea what it meant to so many people unless you have stood down there yourself. It wasn't just a bar! Did you think Owen would bring you into his circle or something?"

"He hasn't gone down to see the bar yet," said Salvador. "But from what he's heard, he's very interested."

Jay scoffed. "Why didn't you tell me that you were going to do this? Man, Robbie trusted me. He's going to find out, and now I've just lost a fucking friend."

"My intentions were good," Salvador reiterated. He reached out across the table for Jay's hand. "The speakeasy you described to me has such an incredible history. It could be reopened as the best gay bar in not just the city, but the country. It will mean something special and bring the community together in such a way that the average gay bar never could. Both of us can be a part of making that dream happen."

"Is that what Owen told you?" asked Jay. "What makes you think he'll keep it as a gay bar? Just because he's bi or gay or whatever the hell he is, doesn't mean shit. He's a businessman, first and foremost. He follows the money. If it's more financially appealing for him to turn it into something else, then he will."

"He doesn't seem like that kind of guy," said Salvador. "You're making assumptions."

"You're naïve," Jay shot back. "You let his charisma and lifestyle and the whole fucking fantasy of this world totally screw with your head!" He placed a hand to his forehead as his heart raced on, his body heating up. "Such a total lapse of judgement, Salvador. Were you blinded by his money and fucking celebrity? Did you do this just to get in tight with him and be one of his connections?"

Salvador sighed loudly and anxiously adjusted himself in his chair.

"Robbie is going to flip out," said Jay, defeated.

"It's a bar, Jay. The reason it was a secret back then is because it *had* to be a secret. There's lots of history there, so what good is it if it's left sitting down there in the darkness? Honestly, fuck Robbie. From what I'm gathering, he's holding it hostage. You think all those people back then would have wanted it wasting away like it is now? That place needs to shine again. You were at Owen's last party. He'll do something great with Roger's. If he has a soul, he won't just rip out its heart." Salvador had a look on his face that suggested that even he didn't believe what he had just said.

Jay got up. "Well, I guess we'll find out. You put the bar's fate into the hands of someone you don't even know."

"He might not even want it," said Salvador. "If he doesn't, he might not even tell anyone about it... Hopefully."

"Might," repeated Jay. "It was a secret held for, what, over a century? How is that even possible? It's because everyone who went there trusted each other. Then, in the blink of an eye, two idiots screwed it all up. It's because of men like Roger and Dennis that I'm able to sit here tonight and call you my boyfriend when back then they couldn't even hold each other's arms like the way we were just fifteen minutes ago. If anything, I'm more disappointed in myself for letting this happen."

Salvador's face softened. "I'm so sorry, Jay. It was a big mistake."

Jay looked down at his phone, running out of words to say, feeling exhausted and riled up. "I'm gonna go." He turned and made for the front doors. Just when he was close enough to walk out, he heard a *boom* and echo of someone tapping a microphone. The music in the room gradually stopped.

"Hello!" said Owen, his voice reverberating throughout the ballroom.

Jay turned to see Owen standing on the small stage, next to the gilded grand piano. "How's everyone doing tonight?!"

All the guests cheered and clapped as Owen smiled down at all of them.

Jay rolled his eyes and kept on walking.

"Look, I've barely opened my mouth and someone is already abandoning ship," quipped Owen with a dry laugh.

Jay felt as though a spotlight had just been planted on him. He turned, and everyone's eyes were on him. Owen was smiling at Jay, eye to eye, like a stare down. Jay's eyes broke contact first, then drifted to Salvador as he sat alone at the cocktail table, hanging his head, the only one not looking at him. Jay sighed angrily, for he could feel every one of his limbs being drawn back to Salvador. His mind was telling him to leave, but his heart wanted him to stay. If he left, there was no coming back.

"Stay a bit longer," said Owen. "Friend."

Jay hesitated, then turned on his heel and went back to sit with his boyfriend.

51

Martin watched Owen's hot friend sit down at one of the cocktail tables where an equally hot Latino guy was sitting. He couldn't help but fantasize about being in a threesome with them. The longer he continued to go without giving in to his increasingly unrestrained desire, the more his arousal grew from looking at every single man that fell within his range of sight. Sex was all he could think about.

Owen commenced his speech with celebratory greetings and thanked everyone who had taken the time to come out and be part of his event. He went on to acknowledge the castle itself and its architecture, telling stories of what he had learned from the caretakers and in history books. He then took a few moments to indulge in his passion for the nightlife scene and his desire to open his own nightclubs, which would establish incredible landmark destinations for Venus Valley and other cities around the globe. The speech concluded with cheers, hoots and hollers from the buzzed audience of fellow entrepreneurs, friends and socialites.

Martin had been receiving hundreds of emails from the various businesses, news stations, radio outlets, bloggers and talent agents chasing him down. It was just a matter of time before Carly herself gave up, knowing full well that his days in the spotlight were numbered because of his stubbornness and refusal to make mountains out of molehills. It felt like he was at square one again–a loser, trapped in a prison cell. His attention drifted up to the balcony where he'd taken his infamous drunken and supposedly drug-fueled leap of destiny.

"Imagine being a washed-up online celebrity," said Martin. He plucked the lemon wheel off the rim of the glass and plopped it into his drink. "If you look up fifteen minutes of fame, you'll see my stupid face."

Zeus finished making a Negroni for a guest then started pouring wine into a glass for someone else. "My break is coming up. Wanna hang out? I'd like to have a conversation with you when I'm not behind the bar for once."

Martin leaned over his drink and sucked on the straw without using his hands like a child would. "Sure," he said.

Zeus examined his face as he poured champagne into a row of flutes. "You look really tired."

"No sleep for the *Jumping Disco Man*," he said, sucking his Long Island iced tea dry of the last few drops and leaving nothing but cracked ice and a sad lemon wheel at the bottom. His head swivelled up. "Double shot of whiskey. Nothing fancy, Nancy." He slammed a twenty-dollar bill onto the bar top.

Zeus leaned forward slightly. "You don't want a repeat of what happened last time," he whispered. "Gotta slow it down, buddy."

Carly's voice suddenly reverberated in Martin's head. *Look happy, baby*! *Look professional, baby*!

There was another round of applause as Owen concluded his speech and Martin spun around to applaud with them. DJ Switch-Blade started up the beats again, and Owen left the stage to mingle with the guests like the good host that he was. Martin watched, admiring him. "Now *that's* being famous for actually doing something great," he said. Continuing the train of random, drunken thoughts, he turned his attention back to Zeus. "At Owen's last party, did you see me as just someone you knew from the internet? Like, if I was some random guy who was a nobody, you wouldn't care about me, right?"

Zeus poured gin and homemade lime cordial into a cocktail shaker along with a scoop of cracked ice. "I was totally starstruck, man. You might not feel like you're something, but you are to a lot of people out there."

"So, you don't care what people say about me? Like, online gossip and... talk and stuff?"

Zeus shook his head and flashed Martin a comforting smile. "You seem pretty cool to me. I'd like to say I'm your number one fan, but I'm pretty sure your wife has taken that title."

"Do you have a girlfriend?" asked Martin.

"He's more of a friend right now," said Zeus with a smirk. "He lives in Brazil, so it's long distance... We'll see what happens. I'm excited to see him again."

Martin looked at him in complete awe. "Can you take me somewhere?" he asked. "Fly me away."

"Where would you like to go?"

Martin's eyes dropped. "It's nice that you're so free... to just be who you are."

Zeus shook his cocktail shaker just above his shoulder, the ice clinking vigorously against the steel. Martin could feel his eyes welling up, so he stood up and stumbled away. He snatched a flute of champagne from a passing server, then strolled through the crowd of talkative guests and cocktail tables.

As he casually ogled some of the guests, he noticed some of them were ogling him in return. One regal woman in particular, wearing a red velvet dress with burgundy feathers around her shoulders, stared at him with a stoic look of vague lust and contempt. He imagined Carly would find out about this exclusive party and demand an explanation for why he didn't take her as his plus one. It was nice not having her at a function with him. Every party he had been to in the last couple years always involved both of them. For once, he didn't need to keep eyes in the back of his head to be aware of her watching his every move.

Martin regretted smashing up his phone earlier, for now he was suffering from muscle memory. He'd reach into his pocket, only for his phone not to be there. He didn't know what to do with his hands now except drink.

There was a sudden tap on the back of his shoulder. He swirled around to see a young girl with black framed glasses and wavy black hair. The iridescent ribbon around the waist of her black cocktail dress made him uneasy–like a bad omen.

"Hi," he said, taking a long sip of his champagne.

"Yay!" she replied, a smile spreading from ear to ear. She pulled her phone out and held it to her side. "You're Martin–the *Jumping Disco Man*!"

Martin smirked and lifted his hands up in surprise. "What gave it away?"

The girl giggled nervously. "It's the beard and blazer! Look, we match!" She pointed to the iridescent ribbon around her waist.

"Hahaha..." drawled Martin.

"Do you have time to take a photo with me?"

"Sure, why not," he said. When the girl nestled herself beside Martin, he bent down a bit, angling his face to make the photo as aesthetically pleasing as possible. Having done this hundreds of times with Carly, he knew the tricks.

"I'm Kitty," she said, angling the phone as perfectly as possible, seemingly not impressed with how he was doing it. She framed the background so that the grand staircase and its torchères was the backdrop, then switched the screen to a filter called *Showtime* that added instant smoothness to their faces, making his teeth unnaturally white. They both smiled as she snapped the picture, then she quickly looked at it to assess the quality.

Martin took a peek over her shoulder to check out the photo. "Cute," he remarked, then turned to walk away. "It's a good one. Anyway, have a good time."

He made his way to the French double doors. The concert stage outside was completely blacked out, as was the catwalk, and the garden lights along the pathways were aglow. Some of the guests were taking a stroll along the paths of the garden hedge maze and around the conservatory and flower gardens. The pools sparkled and soaked up the starlight, and the fragrance from the roses and azaleas filled the breeze and rustled Martin's clothes and hair. His lungs drank in the beauty of their frailty.

There was a small blood orange tent set up next to the catwalk just further up. It was rather enticing, with its gold moons, suns and stars printed all over its exterior. With his champagne in hand, Martin stumbled forward like a moth to a flame. When he finished the rest of the bubbly, he placed the empty flute on the edge of the catwalk and edged himself closer towards the tent. He opened the front flap and found what looked like a dressing room filled with racks of glittering gowns and costumes, wigs and accessories. There was a vanity and seating area with large cushions and a short Japanese coffee table where scented candles were lit. In the glow of the candlelight, two men were making out on one of the cushions, their bodies sinking deeply into it. Martin paused in the entry. He was tempted to leave, but remained rooted.

The two men stopped kissing and looked in his direction. They were both shirtless and toned. Martin took in their pretty faces and muscular legs. One of them leaned upward to acknowledge their new, unexpected visitor. "Hey," said the man in a Latin accent. He wore dangling earrings that bore a red cross. The other man had a tattoo of a shooting star on his left pec, his skin shining like oil in the candlelight and highlighting his toned biceps and broad shoulders. Martin could feel the arousal surging, tempted by the draw of raw male sexuality in front of him, like a warm, moist cake you just had to eat.

The two men started kissing again, gliding their hands down each other's muscular backs. "You can come inside," said Red Cross as his eyes glanced back to Martin.

"In more ways than one," added Shooting Star.

Martin was standing at the point of no return; his fate had been sealed the moment he walked inside. Eagerly and drunkenly, he stepped forward until he stood before them, feeling the warmth from their bodies rising up to him. Red Cross reached up and rubbed his hand along the part of Martin's chest that was exposed through the opening of his button-up shirt, dragging his fingertips along his chest hair, making his entire body tingle. He pulled at Martin's shirt and dragged him down next to them on the cushion. They started kissing in large mouthfuls, not wanting to waste a second tasting each other. Martin put his hands on Red Cross' pecs, feeling the muscle, and down his hard abs. Shooting Star leaned in and started kissing him next.

"You were invited to this party too?" asked Martin between heated breaths.

"We're part of the dance crew for Sabrina Elise's tour," said Red Cross.

"That's so sexy," said Martin.

"You're fucking sexy, baby," whispered Red Cross, biting Martin's lower lip.

Martin lay in between them, one on each side, heat upon heat upon heat. He slowly leaned his head back, feeling the sexual throbs take hold of him, hard. So, this was what it was like. This was what real, raw, animalistic sexuality felt like. He'd never known until now. The temptation was ruthless, beckoning, winking at him, the flames from the candles eroding the shadows from their bodies along the ground. Shooting Star dragged his tongue along Martin's chest, up along his neck and to his earlobe, the light from the fire reflecting off the saliva on his tongue like pretty little jewels.

In the candlelight, Shooting Star stared at Martin as he lay between them. "Aren't you *Jumping Disco Daddy*?"

Martin gulped and delayed his response. "Nope," he said. "You're just high."

"Fuckin' right," he said. "No, but you're him. Don't fuck with me, baby. I've been wanting to fuck you." He picked up his phone from the table.

Martin anxiously pushed himself up.

"Chill," said Shooting Star, reacting to Martin's abrupt movement. "I'm just gonna look you up for a quick sec. You're mad famous."

Martin took Shooting Star's face in his hands, pulling him away from his phone, and putting his lips onto his.

Shooting Star dropped his phone, succumbing to the kiss. Red Cross undid Martin's trousers, then reached inside and grabbed hold of him, gliding his big hands down his thighs. Thinking of nothing but impending sex, Martin's eyes roamed to the front of the tent, drawn by a breeze ruffling the side of the flap. There was a brief glint, a reflection of some kind. Someone was standing there, behind the flap.

"What's that?" whispered Martin, half focused on the entrance and half focused on what was happening below his belt.

Shooting Star squinted at the entrance, then gradually stopped what he was doing. "There's someone there... Yo!" he shouted.

"Fucking peeping Tom," said Red Cross, sliding upright. The

flap was dropped with a swift rustle as the person behind it walked away, grass crunching beneath their feet.

"Nah... You're not getting away," said Martin. He jumped up and made for the flap. When he poked his head out, he could see the person walking away at a brisk pace back towards the castle, the glow from her phone illuminating her like a halo.

"Hey!" Martin shouted, his voice echoing through the clear night sky. After hearing him, she picked up her pace and started jogging. Martin bolted from the tent and went after her, unleashing his inner high school track star. Halfway to the castle, he caught up with her and grabbed the iridescent ribbon of her dress, causing her to stumble backward. He knocked her to the ground and threw himself on top of her, trying to wrestle the phone away from her hand.

"Give it to me," he demanded angrily, trying to pry her fingers away from her phone. Suddenly, the opening to a mid-tempo song started blasting from inside the castle and escaped out into the backyard. Sabrina was performing a song in the ballroom, the instrumental shaking the air around them.

Kitty swatted his hands away as she squirmed underneath him, her glasses askew and her face disturbed. "Get off me! Why are you being so violent?!"

Martin managed to finally rip the phone from her hand, causing Kitty to hurl obscenities at him. "You stupid idiot," he retaliated. He stood and backed up a few feet, huffing and puffing. Her phone was already unlocked, so he went straight to her photos app and tapped on the fifteen-second video she had just recorded. And there he was, with the other two on the cushion, on the verge of what was supposed to be amazing sex. The shadows that were intermingled with the candlelight made it look like an erotic thriller filmed by a novice film student. He looked at her. "What the hell is wrong with you? What were you planning on doing with this?!"

Kitty got up and walked towards him, but he stepped back, out of reach. "Give me back my phone!" she demanded. "You can't just look through someone else's stuff! You need, like, a warrant! It's illegal!"

Next on her camera roll, Martin came across the photo that he had taken with her just minutes ago. Beyond that, there were screenshots of him from the news stories and blogs he had been on, and multiple screenshots from the infamous video of him jumping off the balcony. There was a sinking feeling in his gut that led him to tap on the videos tab in her photo album. As he scrolled through the videos, one thumbnail in particular caught his eye immediately. His eyes widened as he tapped on the video, watching the unaltered real-time video of him standing on the balustrade, then jumping over the edge and being caught below. In the corner of the video was a timestamp of the location and time it was taken. It was an original–*the* original.

Kitty remained silent and anxious in front of him. "I want my phone back, please. I'll delete the video."

Martin furrowed his brow and deleted the tent video, the selfie with her, and the original video of him jumping from the balcony. He went into the deleted files folder and was about to delete the videos permanently from her phone.

"You're famous because of me," she said.

Martin looked at her, his breathing softening. It had just occurred to him that it didn't matter if he deleted the videos or not. This wasn't going to end. His life, going forward, would be a constant stream of scandal, hiding, deleting evidence and drunken anger. The threat of exposure would always be looming in the shadows. What if he just stopped caring? What if he just let go?

He stretched out his arm and handed the phone back to Kitty. She took it from him, tentatively, like it was some sort of trap that she had to be cautious of. "Here... Do what you want," he said.

"Also, here's some exclusive news for you. Ready? I'm gay and married to a woman. Do what you want with that, too." He glanced down at her phone one last time, then turned and strolled over to the catwalk, resting his arms on the edge. Sabrina was singing inside the ballroom, and the lyrics to the song were like the voice inside his head, the conscience in his heart.

Kitty jogged back towards the castle just as Zeus passed her in the opposite direction to where Martin was. He turned his head to do a double take of her, then met Martin where he stood, his face curious. "What happened?"

Martin looked out ahead of him, the stars above bringing him peace for the change he was about to bring upon his life and a fate he was ready to confront. "I'm heading home," he said. "There's, uh, something I need to take care of."

52

Owen's private event was running smoothly. He was impressed by how many of his friends and acquaintances were able to fly out on such short notice. They'd already been made aware days ago of what his newest endeavour was. According to insiders, the gossip on the yachts and inside the country clubs was that this was all a childish reflex to the separation from his ex-business partner–that he wanted to keep up with, or possibly outdo, Teddy.

Owen hadn't extended an invitation out to Teddy for tonight's event, but that wasn't to say the guy would be turned away at the door if he had gotten wind of Owen's soirée and wanted to drop by from London or wherever he was in the world. He imagined Teddy was far too busy, anyway. His nightclub in Liverpool seemed to have been a decent success for him, but as Owen had foreshadowed, not a complete standout. Seeming to have learned from his missteps in opening the first one, Teddy was planning his next nightclub closer to home, in London, Owen had learned. Owen planned on making opening night so he could touch base with Teddy. By then, Owen hoped to have his own nightclub open–and have it be a standout success–so he wouldn't have to show up empty-handed, business-wise. He still cared for Teddy, even after everything they had gone through. If Teddy chose to ignore him, Owen could at least say he tried to patch things up.

Owen's eyes prowled the ballroom of chatty guests until his eyes locked on his dad, who was sitting at one of the cocktail tables near the foot of the stage. He had his glasses on, his face turned down, reading on his phone. It was impossible for Owen to make a beeline to him because guests kept ambushing him to shake his hand and pat him on the shoulder. He smelled at least twelve different colognes and perfumes as they leaned in to converse with him, making his nose agitated. Most of them had a strong buzz going on from the free booze, so conversations flowed effortlessly, and he could float away to the next person without causing any strong offense. He eventually reached his dad and sat down beside him. He removed the strangulation device that was his bowtie, threw it on to the table, and let out an uncomfortable sigh as he looked around the room. "Dad, you're not supposed to be reading right now," he said. "You're being antisocial."

"I'm learning about Larchdale Castle," replied Henry, not taking his eyes off his phone, too entranced with the photographs in the slideshow through which he was swiping. "That little history lesson in your speech piqued my interest." He turned and gestured to the instrument on stage. "Do you know the history of the piano that's up there?"

Owen turned his attention to it. The gilded grand piano was a piece of fine art that fit perfectly in its surroundings; even the torchères offered their light to help it sparkle and shine. "It was donated, apparently," said Owen, tilting his head to the side like he was trying to remember where he might have heard or read that from. "It's not original to the castle. It was made by some guy, Tristan, maybe. The name is inscribed on it. You should use it as inspiration for your next children's book–it has that fantastical look to it."

Henry shut off his phone and removed his reading glasses to survey the ballroom. Just like his son, he was also dressed in a handsome tuxedo. "Impeccable turn-out. On such short notice, too."

"There were more who couldn't make it," said Owen, disappointment evident in his voice. "Sabrina made some calls and got some of her friends to come, so it balanced out." He lifted his wrist and looked at the time on his gold Rolex. "Actually, I'm heading out soon for a bit. I'll need you to keep the place running while I'm gone for an hour or so. Let them wander down the halls and into some of the rooms to keep them distracted, but let Maxwell know first."

"Wouldn't the role you're giving to me be better suited for the actual entertainer in the room?" suggested Henry. He motioned towards Sabrina, who was up on the stage receiving introductions from various guests, one by one. "Is the rumour true?"

Owen looked down at his watch again. "No," he said, knowing what he was getting at. "I'd have told you beforehand if it was. Did you speak to her? Does her vibe make it seem like she's expecting me to get down on one knee tonight?"

"We talked briefly," said Henry. "Just normal talk. She glows when she walks. Are you aware of that?"

"Dad..." said Owen, grinning.

"She's a gorgeous woman," he stated matter-of-factly. "The voice of a turtle dove. Will you be making London your permanent home? You seem to like it there."

"There's a lot going on right now, Dad. There's so much that needs to be done in these next twelve months. I'm focused on the nightclub right now. Nothing else matters." His phone vibrated with an incoming text message. "I'll be checking out a possible location for my club. I'd like to be on the ball with this place before people come sniffing around."

"So, no Teddy?" asked Henry.

Owen got up and gave him an exasperated look. "No, Dad. Teddy is far away. Why are you bringing him up? It's like you do this on purpose to get a rise out of me for your own amusement."

"I thought you two were still pals," he said innocently. "That's all."

Owen sighed and looked down at his phone again. "Mingle... Talk with people, please." He made a quick detour to the stage and stood by the edge, smiling up at Sabrina until his charm got her attention. When she noticed him, she smiled back and knelt down so she could hear him over the music. "I'm heading out for an hour or so," he said. "Sing them something to keep them preoccupied. They'll go insane for it."

"I'll drag your dad on stage to help out," she said, laughing.

"I'd love to see you try and get him up there," he dared her. He leaned forward and kissed her rosy cheek. "See you soon."

He tapped the stage with his hand, then power walked through the crowd towards the front entrance, where Salvador was waiting for him like a nervous first date. DJ SwitchBlade stopped his beats, then announced Sabrina and the first song she'd be singing for them. The guests turned their attention to the stage as the lights in the ballroom were dimmed to create the nighttime ambiance for the mid-tempo pop ballad "Whatever Is Left of Us Now."

The instrumental started as Owen approached Salvador and rubbed his hand on shoulder. "Ready?" he asked excitedly. "I'm pumped, man!"

"Me too," said Salvador. "But, hey... I'm actually having some second thoughts about this place, regrettably."

Owen's excitement dropped like a raindrop sliding down a window. "Why? The way you described it to me made my fucking eyes pop out! I'm all for a speakeasy, especially one that you claim to be, what, two hundred years old or something? It's like a buried treasure, and I'm the explorer ready to snatch it up."

"That's... a great analogy," said Salvador, his voice quickening. "It's just, the owner of the building isn't looking to sell."

Owen furrowed his brow. "Sal, my man, what are you doing to me here?"

"It was a bad miscommunication," Salvador confessed. "But let me see what else there is around the city."

"Everything else is nothing," said Owen, directly. "You told me this place hasn't been used in, what, thirty years? It's from the 1800s? Shit, do you see my face right now? This is sick! Wouldn't you want to step into a nightclub, a speakeasy, where its history is rooted in three different centuries? Aren't you as excited as me?"

"It's just, Owen–"

"Hey," snapped Owen, his voice rising. "You're wasting my time. You can show me where this place is, or I'll find out for myself. I'm telling you, though, if the latter happens, this is where our contact ends. You won't get a chance like this again."

Salvador glanced down for a second. "Alright..." he finally said. "Fine. Let's go."

"Great!" said Owen, his face lighting up again. He walked past Salvador and hurried down the front steps, sliding into the backseat of a vehicle that was already waiting for him. "Let's take separate cars. My guys will follow you. Lead the way, Sal!"

53

July 1987

Tristan pulled two wine glasses from the antique china cabinet in the dining room and brought them into the kitchen, where the aroma of a hot pepperoni and cheese pizza wafted through the air. Accompanying the pizza was a plastic takeout container of saturated Caesar salad topped with bacon bits and garlic croutons. Robbie was already scooping mountains of salad onto a plate stacked high with three slices of pizza. Tristan hopped onto the stool next to him at the kitchen island as the radio station continued playing all of today's biggest hits.

"Your parents have just as much booze as Roger's," said Robbie, acknowledging the bar cart beside the pantry door.

"They've been hosting dinner parties every month," said Tristan. "All their friends like to get drunk and loud... They get gifted a lot of alcohol, so it just accumulates over time. Those are the parties where my mom and dad tell me to come down and play something.

It's kind of fun. They let me have wine." He picked up the bottle of red wine and awkwardly started uncorking it with the bottle between his legs. "They won't notice this one is gone. Do you like red? The white isn't chilled yet."

Robbie stabbed his salad with his fork, causing croutons to shoot out from the plate. "So, don't laugh at me... I've actually never had wine before."

"You're serious," said Tristan, smiling in disbelief, just as he popped the cork open. He poured them each half a glass. "Here," he said, passing him one of the glasses. "You'll do your first wine tasting."

Robbie was just about to take his first sip when Tristan stopped him dramatically with his hand. "You have to swirl it around in the glass first. Then smell it," he said, showing him. "Take a sip, savour it..." He looked at Robbie and snorted at his reaction. "Or just, you know, drink it and skip all that."

Robbie exaggerated all the steps. He took a sip, smacked his lips, then lifted his glass and looked at it curiously, deciding if he liked the taste or not. "Why do you chill the white wine and not the red?"

Tristan tilted his head to contemplate the question. "No clue, actually. My mom and dad do it all the time. I'll open the white one later so you can see which you like better. You might like the white more because it's cold."

Robbie took another indulgent sip. "It's good."

Tristan placed three slices of pizza on his plate, then picked one up and sprinkled some Caesar salad on top. Robbie smiled. His undeniable attraction to Tristan felt so good and he always felt the urge to hug him. Tristan's blond hair was radiant whenever he was beneath any sort of lighting, whether it be kitchen lights or the sun. He was fun to be around, and Robbie always felt disappointment when their time together was over and he had to return to his regular life.

"What do your parents do?" asked Robbie. "Are they professional wine experts?"

Tristan smirked at the mere thought. "They're lawyers. They joke about the creative gene skipping their generation and going to mine."

"My dad is a news anchor and my mom a store manager for a department store," said Robbie. "She always brings home clothes, and my dad gets mad about it."

"She probably gets good discounts," said Tristan, gobbling down another slice of pizza with salad topping. As he ate, he looked at Robbie's reaction. "Sorry, I'm a pig. It only takes, like, minutes for me to eat dinner."

Robbie noticed Tristan's lips were stained from the red wine. "Your lips," he said, pointing at his own for reference. "It's like you're wearing some sexy lipstick."

"It's like those blue candies that turn your tongue blue," said Tristan. "Back when I was a kid, like five years old, I'd bite the tips off markers."

Robbie's reaction was just the kind Tristan was hoping for.

"It was only the one time, though," said Tristan, smiling. "I'd also sometimes taste that glue stuff that we made crafts with in kindergarten–that gunky white glue with the popsicle sticks."

"That's when you know you're a real artist," said Robbie. "You start eating the equipment. Have you tasted your music sheets yet?" He put his hand over his mouth, unable to contain his laughter.

"Maybe they'd taste like chicken," suggested Tristan.

"Sorry, I have this image in my head of you just sitting in your room eating paper now," said Robbie, taking a big sigh after laughing so hard. He downed the rest of his wine in a few gulps as Tristan grabbed a napkin and rubbed the wine stains from his lips.

Robbie couldn't help looking at Tristan's lips now; his mouth was even more pink from the rubbing of the napkin. He leaned forward and kissed him. Tristan put his hand on the back of Robbie's neck and slid it along his shoulder. When they pulled away, they both smiled, then a moment of silence followed as the music carried on to the next song. Tristan rubbed his knee against Robbie's leg, then swivelled back to his pizza and accidentally knocked his glass over with his elbow, spilling wine over his pizza and salad.

"Wow... I'm honestly a klutz," said Tristan. He picked up more napkins and soaked up the wine. He then picked up the wine-coated pizza from his plate and took a bite out of it.

Robbie had a look of comedic horror on his face. "You really are a freaky eater," he said. "It's almost, like, kinky territory."

Tristan cringed when he tasted the mistake that he had just put in his mouth. He fake-gagged. "It's gross. Don't ever try it," he said, getting up and dramatically spitting it into the garbage.

Robbie stared at him when his back was turned. When Tristan was bent over, the backside of his shirt had lifted up, and Robbie could see the top of his underwear band. "Do you work out?" he asked.

"Sometimes," said Tristan. "I'm usually too busy with school and music." He came back to the island and gripped the back of his stool, his eyes darting down to Robbie's chest. "You said the other day that you play rugby."

"Yeah... I've been using the school gym equipment on and off," said Robbie, their eyes meeting again, blue and brown stares. Throbbing, warm-blooded tension followed as their stares lingered, and everything seemed to fall away except their smoldering, intense connection. Summer turned to autumn. Cities rose and fell. The world exploded. The end.

Tristan blinked. "Want to head into the living room?" he asked, taking the bottle of red wine. "I'll play you something."

"Sure," said Robbie, picking up his wine glass. They left the kitchen and walked past the staircase and down three carpeted steps into the beautifully furnished living room that was a mix of modern and antique pieces. Along the left side of the wall was a framed family photo of Tristan with his mom and dad at Christmas from a couple years ago. Underneath it was a black keyboard resting on a stand with a leather bench. Tristan placed the wine bottle down on a side table and poured them more wine. Robbie reached over to the keyboard and started tapping some of the keys playfully with his fingertips. "Will you get a big piano one day?"

"Definitely," said Tristan. He took a few more sips of the wine and sat down on the bench. "My grandparents had one, but it's too big, and there isn't room for it here with all the furniture. So, it's in storage for now. It's kind of ugly, though. That's actually one of the reasons why I've been playing at Roger's. The piano they have there is one of the best things I've ever seen. I'm honestly going to steal it. You can help me."

"Deal," confirmed Robbie, sitting down next to him, wine glass in hand.

Tristan placed his hands near the edge of the keyboard and sent his fingertips into a wild, sporadic frenzy that made Robbie almost drop his glass from bombastic surprise. It was dramatic and quick, like an ominous peal of thunder that rolled across the room. As Tristan continued to play, Robbie felt as though he was caught in a hurricane out at sea, with lightning tearing through the cold black sky like tiger claws ripping into flesh. His boat flailed helplessly in the rushing waters, death inevitable. The howling winds rocked and threw him away from the safety of his boat as millions of rain pellets descended upon his body, smothering him, like the tears of a thousand mourning angels. The waves were monstrous tentacles, rising up to engulf him and drag him down into the bottomless abyss. Then, the music slowed. The storm passed, and he was left vulnerable as the ocean around him calmed to a steady rhythm against the hull. It was a tranquil and transformative moment. The light rain shower rustled birds from their sleep, far away, where they sang songs of rescue and the awakening of springtime joy, out across the sea. He couldn't see the birds, but he knew they were there because he understood what beauty sounded like. Ever so gently, rays of light eroded the darkness and brought its warmth into him.

Robbie looked down into his wine glass and watched the red liquid lap against the sides of the crystal as he rocked it from side to side. He looked at Tristan's fingers as they carried on the sonata, a hostile and tormented force, fear, fading into solace and beauty that brought with it a promise of a long and prosperous dawn. Tristan concluded the piece and took his hands off the keyboard, reaching for his wine glass.

Robbie placed his glass between his legs and applauded. "My entire life flashed before my eyes," he said, awestruck. "It, like, gave me a heart attack."

"Just the beginning part gave you a heart attack," said Tristan, smirking.

"Yeah..." replied Robbie. He looked at Tristan and let out a big sigh, unable to find the words for what he had just felt.

Tristan put his glass down. "I'll show you how to play." He got up and swapped places with him so that Robbie was in the center of the bench. He took Robbie's hands and placed them over the middle keys. "The white keys are like a musical alphabet. The first key on the far left of this keyboard starts with the C note. C, D, E, F, G, then, A, B, C, D, E, F, G. Keep repeating A, B, C, D, E, F, G, until you reach the far right of the keyboard. To help you find the note you want, like D, use the black keys as a visual clue. There are black keys in sets of two and three, but look at the ones in sets of two first. The white key in the middle of each set of two will always be D, which is the easiest to find. When you have that established, the rest of the notes are pretty easy to remember. You can place stickers on the keys to remind you which note is which until you know them all by heart." He looked at Robbie. "Do you kind of get it?"

Robbie registered maybe ten percent of what Tristan had said. He wiggled his fingers a bit, then started tapping random keys from left to right, trying to come up with some kind of decent melody. To a listener, his special composition might have conjured an image of a lost, deformed goat screaming up at the clouds as it was being kicked.

Tristan smiled. "What inspired this epic piece?"

Robbie stopped playing. "I'm kinda better at singing."

"I'm scared of singing," confessed Tristan.

Robbie was surprised to learn this. "You don't ever write lyrics to your songs?"

"Sometimes," said Tristan. "I'll sing when no one is around."

Right away, Robbie started to sing an uptempo pop song he'd heard on the radio. But instead, he sang it as a ballad. He tapped keys that, surprisingly, went well with the melody he was singing. Robbie stopped after the first chorus and sat still, waiting for Tristan's critique.

"You have a really nice voice," assessed Tristan. "You should take singing more seriously. What do you want to be?"

Robbie pursed his lips and stared at the wall in front of him. "I'm not completely sure. My dad suggested media production or a news anchor, like him."

"You should be a weatherman," suggested Tristan.

Robbie wasn't sure if he was joking or not. "Hell no," he said, smiling.

Tristan took Robbie's hands again and placed them back on the keyboard. He pressed Robbie's fingers down on one key, and then to the next, controlling each of his movements as a beautiful ballad emerged from the instrument. Tristan then took full control with his own hands and continued the piece.

Robbie stared at him, Tristan's face so at peace as the melody poured out from him. It was so effortless. "How do you come up with something like that?" he asked.

Tristan stopped. "It just comes. I'll be sitting at my desk in class, bored, and a melody will pop into my head and start to take shape. I'll compose it right away at home, or on the piano in the park. This one was inspired by our time in the park the other night." His eyes fell on Robbie. "It was really easy."

Robbie smiled gently, sighing involuntarily. This warm wash of emotion went from his head down to his toes. He decided to dismiss it as impending drunkenness, and nothing more. He leaned forward, kissed Tristan on the cheek and put his arm around his waist. "I'm kinda drunk," he whispered.

"Same," said Tristan, whispering back to him. "Wait here." He got up from the bench and went into the kitchen, then rushed up the stairs to the second floor.

While he waited, Robbie continued tapping the keys, glancing casually around the living room and spotting a notebook sitting on the couch. He got up and went to pick it up. Flipping through the pages, he saw dozens of compositions. To him, it was gibberish because he couldn't read music. He closed the notebook, and in the center of the black cover was an inscription that read TRISTAN in bold, gold typeface.

Several minutes later, Tristan returned to the living room.

"You should keep this hidden," said Robbie, showing him the notebook. "What if someone breaks in and takes it?"

Tristan took the notebook and placed it beside the keyboard. "Come upstairs," he said.

Robbie followed Tristan up the carpeted steps. There was a

small chandelier hanging down from the middle of the stairwell that wasn't lit up, but dazzling nonetheless. Tristan's bedroom was the first door on the right of the second floor. When they went inside, the first thing Robbie saw was the double bed: ivory-colored sheets and a chocolate brown comforter and headboard. Robbie wanted to dive right into it because it looked so comfy. The walls were a light grey, and the carpeting a nice blue that reminded Robbie of Tristan's eyes. There was also a black electric keyboard under the window next to a desk that had a red, alien-looking lava lamp on it. Posters from pop and classical concerts were tacked to each of the four walls.

Noticing Robbie's interest in the posters, Tristan closed the door to reveal a collage of ticket stubs from all the concerts he'd ever gone to, taped to the back of the door.

Robbie gawked. "Wait, you saw Elton John?!"

"Yeah. His *Ice on Fire Tour* last year," said Tristan as he looked over the door with Robbie. "My parents took me for my birthday. Best present ever. He's one of my idols. Madonna's *Virgin Tour* was awesome as well."

Robbie turned around and strolled over to the desk. There was a framed photo of a black pug sitting next to Tristan on the piano bench as he played the keyboard.

"Aw, that's Rascal," said Tristan. "My parents take him with them whenever they drive out to visit family. I'm playing 'Hound Dog' in that photo."

"He's cute..." said Robbie. "So is the dog."

Tristan smiled and took his arm. "There's something else I'd like to show you," he said excitedly, walking backwards out of the room and pulling Robbie along with him. Tristan took him to the door across from his bedroom and reached behind him to open it. The scent and warmth that escaped from the room hit Robbie instantly. Tristan let go of his arm as they stepped into the bathroom that was lit by only two scented candles on the ledge of the large corner bathtub. It was filled with lavender-scented bubbles, with some oils or scented bath salts that made the room smell like an aromatic spa.

Robbie looked down into the deep bath that was almost like a small hot tub. His reaction was one of confusion, and he found himself feeling slightly overwhelmed and nervous at the same time. It finally clicked in his mind that he was on an actual date again, like the ones he'd seen in movies: romantic and thoughtful. When he thought of romantic dates, he thought of dinner and a movie. He never thought of strolls through the park and kissing under street lights... Piano serenades and wine. It was all so surreal and different and new to him. He felt grown up.

Tristan picked up a bottle of white wine that was chilling in an ice bucket on the counter. "Time for some white wine," he said, dangling it in front of Robbie. But then he paused, his expression worried. "Is this... okay?" he asked, his voice carrying uncertainty.

Robbie exhaled a deep breath and smiled at him, rubbing his hands together. "You are very romantic... It's like Valentine's Day."

Tristan reached around and closed the door, trapping the warm air inside. The room was silent, except for the crackling of the candle wicks and the subtle popping from the bubbles in the water. There was a question emerging on the tip of Robbie's tongue that wanted to be let out, but he felt himself drowning in hesitation. He counted to five in his head, then let it out. "Do you want to be my boyfriend?" he asked, the words falling out of his mouth. "I'm not out, though..."

Tristan twisted the neck of the wine bottle in his hand and smiled. "Yeah," he said. "Pretty please. It didn't even cross my mind that you're not out."

Robbie felt as though his chest was going to burst.

Tristan turned his attention back to the wine bottle in his hands like he had forgotten about it, then looked around the counter space. "Damn... I totally forgot to bring glasses," he said, looking at the door as though he was debating if he wanted to go back down to grab glassware. "Want to just drink it from the bottle?"

Robbie took the bottle and drank multiple swigs. "This is so much better than the red," he said enthusiastically, handing it back to Tristan so he could have some.

Tristan put the bottle down on the counter, then they immediately threw themselves into each other. Their lips were in a deadlock as they lifted up each other's shirts over their heads and pulled down their shorts. Within moments, they both climbed into the tub. Robbie was pushed up against the side by Tristan on top of him, water splashing along the sides in happy little waves. The humidity rose and mixed with the lavender and steam in the air. Tristan kissed Robbie all over, their slippery bodies rubbing against each other, up and down, side to side. Robbie slipped and slid his way on top of Tristan, back and forth, chest to chest, mouth to mouth, in and out, pelvis to pelvis, again and again. Robbie thrust his arm up over Tristan's head and the ledge of the tub, with Tristan's hand tight in his grasp. Their fingers intertwined, each squeezing hard as they both erupted within seconds of each other.

Robbie collapsed onto Tristan, both their chests rising up and down, breathless. He rested his face on Tristan's chest, the bubbles completely decimated, leaving nothing but hot, soapy water behind. The flickering candles lit up the surface of the water and made it dance and sway as it settled around them, the monsoon calming. As Robbie's cheek rested against his chest, ripples of water lapped along his chin. He wrapped his arm around Tristan's torso. "How can something so wrong feel so right?" he said quietly. "Are you ever scared?"

Tristan lay against the side of the tub, his hand caressing Robbie's body. "Sometimes," he said, looking down into the water, watching the reflection of the candlelight ripple across the surface. "My mom cried when I came out to her and Dad last year. At first, I didn't know if it was a sad cry or a happy cry... It could have been a combination of both. She gave me a hug and said she loved me. It was more nerve-racking waiting for my dad's response than hers. He came around the table and put his arm around me, and told me if anyone ever had a problem with me, or called me anything, to tell him right away and he'd make sure it stopped. He also kind of cried. I'd never seen my dad cry before. He said he loved me and was proud of me. I felt a lot better after hearing that from him."

Robbie's eyes drifted down. "I'm scared to do that," he said.

Tristan leaned his head on Robbie, still holding him. "Maybe one day you won't be."

Robbie placed his lips on Tristan's chest and moved them down to his wet stomach, gently and slowly. He pulled himself up so they were face to face, just inches apart, their noses almost touching, seeing all of him. He smiled, and Tristan smiled back, the candle-light dancing in their eyes. Robbie leaned in and kissed him on the lips, and their bodies pressed together as the warm water trickled and slid down their skin.

54

Shaun showed up at Ed and Eddie's house at ten o'clock. The game plan was to head over to Fame at around midnight, which would then undoubtedly transition into an after-party someplace else. Phase one, pregaming, was currently underway. Thumping dance beats were pouring from the living room television speakers, the bass filling the house with killer adrenaline. Being that it was Saturday night, and summer break, if one was to peek through the windows of any given rental house down the block they'd see the same party-prep template of students kicking off their night.

Ben was in the bathroom getting ready, styling his hair with pomade and hairspray. He had gotten a haircut with faded sides that helped send his confidence up to a ten, and the growing anticipation of going to Fame again made him want to look his best. He had also gone to the mall and picked up a white tank top with the brand's logo stretched across the chest and tight blue shorts that rolled up above his knees. Last week, Shaun had managed to get Ben into Fame through trusted connections. It was Ben's first time in a gay club, and it was everything that he had hoped it would be.

Shaun was a social butterfly, and fluttered from one guy to the next, often leaving Ben to himself on the dance floor. Ben wasn't alone for long though, for another guy would quickly slide himself over and take Shaun's place. Sometimes during the night, Ben would forget about Shaun, and the lasting impression he once had on him steadily decreased the more he interacted with other guys. Ben knew that a romantic relationship with Shaun didn't look promising. He seemed like the kind of guy who went after hookups, not romance. Perhaps from being influenced by Shaun's Gay Etiquette 101, Ben wasn't even sure if he himself wanted to date, either. All the men around him looked so yummy.

Shaun came waltzing into the bathroom, thrusting his upper body to the beat of the song. He stood next to Ben, dragging one of his hands over his shoulder and back. He then opened a tiny bag of cocaine and flipped it upside down, emptying its contents onto the countertop like a snowstorm.

"Do a line with me," said Shaun, dividing the powder into two lines. Ben knew without hesitation that he was going to snort it. He'd never done it before, but he didn't want to ask Shaun how to properly ingest it for fear of looking too much like a newbie. Shaun took a rolled-up twenty from out of his pocket, leaned over the countertop, plugged his left nostril with his middle finger, and snorted one line. Ben took the rolled-up bill from Shaun and did exactly what he did, snorting the second line. The whole ritual was done without any words exchanged between them, as though it was a sacred act that required silence. Monkey see, monkey do.

"Hot," said Shaun with a smile. He reached his hand down and touched Ben's crotch. "You should fuck my slutty mouth," he said, slowly brushing his lips along Ben's mouth.

Ben could smell and taste the cherry sugar scrub on Shaun's soft lips. "Are we dating?" he asked.

Shaun looked into his eyes. "No," he said bluntly. "I'm not big into dating–it wasn't much fun. Also, my ex didn't want an open relationship. There's too much dick out there. It's like clothes. You wear something for a few months, but then something new catches your eye in the store, and the thing you were already wearing just doesn't do it for you anymore." Shaun's eyes wandered down Ben's body. "Fairytale endings don't interest me. They're boring, and they're for straight people."

Ben felt a strong lust for Shaun, but he no longer found himself attracted to him the same way he was just a few days before. This was the real Shaun; his mask had fallen off. He didn't make Ben feel butterflies like he once had, or particularly safe. It was just lust.

Shaun rubbed Ben's ass. "Let's join the boys in the living room. If we invited a couple more guys over later, you'd be down with that?"

"Yeah..." said Ben.

"Fuck yeah," agreed Shaun, smiling. He took Ben's hand into his and they went into the living room together. The music flowed into Ben's ears and bloodstream, making him tingle in such a good way. He didn't want this to turn into a situation similar to Owen's party, where he couldn't remember what happened after dropping acid. He knew he was just telling Shaun what he wanted to hear. Shaun was his guide into gay life–a world that was still completely new to him. After what happened the other day with Ed and Eddie during spin the bottle, Ben felt embarrassed. He wanted them to like him, not wanting to come across as vanilla or lame, but his gut was telling him something else... He didn't know what to do with these conflicting emotions.

Ed and Eddie were sitting around the antique chest in the living room with their drinks beside them, looking down at their phones. They smelled of cologne and body wash, all cleaned up and dressed for the night. There was some cocaine on the back of a CD to go along with the alcohol, pot and ecstasy. It was like

Halloween night: goodies and treats galore. Ben poured himself a rum and Coke and stood by the kitchen archway, looking down at his phone.

"Do a line with us, Ben!" said Eddie excitedly. "It has your sexy name on it! Here, we will literally spell your name out with it."

Ben looked up from his phone. "I just did one," he said.

"Do another one, lil' baby," said Ed. "You're getting fucked up tonight. We all are, hunty."

"I'm just gonna drink," replied Ben. "I'll stick with rum."

Ed lowered his face and stared at Ben, like a lion watching a gazelle. "Hey, baby... Whatever you want to try, don't be scared to ask. It's okay to try something to see if you like it or not. If you wish it, we can make it happen."

There was a creeping silence between the four of them as Ed waited for Ben to answer him.

"I've got some Coke already," said Ben, lifting his glass.

Ed scoffed and tossed back the rest of his drink, switching to another song. "Ya lil' smartass. What else?"

Ben looked back down at his phone.

"He took acid," said Shaun, "at Owen's party."

"What about the *Jumping Disco Man*?" asked Eddie, laughing. "He's a tweaker."

"He invited me over to his house a while back," said Ben. "His name is Martin."

"Did you fuck him?" asked Shaun.

"No," replied Ben. "He's married, actually."

"Uh, so."

"I left before anything happened."

"That's a running theme with you," said Ed, looking at him with an obvious sneer. "Giving guys blue balls."

Ben looked down at his phone again as he felt his heart begin to race from anxiety.

"So, what other things do you want to try?" asked Ed. "Other than blow and acid, ya lil' druggie. Any kinks?"

Ben felt his body tingle all over. "None," he said.

"This is a safe space, lil' baby," said Ed. "You don't need to be nervous. Trust me. Eddie here loves being pissed on."

"Hey, can you not?" said Eddie in an embarrassed voice.

"Nah, I'm good," said Ben, returning the same stare that Ed had been throwing at him all night.

Ed inhaled a deep breath then blew out his cheeks dramatically. "Honestly Shaun, your new friend is pretty lame. Can we get a roommate refund?" He glanced at Ben and grinned, watching for his reaction. "Just kidding..."

Shaun looked at Ben and patted the spot next to him enthusiastically. "Come," he said.

"I think I'll go, actually," said Ben.

"Uh... What the fuck? You said you wanted to move out of your boring aunt's place so you could have fun," said Shaun matter-of-factly. "That's what I'm giving to you. You're literally the opposite of what I thought you'd be."

"Likewise," replied Ben.

"Uh, how?" exclaimed Shaun, his voice incredulous, bordering on offended. "This is a party! That's the whole point of pregaming! You're going to have tons of fun, believe me. You're gonna watch the sun come up and smile, baby."

Ed watched Ben as he continued to stand in the kitchen archway, looking at his phone. "Don't just fucking stand there, then," he demanded. "You said you were going, so get the fuck out."

Ben tossed his drink to the floor. It rolled, splashing its contents across the dirty hardwood. "Alrighty. Bye, lil' rapist."

"Hey!" yelled Ed, jumping to his feet.

Ben rushed out of the house, leaving through the back door of the kitchen

"Take your shit and get the fuck out of here!" shouted Ed, his voice merciless, enraged.

Ben went through the overgrown backyard, knocked the tin garbage can over and repeatedly kicked it across the back alleyway until it had several dents in it. He continued down the road and dialed for an Uber to come sweep him up and take him someplace far far away.

55

Liam had finished making himself a whiskey sour when there was a knock on his front door. He wasn't used to having unexpected guests this late, and at his age, he was always cautious in answering the door when darkness fell. He pushed aside the orange curtain of the front window and saw the outline of a figure standing on the top step. Just from the outline, he recognized Johnson by his bald head and beard that he could make out by the glow of the distant street lights. Liam unlocked the door and let him in, but the fierce energy that blew into his house, along with the man, was striking. Johnson stepped into the living room, his face grim. He didn't feel like a friend to Liam. He didn't feel like Johnson at all.

"How are you?" asked Liam, trying a casual greeting.

Johnson stared at him, anger plain on his face, his eyebrows furrowed. He glanced at the television, annoyed by the movie playing there. He picked up the remote and turned it off. "What makes you think you can tell everyone about my private life?"

Liam raised his eyebrows. "What's this about?"

Johnson didn't take his eyes off him. He didn't even blink.

"My concern for you comes from a good place... as a friend," said Liam. "I thought Robbie could talk some sense into you; given that the two of you are friends and work together."

"Friends?!" exclaimed Johnson, his eyes mad. "You can't just go around telling people I'm a crackhead! You put my job–my career–at risk! You're psychotic, Liam!"

Liam looked down. "It was wrong of me," he said, hanging his head as he stepped back into the kitchen to have his drink.

Johnson clenched his jaw. "What do you even do all day? Sad, lonely man who just drinks and smokes pot and cuts hair. Fuck, just talking to you is depressing nine times out of ten. You have no business trying to help someone when you can't even help yourself. Look after yourself first, then worry about other people."

Liam knocked his drink back. "That was my mistake," he said. "Maybe I should just let you die, then."

"Maybe I want to die, Liam!"

"I'm sorry," whispered Liam. "Go on, die then."

Johnson furiously kicked over a stack of boxes next to the front door, then slammed his face into the glass window of the door. He stormed over to Liam, standing before him across the kitchen counter with a fresh cut across his forehead. Blood flowed from the wound and into his eyebrows. "Aw... What's the matter? Why so sad?" he asked in a patronizing voice.

"My life has been a sad ride," Liam replied, staring down into his glass, unable to meet the man's deranged face. He was rooted to the spot, afraid. "You know that."

"Now whose fault is that?" whispered Johnson.

Liam finally looked at him, tears gathering in his eyes.

The menace on Johnson's face suddenly softened as he saw the fear, darkness and turmoil built up over countless years coming to the surface. "I'm not going to end up like you, Liam," he said finally, his own eyes welling up. "Your life can't become mine."

Tears fell down Liam's cheeks. He recognized the reflection of himself in Johnson's face. "I understand now that the best way I can help save you is to have you run away from me. Please, Johnson. For your own good... Leave here, and don't ever come back."

Johnson's face was as empty as could be without any trace of a soul behind his grey eyes. He went around the kitchen counter and extended his hand out to him. "This is goodbye, then."

Liam looked down at his hand and shook it, but held on for a moment longer. "You still have time to find what you're looking for out there," he said. "If you just–"

Johnson ripped his hand away. He turned and walked out of the house, slamming the front door behind him.

56

The empty stage was a distant dream. Robbie sat at the bar, the furthest stool to the left, and in the very spot where he had first seen him play. The light from Robbie's phone brought him no warmth or comfort in such a dark mausoleum. He'd been coming back every couple of days to sit and relive a rusted memory that was covered in dust and grime, any sheen and sparkle long extinguished into darkness. He stood and stared at the stage a moment longer, taking a picture of it with his eyes instead of his phone. Then, he walked out and left the safe haven without looking back. He'd die with the memories he had left of a place... It had changed him. Tristan had changed his life, forever.

When Robbie stepped out from behind the cubby unit and pushed it closed, his phone picked up the data signal now that he was above ground. Sarim had sent him a message earlier in the day, asking Robbie to join him for an exclusive event that Owen was throwing at Larchdale Castle. Robbie had been ignoring Sarim's messages for the last few days. Since his overwhelming descent into the past, Robbie found himself unable to balance the complicated emotions surrounding two people who meant so much to him. His past was robbing him of his present and future. Robbie felt like an empty hull moored to a dock, and no one was going to untie him. Perhaps he didn't want to be untied. He cared for Sarim so much that the very thought of ignoring him, of hurting him, upset him. The pain was becoming too much, and the regret a burdensome anchor. Shame on the man who left Sarim, a pure, loving soul, out on his own in the cold with no loving arms to keep him warm. He deserved to be loved completely, and Robbie feared that love was something that he wouldn't be able to give to him.

Robbie felt his phone vibrate with an incoming message. It was from Jay.

I'm sorry.

Robbie stared at it, confused, wanting to call him. He was just about to when he opened the door of the backroom and looked into the dark hummus bar that was lit only by moonlight pouring in through the windows. The restaurant was closed, but two men were standing outside the front door, waiting to be let in. Christopher, the owner of Lovely, stepped out of the back kitchen and stopped when he reached the front door.

Robbie's heart plummeted to his stomach. Followed by anger.

Salvador anxiously kept his hands in his pockets, dreading the next moments of what continued to prove itself to be a most dreadful evening. Owen and himself, side by side, looked ridiculous in their partywear as they stood outside a closed hummus bar on a Saturday night. Salvador's thoughts was focused on Jay and how much he wanted to drive back to him right this moment, but also the regret for bringing Owen to the speakeasy instead of telling him to fuck off and leaving him at the castle entrance. It was just one bad decision after the next, and Salvador grew more agitated with Owen's shrill impatience and demanding, bloated ego the longer he had to be around him.

Owen was looking over the building, analyzing the architecture, as well as the buildings across the street. He scoffed. "Vegan nightclub chic doesn't exactly make the panties drop. Lovely... What a curious name for a restaurant."

Salvador peered into the restaurant through the glass of the front door. The lights were off, and the chairs were lifted over the tables to signal that the place was closed. Maybe Owen would grow tired of waiting and decide to come back another day, Salvador hoped. But the prospect of this happening fell away when a man appeared from out of the kitchen behind the service counter, startled to see two random men standing outside. Given Salvador and Owen's posh appearance, the man's guard must have been lowered, albeit confused.

He approached the front door. "We're closed," he said through the glass, his voice muffled as he looked the two strangers up and down. The man was in his seventies but still had a head of jet-black hair that had streaks of white at the sides, and a black mustache. His aura was vintage, down to his suspenders and style of trousers, and he spoke in a Mid-Atlantic accent. He seemed strange, like he was a time traveler from the distant past. Salvador had seen him many times before when Kitty dragged him into Lovely to eat lunch with her. It was odd to see a man like him working in a place like this... or seeing him, well, anywhere really.

Owen attempted a friendly, courteous smile. "Hi there. I'd like to talk to you about your business. That is, I'm assuming you're the owner? Do you have a few minutes to spare, or are you preparing to leave?"

The man raised an eyebrow. "Talk to me about what?" he asked gruffly, staring him down with his intimidating, almost scary, green eyes.

Owen's expression suddenly shifted. "The bar," he clarified. "I'm interested in seeing it."

"It's closed," said the man. "You can come back tomorrow."

Owen leaned forward. "You do know which bar I'm referring to, right? I'm not interested in bowls of hummus and pita bread."

Christopher stared him down, and even Owen seemed intimidated by him. Salvador's heart raced, finding the man oddly frightening, but also unusually appealing in his stoic mannerisms.

"Martini?" asked Owen, his voice lowering to a whisper even though there was no one else around to hear. "Roger's?"

The man glanced at Salvador, which caused Salvador to lean back instinctively as though a weapon had just been brandished in front of him. Then, the man reached forward and unlocked the door. His movements were so deliberate and calculated that Salvador knew he was on his game. This man wasn't just some grandfatherly hummus bar owner.

Owen wandered around the front of the restaurant with his hands out at his sides, his eyes trailing the four corners of the room.

The man looked as though he was regretting his decision to let them inside. "My apologies," he said, "who are you?"

Owen cleared his throat and smiled, extending his hand out to him. "Owen Kim. I'm a business owner, just like yourself... You are the owner, correct?"

Salvador rolled his eyes.

The man shook his hand aggressively in a way that seemed to startle Owen. "Christopher," he said, eyeballing Salvador next.

Salvador reached out his hand, smiling, and introduced himself. He couldn't deny it, though. It felt good standing next to Owen, introducing himself and walking alongside him as though they were business partners. He felt powerful, but also deflated at the same time. His thoughts kept straying back to Jay; then he'd return to being upset with himself again.

"Are you two partners?" asked Christopher, as though reading Salvador's mind.

Owen laughed awkwardly, looking at Salvador. "My friend Sal actually told me about your business. I'd like to share an interesting proposition with you, if you're willing to hear me out."

The three of them were distracted by a door opening at the back of the restaurant, intruding on the conversation. Robbie strolled forward, phone in hand, observing them. He positioned himself in front of the service counter and leaned his back against the display case.

"You'll break it," said Christopher, signalling with his hand for Robbie to lift his weight off the glass.

Robbie stepped a couple feet forward and stood tall on the spot, overshadowing them all in height. Christopher turned his attention back to Owen and Salvador. "It's late," he said.

"That's the whole point of a bar, though," said Owen, smirking. "It's open late."

Robbie scrunched up his face as he looked at Owen; it was as though the man's voice alone caused him physical pain. There was so much tension in the room that Owen just laughed. He paced the room, strolling through it like he was in an art gallery, looking up at the walls and down at the fresh hardwood flooring.

"He said leave," said Robbie.

"You really don't want me to leave," Owen chimed in. "There's magic within these walls, isn't there? Like an old folktale lost to the passing of time. Sorry for being melodramatic, guys. My dad's children's books have rubbed off on my imagination. Maybe it's better to think of it as a treasure, buried beneath our feet." Owen lifted his hands to his chest and slowly turned around on the spot, his loafers squeaking when they rubbed up against the hardwood floor. His eyes landed on the two doors at the back of the restaurant. When he walked up to them, he peered at Robbie over his shoulder and slid his hand down one of the doors, his gold ring dragging along the cracked paint.

"Tell me the purpose of you being here, or you can leave," said Christopher, walking towards him. "You have thirty seconds."

"I'd like to see a bar called Roger's," declared Owen, his voice earnest. "That's all. I'm not with the city council or anything, don't worry. I'm not–"

"Just because I'm an old man doesn't mean I don't know who you are," said Christopher. "I've heard of you." He glanced at Robbie, and they caught each other's non-verbal communication.

"I'd like to possibly buy this building from you," said Owen, getting right to the point. "I'm assuming it's yours?"

Christopher folded his arms. "I'm the owner," he said. "This building has been in my family since long before your ancestors ever stepped foot on American soil. Needless to say, it's very unique. What really makes you think I'd sell it to you, someone I've known for a whole five minutes?"

Owen's ears seemed to lift off like Dumbo at the mention of the word *unique*. He turned away from the door and softened his approach. "I'd like to see it first," he said calmly. "There is no pressure, Christopher. Bear in mind, you have a chance of becoming a very... very rich man–your *family* becoming rich. Hm, maybe you already have your fortune and gold, who knows. Then what about fame, Christopher? Do you need help growing your business to unbelievable heights? To the moon. Maybe one of your grandsons will, down the line. He can give me a call, whenever he wants. You *want* to be friends with me. Let's explore some options. If you don't like what you hear, I'll float away, and no one will ever know. Your secret will be safe with me. Trust me."

Salvador felt a tingle go down his body, as though someone was staring at him. Out of the corner of his eye, he saw Robbie's outline, his eyes glaring at him in the ghostly moonlight. Owen was persistent, Salvador knew. There was a menacing quality to him, like sugar laced with rat poison. You didn't screw around with a man like Owen if you knew just how much money and how many connections were at his disposal. Salvador knew it, and obviously Christopher did as well.

Christopher took a moment of introspection, then stepped forward to lead Owen into the back room.

"Christopher," said Robbie, questioning.

Just as he pushed the door open, Christopher turned to look at Robbie. "Nothing lasts," he said, tiredly. The door closed behind him, and the restaurant was left in silence. Robbie used his phone and called Jay, but there was no answer. As he hung up, the headlights from an Uber slid across the windows and a car door slammed just outside the building. Jay appeared at the front door.

Salvador felt relieved to see him, but anxious. Nevertheless, he unlocked the door to let him inside.

"Well... I really have no one to blame but myself," said Robbie, his head hanging low as Jay walked inside. He glanced at Salvador. "Who the fuck are you again?"

"Watch it," said Salvador.

Jay went and stood beside Salvador. "Robbie, I'm sorry."

Robbie sighed and put his phone away. "I'm not angry at you. I'm mad at myself for ever thinking it was a good idea to bring you down there in the first place, Jay." He walked slowly to the back and pushed open the door. "Just go home."

Salvador turned on his heel immediately and left the building through the front door, just as Robbie disappeared into the back, the door squeaking behind him.

Jay was left alone.

57

August 1987

Eleanor's ruby red rhinestones sparkled under the spotlight of the stage as she prepared to announce their expected Saturday night guest. The piano man had been quickly making a name for himself at Roger's, and some of the patrons would stop by the speakeasy just to hear what new song he had deemed worthy enough to share with his loyal audience.

"Before our little piano man graces us with his wondrous talent," said Eleanor, "I'd like to acknowledge a dear friend of mine who has just passed away. Michael was a regular here, and many of you at one point would have seen or spoken to him. He had the loudest voice and the most colorful soul. How many times did he come up from behind you, tap you on the shoulder, and tell you, not ask you, to dance or do a shot with him? Michael was someone who comforted me in my darkest and loneliest times. He got me up on stage when my inner chicken shit held me back from doing so.

He was the call I'd make at two in the morning for a ride home from the bar, drunk off my ass, or when I needed someone to talk to because the silence was too deafening. He'd pull me to my feet and haul my ass into bed so I wouldn't pass out on the side of some road and get mistaken for trash the next morning. Michael was only twenty-seven, but let me tell you, he lived his life on a level that most don't reach until much later in life. He said to me once that I was an inspiration to him. One of my biggest regrets was never telling him that he was my biggest inspiration. He taught me it was okay to be myself, colors and all. He defended and protected me at a time in my life when it felt like no one cared what happened to me. I'm standing here, and not afraid, because of that man. Save my seat at the bar while you're up there, Michael. We'll party together again one day."

Eleanor finished by blowing a kiss up to the heavens as applause and cheers followed its ascent towards the golden lights. "Now, here he is... Tristan!"

The lighting dimmed and the applause carried on as Tristan came out from backstage and took his seat at the gilded grand piano with a smile that was mixed with sadness from hearing Eleanor's speech. He always looked so proud before he was about to play. He had told Robbie that he would sometimes surprise himself at what he was able to create out of his imagination, as though it was second nature to him, like breathing. Perhaps it was the applause and praise from the audience afterward that gave him the ultimate satisfaction. Whenever he looked out into the crowd, before each song, the last thing he looked at before turning his eyes back to the piano keys was Robbie, sitting at the bar.

Liam leaned over the bar top. "Why don't you sit a bit closer?"

"This is where I first saw him play," replied Robbie, not taking his eyes off the stage.

Robbie's face lit up with joy the moment Tristan started playing a familiar melody that he knew almost right away. It was the melody he had played for Robbie at his house, the one he was inspired to write when they were at the park. Robbie's eyes opened wide in surprise when Tristan started to sing lyrics, and from the noticeable gasps in the audience, it seemed to catch others off guard as well. It was the first time anyone had ever heard him sing, and what a treat it was. When Tristan looked away from the piano keys, he briefly made eye contact with Robbie. The performance was a message to him, told through the melody and lyrics of the song. It was love, and regardless of what happened to them through the course of a lifetime, the love they shared would remain intact, and unspoiled, able to weather decades and centuries of changing times until the end of the world. His voice was confident and strong, and he was so beautiful. There was nothing he was unsure about. The chords he played, the notes that flew out from his voice during the sweeping chorus–there was no fear, and there was no judgement. Tristan offered his heart to Robbie, and Robbie took it.

When Tristan finished, another wave of applause erupted from the room. Robbie stood up from his bar stool to clap and cheer for him. Tristan looked at him, smiling, then went backstage.

Robbie eagerly bounced away from the bar and down to the lower floor, grabbing hold of the edge of the stage to pull himself up. He went through to the back, energized as his heart raced, but he didn't see Tristan where he usually was, rummaging around in his backpack as he prepared to leave for the night. From behind him, Robbie felt a sudden jump as Tristan grabbed his hips. When Robbie turned around in surprise, they pressed their lips against one another, a passion like none that had come before. Tristan pushed Robbie towards the wall, placing his hands on the sides of his face, rubbing his chest against him, their hearts beating like rabbits. Eleanor obliviously walked in on them, then she screeched dramatically and turned to leave the way she had come.

Robbie pulled away from Tristan, his face glistening. "You sounded incredible, babe."

"It's not hard... when your boyfriend is the inspiration," remarked Tristan as sweat beaded along his forehead. "I'd like to talk to you about something. It has to do with me coming back to Venus Valley to see you when I'm away at Curtis."

"That's, like, more than a year away," said Robbie, laughing.

"I know!" said Tristan excitedly, putting his hands on his shoulders. "But my parents have a trust set up for me. It's meant to help support me when I'm away at school. I'll use some of it to fly back here every couple months for a weekend. There's also Christmas, summer break and spring break."

"I can't ask you to do that," said Robbie. "Even though... you should."

"You don't have to ask me, because I'm doing it anyway," said Tristan. He ran his hands down Robbie's arms. "Coming to see you counts as one of the things that will help support me emotionally while I'm away at school. We can fly to Mexico or, like, Hawaii for spring break."

Robbie smiled and collapsed on top of him against the wall. "Can you believe we'll be done with high school next year?" He fell into Tristan's blue eyes and sighed in sweet bliss. "I'd give anything to have been able to take you to prom."

"We'll have our own private prom, then," said Tristan. He placed his hands on Robbie's waist and started swaying him from side to side.

Robbie looked down at his sneakers, making sure he wasn't going to accidentally step on him. He looked up at his face again. "You're not real," he said.

Tristan leaned in and kissed him on the lips. He lifted his hands from Robbie's waist and wrapped his arms around his body, holding him close, keeping him safe. They danced as time passed around them, neither wanting to let go of the other. Tristan finally let go and reached for his backpack that was sitting on the floor. "I would have asked you to come over tonight. My parents had this work party to go to, and they always get a hotel room for the night instead of coming back home. My mom got the flu, though, so they didn't go."

"Do you want me to walk you home?" asked Robbie.

"Uh..." said Tristan, "this might sound weird, but I'm actually really inspired right now. When that happens, I'll get into this head-space. Being by myself helps the creativity flow better." He sighed as he looked at Robbie, unable to resist him. "But if you *really* want to I'll make an exception."

Robbie lifted his palms out to him. "I don't want to interfere with a master's craft," he said. "Well... When you finish whatever it is, I'd love to be the first to hear it."

Tristan smiled and kissed him again. "You'll always be my first. I'll see you next week, babe. Bye, Robbie!"

As he started walking away, Robbie called him back. "Hey!"

Tristan turned around.

"You can start calling my house now... Maybe even come over finally."

Tristan smiled and adjusted the strap on his shoulder. "I'd like to see what kinds of posters you have on your bedroom walls. I'll call you on Monday after school."

Robbie was already counting down the hours. "Great."

Tristan waved and left.

58

Christopher shined his flashlight into the speakeasy after opening the door. Owen stepped inside after him and walked slowly towards the gold railing of the main tier, his eyes surveying the space as best he could within the flashlight's limited reach into the darkness. He looked down to where the tables and maroon leather seats had remained in place, untouched, for over three decades. His eyes took in the art deco wallpaper, the plastered ceilings and the glorious chandelier dazzling like twinkling stars in the flashlight's passing aura. He looked at the bar for a brief moment, then turned his attention to the small stage, whose heavy red curtains were parted to its sides.

"You're sitting on something that is just wasting away beneath your feet," said Owen, his voice incredulous. "While you traipse around up there, shuffling customers along in lineups, this world beneath you longs for the lights, music and laughter again. It yearns for the fragrances from freshly squeezed lemons, lime cordial and gin botanicals mixed with vermouth and olive brine." He walked down to the lower floor and took a seat at one of the tables, where he touched the vintage glasswork of one of the lanterns. He dragged a finger along the tablecloth, where decades of dirt had settled.

Christopher sat down next to Owen at the table and flicked off his flashlight, leaving them in complete darkness. It was an eerie thing to endure, having to sit there in complete pitch-black stillness with what felt like centuries of history descending upon them from all directions.

The hairs on the back of Owen's neck stood up, and cold drafts tugged at his clothes. He pulled out his phone and turned on the flashlight, casting him in a shield of light for protection.

"I'd like to see it open again," said Christopher.

Owen looked at him uncomfortably. The old man's terrifying green eyes reminded him of a snake or monster, inhuman.

"But... I'll need help," added Christopher. They both turned at the sound of someone coming through the door of the speakeasy. Robbie appeared out of the dark and took a seat next to Christopher at the table. "So, what are you thinking?" asked Christopher, returning his attention to Owen.

Owen looked at both of them as they waited for him to reply. "Well," he started, "Salvador found me what I've been looking for. It's perfect, Christopher. I'd like to take it off your hands."

"Exactly what have you been looking for?" asked Christopher.

Owen cleared his throat. "I've been looking to establish a new nightclub destination, and to build an even better nightlife community here in Venus Valley..." His eyes trailed around the room, his stomach churning as goosebumps crawled up his skin when puffs of chilled air blew past his ear and down his neck. "It appears this bar hasn't been updated in a long time. I'd like to capture the essence of its past, but bring it into the present. It'll look absolutely extraordinary."

"You do know what this place is, though," said Christopher.

Owen tilted his head, wondering if this was a trick question.

"It's a gay bar," Christopher declared.

Owen nodded. "You're asking me if I'd keep it that way."

Christopher stared at him, waiting.

Owen glanced at Robbie, who, though not as intimidating as Christopher, was still a formidable presence. "It will be an all-inclusive nightclub," he concluded.

"What does that mean to you?" asked Christopher.

"It means anyone can come and enjoy it," said Owen simply. "Trust me on this."

"I don't trust you," said Christopher unflinchingly. "Not since the second you walked into my property."

"Listen," said Owen, "why not use this building in its entirety? Just imagine the possibilities and what it could look like. People will come back, again and again, not just to drink and dance but to soak in the building's history. Forty million tourists visit Venus Valley each and every year, and when they do an internet search for which bars in the city are the best to spend their money at, this place will pop up at the top of the list."

"It won't be some generic... cold and plastic nightclub?" asked Christopher.

Owen shivered at such accusations. "It'll be the best nightclub in the city, and one of the best in the entire country. You don't get that with generic, cold and plastic."

"The best *gay* nightclub," Christopher clarified.

Owen drummed his fingers on the table. "How would you like to have a stake in this venture with me? Both of you. The three of us, plus my other connections, can transform this place into something timeless. Then, we can expand into other cities."

"The name?" Christopher probed.

"Well..." said Owen, "'Roger's' sounds a bit... dated? No? This isn't a hamburger joint."

Christopher's eyes widened. "That was its previous name," he said, not able to contain a vaguely patronizing tone. "It was called Roger's for sixty-seven years until it was changed in 1987."

"To what?" asked Owen.

"You don't deserve to know."

"Tristan," said Robbie.

Christopher shot an annoyed look at Robbie, but then his reaction softened when he saw Robbie's solemn expression as he stared down at the table, his body unmoving.

Owen glanced up at the plastered ceiling, considering the name and weighing it out. "That's... special," he concluded.

"So? What would you name it, then?" asked Christopher.

Owen raised his hands and smiled like he was about to reveal a big *ta-dah* moment. "Ten After Twelve," he announced, pausing for dramatic effect. "It was the precise time when Tremble was officially sold, and it changed my life forever."

"It sounds completely stupid," said Christopher. "Inspired by an equally stupid mobile phone app."

Robbie put his hand on Christopher's arm to calm him down.

Owen let out a brief cough to clear his throat. "The name is negotiable," he said. "I'd like you to come in as my partner and share in some of the profits."

"Eighty is fast approaching for me," said Christopher. "Money is no real concern of mine anymore."

Owen turned his attention to Robbie. "What about you?"

Robbie stared at him. "You want to perform some 'reconstructive surgery' on this place and turn it into something that it simply isn't. It's a slap in the face to every person who ever set foot in here."

"If we keep it as a gay bar, it won't be living up to its full potential," said Owen delicately. "You'd be missing out on demographics that otherwise would pay to come and enjoy an evening in this wonderful place."

"He's not giving you this speakeasy if you won't keep it as a gay bar, you moron," said Robbie angrily. "What part of that don't you understand? It's not about maximizing profits, or having something everyone can enjoy."

"It's a tomb right now," said Owen. "Do you think the people who came here over the last century would want it to keep looking like this? Many of them would have loved the idea of bringing new people in."

Robbie scoffed. "Don't put words into their mouths. You never met any of them. You don't know shit."

"Gay or straight or whatever you are, everyone will have a good time here," prodded Owen.

"Coming from the mouth of someone who isn't part of the gay community," said Robbie. "You don't know what it's like to be me or any of the people who've been here."

Owen's Adam's apple bobbed as he clenched his sweaty fist on the table.

"I've been a black sheep... my entire life," continued Robbie. "Gay bars feel like home to me. I'm surrounded by people who are just like me. You don't know what it's like to have a place you can go to where you can feel safe, where you won't be judged by how you look or who you dance with or who you kiss. This speakeasy has a heart, a history, and you can't just rip that out. You're no different than the assholes who bought your app. They bought something that a lot of people loved, then turned it into shit, didn't they?"

Owen shrugged, completely mute.

"Did you even care about your app in the first place?" asked Robbie.

Owen raised his chin at him. "I developed a fantastic, profitable idea," he said. "My sole intention was to make it popular enough so it could be sold. Tremble meant nothing to me."

Christopher stood up slowly and placed his hands on the back of the chair. "You could offer me all the money in the world, Owen. This place could end up making hundreds of millions. I'd still never sell it to you, or anyone. I'd like to show you something, though."

Christopher walked away from the table. Unsure at first, Owen reluctantly got up and followed him, as did Robbie. They followed Christopher to the rows of framed photographs that were hung on the wall beside the bar.

Christopher pointed up to the very first black-and-white photo on the top left. "That was my grandfather, Dennis, and his partner, Roger."

Owen scanned the photos with the light of his phone, row by row, decade by decade. There were patrons, lots of them, all depicted in moments of happiness, excitement and loving companionship. His eyes fell to the picture on the bottom right, the last photo ever hung. In the photo, there was a silhouette of a pianist playing a gilded grand piano on the speakeasy's stage to a small audience. "I've seen that piano," said Owen in a distant voice. It was like he was looking upon something from his childhood that he hadn't seen in decades.

Robbie looked at him and furrowed his brow.

"It's at Larchdale Castle," said Owen. "What was it doing down here?"

"It was always here. It was donated to the castle when Roger's closed," said Christopher.

"Is it made with real gold?" asked Owen. He leaned in closer to the photo. "That's him... Tristan. Isn't it? His name is inscribed on the piano's fallboard." Owen turned his head to look out at the stage behind him, comparing what he saw in the photo with what he saw in real life. "I'd like Tristan's contact information, if you have it. I'm eager to meet the man who lent his name to this wonderful place."

Christopher reached behind the frame of the photo, retrieved a piece of yellowed paper and handed it to Owen. It was a newspaper clipping. Owen unfolded it and scanned the text.

August 3, 1987

VENUS VALLEY – At approximately 1:25 a.m. on Sunday, August 2, a seventeen-year-old boy was determined to be the victim of a suspected hate crime after being found unresponsive on a sidewalk in Pleasant Bay.

According to a resident who witnessed the incident from a window of her home, the boy was approached by two males in their twenties, and they were overheard asking him if he was gay. The boy replied "yes" and a violent scuffle occurred. The victim was reportedly thrown to the ground and attacked repeatedly as the two men could be heard blaming the boy for the AIDS epidemic. The witness says the boy pleaded for his life through fits of choking. The eyewitness' parents ran outside to help, but the assailants had fled. The victim was declared dead on scene by paramedics.

Anyone with information is urged to contact police.

Owen lowered the newspaper clipping and handed it back to Christopher. "I'm sorry," he said softly.

Robbie stared down at the paper with sullen eyes, a wash of emptiness spreading across his face.

"At the time," said Christopher, "it felt like we'd all end up living short lives. If the gay cancer didn't get you, the violence sure would. Or, ultimately, your own self-resentment. No one had the ability to light up a room the way Tristan could with his music. After his death, faces I'd come to know were no longer showing up here. The light kept fading as more and more lives kept leaving. So, for the first time since 1920, we closed the bar. It was only supposed to be a temporary closure. There was always the intent to come back here one day, to reopen the door. Liam, one of the bartenders here at the time, suggested the name be changed. To honour not only Tristan, but all the others who had died as well. Tristan stands for something. Not just a boy, but a hope. Like the Pink Flower, and Roger's that came after. Roger's was a hope that one day love would win. But in 1987, almost seventy years later, it felt like all the progress that had been made up to that point was for nothing, and what happened to Tristan was proof of that. Even though..." Christopher turned to Robbie, "there was still so much love to be had."

Robbie looked to Christopher with tears in his eyes, then to Owen. Their eyes connected, and Owen saw a whole life unfulfilled, a life that had been snatched away from this man. Owen extended his hand in surrender, his face mournful. "I'm sorry for the inconvenience of my visit." Without another word, Owen turned and walked out of the speakeasy.

Robbie lifted his hands to his face and sobbed, his anguish echoing throughout the room. Christopher put his arms around him. "I'm giving it to you, Robbie."

"I can't," he said.

"My years are running out," said Christopher. "You're still young. There's no one in my family who will understand the importance of this place like you do. I'm not selling it to you. I'm giving it to you."

Robbie's face was wet with tears as they continued to fall from his inconsolable eyes.

"Will you accept my gift?" asked Christopher.

Robbie grasped onto Christopher tighter, like he was a life preserver threatening to slide away from him. "Don't you leave me too," he cried desperately. "Why does it still hurt so much after all these years? He's supposed to be here!"

Tears spilled from Christopher's eyes as he rubbed Robbie's back. "You sail onward, Robbie. You have to."

59

Martin stumbled into the foyer as the Uber reversed out of the driveway. Drunk, he slid his loafers off and dropped his keys onto a nearby table along with his wallet. It was just past ten, earlier than usual for getting home after a party. Carly was talking to an online friend through video chat as she snacked on a grilled chicken Caesar salad she had ordered through a food delivery app.

Martin sat down next to her on the couch, moving aside the pillows and resting his hand on his cheek as he waited. Waited for what, exactly? He didn't know.

Carly laughed as she and her friend chatted away. She glanced at Martin out of the corner of her eye, noticing his unusually melancholy energy.

"Sarah," she said. "I've gotta go. Martin just got home...We'll talk next week? Great!" She disconnected from the chat and carried on eating her salad, stuffing it down more quickly now that she wasn't on video with her friend. She extended her plastic fork out to Martin, a piece of Caesar-drenched lettuce falling onto her sweatpants. "Try some. It's from Fresh, Oh My! They sent me a gift card for one thousand dollars for tagging them on a post a couple weeks ago."

Martin leaned forward and let her feed him a slice of the grilled chicken and soggy lettuce. "It's good," he said. "Salty, though."

"How was the party?" she asked, dropping a small crouton into her mouth. She looked perfectly dolled up, like she always was, with her hair done up in a bun.

"Are you upset that I didn't bring you with me?" he asked.

Carly flapped her hand at him and shook her head. "As long as you had a good time," she said, reaching for a napkin and wiping her mouth. "I'd like to say sorry for how I've been acting. It didn't occur to me how much pressure you've been under lately. It's been stressing you out."

He smiled and put his hand on her leg. "It's okay."

The room fell into an abrupt silence. For Martin, it was like he was peering over the edge of a precipice, his heart racing, about to jump.

"Who was there?" she asked.

"People," said Martin. "Super rich people who'd probably never give me the time of day. You didn't miss anything. It was a waste of time, actually." He paused. "I've been wanting to talk to you about something."

Carly slowed her chewing and looked at him, caught off guard. Martin looked back at her with downtrodden eyes, his chest heaving before the plunge.

She put her fork down. "What?" she asked.

Martin sighed and sat upright, his hands on his knees. "Carly, I'm gay."

Carly was still, frozen in place. Martin couldn't bring himself to say anything more until she responded. He stared at her, waiting. The longer she went without saying something, the more desperate he became. His eyes were beginning to tear up, his mouth agape, breathless.

She twisted her fingers and the bracelet around her wrist. "How long have you known?" she asked finally.

"For a while... Something finally clicked," he said quietly. He could tell a million and one things were running through her head. "I'm sorry."

Tears filled Carly's eyes and she looked away. She placed a hand to her forehead, her wedding band glaring at Martin. Then, she cleared her throat and stood up. "Well... That's that."

Martin furrowed his brow up at her. "What does that mean?"

"No, um... Thank you for telling me," she said as she picked up the open container of salad and walked towards the kitchen, but she stopped halfway and returned to the living room. She sat back down and placed the salad right on the edge of the table, accidentally letting it fall to the floor and scatter lettuce and chicken everywhere. She curled herself into a ball and started crying.

Martin leaned forward to hug her. "I'm sorry for doing this to you."

"It was something that did cross my mind," she said through fits of sobbing. "Even before we got married."

Martin leaned in closer and rested his face on her shoulder.

"I just want you to be happy," she said quietly, "and I'm sorry you're not happy right now being with me."

Martin wiped some of the tears from her cheeks. "You were great, Carly. You really were like a ray of sunshine in my life... You still are." He held his gaze on her. "If you had your suspicions, why did you agree to marry me?"

More tears rolled down her face as she turned to look at him. "Because I love you," she said. "Do you love me?"

"Of course," he said. "I'll always love you." He put his hand into hers. "I just... I can't give you the kind of love that you deserve to have."

Carly nodded her head, tragically, as her kingdom fell from under her feet. She smiled and placed her hand on his arm.

Martin hung his head. "Can you forgive me?" he asked.

"There's nothing to forgive," she said. "Thank you for telling me, and not choosing to wait until ten years from now." Her face broke down again, but this time she started laughing, and crying, at the same time. "Leave it to me to marry the gay boy."

Martin laughed along with her, but he too started to cry from feeling the burdensome weight finally lifted from his shoulders.

"I have one last favour to ask from you," she said.

"What is it?"

"Can we do a video together?"

Martin's face dropped. "About what?"

"You coming out."

Martin's eyes widened in disbelief. He scoffed at her. "Like one of those 'my husband is gay' videos? No."

"Please," she said, grabbing his hands. "It'll be great!"

"You're not going to monetize this moment," said Martin, frustration building. "You can't monetize my pain."

Carly's face recoiled into annoyance. "What about my pain?"

"Recording a video for millions of strangers to watch and judge me, and you, isn't the answer," he said. "I've had enough of that. I'm not ready for the comments and... bullshit. Why is it that every little thing we do needs to be recorded and shared?"

"That's what you signed up for when you married me," stated Carly. "It's my job–it pays for everything!"

"No, then," he concluded. "That's my answer. I'm not going to make some confession to the world about something so personal and hard for me, just for the sake of clicks and ad revenue."

"It's not all about that," she said defensively. "Maybe your story will help others."

"Money is all it's ever about!" exclaimed Martin. "Actual dollar signs are flashing in your eyes as we speak! Helping others comes in at a distant second place, believe me."

Carly got up and bent down to push the fallen scraps of food back into the container like it was a dust pan. "You're really lucky I'm supportive of this new direction in your life," she said dramatically. "Many women wouldn't be."

"This is all my fault," said Martin, "I'll admit to that. I'm sorry for doing this to you. But if you think you can exploit me, all in the name of your job, then no, sorry."

"Do I have your blessing to do a video by myself, then?" she asked, looking up at him.

"It's your life, Carly. You can do whatever you want."

"It's just... I don't want to do it without our families knowing first," she said.

Martin had completely forgotten about telling his family. The weight of his burden returned, and it must have been obvious because Carly sat next to him and put her hand on his thigh.

"Do you want me to be there when you tell them?" she asked.

Martin shook his head and cupped his face into his hands. "I don't know if this is even worth it. But it's too late now, right?" He pulled his hands away and looked at her. "I'm straight, actually."

Carly gave him a small smile. "You need to live your life open and honest," she said. "You made the right decision doing this now rather than later. I'll still come to your wedding."

Martin returned a smile. "I'll be at yours, too."

Carly sighed and slumped down on the floor. "Here's to doing it all over again. Maybe I'll just die alone, with no kids." She took his hand, her eyes welling up when she looked at his gold wedding band. "You were my white knight," she said quietly. "You made me so happy... You weren't a mistake... Please know that." She let go of him and ran upstairs, shutting the bedroom door behind her.

Martin looked around the living room. He got up and stood in front of the fireplace mantel, where some of their framed wedding pictures were arranged like a shrine. Carly's smile from that day was the brightest he had ever seen it, and his was equally joyful. Looking back, he had done what he thought was the right thing to do.

There would be no more hiding now. The fading night would bring a new dawn tomorrow, and with it a new life with an uncertain destination ahead.

60

Fame nightclub was busier than usual for a Saturday when Robbie arrived. He had come here as a reflex for what had happened earlier in the evening, wanting to drown his sadness in shots of tequila. Everything was crashing down on him and burying him alive. He was experiencing an existential crisis, looking back on his life, and punishing himself for the choices he had made that led him to where he was now. He thought about Tristan, and how he would have been disappointed in him for all the things he hadn't done with his life. Robbie's last year of high school was bleak. He locked himself inside his bedroom for the entire year whenever he wasn't in school, never wanting to come out. He'd lie in his bed thinking of ways to end his life. But something held him back from pulling the trigger. He thought about Tristan, and how his promising life was taken from him, and here Robbie was, contemplating taking his own. He wanted to keep on living, for him. Robbie regretted, every day, that he wasn't there to protect his boyfriend from what had happened to him. If he had only gone with him that night, Tristan would have made it home. Tristan died alone, with no one there to save him. He died in fear, in the dirt. Tonight, all the emotions Robbie had felt back then were eroding within himself. He felt like he was seventeen again, helpless, and afraid. He had wasted his life. He amounted to nothing.

Robbie managed to scoop a table for himself after downing two shots of tequila. He sat alone, with his fist under his chin, staring vacantly into the void as a multitude of men filled the open spaces around him. To some, it might have appeared he was staring right at them, when in actuality he was staring at nothing, for his mind was in a clouded wasteland. He caught the attention of a boy who was sitting at a table just in front of him. The array of lights from the dance floor lit up the surface of his earring and his dreamy eyes that were searching for a connection in the crowd. The boy was with two of his friends, who wore backwards ball caps, one of which was black mesh on the backside and the other bejewelled with blue rhinestones. All three casually looked at Robbie with *the eyes*: lust, and want. The boy with the pierced ear came forward with his beer in hand and took the stool beside Robbie.

"Hey," said the boy.

"No," said Robbie, not even looking at him at first, but then his eyes wandered to the boy's shirt that read *Helluva Bottom* in a juicy pink typeface.

The boy scoffed at Robbie's rejection and stood up. "Okay... Whatever. Imagine getting lost on your way to the retirement home. Don't break a hip when you leave here."

"That was quite the speech," said Robbie smoothly, flashing a smile at him. "Gold star for you."

Robbie's unusual smile seemed to have done something to the boy, because he seemed to regret his insult. With nothing more to say, intimidation got the better of him and he went back to his table. Soon after, Helluva Bottom and his two friends got up and went elsewhere.

Robbie left his table and made his way through the cluster of bodies to get to the unisex bathroom. Inside, there was an alcove to the left with a built-in padded bench where patrons would sit and wait for their friends, or engage in lively conversation. There was a man at the washing station who was offering hand towels, spurts of cologne and deodorant to anyone who left a tip for his services. Robbie didn't have to wait long to use a urinal, and when one opened up for him, he took his place next to a muscular man with a shaved head.

The man looked at Robbie, giving him *the eyes*. The veins were prominent down his arms, and his nipples stiff through his white muscle shirt that said *Work. Lift. Fuck*. He had a scruffy face and big, beautiful brown eyes with long lashes, probably in his thirties. It was just so easy to get sex. There was barely any effort required, and if you looked like Mr. Scruffy, zero effort was needed. If you flashed him *the eyes*, and had nerve, you only had to wave your dick wand in his general direction and it would be a party inside your mouth in no time. When Sarim was away on Sabrina's tour, Robbie wouldn't have sex with anyone else. In the four years they'd been together, the only time he was with another person was when Sarim was home and they were looking for a third or another couple to have fun with. Those hookups were always a great time, and added more adventure to their life by helping them make new friends along the way. But, ultimately, no other sex was as passionate and intimate as what he and Sarim shared. The other guys were fast food, something to indulge in for the moment. Sarim was the bed that kept him warm at night during the cold winter months. He was the arm that wrapped itself around him as they fell asleep together, and the face that greeted him in the morning. He was the home he looked forward to seeing every day. When Robbie made eye contact with the man next to him, it was empty lust.

Robbie left the urinal and washed up, dropping a five-dollar bill into the attendant's tip jar after being offered a towel. He stopped to pull out his phone beside the alcove where two girls and a boy were laughing, their eyeshadow done in brilliant shades of purple and blue. Sarim had messaged him a couple hours ago telling him that he was staying another night at Larchdale Castle to finish with last-minute rehearsals for Sabrina's concert tomorrow night. Then, Sarim would be leaving Venus Valley to continue with the rest of the tour for another two months and wouldn't be back again until autumn. Robbie knew just how little time he had spent with Sarim during the last week. They could have done more things together, like go out to eat or just share each other's company. Robbie's heart dropped. He felt angry and frustrated with himself. He was sabotaging this relationship. His inner demons were getting in the way of loving Sarim to the full extent that he should.

Robbie replied to Sarim's message, and Sarim responded almost right away.

Hey, sorry for the late response. Can we meet up tomorrow?

Ok :)

The added smiley face from Sarim made Robbie feel better. He just wanted to love Sarim. But it felt like loving Sarim was a betrayal when his heart already belonged to someone else.

He looked at the kids having a good time in the alcove, and it infuriated him, seeing them happy. He stormed out, only to be met with two boys kissing against the wall, their bodies coated in a ghostly red light that shone down from over the bathroom's entrance. Robbie looked at them, pressed up against the wall, one boy's hands on the other's face as though it was the last time they'd ever see each other again. He ripped himself away and headed for the crowded bar of wild partying drunks to down another shot of tequila. He stayed at the bar instead of returning to his seat because a group of people had already commandeered his table and decided to dance around it. At that precise moment, the DJ started spinning a dance remix of Elton John's "Nikita." The familiar melody reverberated down on everyone like a wave of celebratory ecstasy. The table where the three boys had been sitting previously was now occupied by another boy, sitting by himself. He was the kind of boy who wouldn't be sitting by himself for much longer amongst all these prowlers of the night. The lights flashed across his face, perfectly perfect, just like how Robbie remembered him to be. Robbie's mouth hung open; he felt like he was hallucinating. It was *him*. The ghost.

It wasn't long after when two men dressed in black shirts and jeans came over and took a seat on the stools at either side of the boy. This wasn't an introductory interaction, for they all seemed too casual and laid back together. All three were smiling, talking and drinking like they knew each other already. Both of the men were masculine in appearance, possibly friends of the boy, or maybe they had just met him earlier in the evening. They were also older than him, perhaps in their thirties. They looked the boy up and down as they spoke, eyeing him like a prized slab of gourmet chocolate in a chocolatier's window display, their mouths all but drooling as their tongues rolled out of their mouths for such a young, handsome thing to be devoured. The boy was drinking from his own glass when one of them offered him a shot, and they all did one together, throwing their heads back.

Robbie felt a knot developing in his throat, but he wasn't exactly sure why. He tried looking away, surveying the silhouettes of people around him instead, but his eyes would always return to them like a magnet. Robbie looked away every few seconds, trying not to be obvious. The boy was clearly buzzed, as were the two men, and he appeared eager to indulge in whatever the night had to offer him. One of the men leaned into the boy's ear and said something over the music that blared from the speakers around them, sending the dance floor into a frenzy. Then, the three of them stood up in unison. Robbie looked away again, just assuming they were headed for the dance floor or bar to grab more shots. Instead, they went in the opposite direction, away from the dancing and drinking and towards the exit. The two men walked behind the boy, like a pair of bodyguards, with one of them placing his hands on the boy's shoulders. Robbie watched as the two men stopped for a moment to whisper into each other's ears, laughing, then continued on in the boy's wake.

Robbie stood at the bar, not ordering anything. The bass of the music was in sync with his own pulse as his body heated up. His gut was twisting inside of him. He couldn't shake the boy from his mind. He looked just like *him*. Then, a sudden chill crept over him, a draft of wicked foreboding. The Elton John song rang in his ears, the alcohol clogging his judgement. Suddenly, a glass had fallen and shattered on the floor right in front of him, its shards glowing blue in the passing lights.

Robbie pushed his way through the crowd and made for the exit just as the three that he'd been watching left the building. He paused where he was; waiting, thinking... frustration overpowering him. He glanced over to the VIP lounge next to the exit, where there was an elevated platform furnished with couches and tables where groups would pay for exclusive bottle service treatment. He edged towards the exit, his mind going in several different directions. Then, a bottle of vodka in the VIP lounge caught his eye. The clear bottle was nearly empty, just sitting on the table. Robbie was used to making snap decisions, and given that he was intoxicated, this one came easy. He made his way up the few steps of the VIP lounge and stood before a group of five girls on a white couch. The girl in the middle, wearing a cotton candy pink cocktail dress, was also sporting a cheap birthday crown that signaled to all that it was her twenty-first birthday.

He flashed them a smile and extended his hand out in a welcoming gesture. "Hello, birthday girl!" he said enthusiastically. "I'm the manager, and thought I'd check in to see how the party is going tonight!"

"It's so amazing!" yelled the birthday girl, laughing with the others.

"You're really hot," said one of her friends. They all continued laughing as Robbie looked at them, his face dumbstruck.

"I've been wanting a sugar daddy for my birthday present," said the birthday girl, looking up at him with happy, drunken eyes. "I'll be the secret bar ho that you can keep under the counter for after hours play time."

"Natalie! No, no, no," said one of the other girls, cringing, as she put her hand over her friend's mouth.

"Yessssss," said the birthday girl matter-of-factly, placing a finger on her friend's lips. "This a gay bar, so it's all good. I'm gonna make out with a gay guy..." She rolled her head back and laughed hysterically. "Can we get some food up in this bitch? We're all hungry as fuuuck."

Robbie picked up the vodka bottle. "I'll get this out of your way and bring you something else. The food is on its way out. Stay out of trouble!" He turned around, ignoring their drunken praise, and rushed back down the short flight of steps towards the exit. As he casually looked around, he slid the bottle underneath his bomber jacket and held it in place against the side of his chest with his arm. He exited the nightclub and saw the usual late-night shenanigans of people coming and going, as well as the interested glances from guys as they walked past him. Robbie's frustration was that he had stalled for too long. He only had seconds to see which direction they had gone, whether they'd gone in a vehicle or on foot, so he looked up and down the streets and glanced into cabs, his heart panicking for no real reason. If he couldn't see what he was looking for in the next minute, he would go home. This was madness.

Robbie walked further down the sidewalk for a new perspective. Across the street, the two men in black and the boy had just rounded a corner onto a side street. Robbie's pulse quickened and he jaywalked across the street, where he got an angry, extended blast from a car horn. He made it to the corner and turned down the side street, keeping his hands inside his pockets as he walked casually, but quietly, like a ghost.

For several minutes, Robbie followed them from a safe distance, not knowing what he was actually doing here. He felt intrusive, like a creep, and wondered if he should just turn around and leave them be. They were just three guys, friends perhaps, having some fun. They were going home from the bar to continue with the party, something Robbie was all too familiar with from when he was younger.

He stopped where he was, looking onward, his feet paused on the cement. He stopped because his gut was in knots again. There were far too many times in his life where he had chosen not to listen to his gut. He started walking again and told himself that he'd only keep going until he was satisfied that fate was no longer in his control. Just a few more minutes, then he'd turn around and go back to the club, grab an Uber, and head home like he probably should have done in the first place.

The group of three turned down a couple more side streets, further away from Fame and the vibrancy of the gay village. Everything in this area was closed, and there were no signs of any human life except for the occasional person or duo. Uneasiness overtook him when a dark shadow crossed the street ahead. He sometimes forgot just how intimidating he looked to some people, and often had to remind himself that to them, *he* was the guy they should be keeping a distance from, not the other way around.

Just when he thought about turning back, feeling like this was all a waste of time, the two men paused up ahead and halted the boy, causing Robbie to stop where he was and sink into the shadows of a bakery storefront. When he craned his head around the railing of the stairs, he witnessed one of the men grab the boy around the neck and drag him in between two buildings to their right, with the other man following.

"Fuck..." said Robbie quietly. Every second counted now, and he couldn't hesitate. He felt immersed in his sudden panic, anger awakening inside himself. He jogged forward as quietly as he could. The space between the two buildings was narrow, and Robbie peeked his head around and saw them, the street lights weakly illuminating half the scene. One of the men had the boy pinned to the wall, pressing his hand against the back of the boy's neck and shoving his face into the dirty wall. The boy had already given up on fighting back, knowing how weak he was compared to the two of them. The other man stood on the other side of the boy, facing in Robbie's direction. However, he was too distracted by what was happening to notice Robbie. The man who had the boy pinned against the wall started unzipping his pants and loosening the belt. The sound of the metal buckle eclipsed the quiet of the night.

"Pull down my pants," demanded one of the men, taking his hand off the back of the boy's neck and slapping him across his cheek. He forced the boy around so he faced him, and the boy reached down and pulled down the man's pants, doing as he was told, unknowable thoughts running through his head.

Robbie gathered up the courage he needed to be strong, invincible. Then, he pulled out the bottle from underneath his jacket, grasped it firmly, rushed forward, and slammed the side of it against the nearer man's head just as the other shouted when he noticed

Robbie's presence. The man grabbed hold of Robbie, but Robbie shoved the flat base of the bottle into the man's forehead and kicked him in the crotch, sending him backward. The man that Robbie struck was holding the side of his head where the bottle had hit, yelling obscenities. He slammed his fist into Robbie's face, but Robbie came back and struck him with the bottle again, this time sending him to the ground. Robbie focused all his attention on the other man now, kicking him in the crotch and slamming the bottle at his head. The man was sent stumbling backward towards the wall with a small, jagged shard of glass sticking out of his skin. Robbie heard brisk footsteps as the boy ran out of the alley, so he took advantage of the men's delirium and pain and bolted away with the broken bottle in hand, following the boy, who was sprinting like his life depended on it. The boy went down another side street, and Robbie did the same. Robbie turned his head back to see if the men were following them, but there was no one, not a sound, so he tossed the broken bottle away.

"Hey!" yelled Robbie, seeing the boy getting farther and farther ahead of him.

The boy looked over his shoulder but kept on running. They ran for some time, and Robbie's body was unable to keep up. He was no longer the rugby star he'd been in high school. There were cramps in his chest, and his legs were buckling. He had to stop and breathe. He leaned over, grabbing hold of the nearest wall for support, his face sweaty, his shirt feeling like he'd been out in a downpour from the amount of sweat running down his back on such a humid night.

The boy kept on going. Robbie was heaving hard, and just when he thought the boy was going to turn the corner, the boy stopped and spun to his right. He leaned over to throw up. Robbie didn't want him to stop running. He wanted him to keep getting away, to get out of here, to find somewhere safe. The boy leaned back up and looked in Robbie's direction, his body heaving up and down. He collapsed onto the sidewalk.

Robbie pushed himself off the wall and jogged down the street until he reached him. The boy had tried to pull himself up but had collapsed again, his own vomit smeared on his shorts and legs. Robbie took his arm and helped him up to his feet. "Hey, I'm here to help you," he said.

The boy grabbed Robbie's other arm for support, and Robbie guided him away from the mess on the ground. "Can you walk?" he asked, slowly letting go of him. The boy seemed able to manage on his own, just stumbling slightly.

Cars appeared from around the corner, one by one, like a steady train. The headlights flashed across Robbie's sweaty and bruised face. Just around the corner was the entrance to a local park, its front iron gates wide open as cars exited.

"Let's get in there," said Robbie, leading the boy inside. He thought maybe the boy wouldn't follow him, but he did. The boy took hold of Robbie's arm, which surprised him. It made him forget about the pain he felt in his body for just a little bit. Once inside, they went down the park trail that diverged from the main road. "You're safe with me, okay?" he said.

"Mhm," said the boy.

Robbie was able to find the outdoor bathrooms, where he was hoping there would be a water fountain. When he spotted the small wall fountain between the men's and women's bathrooms, Robbie led the boy to it and they both chugged probably half a liter of water each. The several trails were aglow from the overhanging lights of the park, and Robbie thought he would see the play structure… the swings. But they weren't there anymore; it was just a small, empty field. The old, abandoned stage, however, was still present. Mostly overgrown, it had been turned into a mural by various local artists. Its domed ceiling was a ruin, but decorated with art to cover up the decay. Seeing how exhausted the boy was, Robbie took his arm and led him to it. "I'll order you a ride," he said. "It'll be ten or fifteen minutes."

When they crossed the field and reached the stage, they collapsed on the steps. The boy crawled up to the stage and leaned over the edge, probably to throw up again. When it didn't happen, he instead fell backwards and lay spread eagle on the stage floor.

"Are you okay?" asked Robbie.

The boy wiped his mouth with his hand and nodded.

Robbie pulled out his phone and opened the Uber app. "I'm ordering you a ride now."

The boy made a groaning noise and rolled over to his side.

"Are you sure you're okay?" asked Robbie again, lowering his phone and looking at him. "Are you hurt?"

"No," replied the boy, tears forming at the corners of his eyes. "Just really drunk. My head and face hurt." He reached around to rub the back of his neck. "I'm kinda sore."

"Just take it easy," said Robbie. "The Uber shouldn't take that long. You'll be home soon. Would you like to tell me your name?"

"Ben," he replied, looking at him.

Robbie smiled slightly. "My name is Robbie."

"What happened to them? Where did they go?"

"They're gone. What matters is that you're okay."

"I shouldn't have gone with them," confessed Ben. "I just met them at the bar... and wanted to have a good time. It never turns out to be a good time."

"People have different ideas of what a good time is," said Robbie. "You should try going with a friend next time or someone you know–like a buddy system."

"That was the original plan," said Ben. They made silent eye contact with each other, and Robbie looked down, unable to look at him for more than a few seconds at a time.

"What's your address?" he asked, reopening his phone. When Ben didn't reply, he asked him again.

Ben looked down, his jaw clenched, like he wanted to say something, but couldn't.

"I'm ordering you a ride home," clarified Robbie. "I'll pay for it."

Ben reached for his pockets in a panic to check that he still had his wallet, phone and house key on him. He then put his hands down and froze, unmoving. It became eerie, like he had suddenly turned to stone. There wasn't a single sound, anywhere. Spooked, Robbie glanced out into the field to seek out something that was moving, a leaf or a branch in the wind. Ben finally blinked and moved his body.

"Do you live with parents or a family member? Roommates?"

Ben wouldn't speak. His eyes were so lost.

Robbie was becoming concerned over Ben's inability to answer such a simple question. "Where did you wake up this morning?" he offered, rewording the question.

Still, no response.

Robbie put his phone down. "I'm not leaving until you tell me." When he said those words, Robbie thought maybe he was being too forward, that maybe Ben would run off. He looked down and sighed. "Is it complicated?" he asked.

Ben looked at him and nodded.

"Where were you planning on staying tonight?"

"I'm not sure," said Ben. He looked at Robbie again, his blue eyes crumbling. "I don't want to be gay."

Robbie furrowed his brow, caught off guard, the words hitting him hard. "What makes you say that?"

"It's really lonely," said Ben.

Robbie glanced down and placed a hand on the stage floor. "It's important to have people in your life who love you for who you are, and will always be there for you... People who help you feel like it's okay to be yourself. Sometimes there are people who you thought were those things, but actually aren't. It's the people who really love you for you, the ones who are there for you no matter what, that you need to keep by your side."

"What if you don't really have anyone like that?" asked Ben.

"You're looking at one," said Robbie. "Right here."

Tears filled Ben's eyes, and they spilled over down his face. "I'm scared," he whispered.

Robbie moved closer to him. "I used to know lots of guys just like you, Ben. Guys who were scared, myself included. Then there were others who seemed so sure of themselves, colorful and proud. They cross my mind all the time. But, as time goes on, it gets harder to remember them. Many of them never had the chance to live out their lives. They didn't get to make it to thirty, or forty, or fifty... or twenty." Robbie's eyes scrunched as his words ripped through his heart. "Sometimes I'd question if heroes really exist, because if they did, why couldn't I save any of my friends? Why did I get to live, and they had to die?"

Ben looked away when it became too hard to look at Robbie's face when he spoke, when his words turned into pins in his heart.

"Many years ago, there was someone who was really important to me," said Robbie. "But he was taken from me. At the time, it felt like he was the only one who really understood me. When he died, I spent a long time believing that the only love I'd ever know had died with him. That loneliness you're feeling, Ben, it'll pass. Someone will come into your life, and you'll wonder how you could have ever come this far without them. They take a lot of that loneliness away and replace it with their love." Robbie looked down at his phone's background photo of Sarim and himself, together. "Sometimes they're even right in front of you, waiting patiently for you to love them back." He faced Ben again, and his emotions and entire life story were written upon his face.

Ben hesitated before speaking. "Is it okay if I stay at your place tonight?"

Robbie's face softened. He could see Ben's desperation, and he knew if he said no, it would leave Ben even more aimless and alone. "If you're comfortable doing that," he said.

Ben breathed a sigh of relief and cried. "I'm always getting thrown away. I don't even know what I'm supposed to do, or where I'm supposed to go."

Robbie pushed himself closer to him. "Listen, if anyone ever has a problem with you, or you feel unsafe... If you need a ride home or don't know what to do... You can call me. I'll be there to help. You never have to feel alone."

Robbie held the door open for Ben when they arrived in the foyer of his spacious single-story house. It was brand new, having been built less than a year prior, and captured the essence of a sophisticated modern lodge. The sunken living room featured a fireplace and contemporary sectional sofa, and long windows ran vertically all the way to the high ceiling beams. Eye-catching bursts of green from well-placed potted plants complemented the vibrant paintings down the hallway. The flooring was dark hardwood and had a sleek, polished finish, and beautiful framed photos of Florence, Moscow and India were blown up and hanging on the walls. Ben assumed that Robbie was rich. He also wondered if he was an artist, or if he just had really good taste in art and design. The house was warm, inviting and–on some level–mysterious.

Robbie saw Ben's subtle reaction and smirked. He turned on

the kitchen light and took a glass from the cupboard. "Do you want something to eat?"

Ben stood beside the fridge like a puppy waiting for his owner to give him his evening dinner. "Honestly, the thought of eating food right now makes me want to throw up," he said with a hint of queasiness in his voice.

"Well..." said Robbie as he poured Ben a fresh glass of water. "We'll just stick with fluids, then. I'll show you to your room. Do you need something for your head?"

"I'm fine," answered Ben. He took the glass from Robbie and chugged back the water. When he was finished, Robbie led Ben past the living room and down the hallway and, along the way, Ben surveyed the oil paintings that lined the walls. There was one that depicted an enchanted forest from a fairytale, with two wooden swings hanging from the limb of a large oak tree below a full moon that cast its light across a mystical landscape.

Robbie turned on the light to the beautiful guest bedroom. It had a queen-sized bed with a dark brown duvet and aqua blue sheets, and a simple set of drawers with a sculpture of Saint Basil's Cathedral on top. "Bathroom is just down the hall," he said, pointing behind him. "My room has its own, so the one in the hall is all yours. There are fresh towels in the cupboard if you need to shower, and toiletries. Help yourself to anything in the kitchen... But maybe stay away from the vodka." He met Ben's blue eyes and held them in his gaze for a beat longer, then realized that he was just staring at Ben now, and quickly recovered his composure.

Robbie turned and left the room, heading back to the kitchen to pour himself a glass of cold water. He chugged it back. When he finished, he folded his arms over the countertop, leaned over, and rested his face on them, letting out a deep sigh of exhaustion. He went over everything that had happened over the last couple of hours, and was led down mind mazes of events that had occurred during all facets of his life.

He pulled himself out of his thoughts and refilled the glass one last time before heading to his bedroom, bypassing the open guest room door. He forced himself not to glance inside for fear of coming across as a creep. When he entered his ensuite bathroom, he looked himself over in the mirror, groaning. He hadn't been aware that his nose was covered in dried blood. It complemented his bruised cheekbone perfectly, and his overall dishevelled appearance. His face was oily with dirt, his hands bruised, his clothes grimy. He closed the bathroom door, stripped down, and stepped into the shower. When the water hit his back and head, he rejoiced, and ran his fingers through his thick silver hair, letting the hot water cleanse him. Hot steam clouded around him, and condensation drizzled down the door of the shower, walls and mirror.

When he finished, he put on a clean white t-shirt and sweatpants, then collapsed onto his bed, closing his eyes. He was ready to pass out after feeling the warmth and cushioning of the mattress and duvet beneath him. Ben was in the other bathroom, so Robbie waited for him to finish up before turning in for the night. He just needed sleep, feeling more exhausted than he'd felt in years. Perhaps the exhaustion was getting to him, for suddenly, he started crying. Reality was hitting him, in one overwhelming swoop.

When Robbie heard the shower turn off, he quickly wiped his hands over his face in an effort to get himself under control. He went back into his bathroom and brushed his teeth until he heard Ben emerge from the hallway bathroom. Minutes later, Robbie went to check in on Ben, who was sitting in bed, his back leaning up against the headboard, shirtless. Robbie's entire body stuttered. He felt awkward, and it probably showed on his face. "Feeling a bit better now?" he asked, his hand on the door knob.

"Yeah," said Ben. His eyes broke from Robbie's first, dropping down to the duvet cover.

Robbie gave him a small smile and started to pull the door closed. "Goodnight."

"Hey, Robbie," said Ben.

Robbie held the door halfway open. Hearing Ben say his name caught him off guard. "Need anything else?"

Ben looked at him, hesitant. "I don't want to be alone tonight."

Robbie's eyebrows went up in surprise. His mind went blank. "Are you sure?"

"Yeah," said Ben.

Robbie flicked off the light switch, then closed the door. He went around to the left side of the bed and gently lay down on his back. The rustling of the feather duvet indicated that Ben had slid himself down so he could rest his head on his pillow. Robbie lay awake, staring into the darkness above. Believing that Ben was falling asleep, he rolled over onto his right side to face the wall beside the bed. Light from the moon crept into the bedroom through slits in the blinds, and Robbie thought about replacing them with blackout curtains instead.

There was a rustling of the sheets, then a warmth fell over Robbie as Ben slid closer, wrapping his arm around Robbie's chest. When Robbie rolled onto his back, Ben placed his head on his chest like a pillow. Robbie wrapped his left arm around Ben's shoulder and placed his hand on his waist, pulling him close. He sank lower into the sheets so that he was on the same level as Ben, eye to eye, their noses aligned.

"This is the safest that I've felt in a long time," said Ben. He put his forehead against Robbie's. "Can I kiss you?"

Robbie felt the warmth of Ben's skin under his hand. "If you want to," he said quietly. Ben leaned forward and gently pressed his lips against his. Robbie touched the side of his face, feeling his soft skin and blond hair. He pulled away from the kiss, feeling like he must have just been given a pair of angel wings so he could wrap himself around Ben to protect him. Ben nestled his head in the crook of his arm, and Robbie's hand once again rested on his waist, his fingertips gliding gently along Ben's skin. Moments later, Ben had fallen asleep.

Ben's slow breathing, and the barely perceptible beating of his heart, told Robbie that he was at peace.

61

It was just after one in the morning, and all the guests had left. Henry must have failed in his duty as his son's proxy, for he'd been too enthralled with exploring the rooms and halls to take notice of much else. He had no real desire for parties–unlike his son, who seemed to have a routine addiction to them. Henry's intoxication enhanced his prowling of the castle, making him feel like a bright-eyed child full of restless curiosity. His head was tilted back as he marveled at the detailed frescoed ceiling of the ballroom; a sweeping piece of divine art among the extraordinary architectural displays of the castle. His feet twisted and turned as he repositioned himself so he could discover hidden details in the ceiling's fresco that had slipped past him upon first glance.

When Henry glanced at the grand staircase, he was surprised to see Owen sitting at the gilded grand piano that was still on stage, the torchères emitting light upon it. He had thought his son was out celebrating his new endeavour with his peers, and wasn't made aware that he had already returned to the castle. Henry climbed up onto the stage and sat down next to him on the bench, watching his son as he stared blankly at the piano's fallboard.

"Did you know," said Henry, "that this castle was built between 1889 and 1895? The original occupants were known to throw the most decadent of parties, inviting people from all over the country. Guests traveled for days just to visit one of their celebrations... To indulge in the food, the wine and to dance to music and frolic in the gardens. There used to be a throne somewhere in here, too. I'm curious to know what happened to it."

Owen continued to stare at the piano's fallboard. "Maybe that's the next question you should find the answer to on your wandering travels," he suggested. "There was a fake throne at the other party, but it broke."

Henry's eyes trailed the towering height of the grand staircase and its torchères. "How did it go, your scouting mission?"

"Not good," Owen said vacantly. "It was a bust... and a total waste of time."

"There seemed to be a large degree of interest from those who showed up to support you," said Henry enthusiastically.

"Sure," said Owen.

Henry surveyed his son's face and saw his obvious disappointment. "Teddy was here."

Owen furrowed his brow. "What?"

"He showed up twenty minutes after you left. Fashionably late, of course. He walked in and all eyes were on him, like Cinderella arriving at the ball in search of a prince. Only... The person he was looking for wasn't here."

"Did you at least say or do something?" asked Owen in a condescending tone.

"He mingled with the others," replied Henry, shrugging his shoulders. "At least, I'm assuming it was Teddy. He looked like the picture that you showed me of him–the one you stare at for hours every day."

"I don't stare at his picture for hours," said Owen defensively as he adjusted his position on the bench. "You were supposed to be the host in my absence. That meant greeting everyone and socializing, not getting boozed up and waltzing from room to room looking at pretty tapestries. What part of that didn't you understand?" He unlocked his phone and browsed through his unread texts and emails. "When did he leave?"

Henry bit his lip, not wanting to infuriate his son even more with his reply.

"Never mind," said Owen. He sighed and closed his phone. "I just… I can't stop thinking about that speakeasy."

"What's so great about it?" asked Henry.

Owen stared ahead, into the void.

"The owner won't sell it to you?"

"It's not about him not selling it to me," said Owen. "It's about me not deserving it."

"Did you make him an offer? Does he know who you are?"

Owen sighed. "Dad, you can't solve everything with money. There are some things you just can't buy."

Henry was still confused about what the root problem could be. "Well, you were there, not me. So, you look for someplace else. Are you sure Venus Valley is the right location?"

Owen exhaled deeply. "I don't know what to do with my life anymore."

Henry was taken aback by his son's statement. "I haven't heard you say those words since middle school. The phrase 'I don't know' isn't in the Kim vocabulary. Indecisiveness isn't, either."

"What about a disappointing son?" asked Owen.

Henry paused for a moment and scoffed, laughing gently. "Disappointing son? On the list of things that have disappointed me in my life, the pen hasn't even come close to the paper as far as your name is concerned. You were well on your way to doing great things long before Tremble came along. I'll remind you of what your mother and I told you back when you were still a teenager: you can do whatever you want, as long as it makes you fulfilled. Whether that's making a little bit of money, or a lot of it. As long as you can keep a roof over your head and a fridge full of food."

Owen smiled, but just barely. "That's great. But that's not what I'm really getting at."

An expression of perplexed curiosity crossed Henry's face.

"I'm your only child. Because of that, I invented all this pressure for myself. When I realized that liking men wasn't some obscure adolescent phase, my concern was that I'd disappoint you because I wasn't what you would have wanted in a son. What dad wants his son to like men?" Owen looked down at the ivory piano keys. He reached forward and gently tapped one of the keys with his finger. "Developing the app gave me hope that you'd accept me because of the success it could bring. After selling Tremble, I revealed to you that I liked women as well as men, but would perhaps want to pursue a relationship with a man. My thought process behind coming out to you was heavily influenced by where I was in my life. That even if you rejected me, I'd still have the money to fall back on to keep me happy. When you told me that it didn't matter who I dated, it dawned on me that I had wasted so much of my life not being me. I could have saved myself so much stress and anxiety if I had just told you and Mom sooner."

"You were our miracle baby," said Henry. "When your mother lost your little brother, she didn't want another. To bring meaning back into her life, she needed something that would make her happy again, and that something was you. She would always call you her beautiful boy. Something so minuscule as who you kissed or chose to love... Not a single damn was given by either of us. All we wanted was for you to be happy and passionate, regardless of the road you chose."

"She never got to see any of this," said Owen meekly. "I wanted her to be proud of me."

"She was," said Henry.

"No," said Owen sharply. "She didn't live long enough to see what I was capable of doing, or to see you write your children's books. She died, never knowing." His eyes trailed around the ballroom. "Imagine her walking through the front doors of this castle, stepping into the ballroom, and seeing this beauty all around her. She would have felt like a queen."

Henry smiled and placed his hand on Owen's shoulder. "She probably would have fainted, to be frank. Afterward, she would have told you to buy the place." He paused. "So, why don't you?"

Owen raised an eyebrow and gave him a dubious look. "Be serious."

"I am," said Henry.

"I'm not buying a castle," he said, incredulous. "I'm tired, Dad. I'm tired of having to play the fucking game. I always have to keep doing better until it's enough: to keep growing my brand and to keep creating and to keep making more money. It's never enough, though. There's always an even bigger level above with higher expectations. If I'm not growing, I'm losing. On and on it goes, never stopping. If this is what I have to do to be accepted by my peers, to hell with it. I spoke with everyone who was here tonight, from one to the next, every fucking person, and it was all an illusion–their fake, plastic smiles hiding behind their cocktail glasses. Some of them don't try to hide it anymore. I'm beginning to realize that perhaps I'm not cut out for their world. If that's the case, then they can fucking have it. They can have their money, their cars and their castles. Give me a deserted island out in the middle of nowhere that has white sands, clear water and a perfect sunset with the love of my life next to me for the rest of my days."

Henry smiled proudly at him. "Seeing you as the man you are today is my greatest success story, Owen. You have nothing left to prove. Not to me, not to the world, and most importantly, not to yourself."

62

Jay was thinking of the colors he'd want to wear. He had checked to see what the weather would be like once he landed, and the forecast predicted nothing but sunshine and warmth for late July and early August. He packed linen shirts and shorts, but he only owned ball caps for headwear–he'd find something more appropriate once he arrived in Paris. He dreamt about the fresh bakeries and chocolatiers, the fine French dining and European men's fashion... The men. He could hardly wait. His suitcase wasn't too heavy, nor was it packed to the brim, but it didn't need to be. When it came to his head and heart, he wasn't bringing baggage with him. He couldn't shake the feeling that he was forgetting something, though.

Jay looked down at his phone when he received the text message that he'd been expecting. He buzzed Salvador into the building and replied to say that the front door to his condo was unlocked. Minutes later, he heard his front door open and close, then silence.

"Hello?" hollered Salvador, his loafers clicking and clacking against the floor.

"I'm in the bedroom," said Jay.

Salvador strolled in, and right away Jay could smell his cologne, like it had blown in on a breeze through an open window. It was impossible not to feel warmth from Salvador the second he walked into a room. He was so adorable, like a puppy wearing a birthday bow. Today, he wore a black quilted vest and navy Henley with the usual gold jewellery dangling around his wrists and neck.

Salvador looked at the suitcase at the foot of Jay's bed. "Where are you heading?"

Jay dumped a few socks into the suitcase. "Paris."

Silence fell between them as Jay's hands rustled through his clothing, the zippers of the suitcase flailing about.

"Listen, I'm really sorry," said Salvador softly. He cleared his throat and looked down at the floor. "If you don't want to talk to me again, I'll understand. But..." He sighed and leaned against the door frame. "I've been beating myself up, hard."

Jay saw just how far Salvador was standing from him, the open space between them so distant and cold. "Everything is a blur right now," he said. "My head needs to be cleared. I'm trying to reorganize my life."

"When are you coming back?"

"I'm not sure," replied Jay. "I'll be in Paris for two weeks, but I'm thinking of going somewhere else after that, and another place after that... To the edge of the world, maybe."

"That sounds like an exciting adventure," said Salvador, smiling. "Seeing the world."

"Yeah..." said Jay, looking down at his suitcase and dropping a pair of white boat shoes inside. He looked around his bedroom before fixing his eyes on Salvador. "Hey... Please, don't wait up for me."

Salvador furrowed his brow.

"If you need to move on while I'm gone, then do it. If you find someone else, I'll understand. My life is a big mess. It's not really going anywhere. If you find love when I'm gone, then don't let me hold you back."

Salvador's expression softened. "But what if I already found it?"

Jay's lips parted as the air was sucked out from his lungs. He could almost hear the thumping of Salvador's heart from across the room.

"There's lots of other guys out here, for sure," said Salvador, stepping closer towards Jay. "I really like being around *you*, though. Last night, all I could think about was how lonely I felt without you next to me... with our arms wrapped around each other, cuddling. You bring something to my life that I've never had before with anyone else. You're unselfish and kind... You make me happy, Jay." Salvador shrugged his shoulders, like that was all he had to say.

"I thought about you last night too," confessed Jay. "Instead of counting sheep, I counted how many times we've kissed in the last week."

Salvador placed both his hands on Jay's arms and dragged his fingers up to his shoulders. "I'm always counting Blue Jays, baby."

Jay leaned in as fast as he could and kissed Salvador on the lips, a sudden gesture that quickly escalated into a passionate embrace. Jay pushed his suitcase off the bed so there was room for both of them to fall back, their bodies pressed up against one another, the sheets becoming a wave of rustling, swallowing up their movements.

"Someone will have to be there to swat all the French boys off of you," said Salvador, breathless, as he hunched over Jay.

One of Salvador's gold necklaces hung low above Jay's neck, so he grabbed it with his teeth, hungry for him, starved for his touch. "If you're coming with me, you're only bringing one suitcase."

Salvador cocked his head. "That is near impossible, and you know it... By the way, do you know any French?"

Jay ran his hand through Salvador's curly hair. "Bonjour. That's pretty much it."

"My God..." said Salvador, collapsing on top of him in defeat.

Jay spun Salvador to his side and climbed on top of him."I'm fluent in French kissing, though," he whispered, pecking him on his fuzzy cheek.

Salvador smiled as he looked up at the man of his dreams. He then pulled himself out from their entanglement. He jogged out of the bedroom, his loafers thumping down the hall. Confused, Jay sat up on the edge of the bed. Seconds later, Salvador returned with a framed photo in his hand. He knelt down and positioned the open suitcase properly on the floor before pulling the photograph out of the frame. He laid the photograph of Jay's mom and dad down on top of the clothes in the suitcase.

Jay smiled at him. "I'm happy you're here with me, Salvador."

63

Robbie awoke face down with the duvet partially covering his body. His arm was slightly outstretched, with his right palm on the right side of the bed. He stared at the empty space on the bed beside him, dragging his hand along the sheet and feeling the cold fabric along his fingertips. The room was partially lit with early morning sunlight, and the blinds over the window made the colors of the room appear desaturated of life. He sat up and leaned his back against the pillow and headboard, confused, like he didn't know where he was at first. Robbie had his own internal alarm clock and always woke up at seven in the morning. As an added precaution, he'd set his phone's alarm for the days when he accidentally slept in. The alarm tone would begin quiet, then gradually become louder as the seconds passed. It was happening right now, forest birds singing songs in summer orchids and daytime rain showers in a dewy meadow.

He got out of bed and followed the harmony of chirping birds to his bedroom. His ears perked up as he gauged where his phone's location was and homed in on a pair of pants that were sprawled on the floor alongside the shirt and bomber jacket he had worn last night. He reached into the front side pocket of the pants and pulled out his phone, turning off the alarm. The battery was nearly dead at four percent, so he placed it on the cordless charging dock on the nightstand. As the phone lay on the charger, he scrolled through his notifications and saw that he had one missed call from Liam from late last night, and a text message from Sarim.

Goodnight baby.

Robbie stared at Sarim's message and wept.

Johnson lay on his bedroom floor after having been up all night. He was staring at the wall, the side of his face against the carpet, having not moved in several hours. There was little desire for anything. He wanted to starve, to grow roots and lie dormant without ever caring to feel beauty or sunshine again. He deserved to rot in a dark, empty dungeon filled with dirt and dust, locked away without a chair or bed, forced to lie on the cold, hard earth.

His phone started to ring somewhere nearby, but he didn't answer the call, choosing instead to believe that it simply didn't exist. When the ringing stopped, it was soon followed by the *ding* of a new text message. As much as Johnson wanted to die, knowing that someone had tried calling him gave him hope.

Johnson sat up and stared at the floor, feeling sullen and exhausted, his stomach empty from not eating anything for a couple of days. He reached for his phone and tapped it, looking at the message from Robbie.

Liam is dead.

Johnson rushed from his car, opened the front door, and pushed his way inside. Liam was on his back, on his couch, his right cheek slumped against his shoulder and his face ashen. Both eyes were closed, and his mouth hung open. His right arm lay over the edge of the couch with his hand open and his fingers slumped downward. Just below his hand were upright pill bottles and an open bottle of bourbon on the floor.

All at once, Johnson's composure dropped, and his entire body tensed up from absolute, horrifying shock. The corpse was bathed in early morning sunlight from the living room window. Robbie was in the kitchen, his eyes bloodshot.

Johnson looked at Liam's body and crouched low, breaking down. He stumbled backward and knocked into a low shelving unit underneath the window. Incredibly weakened, Johnson's body gave up and slumped down against the unit and onto the floor, hot tears running down his face. Robbie walked over and handed Johnson a piece of paper.

Well, that's it for me. I'm sorry for the way you found me. I can't wait any longer, so it has to be now. When people look back on the story of my life, there won't be anything worth remembering. My life wasn't what I had hoped it would be. Maybe my next life will be a better one. Please don't feel sad for me. As my parting word, I'd like to say this to you. That is, when you find love, don't let it go. Hug it tight. Keep it safe. Life isn't worth living alone. Success isn't worth anything if you don't have someone you love to share it with. There may come a time when love leaves you. It's taken away. But with strength and courage, love will find its way back to you again. When it does, don't ever let it go. Live your life with someone who brightens your heart. Good luck to you, and we'll meet again one day.

Your friend, Liam.

Johnson held his hand over his mouth as he read the note. His tears fell down his face and over his hand, his whole body shaking. He put down the note and remained slumped against the shelving unit, staring at Liam's body.

For several moments, neither he nor Robbie could speak as devastation rolled over them both. Weakened and diminished, Johnson pushed himself forward on all fours and crawled towards the couch. He picked up one of the pill bottles and dumped the remaining capsules into his palm, dropping the empty bottle to the floor with a clatter.

The sound of the bottle hitting the floor made Robbie look up from his mourning in the kitchen. Johnson was on his hands and knees, one hand raised and hovering at chest level, his palm filled with dozens of pills, seconds from being dropped into his mouth. Robbie bolted forward and tackled Johnson, sending them both down onto their sides and the coffee table several feet across the floor. Robbie pinned Johnson's outstretched arm to the floor as Johnson clutched the pills like a vise. His fingers turned white from the pressure as his fingernails dug into his palm, refusing to let them go.

"You're needed here, buddy," said Robbie.

"Fuck..." mumbled Johnson. His tears pooled where his cheek met the floor. He looked at his arm that was lying useless under the pressure being applied by Robbie

Robbie reached over and placed his hand on top of Johnson's enclosed fist, wrapping his fingers around it tightly. "Let go," he whispered to him. "You have to let them go."

Johnson heard Robbie's words in his ear, then felt his grasp around the pills loosen. He opened his fist, feeling the cold air sweep against his sweaty palm and fingers as the pills shifted delicately against each other. Robbie scooped up all the pills and tossed them to the side.

"Come back..." pleaded Johnson, his mouth quivering.

Robbie closed his eyes as tears continued to build behind his eyelids. He kept one arm wrapped around Johnson as they lay against one another on the floor.

64

Bailey rummaged around inside his satchel and pulled out a pair of black Versace sunglasses with gold medusa studs on the temples. He and Lisa were standing at the drop-off curb in front of the airport to say goodbye to Zeus, who wore his flight attendant uniform consisting of a tailored black suit, blue silk tie and white button-up shirt. Bailey handed him the shades, and he slid them on, flashing them both a suave smile.

"It's so you don't forget about me," said Bailey in a dramatic voice. He extended his arms out and embraced Zeus. "*Hasta pronto, querido*!"

Lisa joined in on the hug, her sunglasses accidentally bumping into Zeus' face. "Where are you headed to?" she asked.

"First, it's Chicago," said Zeus. "What time is your flight to London? Midnight, you said?"

"Yes, right after Sabrina's concert tonight," replied Bailey. He turned to Lisa excitedly. "Are you ready to see and hear the sights and sounds of Europe for the next two months, Ms. Liza Sherri?"

Lisa put her hands to her face in anticipation of what was

waiting just around the corner in the next phase of her career, and her life. "It's the most excited I've ever been, honestly."

"You'll start feeling like Sabrina's groupie by the third city," Bailey said casually.

"Wait, Liza Sherri?" asked Zeus, taken aback.

Lisa scrolled through her phone and showed Zeus one of her social media accounts with the new name change.

"Holy shit," said Zeus, gawking, as he marveled at her rebranding. There was a new profile picture of herself, taken at Larchdale Castle on the grand staircase with a makeup brush in hand, the pink bristles rubbing her chin as she smiled seductively.

"Bailey suggested I use Liza, as in Minnelli, for my alias. It was my idea to incorporate my middle name, Sherri."

"So now when you start meeting all those European makeup artists, you'll be introduced to them as Liza Sherri!" said Bailey in a celebratory voice. "When people say to me 'Hey, nice makeup,' I'll be like, 'Thanks bitch, it's brought to you by Liza Sherri; check out her socials and follow her. Here, try out some of the new products from her line.'"

Lisa scoffed, a sardonic smile spreading across her face. "No one would buy my line," she said in a self-deprecating tone.

"We gotta work on that confidence, girl!" said Bailey, raising his voice as though he wanted the whole city to hear. "When your brother sees you next time, you'll be dripping in it!"

"Like you," said Zeus with a smirk.

"You don't do extraordinary things by thinking you suck," said Bailey. "You, Ms. Liza Sherri, do not suck. Say it with me: Liza Sherri is talented and extraordinary."

"Liza Sherri is talented and extraordinary..." repeated Lisa, humoring him.

"Zeus is talented and extraordinary," Zeus chimed in.

Bailey rejoiced and extended his hands out like a pastor would at a Sunday morning sermon. "Believe in yourself. If you don't, others won't."

"Word," said Zeus.

"People are literally looking at us like we're crazy," said Lisa, laughing. She turned her attention back to Zeus. "So, are you still coming to Thanksgiving at Mom and Dad's?"

"Gotta see the fam," he replied. "Definitely."

Lisa smiled at his response. Bailey's eyes went back and forth between them; then he casually sauntered away towards their ride. "I'll just be chillin' in the car, blowin' the driver."

Zeus quickly checked the time on his phone. "Okay... I gotta get going now."

Lisa looked down at his suitcase, then shifted her weight on the spot. "Thank you for helping me," she said.

"It's what big brothers are for," he replied, smiling at her. "I'm happy for you. You're going to have a lot of fun and learn a lot out there."

"I'm still nervous," she said, clenching her teeth.

"It's good to be nervous sometimes. It shows that you're going out of your comfort zone. Happens to me all the time, especially when I'm asked to bartend massive castle parties hosted by super rich dudes."

"So, working for Owen..." said Lisa. "He changed his mind on that?"

Zeus shrugged, indifferent. "He told me the circumstances have changed and needs more time to pursue other options for what he wants to do. He said he'll stay in contact with me, so that's promising. Fingers crossed!" He leaned forward and gave Lisa a big hug. "Love you."

"Love you too," she said, patting him on the back.

Zeus let go and made his way into the airport, his suitcase rolling behind him. "Text me when you land in London," he said.

Lisa nodded and waved back to him. She released a deep sigh and smiled.

Martin had concealed himself in sunglasses and a grey hoodie as he sat on a bench across from the airport entrance. Given his viral online infamy, and the current state of his marriage, he didn't want to draw unwanted attention to himself. He was completely inconspicuous, as the summer tourist season was now in full swing. There was a constant flow of happy travelers arriving to bask in the sunshine and adventure that was Venus Valley, with hopes of being able to see the castle where Owen's viral party took place.

He casually scrolled through his phone, looking up every ten seconds to see if Zeus had come through the entryway. When Zeus finally did swing through the carousel entrance, Martin stood up, catching Zeus' eye almost immediately.

Zeus strolled forward, smiling from ear to ear. "Hey, buddy," he said as he put his luggage down and hugged him.

"Nice shades," said Martin.

Zeus reached out and adjusted Martin's sunglasses. "Likewise." He took his new Versaces off and slid them into his trouser pocket. "Your incognito is working great. How have you been these last few days?"

Martin exhaled deeply. "Ask me that question again in a year."

"You're really brave," said Zeus, his voice honest and admiring. "You'll land on your feet... Unless it's jumping off a balcony. Don't do that."

Martin rolled his eyes behind his shades. "Only if I'm planning on offing myself, maybe," he joked, but then cringed at what he just said.

"Video chat me soon," said Zeus in a serious voice. "If you need a friend to talk to."

"Thanks for seeing the real me," said Martin, "and not just as a meme."

"You gotta keep up with your videos and the streaming," replied Zeus. "There are tons of people who want to see what you're going to do next."

Martin nodded in reluctant agreement. "Yeah. I'll be changing it up a bit. I've been playing video games for eight years now, and it's just not hitting the same as it used to. Actually, Marc asked me to be a recurring co-host on his podcast."

Zeus' reaction was just what Martin was expecting when his mouth dropped open in surprise. "*MarcVsMartin* back together! For real?"

"I'm not doing it," Martin clarified.

Zeus' reaction went from excited to crushed in a second.

"It'd be cool and all," said Martin, "and tons of fun. It would for sure open doors for me. But it's not really my thing, just sitting behind a mic having conversations and interviewing people. That's his schtick now, not mine."

Zeus nodded, seemingly embracing the change. "Well, whatever you do, I'll be watching... or listening... or both. You're good at what you do, this streaming stuff."

"What's happening with your bartending and mixology?" asked Martin.

Zeus drummed his fingers on the handle of his suitcase. "It's an ongoing thing... Stoking the flame."

"We'll have to hang out again sometime," said Martin. "You've gotta make me some new drinks, man."

"I'm looking forward to it," said Zeus. "We'll rent out a penthouse or something and throw a New Year's Eve party."

"Larchdale 2.0 all the way," suggested Martin, smiling.

"Disco themed," added Zeus as he checked his phone for the time. "Alright... Gotta go. Chicago, and the world, are calling my name. Take care, Martin."

They leaned in to hug, then Zeus grabbed hold of the extended handle of his suitcase and rolled it away with him, waving one last time.

Martin watched him disappear into the hustle and bustle of the airport, then bent down to retrieve his duffel bag, which was sitting underneath the bench. He slung it over his shoulder and strolled over to the electronic boards overhead that displayed the various departures, his eyes scrolling from city to city, country to country, pondering. He unlocked his phone, opened his streaming app, and pressed the red LIVE button. His face popped up on his phone and the chat bar appeared along the lower half. Within seconds, five of his subscribers clicked on to watch. Then, fifteen... twenty-three... thirty-eight... fifty-two...

65

At four o'clock in the afternoon, Robbie drove down the Forever Road and through the hills of Larchdale Grove. When he pulled up to Larchdale Castle's estate, he was stopped by security at the open gate and was required to give his name and purpose of arrival. When the security personnel spoke with someone through their headset, Robbie was granted access by the guard, rather begrudgingly, after being searched. Given the castle's recent rise in worldwide notoriety, security had tripled within the last week, and the place didn't feel as welcoming as it once had. The driveway was packed with idle SUVs, airport shuttle buses and a large tour bus that was used for the American leg of Sabrina's world tour, which would be concluding tonight in downtown Venus Valley. Several members of Sabrina's team were milling around with piles of luggage and duffel bags all about, with the castle's security personnel stationed among them. Robbie noticed a pair of legs dangling out from the backseat of one of the SUVs, and he was curious to know whether the person inside was sleeping, dead or just lying down out of boredom.

After parking his vehicle and getting out, Robbie noticed some were throwing curious glances his way as he passed them and made his way up the stairs to the open front door of the castle. He entered apprehensively, for he felt like an intruder entering a space that, first, was historically intimidating, and second, had two celebrities inside.

Stepping into Larchdale Castle's ballroom this time around felt much different. Gone were the fantastical accoutrements, marble bar tops and showmanship of a world-class party for eccentric party guests. What remained was the castle's original splendor, untouched by modern influences. Robbie felt unworthy to be standing inside a world so regal and enchanting. The party was, indeed, over.

As he stared up at the fresco above, he heard footsteps coming from behind. He turned around to see Sabrina, all made up for her concert that was scheduled to begin later tonight. She slowed her pace when she saw him, a curious surprise on her face.

Robbie smiled awkwardly, feeling like an uninvited guest in someone's house.

"Security? Never heard of them," she said sarcastically.

"Oh," replied Robbie, "Sarim knows I'm coming. He apparently told security about my arrival, and also ran it past Owen."

"Ahhh..." she said, looking him up and down and putting her hands on her hips.

Robbie stared at her, intimidated in the presence of a celebrity of her calibre, alone in a room, with no one else around. It didn't help that her blue and silver outfit made her look like Aphrodite herself, completely untouchable.

Seeing his obvious case of starstruck nerves, Sabrina circled around until she was standing in front of him, facing the open door. "You're Sarim's boyfriend," she said.

Robbie nodded. "Yeah."

Sabrina smiled warmly and raised an eyebrow. "He talks about you a lot."

Robbie felt his face blushing. "Yeah?"

She stepped closer to him. "It's like a fairytale, and I'm the wicked witch keeping the two princes away from each other."

"It's his job." Robbie shrugged. "He enjoys what he does. My job is restrictive too, otherwise I'd have flown out to see him."

"He's such a wonderful person," she said. "He's really kind, and especially sweet. When the tour was in Miami, we all went out to the club for what was supposed to be a fun night. But once the public found out we were there... Well, they ruined it. We left after five minutes. But Sarim didn't even come. He stayed back at the suite and video-chatted with you."

Robbie looked down and smiled. "Video messaging is great. But it's hard, because you can't reach through the camera and touch the person you're talking to who's on other side of the world. They're still so far away, even though they're right in front of you."

Sabrina smiled wryly. "I've felt that way many times. It's never easy being away for such long periods of time. It's admirable that you two are keeping that connection going by doing those sorts of things. You're incredibly lucky to have someone who loves you as much as he does, someone who wouldn't be able to breathe if you weren't in his life."

Robbie opened his mouth, then closed it again. He saw Owen over her shoulder, walking towards them from across the ballroom. Owen went and stood next to Sabrina, the three of them looking at each other awkwardly as though they were at a high school reunion.

Sabrina quickly cut the awkwardness. "This is Robbie," she said, introducing him. "Sarim's boyfriend."

Owen smiled and reached out to shake his hand. "I'm sure we've met before."

Sabrina ran her hand through her hair, then placed her hand on Owen's shoulder and walked away, leaving Robbie with a lingering smile.

"I'd just like to say," Owen started, "that the other night was a very profound moment for me. My sincerest apologies for my insensitivity and rudeness. I'm still rather upset with myself."

Robbie knew he should say something, but couldn't form the words.

"Just out of curiosity," continued Owen, "is there any intention of reopening it? Not by me, but by Christopher or whomever?"

"It's mine," stated Robbie, looking him in the eyes. "Christopher gave the speakeasy, and the building, to me."

"Ah," said Owen, glancing to the side and nodding his head. He stepped forward. "You don't have to take my advice. Throw it in the trash if you wish. But why not let Tristan come alive once more? Open the place up, and make it a must-see destination for the gay community. Let people enjoy it like they used to. But this time, let them enjoy it out in the open, not in secret. We don't have to hide anymore."

"We?" Robbie asked curiously.

Owen smiled gently. "No more hiding." He held his hand out once again, and Robbie looked down at it for a few seconds before accepting the gesture and shaking his hand. Owen nodded, then walked past him, leaving through the open front door and down the steps.

Robbie lingered for a moment longer, then he continued his trek across the ballroom and through the terrace that spanned the perimeter of the main floor. He went down several grandiose hallways, keeping himself focused on his destination rather than allowing the surrounding pleasantries to distract him. He came to the familiar door of the dancers' quarters next to the steps of one of the corner towers. He casually walked into the armoury, where luggage and boxes were lined up in front of the door, waiting to be taken outside. Robbie went through the archway below the second-floor balustrade and stepped into the back room, where a few of the dancers were still swishing about with last-minute packing. Sarim was sitting on his closed suitcase near the back windows, wearing a leather jacket and dark pants. He was playing a song from his phone on low volume while he scrolled. Just as Robbie entered the room, Sarim stood up at the first sight of him, a smile immediately brightening his features.

Robbie returned the smile, looking him in his eyes. Everything else faded into the background. He took Sarim in his arms and held him closely, feeling as warm and safe as he could be.

Sarim took Robbie's hand and held it tightly as his smile revealed the subtle crow's feet at the corners of his eyes, adding life to his face. "Come with me," he said.

Robbie let Sarim lead him out of the armoury and up the steps of the corner tower, the echo of their footsteps bouncing against the stone. When they reached the top landing, Sarim opened the ancient wooden door and revealed a room inside the turret that was being used as a storage attic for various works of art in gilded frames. Most were leaning against curved walls or pieces of furniture, while others were hanging on the walls. There were oil paintings of sweeping landscapes, Elizabethan ships on open seas, foreign architecture and mystical creatures ranging from sirens and sea monsters to African beasts and tropical birds of paradise; such creatures that Robbie had never seen before.

"Check this out," said Sarim, reaching behind one of the paintings that was leaning up against the wall. He pulled out what appeared to be a gold and black sceptre. It was the length of a man's forearm, from his elbow to his fingertips. The tip was a bulbous black and gold head with wavy tentacle-shaped arms extending out from its base like those of an octopus or sea monster. The stem was twisted and gnarled like an old tree limb, and was etched with complex gold and black engravings and raised markings that bore no real meaning upon first glance.

"Cool, huh?" said Sarim, holding it in both his hands like a trophy, its weight obvious.

"Where did you find it?" asked Robbie.

"Exactly where you saw me pull it out from. Maybe someone was hiding it."

"Like, someone was planning on taking it?"

"Not one of the dancers," Sarim reassured him. "Security is extremely tight. There are cameras everywhere. Every single person has to be checked thoroughly before we can even leave. That's why it's taking so long to get out of here. Security also have to go through each room to make sure nothing was damaged, even the places we weren't allowed into." He lightly tapped the sceptre against his palm. "This sucker isn't going anywhere."

As Robbie stared at the sceptre, Sarim noticed the curiosity in his eyes and reached over to hand it to him. Taking it gingerly in his grasp, Robbie felt the heft of it as his fingers bumped along the gold and black markings of the stem. "It looks like the staff of a pirate king," he said with a smirk, drumming his fingers on it. He turned his back to Sarim, his attention no longer focused on the object in his hand. Silence fell upon the room, a quiet that was as still as the paintings themselves.

Sarim stared at Robbie's back, his face transitioning from happy to concerned as his heart raced. "You've been hurting," he said "Perhaps I'll never know why. It's okay if you never share it with me. Maybe there are some things that are better left unsaid."

Robbie's mouth opened as he looked down at the floor, reliving moments in his life that weren't healthy to be reliving time and time again, especially right now.

"All I've ever wanted from you was to see you happy, Robbie," said Sarim.

Robbie closed his eyes as the warmth and sincerity of Sarim's voice broke through and caused him to tear up.

"There's someone standing right behind you who loves you," said Sarim. "Who would do anything for you. When I'm with you, it's like Christmas morning, every day. The ones who I thought would love me the most left my life a long time ago. Then you came along, and everything made sense to me. If I could take out my heart and give it to you, I'd do it." Sarim's voice began to shake, his anxiety peaking while he struggled for control. "I don't want to feel like this is all for nothing. When I fly out tonight, do you want me to come back?"

Robbie felt instant fear setting in, bordering on panic. He felt a cold chill run down his body; the possibility of never seeing Sarim again, of Sarim leaving him behind, was horrifying to Robbie. He turned to face him, letting the tears fall down his cheeks. "I want you to come back, Sarim. I love you." He put the sceptre down on the floor and took him in his arms. Worried that Sarim might turn to dust and vanish in front of him, Robbie kissed him, grabbing hold of his face and pulling him closer. He nestled his face into the crook of Sarim's neck and held on to him with all his strength. "Please, always come back home."

Sarim reached into the front pocket of his jeans and withdrew a gold ring. His fingers were shaking as he lifted it up to chest level. He rubbed both his eyes with his other hand, ridding himself of the tears. "Do you love me enough that you'd want to spend the rest of your life with me?"

Robbie gently took the ring and let his fingertips glide along its delicate surface. He slipped it on his left ring finger. "I do," he said.

Robbie walked back across the ballroom to leave. Looking around the room, he noticed that he was completely alone. Most of the lights had been turned off as though everyone had already left the castle. Only the grand staircase's torchères remained lit. Robbie gradually slowed and stood still in the silence. He scanned the balconies above that were shrouded in darkness. The place felt like a forgotten dream where starlit smiles, sparkles and glitter had all vanished from sight. What remained was reminiscent of a glorious cathedral where gold accessories and stone architecture lay hidden behind a blanket of stillness and shadow. It was as though the torchères were holding the darkness at bay, a darkness that eagerly sought to extinguish the lights.

Robbie turned towards the small black stage that was still positioned in front of the grand staircase. The rest of the catwalk had been removed, but the stage was a mere prop for what sat on top of it. Glowing under the radiating lights of the torchères, the gilded grand piano sat in ethereal glory, as beautiful as when he first looked upon it. Robbie strolled up to the stage, preparing to hoist himself up, but noticed some steps leading up along the left side. When he climbed the steps and reached the top of the stage, he took a seat on the piano bench, his hands resting on his knees as he stared down at the ivory keys. He turned to face the ballroom, the six balconies rising to the left and right along the mezzanine of the third floor. He looked further upward at the immense chandelier that hung over the main entrance, the crown jewel of the room. The torchères sent out their light to it, dazzling parts of its surface as the rest hid in darkness.

Robbie returned his attention back to the piano and placed his fingertips on the keys, pausing for a moment to take in the name that was inscribed on the fallboard. "This is for you," he said.

Delicately, he pressed his fingers down on the keys. They released a melody that Robbie had kept locked within himself, a story that had been anchored to his heart for decades. It flew out from him, as did the lyrics from his voice as he sang. He'd written and composed the song during a time in his youth when he was hopeful his life would get better, that darkness would not prevail and would instead fade away from him. He'd spent his life mourning the person he should have become, and the roads that were left untraveled by his weary feet. Now, he could no longer deny himself the happiness of a new love. Robbie missed Tristan's smile. He'd never again look into his blue eyes, or sit and listen to him play for the millions who would have adored his music. There were souls Tristan never got to touch, and applause he never got to hear. Melodies were unwritten, and stories left untold. He was just a fantasy now, a faded photograph in Robbie's mind, and a memory from an unreachable alternate life that he'd never touch or see again.

As Robbie reached the final arc of his song, he looked out again into the empty ballroom where thousands should've been listening. He looked up to the balconies where hundreds should've been weeping with joy, and to the world outside where millions more would've been applauding had Tristan been here instead of him.

Robbie ended the song, his fingers lying still on the keys. He took his hands off the keyboard, stood up, and walked away.

66

Jay sat on his kitchen island with his suitcase and duffel bag by the door, ready to go. His flight was departing in three hours, and he was meeting Salvador at the airport. But there was one last person he was going to see before heading out.

Yesterday, Johnson had messaged him, asking if they could talk. There was a part of Jay that wanted to be petty, to ignore the message or to blatantly tell him to leave him alone. When Jay went over those scenarios in his head, there was another part of him that wanted to go through with accepting Johnson's request. So, he'd speak with Johnson face to face, to get closure to a situation that had brought him significant pain and embarrassment. It was a humiliation that would follow him for the rest of his life, and all he could see now, burned into his vision, was Johnson smacking his lips as he tossed popcorn into his mouth, gleeful and mocking at the sight of Jay squirming helplessly at his mercy. Jay was a grown man, and the way Johnson treated him made him think less of himself. He was angry for his own foolish actions that led to the destruction of his career, but Johnson was the catalyst for that anger. Jay despised that he had let another man so recklessly tear him down.

After today, he had no desire to want to hear from Johnson ever again.

Jay's previous life had ended when he walked out of the office on that late Friday morning. In the months and years ahead, he'd look back on his younger self and see just how normal everything was at the time, how unmoving and unchanging, when he thought everything would last forever and stay as it was like one long summer. There was no going back to that man or that life. That existence was long gone, and the threads of his memory would continue to cling to it until the final chapter closes on his life. The coming decades would be a mystery to him, but he knew moving forward that he wouldn't be alone. He'd meet new people, make new dreams and find love in the most unexpected of places.

He received Johnson's text, saying that he had arrived, so he buzzed him in. After exhaling a deep breath, Jay jumped off the kitchen island and stood by the door with his hands in his pockets, staring at the door handle. When he heard the knock, he reached for the handle and pulled the door open. There was Johnson, looking right at him. Jay's mouth fell open at the sight of him. Johnson's eyes were downtrodden and sleepless, with heavy bags beneath his lids. His frown was weighted down with an obvious disturbance that made Jay reconsider what he thought his own reaction would be when he opened the door. There were things Jay wanted to say to Johnson. He knew the energy and demeanor and attitude he wanted to convey when saying them to him.

Johnson walked into the kitchen like a scared dog who was entering his owner's place for the first time, unsure and anxious.

"How are you?" asked Jay, closing the door.

Johnson looked around the condo. He was lost, as if he had just stepped into his own place but didn't recognize the cabinets or the layout. "I've come here..." he said, his eyes filling with emotion.

Jay's expression softened. He was caught off guard, surprised to see Johnson in this state.

Johnson looked at Jay with sudden desperation, tears welling up and threatening to spill over. He struggled with what he wanted to say, and after some time, the words finally came. "Can you forgive me for what I did to you?"

Jay tried holding back his own emotion while he registered what Johnson had just asked him. His extended silence must have been numbing for Johnson, for the longer he went without saying anything, the more Johnson broke down in front of him. He turned his head to the side, away from Jay. His hands were planted firmly at his sides as he tried to remain composed, but he couldn't help himself as his weeping overwhelmed every part of him. At that moment, Jay didn't have to think about or question what he wanted to do. He stepped forward to give Johnson a hug.

"Can you?" pleaded Johnson.

Jay stared at the kitchen wall behind Johnson as his chin rested on his left shoulder. Everything he had wanted to say to Johnson went away. There was no use for it. It didn't matter anymore. "It's okay," he said. "I forgive you. For everything."

Johnson pulled away, his face red and wet. "I'm moving back to Tennessee to stay with my parents for a bit," he said.

It finally dawned on Jay that something might have happened to Johnson to result in his current state. "Were you let go from work?" he asked.

"No," said Johnson, rubbing his face with his fingers. "I need to be somewhere right now where I feel safe."

After looking at him for a few seconds longer, Johnson didn't waste any time in reaching for the door handle and opening the door.

Jay's expression was now one of concern, but he didn't want to pry further. "When you come back to Venus Valley, we can grab some dinner and drinks," he offered.

Johnson turned to look at him. "Okay," he said quietly, with no trace of hope on his face. He looked down at the floor, paused, then left, closing the door behind him.

67

Liam's ashes were interred in his family's plot. The funeral attendance was small. It was hard to say exactly how many people knew Liam, and of those who did, it was hard to further guess how many of them didn't show up because they simply couldn't be bothered to be there. When his will was read, his siblings were named executors of his estate, which meant they could now sell their parents' home that Liam had been living in. Within weeks of his passing, there was a bold FOR SALE sign hammered into the front yard with the realtor's toothy grin on full display. His brothers were all too eager to finally sell the man's home from his cold dead hands. Liam's savings and investments, on the other hand, were left to Robbie and Johnson, fifty-fifty, which came as a surprise to both of them, and brought wrath to Liam's brothers. They detested the idea and wanted to fight it. The glares that Robbie received when he went to see them at Liam's house made it clear that he wasn't welcome in their lives. They didn't know who he was, nor had they ever met Johnson, and they couldn't understand why their brother would leave his money to strangers when his brothers had been in his life for close to seventy years. Robbie wasn't quite sure himself, but the reason had died with Liam. One thing Robbie did know: he would forever be thankful to Liam.

Robbie and Johnson were the last ones left at the open plot. Liam's family was at the service, including his brothers and some of his loyal clients whose hair he had cut over the decades. Besides the obvious relatives and barbershop patrons, there were others... Strangers. Robbie could have sworn he recognized some of the others as faces he had last seen long ago. Some of them glanced his way and gave him the sense that he had seen them in passing, once upon a time, in a speakeasy called Roger's. None of the other men at the service spoke to him, though. In the end, they went away, back to their lives. Liam was just another familiar face they had once known, now turned to ash and put in the ground.

Liam's urn sat alongside those of his mom and dad, surrounded by flowers from those who had been at the service. Robbie stepped up to the open plot and knelt down beside it. He held a framed photo of Liam from when he had bartended at Roger's. In the photo, he was standing behind the bar holding a cocktail shaker just above his shoulder in mid-shake, looking down at a whiskey glass in front of him.

"I'm getting married, Liam," said Robbie, smiling fondly as he looked down at the photo. "You're going to be there, right?"

After staring at the photo for a moment longer, Robbie placed the frame next to the urn, nestled amongst the flowers. "Thank you for helping me. Thank you for giving me the courage to go up and talk to him."

TRISTAN
February 19, 1970 – August 2, 1987
What a gift for the angels,
to hear you play your music forever.

Robbie flicked through the pages of Tristan's black songbook of original compositions as he knelt down in front of his tombstone. "I brought you your songbook... in case you've gotten bored up there," he said. After having maintained his composure the entire day, Robbie's face finally broke. He closed his eyes, but couldn't keep them closed for long, for the tears wouldn't allow it. "I'll always love you. But I have to say goodbye now."

The words left a sudden knot in Robbie's throat, making him feel as though he couldn't breathe. Tears rushed down his cheeks as he placed the songbook right up against the tombstone; then he leaned forward and placed a kiss on his boyfriend's name. He held his kiss on the inscription for several seconds, as though doing so would summon a miracle that would bring Tristan back to him. His tears slid off his cheeks, the cold chill from the stone pressed against his skin. "I love you," he said, in a voice that was definitive and final. He stood up, turned around, and left without another word. He walked away not because he wanted to, and not because he was choosing to leave Tristan behind, but because it was now time for them both to finally be at peace, forever. He had to just let him go.

Robbie slid his hand over his face as he walked away, the tears being cleared away by his fingers, his heart breaking, and his soul screaming for him to go back. He couldn't, though. There was only what lay ahead now, his future, and it made him proud. There was something beautiful waiting for him. He looked down at the ring Sarim had given to him, a promise from someone who loved him just as much. Love didn't die; it was still there for him, to hold, kiss, rely on and be with for as long as life would allow.

As Robbie walked on, a strong gust of wind blew past, making him look back. He caught sight of the black cover of Tristan's songbook that he had left at his tombstone, but it had been blown several feet towards Robbie. It lay there, open, its pages flapping in the wind. Robbie stared at it, desperation forming on his face as the book slid from side to side along the grass as though at any moment it would be swept somewhere unknown, lost to the wind. Panic stricken, Robbie jogged forward and grabbed it, holding it securely in his hand. He looked at the cover for a moment longer, then slid it beneath his jacket to keep it safe.

Eleven Months Later

The afternoon sunlight spilled through the open window and into the ornate sitting room as the violinists from inside the ballroom drew their bows across their instruments' strings. Larchdale Castle filled with harmonious melodies as hundreds of awestruck guests filed through the front entrance. The castle's glorious architecture was accentuated by the lavish floral arrangements adorning the rows of chairs and polished parquet flooring. The torchères from the grand staircase radiated warm, divine light that blended with the golden haze of the overhanging lights, and the great chandelier's crystals winked and twinkled at each and every person below. Many guests had already taken their seats for the ceremony, with many more choosing to stand along the mezzanine that spanned the perimeter of the third floor, looking down over the balustrade. Five of the six balconies held even more guests, with the sixth, farthest from the staircase, housing the violinists.

Robbie stood in front of an oval floor mirror. He wore a handsome, custom-made black tuxedo with a pointed collar and double vent. There was a powder blue boutonniere pinned to the left side of his chest, and his silver hair was elegantly styled with a strand positioned over his forehead. He reckoned this was probably the finest he had ever looked, and his mom seemed to agree. Robbie's siblings, Miranda and George, had flown in from out of town. His mom, Judy, was rolling a lint remover down his arms and shoulders, collecting last-minute lint and dust that had fallen onto the fabric. At his feet, a man was polishing his black loafers to perfection.

"No one is going to be looking at my shoes," he said, glancing down at the man as he worked away.

"You'd be surprised what people notice, Robert," said Judy casually. "Shoes are almost always the first thing someone notices. You can't be wearing a wonderful suit and not be wearing an equally wonderful pair of shoes."

"For such a wonderful occasion," continued Robbie, looking at her in the reflection of the mirror.

"On such a wonderful day," she chimed, smiling.

Robbie scoffed, following it up with a small laugh. "Okay, let's stop please."

When he'd told his mom that he was engaged, she reacted in a way that was to be expected upon hearing such an announcement made by a son: tears of joy, hugs. He was the last of her children to walk down the aisle, more than twenty years after his brother and sister. His whole life, Robbie was always the gay son, the gay brother, the gay uncle, the gay cousin who never married and never had a long-lasting relationship of any consequence. Until Sarim came along, he had never introduced a boyfriend to them, never brought one to Christmas gatherings or weddings. Early in his young adult life, when he'd first come out to them, his mom and dad believed that, being who he was, he would never follow the same relationship trajectory as his siblings had. No wedding to celebrate, no grandchildren to look forward to, and a much different way of life than what they would have imagined for him. Not having his dad here made him think of what he might have said to him today if he was still alive. Doubtless, there would be words of encouragement showered upon him.

There were many others whom Robbie wished could have been here today to celebrate with him. Three months earlier, Christopher had died. The secret he had guarded all those years was now in Robbie's hands. Roger's would either live on while Robbie was still alive, or it would die, never to feel the warmth of comradery or the sound of music ever again. Christopher had made it clear before his passing that it was Robbie's choice. "Do what you think is right, Robbie."

The wedding director opened the door, letting in music and chatter from the ballroom. Robbie sighed and blew out an anxious breath. "I'm nervous," he said.

"Everyone always is," Judy reassured him. "Your father had a terrible sunburn all over his body on our wedding day, so you can imagine the whining everyone had to endure."

Robbie smirked.

The wedding director, Shawna, was smiling from ear to ear. "We'll be ready to begin in fifteen minutes," she said.

Robbie smiled nervously. "Alright."

Judy followed Shawna out of the room with Robbie trailing behind. He slid his right hand over his face, then placed his arms at his sides, his fingers flexing and twisting in anxious knots like he was trying to cast a secret spell on her. They walked along the darkened terrace beneath the balconies, and Robbie glanced over at the rows of seats filled with people and people and more people, the chatter and music filling his ears. He had to remind himself that there was nothing to be anxious about anymore.

Near the right side of the castle's front entrance was a makeshift room with walls constructed out of white curtains. It was meant to be an area for Robbie and Sarim to wait in before walking out to begin the ceremony. Beside the room was a long display table decorated with flowers and small silver lanterns glowing with tealights. There were framed photos of Robbie and Sarim during various stages of their relationship, with a blown-up official engagement photo as the centerpiece. With the exception of a few stragglers who were quickly making their way inside, the front entrance was now empty and most everyone was in their proper places for the ceremony to begin. Robbie and Sarim had both agreed that there wouldn't be any bridesmaids or groomsmen, just the officiant. Though their two different religious backgrounds came with their own ceremonial traditions, their service would ultimately be non-traditional and secular. They had planned to focus purely on the love they shared for each other, rather than stress over the religious politics and expectations.

Robbie knew from the moment they started planning for their wedding that the situation of Sarim's family would be a sensitive one, and he'd decided that he didn't want to initiate a strategy until Sarim brought it up. He never did, though. When Robbie was making the guest list, he could tell by Sarim's face that he was thinking about them. He had never found the courage to reach out and tell his family about his engagement, for after twenty years of not speaking with them, Sarim didn't have the heart to make the call. He didn't even know where they lived after twenty years. Perhaps Sarim's heart had been broken too many times already, and the constant burden of reliving what happened to him over and over again in his head meant that it was impossible for his heart to break even further. It was a reality that Sarim had accepted a long time ago, and one he was now numb to. He had a new family who welcomed him, thanks to Robbie's family and friends. It was the first time in Sarim's life that he could feel what it was like to be surrounded by a family who loved him for who he was.

Robbie stepped into the curtained room from the back and saw

Sarim. His face glowed when he saw Robbie; he was dressed in a silver Nehru jacket with floral embroidery that wrapped around his torso like a chest of armour, and a powder blue belted drape that hung over his right shoulder, falling perfectly down his white kurta to his pants. Robbie hugged him, his heart beating rapidly as though the moment they were sharing couldn't get more surreal than it already was.

Sarim reached forward and felt the soft blue petals of Robbie's boutonniere. "I'm really excited," he said, his voice soft, just like the petals he was touching.

"Me too," replied Robbie, wanting to lean in and kiss him, but he held back, preferring to wait. Sarim appeared to have the same sentiment, for as they looked into each other's eyes, they both wanted nothing more than to just throw themselves at each other, scatter the contents of the display table to the floor, and uncage their passion right there and then. Robbie's eyes drifted over Sarim's shoulder to see the greeter at the front doors checking her watch. It was almost time. Robbie looked over his own shoulder and saw his mom talking with Shawna. The violinists on the balcony above came to the end of the current melody they were playing and segued into the processional song. Robbie patted Sarim on the arm, holding tight for a moment, then turned around to check on his mom.

Sarim passed the time by swinging his arms and pacing, and he caught a glimpse of the long display table just outside the curtained room. He smiled as he scanned the photos of Robbie and himself. When he looked past the end of the table, his eyes drifted to the front entrance, where a group of four people was speaking with the greeter only minutes before the ceremony was about to begin. As the butterflies grew inside his chest from the impending walk down the aisle, he was about to retreat back into the curtained room when something inside of him forced him to stop. The greeter pointed in Sarim's direction, and the group of four followed her gaze–right at him–just meters away. They didn't move as they made eye contact with him. Sarim was a sudden apparition to them, a ghost from their past materialized into flesh before their eyes.

Sarim's heart beat more wildly, a new nervousness overtaking him. These people whom he initially thought were strangers were transforming into people he once knew, a long time ago. Sarim's mom and dad, Bilal and Aleena, began walking towards him, a shyness in their steps, as though the man in front of them couldn't possibly be the seventeen-year-old boy they once knew. Their shyness escalated into an urgency as their pace quickened. Sarim's fingers clenched into fists down at his sides, his eyes wide and welling up, breaking and hurting, feeling like he couldn't move as they came ever closer to him with each passing second. Their features became clearer, as did the detailing and embroidery of his dad's powder blue sherwani and his mom's purple peplum kurta and white lehenga. His sister, Shaima, followed behind them, ecstatic, like all her dreams had finally come true, seeing her brother as a grown man, and her, a grown woman.

His mom and dad stopped just in front of him, their faces overjoyed, his mother beginning to weep. Sarim's face was a storm of shock and emotion, then became stoic. He hung his head as they faced him, frozen and crying, as he stared at the ground, tears rolling down his cheeks. He stood helpless, his arms at his sides, rooted, and hiding his face in shame. Then, he felt the gentle touch of his mom's fingertips as she touched his enclosed hand, coaxing him to loosen his fist and unfurl his fingers. He slowly raised his eyes to meet hers as tears slid from his eyes, the burden of twenty years impossible to hide anymore. His mom reached forward and put her arms around him. Sarim had thought he would never feel a hug from his mother ever again. He looked at his dad, who smiled back at him, and gave him a hug–a hug that was strong, affirmative and loving.

"We've missed you so much," he said as his face fell into Sarim's shoulder.

Sarim's tears fell onto his father. He didn't want to ever let go. When he finally did, Sarim turned around with wet eyes and saw Robbie, smiling from a distance. All the people Sarim would ever need were here with him. He was home again.

Beside his sister stood a boy of seventeen. Shy and reluctant, he met Sarim's eyes with his own and they stared at each other. It was like looking into a mirror: the boy's dark brown eyes were his... The boy's facial structure was his... This boy *was* Sarim, when he was seventeen.

"Aysar," said his dad, "this is your brother, Sarim."

They both stared at each other, Sarim's mouth agape, the thumping of his heart almost visible through his chest. He made the first move and slowly leaned forward to hug his baby brother.

Robbie and Sarim walked out of the curtained room as the violins above went on with the processional melody. Soaring and delicate, the music lifted the guests to their feet as the two men took their place in front of the castle doors and walked forward, side by side, until they reached the start of the aisle. On either side were Robbie's mom and Sarim's parents, patiently waiting for their sons to reach them. Robbie linked his left arm around his mom's. Sarim took his parents into both his arms, one on each side, intertwined. The moment was so much more than Sarim could have ever hoped it to be. All he could do now was look straight ahead, smiling, while trying hard to keep it together. The five of them began the journey forward down the aisle, row by row, towards the grand staircase ahead where the small black stage was nestled between the diverging stairs of the bottom landing.

Robbie kept his eyes forward, knowing hundreds of pairs of eyes were on him. The photographers were going wild, doing their own dance around the aisle as they caught the perfect shot of every step they took. He concentrated his attention on the torchères instead, their lights like little suns beckoning him forward; warm, inviting and pleasant. He couldn't reach them fast enough. It was like a plane he was excited to board that would take him somewhere new and unknown, but worthwhile and permanent, everlasting. Robbie turned his head to look at Sarim, whose eyes were going every which way, emotional for what was happening around him and inside of him.

When they arrived at the end of the aisle, the three parents took their seats in the front row, leaving their sons to walk up the stairs of the stage, side by side. As Robbie and Sarim took their place in front of the officiant, Robbie looked up, over Sarim, to the balcony behind him that was nearest to the stage. Amongst the crowd gathered at the balustrade, Ben was there looking down, his blond hair bright against the gold auras of the room. They locked eyes for just a brief moment, and Ben smiled, happy.

Robbie's eyes welled up. He brought his attention back to Sarim, and Robbie smiled at the love in front of him, fortunate to be able to take this man's hands into his. The officiant started to speak, and as he did so, a tear spilled over Sarim's eyelashes, spurring Robbie to reach forward and gently wipe it away. As he did so, he thought about what they would do together. He thought about the experiences they'd share, the places they'd see, and the new memories they'd make after today. It would be a most thrilling adventure.

The doors of the castle opened for the reveal of Robbie and Sarim as they stepped out onto the front steps, the sun bathing everything around them in its light. All the guests were applauding and cheering at the bottom, every single face looking up at them in celebration. White confetti was released from both sides and cascaded down upon them as Robbie and Sarim smiled and waved and held each other's hand, their gold rings catching the glint of the sun. They turned to each other and kissed, smiling, as the sides of their noses rubbed up against one another. From the steps, the videographer zoomed in on their faces, immortalizing them.

Ben looked up at Robbie and Sarim. It seemed so out of reach, to have what they had. Ben thought of what it would be like to walk out into the daylight with the person you loved and see all the people who cared for you and wished you well as you started your life anew with the one person who made all the difference to you.

For a moment longer, Ben's gaze lingered on Robbie and Sarim; then he turned and started the long trek down the road, on his own, to a place he couldn't quite call home yet. Perhaps a day would come when all their paths would cross again, and he'd tell them the story of how they became his heroes. Ben felt unwavering hope that eventually, someday, he too could find what those two shared together.

Acknowledgments

First, I'd like to express my utmost thanks to Jennifer for sifting through and editing the first draft of *Tristan* in its bloated 183k word glory and marking up each page with walls of red ink. You helped *Tristan* sing.

Thank you to the four Fiverr beta readers who gave me invaluable advice and suggestions to help tighten the story even further: Kenneth (@kennethbc), Matt (@matt_ljr), Amber (@ambercampbell21) and Ritika (@ritika_97).

Thank you to Alemão Carpinteyro-Sanchez, PhD for correcting my horrible Spanish translations.

Thank you to my Fiverr proofreader Madeleine (@madeleine01) for tying up loose ends and helping *Tristan* shine in its final stages.

This might sound corny, but thank you to music. It became one of the biggest inspirations for me during the writing of this book.

Thank you Mom and Dad. This book wouldn't be what it is–and most likely wouldn't exist–if it wasn't for you.

Lastly, thank *you* for reading this book and taking a chance on it, and me.

Photo © Jesse Roman

Jesse Roman lives in Canada. He's been writing fiction since high school and has a constant need to tell stories from his vast imagination. When not writing books or creating YouTube videos, he's making cocktails, watching movies and getting lost in music. Tristan is his debut novel.

officialjesseroman.com

Coming Soon From Jesse Roman

BLAZING CITY

Book 1 of the "*A World Divided*" series

COMING 2025

&

FALLEN GUARDIN

Book 1 of the "*Fallen Guardin*" trilogy

COMING IN, LIKE, A FEW YEARS

&

T / PT / 2

---

cory roman natuik

Music That Helped Inspire The Book "Tristan"

- *"Gift of Life"* by Nick Murray
- *"All the Lovers"* by Kylie Minogue
- *"This Is Your Night (House Mix)"* by Amber
- *"Heartbreak in This City (Single Mix)"* by Steps & Michelle Visage
- *"Bleeding Love (Jason Nevins Original Radio Mix)"* by Leona Lewis
- *"On a Night Like This"* by Kylie Minogue
- *"Acid (from The Perks of Being a Wallflower)"* by Michael Brook
- *"if this is the last time"* by LANY
- *"Anyone to Love"* by Michael Bublè
- *"I'm Forever Blowing Bubbles"* by Albert Campbell & Henry Burr
- *"Lovers In a Dangerous Time"* by Barenaked Ladies
- *"Reckless"* by Leathers
- *"Asking for a Friend"* by CHVRCHES
- *"An Unusual Prince/Once Upon a Dream"* by Mary Costa, Bill Shirley & Sleeping Beauty Chorus
- *"Jimmy Jimmy"* by Madonna
- *"It's a Sin"* by Pet Shop Boys
- *"What Am I Gonna Do About You"* by Reba

- *"Sunday Night 1987"* by M83
- *"Please Be Naked"* by The 1975
- *"When You Kiss Me (Red Pop Version)"* by Shania Twain
- *"Agenais"* by Donna Lewis
- *"The Mysteries"* by David Bowie
- *"Bridge Over Troubled Water"* by Simon & Garfunkel
- *"I Have Nothing" by Whitney Houston*
- *"Nikita"* by Elton John
- *"Night Trouble"* by Petit Biscuit
- *"The Drugs Don't Work"* by The Verve
- *"Silent World"* by Donna Lewis
- *"Midnight Souls Still Remain"* by M83
- *"Rainbow"* by Kacey Musgraves
- *"When We Were Young"* by Adele
- *"I Wanna Grow Old With You"* by Westlife
- *"Run (Single Mix)"* by Leona Lewis
- *"I Know What Love Is"* by Céline Dion
- *"So Was Red (from The Shawshank Redemption)"* by Thomas Newton
- *"End Title (from The Shawshank Redemption)"* by Thomas Newton
- *"(Everything I Do) I Do It for You"* By Bryan Adams

Check out this playlist and what other music Jesse is listening to on Apple Music @enlightenjesse

Printed in Great Britain
by Amazon

39933259R00300